Lakota Cowboy

Books by John Hafnor

Lakota Cowboy
Black Hills Believables
Strange But True, Colorado
Strange But True, America
Trekking the Last Badland, a Natural History

Wahres aus dem Wilden Westen
(Translation to German by Edith-Maria Redlin)

Lakota Cowboy

John Hafnor

SPEAKING VOLUMES, LLC
NAPLES, FLORIDA
2021

Lakota Cowboy

Cover direction from StorySpring Consulting LLC.

ISNB 978-1-64540-572-6

If you come across one of the occasional Lakota words in the book that is puzzling, refer to a compact Lakota-English dictionary on page 418.

Curious about the native contributors to this work, including cultural editor and esteemed Lakota elder Jhon (not John) Goes In Center? See the Acknowledgments section at page 415.

There are several ranches and dwellings mentioned in this book, some fictional but others very real. Please respect private property and understand that uninvited persons will not be welcome on a working ranch or certain tribal lands.

This book is a novel. Not a history. Yet who can ignore the many worthy novels carrying echoes of real people, real events. This principal guided the crafting of *LAKOTA COWBOY*.

The original inspiration for this book hung on the walls of my childhood home—photos of my maternal grandfather, and nearby his great Lakota friend and neighbor.

As a boy beholding these portraits, I saw archetypes of the last nomadic Indian and the last open range cowboy. But could I fully capture two lives that spoke so universally of the pathos of race relations; of cultures that win and that are overwhelmed; and of the myth of the West? Two decades ago, I bent to the task, seeking out those few people with personal recollections, then moving to archives to glean more of the pair's adventures, loves, enemies. For the past ten years I've pressed pen to paper, results of which you now hold in your hands. Because this novel features flesh-and-blood characters, it is my fond wish that you, the reader, can more easily enter into this 100-year-long saga.

Chapter One

New Horizons, Blue Horizons
1913

Cannonball towered sixteen hands at the withers, a high-stepping sorrel gelding. Baked into his marbled muscles and large head were bloodlines and spirit to win any rider's favor.

The tan-faced cowboy on Cannonball's back had grown up in that last generation for which horsemanship was not an option, but rather part-and-parcel of full manhood. His hawk-like gaze could take quick measure of any horse, or any stranger.

Cleve Berry and Cannonball were in many ways one creature. At 5'9" and a sinewy 140 pounds, Cleve was light burden to a cow pony. The result was two living things moving as one. There were no over-weight cowboys in those days, if ever there had been. Working horses had a way of enforcing weight limits by bucking off the unwanted.

Cleve was nearly twenty-seven now. For years the saddle had been his only home. Time to find a patch of prairie to call his own. Maybe in his native Nebraska. Or maybe near big brother Tom, who'd started with a modest homestead in the South Dakota badlands and already had a burgeoning spread. Folks called it the XX Ranch. In a short letter to Cleve he wrote ". . . come on up, have a look see. There are still a few homesteads for the taking. The flat farming land is all taken. But heck, I've got bad news for the sodbusters—this ain't farming country. This is cattle country."

Cleve wrote back that he would be there before the June berries ripened. And so he urged Cannonball westward into a smooth-jointed trot.

Plunging down into Cottonwood Draw, Cleve reined Cannonball to a halt and dismounted in search of water. An old-timer had warned Cleve:

"This is the last chance for many miles to refill your canteen and water your mount." But on this day the draw held only cracked mud. Nothing to do but press on across an increasingly dusty land of sparse buffalo grass, cactus and yucca.

Not a fence post or tree broke the lateral lines, least of all the far-flung horizon below arching skies. It was the kind of nothingness so disturbing to earlier immigrants stepping past the last forests of Minnesota, Illinois, Missouri. Whether from Europe or eastern America, they had seen no such wide-open spaces. But Cleve, born of this country, gave the agoraphobic scene nary a thought.

He proceeded in the cool-headed manner of his kinfolk, though having neither compass nor map. Instead, he had an animal instinct for direction and route.

This was 'tweener' country, 'tween the tall-grass garden prairies of Iowa and east Nebraska, and the huddled shortgrass steppe of the American West. By now the golden destination, Cedar Butte, was in distant sight—to Cleve's eyes Cedar Butte's long eastern flank floating like some low-slung battleship. The heights sported dark patches of what must be evergreens. This promise of shade soon had Cleve urging his horse into a higher trot. As they drew nearer, the flat prairie built slowly into hills that rolled like waves toward the base of the butte. The land was becoming more interesting, more muscular.

Man and beast were for the moment energized by entering a seemingly foreign world. Perhaps it was the rise in elevation and drop in humidity conjuring that stunning and very Western clarity of air.

Cleve had little idea of what this land's native population would be like. He had seen a Ponca or two on the dusty Nebraska streets of his youth, and occasionally the Lakotas would assemble in Valentine to drum and dance on Main Street. He had also seen Cree, Assiniboine, and Blackfeet in his year in the Canadian wilderness.

But what lay ahead would be an eye-opener, for his new neighbors would be very traditional *Wazhazha* Lakotas of the Rosebud Reservation.

Having traveled cross-country through unfenced reservation terrain, Cleve now joined a dirt trail rolling westward. On this lightly-used trail he came across his first Rosebud Indian—a small boy standing beside a dead pony. How long had he been there? Where were his parents . . . or indeed any other adults?

As Cleve rode closer, the doe-eyed child moved not a muscle. He neither retreated nor advanced but simply stared unblinking right through this blue-eyed, light-skinned *wasicu*.

Having reined up long enough to determine assistance would not be welcome, and seeing the child had a water canteen and wasn't in visible distress, Cleve continued on.

Time and distance had by now surrendered to the horse's rhythm. Slow, but not too slow—a horse cadence will in time affect the way a cowboy talks, or so he was told by a city friend in response to Cleve's drawl.

Four miles further west, Cleve noticed wolf tracks paralleling the trail. He smiled, for the tracks brought back old feelings of being on the edge of the unknown. Feelings he remembered from Wyoming, and from the Canadian Rockies.

But the tracks—was it three animals or four?—brought a twinge of apprehension. A small rancher could not succeed in the long run if he lost even two or three calves annually to wolves. *Does this mean war with wolves*, he thought, *and will I win?*

With Cedar Butte now dominating the west horizon, there was no danger of getting lost. But the going was slow, given the single track's braided and unimproved nature. Now seemingly on a game run, but then what appeared to be a wagon trail, these parallel pathways wandered through ever rougher terrain and not always towards Cleve's destination.

The young cowboy was curious as he rode for the first time among badlands. These canyons held no grass for cows but something even better—shelter from freezing winds and blizzard snows. Every shade of sepia and buff, the badland walls smelled of soft rock and a chalky dampness.

As Cleve approached the ever-sharper flanks and hoodoos of Cedar Butte, he intersected a much more efficient trail. This one was well traveled; the solid double ruts of a real wagon road promising smoother travel the remaining miles westward to his brother's XX Ranch. But now Cannonball, head down, was visibly suffering from a lack of water.

After traveling less than two miles, for reasons he couldn't put his finger on, Cleve hobbled Cannonball in the shade of a treeless hill bordering the trail on the north side of the Butte.

He climbed the steep hillside to the very top. Perhaps for a better view of the countryside. Perhaps mysteriously half sensing this hill overlooked that patch of ground on which one day his Berry house and barn and corrals would rise.

His conscious mind, however, was focused on this road he'd stumbled upon, meandering as it did miles to the west. All the way to his brother's established ranch. Where he was bound—and where just maybe he'd claim a homestead by building a tar paper shack for he and his bride-to-be in a nearby draw.

Whatever possessed Cleve to climb this hill, he was now content to sit a spell in the hilltop's cooling breeze. And to run his fingers through sandy soil that was still damp from some recent stray thunderhead.

That's when he felt it—an uncharacteristically hard smooth rock, prompting the cowboy to brush aside sand until he spied the arch of something red. Unsheathing his knife, Cleve easily dug deep enough to pull up the stone bowl and crumbling wooden stem of an Indian sacred pipe. Its rosy color told Cleve this must be from the famed quarry of similarly colored pipe-making rock at Pipestone, Minnesota.

Cleve had seen a few of these valued red pipes in store museum cases and among the Sioux in Nebraska and the Blackfoot in Canada, so he did not question how it traveled here. But who had chosen to bury a holy relic on such an obscure hilltop? And why?

Still pondering this, his gaze flashed downhill upon hearing a creaky Indian wagon rolling eastward. The elderly driver urged his laboring team forward.

Years later Cleve learned things about this pipe and this road that the old driver would have always known. Things like the pipe being buried parallel to the route presently plied, and being a metaphor for *Chanku Luta*, the Red Road.

The lovely pipe bowl in Cleve's right hand, as buried, pointed to the Pipestone quarry beyond the rising sun—where the stone originated. The mouthpiece pointed west, towards the famed Wyoming stone quarry known as the Spanish Diggings—beyond the setting sun, hidden near Rawhide Buttes.

And the long wooden stem connecting the two—representing the Red Road and those many other east-west roads connecting these two great quarries of Middle America.

Cleve discarded the hopelessly rotted wooden stem and slipped the stone portion of the pipe into his vest pocket.

Digging boot heels into the steep hill, Cleve used short, stiff steps to descend. Once on the level his gait, young man though he was, hinted at the bow-legged years to come as consequence of a life on horseback. At Cannonball's side, he deposited the pipe bowl securely in the saddlebag. Before mounting, he felt without looking to make sure the cinch was not rubbing, then he adjusted the latigo and took up the reins.

Having earlier placed a red bandanna round the sweatband of his hat, Cleve undid it to wipe perspiration from his neck. Wearied now by thirst and the journey, he surveyed the deep ruts of the road, surmising that the Indian rig he'd seen was but one of many.

Cannonball faithfully plodded westward, but his carriage lacked spirit. For the day had reached a sizzling point, prickly heat meeting man and horse in midget waves from both sky and ground. All at once Cleve felt a quiver pass through Cannonball—then a sharp lifting of head and ears. The cowboy knew his mount had scented water. Together they quickened the pace. There. Over there, a green patch of grass that must be a spring!

Riding on, Cleve saw a modest four-square frame house near this verdant grass. It was not the typical log cabin affair of the Lakotas, but clearly an Indian abode—no curtains in the windows, a circular patch of bare ground suggesting a tipi location for the summer, and nearby the low-slung willow frame of a recently erected sweat lodge.

Various wild herbs hung drying from cords of rawhide under the eaves, including the wild gourd *Wagmu Pejuta*, the plant of mystic properties not to be handled by ordinary tribesmen. Nor could it be brought inside a lodging where human thoughts might corrupt its potency.

The scene suggested that no one was home. Surely they'd not mind if a weary traveler rested in the shade of the house and slaked his thirst. Even a cowboy.

While tying off his horse Cleve looked up to see a full-blood, perhaps in his early 50s, walking in the hushed, light-footed way of those who spend a lifetime in moccasins. Jet black hair mixed with a few grey strands tumbled nearly to his waist in two loose braids. His equine head was made noble by slabs of muscle hung from high cheekbones. An untucked muslin shirt was topped with a red silk scarf tied at the neck.

Well-worn moccasins were below beaded leggings peeking from under woolen pants.

He was hatless, with a face that seemed more leather than skin. The man's demeanor wordlessly received the weary wasicu before him. It was clear his spring water and shade would be shared.

The two took the measure of each other, as is customary on the prairie. In this sizing up there welled for both an odd familiarity transcending their obvious differences. Perhaps they recognized that each was the last of a breed. The archetype cowboy and Indian, meeting again . . . but never thereafter in quite this way.

To shake hands, or not. Cleve smiled before offering his handshake, sure to be firm. The native hesitated briefly before offering his gentler handshake. To a Lakota, touching between non-familial males was rare . . . the hard handshake always feeling like a way of keeping the other from pulling away. In his world thrusting forward with the right hand, the weapon hand, was an indiscretion. He would, though, not refuse what for him was a meaningless wasicu custom.

The older man motioned Cleve to lead Cannonball to a nearby livestock water trough. Then the men walked together towards the spring. Cleve couldn't ignore the reverence with which his host approached the modest fountain of water.

The native made a "cupped hands" sign by way of asking if Cleve had something to drink with. When the cowboy shook his head, the older man diverted to retrieve a dented tin cup concealed under a bush beside the spring. Cleve accepted it with a smile, drinking long and deep of the sweet spring water. Only then did he notice his host's hands. Hands so big, so capable, as if sculpted from a heavy mahogany limb.

Here, Cleve thought, was just the type of man his big brother suggested he seek out: An older Lakota who was intimate with the land—a valued ally with generational knowledge to select favorable building sites—the place where grasses green earliest in spring, where winter winds are gentler, where flooding is unlikely. A place tender Jessie Iddings might like, if his courting of her became something more.

For his part, the host instantly liked this young white man's calm ways with no hint of the condescension felt from some other settlers. He smiled a genial smile before pointing to his chest and sharing his Lakota name, *Nawica Kicijin*. The cowboy smiled but didn't attempt to repeat it, then in reply, "Cleve is my name. Cleve Berry." In coming years his Lakota neighbors would struggle with pronouncing this name. For them, Cleve Berry was always "Clib Belly."

Below the meeting's budding amiability there floated a faint tension, the residue of 400 years of warfare. Cleve turned to leave, hesitated on hearing footsteps, and looked back to see a diminutive woman exiting the house. She was holding a small lifeless animal by the back legs, its hair singed off. Only as she slipped the creature into a large cast-iron cooking pot did Cleve realize it was a pup. Only then did he sense how much he must learn about his future neighbors. A shadow enveloped the scene—whether by dark cloud or flock of geese Cleve could not tell.

Just then the words of his part-Indian brother-in-law came to him: "These Lakotas will watch you with their sad eyes, always. Years of watching. Then, together they will accept you or reject you."

Cleve easily found brother Tom's nearby cabin. It looked so small, perhaps just one room, but built on a good foundation hinting at more rooms to come soon. Ever the big brother, Tom bearhugged Cleve and applied three slaps on the back. Tom and wife Rena smiled broadly on hearing Cleve had already met a neighbor as important as Nawica Kicijin. He eyed the solid look of the cabin and Rena's big garden. "You two have done a whale of a lot in two years."

Within days Cleve had staked out his homestead claim and begun hammering together a homestead shack. He and Nawica Kicijin often and easily crossed paths, beginning to fashion lifelong ties. They did after all both live upon the same trail, the Red Road or as Nawica Kicijin knew it *Chanku Luta*.

For Nawica Kicijin the hallowed road was the most direct route to his parent's allotment east of Cleve's mailbox. Also, *Chanku Luta* connected him to many tribal friends living east of *Hunte Paha* (Cedar Butte) and the Rosebud Agency. A smooth pathway to friends like the Standing Bears. On this day as he stood beside the road, his eyes looking west then east, but his mind lifted then floated back to a childhood memory.

He was then known as *Heyŭktan*, meaning curved or bent horn in reference to a yearling buffalo. Those were days his band moved over the land with such utter confidence. Cedar Butte and the Red Road were in the heart of traditional Lakota lands, if a bit southeast of the usual *Miniconjou* Lakota hunting grounds. But Heyŭktan's sub tribe, the *Shunka Yute Shni,* were a far-ranging group.

Grandfather had told Heyŭktan rather sternly to remember this road, for it connected western and eastern hunting grounds. More vitally it was a summer wildfire escape route, for it cut cleanly through *Mako Sica*, badlands devoid of vegetation.

Grandfather further said Lakotas were not the first owners of the Red Road. "Grandson, we inherited this trail, already ancient when our people first moved westward from the great river. Surely the Kiowa, Pawnee, and Arikara made good use of this road. And before them the ancient and mysterious ones who hunted with such mighty stone points."

It was then early winter. *Shunka Yute Shni*, the Eat No Dogs, were moving to the Black Hills for such winter shelter as her foothills typically offered. Behind certain horses dragged long tipi poles upon which were balanced the distinctly black-topped tipis, hallmark of the Eat No

Dogs. Horse hooves made sucking and popping sounds in the trail's damp gumbo.

On reaching the lowest point where the storied trail crossed a dry creek, everyone stopped to adjust several heavily-loaded horse travois. The smell in the air was of a winter storm, expressed in the upturned noses of camp dogs and horses alike.

Fortune had shined on *Eat No Dogs* hunters on the plains to the east of Cedar Butte. Each hunter had brought one or more buffalo crashing to earth. Owl On Mountain had killed three, Heyúktan's father Elk Robe had claimed two. Butchering and then moving these mounds of fresh meat and green hides strained a band already carrying tipis, poles and all household items meant for winter camp.

"Tie that big bundle more tightly, Heyúktan," Elk Robe admonished, "and move the heavy items low and to the front for the sake of your horse." After this short pause, the Eat No Dogs again moved westward and upward from the creek bottom—the Red Road steeply rising. Rising.

That's when Heyúktan looked up to see what at the moment seemed the sighting of a lifetime.

Others saw it too, and together every foot hesitated as every jaw dropped. For coming down the hill and scattered among the dark cedar trees along the Red Road was the inconceivable: White Buffalos! Not two, not five, but an entire herd.

Holiest of holy, a white buffalo might be glimpsed once in a generation. But here were scores of these beasts moving urgently downhill, just as the band labored uphill.

Heyúktan and the others split left and right so that the herd might pass, all watching the spectacle that could not be real.

And indeed it was not real—these buffalo had come over the divide and through the approaching storm. They were caked with snow.

But it was hardly less impressive for young Heyúktan, his first close encounter with living buffalo. Silently he joined in watching the herd drift past, as indeed the people had no need to harvest more animals. By their closeness the beasts acknowledged that they felt safe.

Wide-eyed Heyúktan watched the magnificent creatures. Swinging their outsized heads side to side and pumping their great shoulder blades round and round beneath wooly humps of muscle.

He watched especially the yearlings, those "bent horns" after whom he was named. Already substantial beasts, they seemed to know their task, plunging stoically forward in the ageless migratory way of all buffalo.

Heyúktan now understood how buffalo and elk and grizzly must have trod the Red Road long before *Wakan Tanka* brought people to this land. Was not an easy pathway for Lakotas the same easy pathway whatever the creature?

With the herd's passing, the Eat No Dogs adults smiled at their own folly.

As the band resumed their uphill trek, Elk Robe moved his horse so as to ride beside Heyúktan, "Son, today *Wakan Tanka* was a trickster, but even so this moment adds luster to the Red Road."

Then in a cautionary tone, "Remember this simple road, for one day I will show you another road to the south, one with deep ruts and carrying white-topped wagons beyond counting. A road so busy with wasicu that it splits our buffalo into two great herds, north and south."

Heyúktan tried without success to imagine such a mighty road.

"You are young, but a day may come where both you and I take up the spear to stop more such wasicu roads."

Lakota trails were fainter than wasicu roads, for travel on even well-known trails was sporadic—the drag marks of the travois often quickly covered with new plants. Roads faded to trails, trails faded to traces, and beyond these correct directions were found only by landmarks—just the way young Heyúktan liked to travel. It was along such a faint trace far to the northwest that Heyúktan's band traveled to a summer camp in 1865.

Hiding behind one black-topped tipi after another, Heyúktan shadowed the big man in such a way that few would notice. Ten years Heyúktan's senior, *Canku Wahatuya* was this man, his name roughly translated as High Backbone. Barrel-chested and a formidable warrior, he was on a path that would one day elevate him to *Intancan* of the Shunka Yute Shni band. Presently he was *Blotahunka*, a war party leader.

Heyúktan knew High Backbone as one to be carefully watched, to be emulated. This was especially so because High Backbone had been blessed with not one but two vision quest dreams . . . and was whispered to be a holy one.

One gentle summer evening High Backbone assembled the young boys of the Eat No Dogs, so as to address their many questions. The boys were especially eager to hear how he had once done the near impossible—glimpsed the thunderbird among the steel-grey clouds of a winter storm. Or how he had elevated the standing of every Miniconjou Lakota by riding so fearlessly as a decoy in the entrapment of *mila hanska*, the long knives—the battle later wasicu books would call the Fetterman Massacre. Heyúktan was in the front row of these rapt young listeners.

High Backbone chose to speak to this next generation of warriors in response to the fresh armies of soldiers streaming westward with the conclusion of a great Civil War in lands beyond where the sun rises. He was aware of the infamous order given on June 1865 by General Pat Conner, aimed specifically at the Lakotas and Cheyenne: "Find the hostile tribes and kill all males over the age of twelve." Many of those before him were approaching twelve winters.

Heyúktan knew High Backbone as one who spoke only when sharing something truly important. After the manner of his friend and cousin Crazy Horse, High Backbone believed silence to be the perfect balance of body, mind, and spirit. Heyúktan had never known him to address anyone younger than warrior age in private conversation.

But once, between his tenth and eleventh winter, Heyúktan had a special "as one" encounter with High Backbone. It was the season of ripening plums, and near here on the banks of the Little Missouri River Heyúktan discovered and kept secret a perfectly ripe plum patch far from camp.

The Eat No Dogs journeyed to this campsite each summer to hunt the now dwindling great northern herd. Still too young to join a buffalo hunt, Heyúktan was none-the-less free to roam as far as his legs and courage could take him. Off to the east lay this wild plum thicket where alone on this day he dreamed and sunbathed and gorged himself on this sugary prairie dessert. Heyúktan liked being alone, away from his teasing peers. For a bout of smallpox had rendered him weaker and less skilled than most others his age. This despite his taller-than-average frame.

When the sun swung low in the afternoon sky, it was his signal to start for home. His belly ached from too many plums. He moved as he'd been taught, wolf-like, always below the ridge tops. That's when Heyúktan saw a lone horseman descending from the north. Could it be a Crow or Shoshone? In a panic, he dropped and rolled into the concealing cover of the plum thicket. In the harsh inter-tribal warring of those days, such an encounter could mean enslavement or even death.

Heyúktan crouched lower, a pounding heart so loud he feared it might give him away. He waited, breathless, until seeing the unmistakable trappings of a male Lakota hunter in his prime. A moment later he recognized first the horse, then the rider—it was the esteemed one of his own clan. High Backbone!

With more than a little relief, Heyúktan scrambled out of the thicket in hopes of hitching a ride back to camp. But he also noted High Backbone's pony carried in addition to the hunter a sizable quarter of meat from a successful kill.

No room for a boy, surely. But a safe someone to follow home on foot. Heyúktan trotted into the sun at an angle that would intercept the rider.

On seeing Heyúktan a surprised and somewhat amused High Backbone reined up, leaned over his horse's neck, and contemplated the youngster.

"You seek an escort to camp, little brother? And maybe a ride?"

"Hau, please."

"My horse says 'no,' but today I shall say '*yes*'." To which Heyúktan grabbed the powerful extended forearm and vaulted nimbly onto the meat-filled parfleches arranged on the horse's rump. Careful not to otherwise touch High Backbone once in place, Heyúktan basked in the aura of muscle and might of such a man.

And so began Heyúktan's hour alone with a future "big belly" of the Miniconjou band. For a long time, High Backbone rode silently. Heyúktan dared not utter an unsolicited word.

When they reached a high bluff and could see afar the village staked out along the waterway, High Backbone dismounted to rest his overloaded mount. As they sat on haunches facing the south, the man's direction, High Backbone finally spoke. "Surely you have noticed how our people treat future warriors. You will be conferred certain privileges: the best cuts of meat, warmer clothing crafted by others, superior horses when compared to one's sisters. But in return a price is levied—boys like you must be our band's only line of defense in this world. We ride always under Lakota skies. If the sky is blue or gray or black, it is our sky. But we are surrounded by blood enemies like the Crow, Arikaree, Ponca, and Pawnee. And now the fearsome bluecoats."

"So whatever your life calling," said High Backbone, "you will be expected to take up arms in defense of our women, our children. Without you and your playmates, a day will come when our helpless ones are slaughtered like so many rabbits. Only with you as a defender can Lakota women take their place as the true strength, the beating heart, of our nation."

Heyúktan found the pluck to ask a question, not knowing if he'd like the answer: "When, big brother? When is one such as me asked to take up the spear?"

"The call may come soon," said High Backbone while motioning Heyúktan to the horse. "I will tell you a story as we complete our journey."

High Backbone swung a big leg over the back of his mount, and Heyúktan repeated the leap to take his place on the parfleche full of meat.

High Backbone did not have to direct his mount as to the way home. He cleared his throat. "This true tale begins at Summit Springs, the southern edge of our Lakota nation. There clustered forty lodges of the Cheyenne leader Tall Bull, and a few visiting lodges of our own *Sicangu* Lakota."

"It was a day following a successful hunt, with most men and boys back in camp as the sun passed its high place. One apprentice warrior, Little Hawk by name, was far from camp. His assignment that day—take a position on a hillside and watch over the tribe's prized horses as they grazed."

Without touching High Backbone, Heyúktan leaned forward to better hear.

"I am sure Little Hawk assumed the quiet alertness of the apprentice "scout" by swiveling his head from vista to far vista. He also knew that human watchfulness was no match for that of the horses themselves—their senses detecting a wolf, mountain lion, or a mounted stranger before any human ear or eye."

"So, when equine heads and ears lifted towards the northwest, Little Hawk knew he'd soon see something of interest. Never did he imagine what shortly unfolded—Riding hard upon their large horses, a force of almost 250 bluecoats, and led by 50 hired Pawnee scouts.

"Little Hawk had but one instant to make a choice—escape on his childhood pony tied close by . . . or . . . though time was short, round up the best war horses and gallop them into camp so as to sound the alarm and provide mounts."

"Such was his choice, and soon he was thundering into camp behind the horses and just ahead of the invaders."

Heyŭktan hung on High Backbone's words, easily imagining the bedlam as a hundred shocked warriors lunged for both their weapons and their own war horse.

"Even Little Hawk took up his bow and arrow and found a place in the line of adult warriors. For his valor, Little Hawk was later celebrated by the Pawnee scouts . . . though this did not stop these scouts from killing "short man," as they called him."

Lesson complete, point nearly made, High Backbone looked back to make eye contact with his passenger and then with seeming nonchalance: "Heyŭktan, the martyred Little Hawk was twelve winters. You will soon be twelve winters."

A long pause while he let it sink in, then, "Let us now ride in among the black-topped tipis in the proper way, little brother. In silence."

Chapter Two

Prairie Smoke and the Red Buffalo
1914

In those early years, 1914 and 1915, Cleve's small ranch didn't have much fencing in place. Neither did brother Tom's spread, just to the west on the banks of Black Pipe Creek. A little later and further west, brother Claude's Pass Creek Ranch would border open range until 1926.

With cattle safely branded, it was common practice before and during the Great War to let 'em roam the open range. This required occasionally riding out and herding the stock back closer to home. This was the end of the era when settlers fenced crops or gardens to keep livestock out—livestock had the run of the land. Henceforth, cropland would not be fenced in, but rather the livestock.

"He who controls the water controls the grass. And the cows." Like every rancher, Cleve said this, believed this. That morning Cleve found himself standing beside new neighbor Cornie Utterback at Belvidere Hardware. Together they examined the newest offerings of barbed wire.

Cleve pushed the brim of his hat up to better examine a sample length of Bain Reverse "H" Barb. With a wry smile Cornie said, "Guess we're all gonna have to barb wire fence every damn bit of this land. No wonder they call it the devil's rope."

Cleve held the barbed wire up to the light, "Yup. This'll be the death of the open range. Not much of it left even now. Most is Indian land."

Cornie nodded agreement, then passed along the morning's latest rumor: government-hired cowboys would begin rounding up reservation cows—to be distributed to the natives as part of their treaty mandated beef issue. Privately owned steers would likely be caught in this net as well.

If a rancher wanted his branded but trespassing cattle back, he'd have to pay $1 a head. If a critter was unbranded, it was fattening on Indian land and the owner'd likely never see it again. So Cleve walked out of the hardware store with purpose in his step, a roll of barbed wire over his shoulder, and headed straight to brother Tom's place.

As in the recent past, the brothers would work together to round up their cattle in advance of the government cowboys. Within hours they were riding hard, camping under the stars in an all-out effort to make sure their animals weren't caught by agency riders.

It was on the second overnight that Cleve saw it. Peering out from under his tent flap, a sleepy-eyed Cleve wondered if he was dreaming. There in morning's first light was the American antelope, a sleek pronghorn buck not twenty yards away.

The moment was beyond unusual—it was unheard of. In those years there was no big game in the badlands, unless you counted wild horses. It would be decades before Cleve even began to see the deer return. When buffalo hunters flooded the plains from 1860 to 1880, they not only slaughtered the buffalo but also decimated the only other four-legged roaming the plains in millions: the antelope.

Brother Tom was in a nearby tent, snoring forcefully enough to fluff a tent wall. This seeming mirage would be Cleve's alone. "Do not wake me early, Cleve." Tom was seven years Cleve's senior, and never shy to use the authority those years bequeathed.

He was an inch shorter than Cleve but of stockier build with a personality just as robust. Tom's toothy smile and Will Rogers-esque sense of humor invited loyalty. But his stance, boots a good foot apart, said here stands a man unlikely to compromise.

Returning the gaze of his four-legged visitor, Cleve rubbed his eyes to better believe what he was seeing. Reaching slowly under his bedroll, he felt for the cold blue barrel of his 1910 Winchester 401. Meat was meat.

Rearranging himself among canvas and bedroll, Cleve steadied his breathing and held a stone-cold eye on crosshairs over this gazelle-like creature's heart. Just as he commenced to squeeze the trigger Cleve noticed the cows they'd rounded up yesterday grazing in the same line of fire.

By now the horned speedster was drifting, head up—head down—head up, right in among the bovines. And then, before Cleve knew it, this prairie ghost was trotting to the northwest and beyond rifle range.

Watching it float out of sight, Cleve pondered his good luck in the sighting and bad luck in the shooting. He spent the day gathering cattle on the butte's high slopes. Oh how he loved riding among the ponderosa pines atop the butte, for the broad prairie seemed a rather unlikely place for a pine forest. To hear the eerie whistling sound of the wind as it passed over long needles. To see the jigsawed bark, cinnamon in color. And when the sun warmed the bark, to smell this fine tree's hint of cinnamon and vanilla.

In these early days, Cleve spent more than half his time hammering together a homestead shack, using some cast-off and some store-bought lumber. He had to build the barn of sod, then the bunkhouse of sod. Pausing for a drink, he surveyed patches of brown grass that just yesterday were green. He reckoned it would be a hot, dry summer. Old buffalo wallows held deep cracks instead of water. Last year's toads hadn't bothered to emerge from their mucous-lined burrows. His neighbor Nawica Kicijin noted Cleve's horse tied at the hitching post, signaling his new friend was home. So the old headman stopped in for a visit.

A vaulted sky was more sun-bleached than blue, not a cloud in sight. On this day the heat drove the pair directly to their small shade tree. Hats came off, foreheads were wiped, and shirts unbuttoned. A dipper and bucket of water was stationed between the pair. Cleve savored time with Nawica Kicijin, for a good reason. Badlands homesteaders were universally young or middle-aged men—hardly any old men to be seen.

Here sat a man three decades his senior. Cleve, the young man, had always sought the company of old men. Tough times seemed less so when an old man was across the corral or on the next horse—because that oldster had also been down to his last match, had seen troubles as bad, and worse. Cleve looked now at Nawica Kicijin's eyes, at the always present sadness therein. As the older man looked away at the land, Cleve's land, it struck him that his homestead was but yet another piece of Indian land gone forever. He of the conquering nation, Nawica Kicijin of the defeated nation. A sad smile from both seemed to acknowledge the native loss of land, of language, of religion, of livelihood.

Just then as Nawica Kicijin leaned down for a dip for water, Cleve glimpsed at the open collar deep scars evenly spaced across the old one's upper chest. The meaning seemed clear. So, when the headman returned the cowboy's wide-eyed stare with a self-effacing smile, Cleve's hunch felt confirmed—as a young man Nawica Kicijin must have stepped forward to suffer for the people at the pole of the Sun Dance. Nawica Kicijin lifted his head and narrowed his eyes, this squinting the damage from having stared too long at the sun during this long-ago ceremony.

Cleve imagined the roped thongs being plunged through pectoral muscles, so that the man before him could be suspended several feet above the ground. Staring directly at the sun. Agony elevated to transcendency. *Wi-wanyang-wa-c'i-pi*, the high holy Sun Dance.

Cleve assumed the rather elderly Nawica Kicijin's participation in the Sun Dance was a long-ago thing. It was a young man's challenge, plus the Sun Dance in its most self-mutilating rendition had been illegal for some decades.

Having seen the scars and the squinting, Cleve took in his guest's patriarchal features with fresh deference. What he did not know was that during these years of the Great War a milder form of the Sun Dance was being allowed . . . and that the old man sitting beside him was often honored as high ecclesiastic at the Rosebud Sun Dance.

Presently Cleve's eyes trailed off the stately face, to a pointing brown arm and index finger, hence to the far-off plume of white smoke that must have only recently popped up on the southeast horizon.

The men shared a knowing glance and raised eyebrows, both aware that white smoke declared prairie fire, dark smoke a forest fire. Either would be a threat in the dry conifer-stubbled range south of the ranch. Perhaps even to the place where they sat.

Faint frowns crept across both faces, but then the older man chuckled softly—for the pair were poles apart on how they viewed fire.

When Nawica Kicijin was little, when his name was Heyúktan, his people called fire the "Red Buffalo." A restorer of the prairie, bringer of new grasses and new herds. Fire was first a friend and secondarily a foe—intentionally set to drive game, to thwart an enemy's advance, or to clear smaller trees and brush (making for easier hunting). Some tribes would even intentionally set a "fire surround" to trap and roast protein-rich crickets and grasshoppers.

For Cleve's people fire was never a tool, always an enemy. Destroyer of the prairie. Destroyer of buildings. Destroyer of cattle and horses cornered by fences. Destroyer of cedar trees which he and other ranchers needed desperately for fence posts and fuel.

Without taking their eyes off the column of smoke, Cleve and Nawica Kicijin each noted how the wind blew unsteadily—now from the north, then the east, then the southwest. After watching the smoke some moments longer, both men stood and considered their options should the winds shift yet again.

21

Nawica Kicijin thought it prudent to untie his patient team and head for home. Cleve strode to the bed of his buckboard to double check a rancher's common kit for fighting wildfires—the short-handled shovel, the large gunny sack, and a 10-gallon jug of water for wetting that gunny sack.

When the smoke thinned, then disappeared, Cleve breathed deeper, easier. With that relief came a boyhood memory of his first wildfire. A memory he had not resurrected in many a year.

Had it been the drouthy summer of '92 or was it 1893? he wondered.

Cleve, then six or seven, was with little brother Claude cane-pole fishing in a side creek of the Niobrara River, intently watching the cork bobber. Then he jerked his head around on hearing a shout from father. And there he was, high on the river bluff some 80 rods distance, motioning urgently for the boys to join him.

Cleve was first to scramble up the bluff. Father pointed upriver at the grim sight: a dark wall of smoke, beneath which was a slightly smaller wall of advancing flames.

"Prairie fire, son! We've talked about this. I need you to run to the horse pasture to fetch Pilgrim and Donner. Pilgrim might be easier to catch. Whichever you can catch quickest, know that the other will follow."

With this, father paused only long enough to ensure Claude was ske-daddling for the house. In the instant before turning to fetch the draft horses, Cleve looked back to the house where a bucket brigade of older siblings and mother were even then wetting down the wood shake roof.

Lickety-split, breathless, Cleve was at the big horse pasture and rummaging for a tin of oats under a board covering a hollow tree stump. This he shook as he enticed the horses in. Before long he'd secured Pilgrim on a lead rope and was urging the big horses homeward. As they trotted for home, smoke and ashes were in the air, carried by a roaring west wind. Shadows disappeared as burning embers floated here and there.

In the excitement Cleve hadn't considered why father needed the draft horses. After all, there were big horses nearby in the stables. But approaching home he could see father bent to the labor of harnessing two horses to his biggest disc, an implement to turn the soil faster than a sod-breaking plow. Donner and Pilgrim would complete the powerful four-horse span, and James Baxter was soon feverishly urging them to cut an ever-wider black earth firebreak 'round and 'round the house.

Cleve briefly joined his siblings on the bucket brigade to the roof. But as flames roared closer, all scurried inside where mother passed out rags to be wetted and used to breathe through.

By the time father completed the plowed swath and tied the heaving team on the leeward side of the house, he had time only to slam the door behind him before the inferno stampeded up, over and around.

Cleve even now could recall the sheet of darkness, the freight train racket. And how the fire and smoke sucked all oxygen out of the house, making it momentarily impossible to breathe.

Then the stillness, as if time itself had ended.

The fire break and sodden roof had saved them. James Baxter Berry would not cry, but none forgot the trembling chin and eyes glassy bright as he enveloped each child in a bear hug.

Looking up now as Nawica Kicijin departed, Cleve wondered if perhaps this old man had been involved in another old Berry family story. He would be about the right age.

Cleve had not lived this family memory, but rather heard it told and retold at his mother's knee: the tale of the inter-tribal Indian battle that unfolded on a river bluff within easy sight of their Nebraska homestead in the 1870s. Mother had wanted to look away, but in that way we're all drawn to gruesome sights, she watched transfixed as mounted Lakota warriors circled a cluster of Ponca fighters dug into one of the farm's hilltops. She watched as men fell, to be dragged from the skirmish grounds by their compatriots.

The next day, Cleve's oldest brother had found a badly wounded warrior in a thicket below their house. Cleve's parents provided him water, food, and rags to bind his wounds. When offered shelter, he would not approach the wasicu buildings, and by next morning he was gone.

Three weeks later he returned briefly to the Berry homestead, healed now, and through sign language expressing thanks. Then vanished again.

As he mulled these memories Cleve bent to the task of pulling a drawknife to debark cedar logs, for only cedar made fence posts to last a hundred years. So many fence posts needed. So little time.

Chapter Three

When Names Were Earned
1867

Heyúktan peered sleepy-eyed from beneath the heavy softness of a buffalo robe covering his bedroll. With hands propping up his chin, fingers examined teeth for any tiny morsels that might have wedged there from last night's feast. As on most mornings, he felt no great urge to get up, for he was a somewhat different one, a weaker one among adolescent peers despite the irony of a rather formidable frame.

"The fragile one," sneered many of the other boys.

Not so long after Heyúktan learned to walk and talk, Lakotas endured what people remembered as the Winter of Babies-All-Sick-Many-Die. No one knew what the disease was or where it came from. A new sickness, Heyúktan's mother Sitting Bird believed it came from the east, from the wasicu.

Heyúktan did not die from the new sickness. But he suffered.

The sickness put him behind the other boys in skills learned, games won. So, despite eventually growing to larger than average size and unexpected robustness, Heyúktan's playmates doubted he would ever be a warrior. They mockingly called him "Walks Coughing." Such low expectations clung to and could not be shaken from his shoulders as he navigated his tenth, eleventh, twelfth winters.

But hunger beckoned, so earlier than usual Heyúktan flung back the buffalo robe and dressed for the day. First he would, as always, walk to the pony herd and see if he could spot all of his father's fine horses. Then he ran on tiptoes towards the smell of a nearby cooking fire.

Heyúktan rounded the tipi of Elk Robe's Wife Number One, the eighteen-hide tipi of his mother, Sitting Bird. He was just in time to see six-year-old half-sister Eagle Lodge chasing her favorite puppy—the animal playfully nipping the heels of a like-aged boy named Skunk. This neighbor boy was just then scampering past Sitting Bird's cooking fire, a child's bow in one hand and a dead meadowlark in the other.

Heyúktan had the power only to watch as Eagle Lodge shrieked on seeing Skunk spin around and kick the puppy, then begin firing toy arrows at the animal from his toy bow. At first the arrows, sharpened sticks really, bounced off the startled pup. But as a quick-forming circle of adults cheered on, the pint-sized future warrior stepped much closer and now his arrows were drawing blood.

Heyúktan felt he must rescue the puppy on behalf of his wailing little sister. But he hesitated. Lakota tradition demanded encouragement of pugnacious traits in little boys—the nation's future hunters, future warrior. In fact, male children were almost never punished—certainly not for displaying aggression.

Heyúktan's family loyalty vied with societal taboo, so he made only a tentative step and motion to disarm Skunk.

Before Heyúktan could lay a hand on Skunk's shoulder, a larger, firmer hand seemed to swallow up his lean shoulder.

Heyúktan's heart sank as his eyes followed the arm to the scowling face of Shirt of Bones.

Older brother to Skunk, and perennial thorn in Heyúktan's side, Shirt of Bones shouted, "Stay away! This is only a cur dog, surely destined for the stew pot." With this, he shoved Heyúktan to the ground.

Heyúktan could offer no resistance. Not with the growing circle of adults goading on Skunk and even laughing as Heyúktan assumed a sitting position and commenced dusting himself off. So many witnesses meant he would forever be seen as less than a natural-born warrior in a warrior society.

Before Heyúktan regained his feet, Eagle Lodge managed to snatch the bleeding puppy, its condition grim. She darted into her mother's tipi.

Just a year older than Heyúktan, Shirt of Bones had tormented Heyúktan for some years. The animosity had started so early that neither could recall the origins.

Perhaps it stemmed from the boy's fathers, both headmen, whose decades-old dispute over the ownership of a long-dead dappled stallion was rarely visible—but known to insiders. Perhaps it was that both boys were the tallest among their peers—Shirt of Bones robust in every way, Heyúktan still awkward in his leggy, newly muscled frame.

But Heyúktan's summer would come. The summer of noticing hairs on his body, hairs to foreshadow his manhood. The summer when two events put him forever beyond reach of any childhood rival.

The first came on the heels of the puppy incident, arriving as a lightning bolt for Heyúktan.

"Could it be?" At his feet lay a antelope-skin bundle that he opened with relish. Inside was a polished long bow, a man's bow to replace his much smaller practice bow and arrows. So unexpected because it came a season earlier than was Lakota custom. And so unexpected because the giver was not a relative, or even a family friend.

The giver had each summer been watching the next generation for a worthy boy on which to bestow the fine old bow, an heirloom of his *tiyospaye*, as he had no sons.

He was Spotted Eagle, a *Sans Arc* intancan of note . . . charismatic in the way of Crazy Horse, mystical in the way of Sitting Bull, fierce in battle, notably generous and self-effacing when among his own people.

And he had chosen an unlikely recipient for his gift from among the allied Miniconjou tipis. Spotted Eagle himself brought the gift to the Miniconjou tipi circle, conferring briefly with Elk Robe before sitting and talking with Heyúktan for the smaller part of an evening. Then he was gone. As Spotted Eagle walked away, Heyŭktan noted with a start the soft white antelope-skin bundle at his feet.

Though it was nearly dark, Heyŭktan quickly unfolded the bundle, strung the bow and ran straight away to test his skill on a fallen log behind the last of the tipis. Thus ended the day of the first miracle of his youth.

Heyŭktan and his tiyospaye would keep the news of Spotted Eagle's honoring gift to themselves for a few days. In this way its power would multiply.

Next morning Heyŭktan was dressed and sitting beside the cold morning ashes of his mother's evening cooking fire. Sitting and watching other children playing was a hard but not uncommon way to start his day. For certain elders noting Heyŭktan's wheezing breath had counseled him to be a sitter and watcher, not a doer.

And though a tribe could dream of future security only by counting the number of strong young boys in camp—the "citizen soldiers" of tomorrow, the elders said ones such as Heyŭktan were needed too. Men with minds and spirits capable of healing the sick, predicting the weather, finding and sharing the divine spark.

Still, the boy could hardly imagine a life as something less than a warrior. A solitary life without a warrior's name.

Heyŭktan, "to have bent horns," was hardly a name to shun, for it alluded to a yearling *pte*, or buffalo. Yet Heyŭktan dreamed of earning a name fit for manhood.

Any name given at birth was somewhat provisional. How could parents name a member of society before that child had declared his or her vision, or vocation, or experienced a defining moment? Only then could an adult name be truly owned, earned, chosen.

How strange by comparison seemed the wasicu custom, permanently naming a baby at or even before its birth.

At special times came grounds for a community naming ceremony—the new mantel bestowed on a youth aged nine, or fourteen, or twenty-one . . . based on unique signs or circumstances.

But, for the present, such matters were far from Heyúktan's mind. Rather, he hoarded waking moments in practice with the newly bestowed long bow.

Some days after the gift from Spotted Eagle, Heyúktan dared to take a back-row seat at a hastily convened council fire. First to speak was Eat No Dogs headman, High Backbone. Adorned in his buckskin scalp shirt, it was plain that today he was speaking not of hunting parties or trading or other peaceful matters, but of war.

High Backbone never needed to gesture for quiet, he needed only to rise, for his broad chest and fierce visage commanded attention. "We gather today because of an important bundle that arrived this morning by courier. It is from our brethren in the band of Touch the Clouds."

He cradled the bundle before lifting it for all to see.

With rising emotion now, he said, "The Touch the Clouds camp is on the Powder River, only one sleep away. The runner tells us Crow raiders killed two sentries and made away with a herd of almost two hundred Lakota ponies."

With this High Backbone abruptly found a seat within the inner-most circle as the august Black Shield rose, assumed the bundle, and walked close to the council fire. He wordlessly unwrapped the bundle to reveal a war pipe, and held it high for all to see. Fetching a burning twig, Black Shield lit the pipe. Soon the men nearest the fire, all noted warriors, were passing the lit pipe in a clockwise fashion.

To smoke the war pipe. To string one's bow. To go to war.

This meant Heyúktan's band would begin immediately to move camp a day's journey away to a point near the northern tip of the sacred

Black Hills. Here they would be in position to join Touch the Cloud's band in assaulting the Crow camp.

This last major battle between these traditional enemies was fought in a howling gale. Those remaining in the village huddled in nervous groups. Most could only imagine the violence unfolding in the next valley. Each silently wondering, would their loved one return with a scalp, with a wound, or face down over the back of a pack horse?

As happened more often than not, the dominant tribe of the Northern Plains, the mighty Sioux, prevailed.

Winds dropped from gale to breeze to misty stillness on the afternoon when runners brought news of the morning's victory. Heyúktan heard it from his mother. On a battlefield even closer than expected. Now blazing sunshine was competing with growing ranks of clouds, and atypical patches of fog. It is August, 1870 by the white man's calendar.

The group of youngsters shoved one another playfully, then jumped up and down in excitement. They had just received permission from a certain elder to scavenge the battlefield for useable arrow-points, shafts, cartridges, clothing . . . any items which might gain a second life. The instructions from Touch The Clouds were firm—"You may touch the body of any fallen Crow, be it warrior, woman, or child, only for purposes of retrieving useful items. Remember that their relatives and even their spirits, our true enemies, may yet be close at hand."

Heyúktan was among the small group gravely absorbing Touch The Cloud's admonitions.

Years later the wasicu would know this place of death to be the lower slopes of Crow Peak—a name immortalizing the hardhearted Lakota win in this final act of a centuries-old rivalry.

The youngsters set out then, seven in all, at a purposeful walk—moving, as taught, always below the crest of any ridge or hill. Twelve-winters Heyúktan was not the oldest of the group. But he was easily the tallest. As the children walked, Heyúktan was not-so-gently goaded for lacking bravery worthy of his size.

Acting as though they would assume group leadership were twins Bad Thunder and Bear Shield, fourteen-winters. Also along for the adventure were the youngsters Little Knife, Dog Eyes, and the plucky prepubescent girls Pretty Bird and White Shell.

Ten minutes from camp, White Shell pointed out turkey vultures riding thermals over the battlefield in broad circles, gliding lower, lower.

The children followed a creek down into a light ground fog hugging the bottomlands, all the while discussing what might await them.

"I may collect a grownup's bow, and this I will gift to my big brother," said White Shell. "With it he will hunt the forked-horn, bringing me the hide that makes softest moccasins."

"It is possible we will find a Crow still breathing." Bad Thunder clapped his hands at the prospect. "If this may be so, I will count coup. Then our warriors will call me one of theirs. They will allow me on the next horse raid." Bear Shield grunted his approval.

Heyúktan frowned, "Have you so quickly forgotten the instructions of our elder Touch The Clouds? Must you hear it from Black Shield himself?"

Bad Thunder stopped and stared hard at Heyúktan. As did Bear Shield.

Heyúktan simply kept moving, but maintained a sideways glance as he walked past Bad Thunder. All others scrambled to keep up with Heyúktan. The twins could only shrug, then follow from the rear.

Heyúktan could feel many pairs of eyes warm on his back as he moved out ahead. This told Heyúktan he was now the little group's leader, if only for today.

Rounding the crest of a hill, Heyúktan slowed, and put his hands up as he saw the first sacrificials of the battle. Two war ponies lay side by side amid dry rivulets of blood. One carcass was a pincushion of arrows, the other riddled with bullet holes.

As Heyúktan and the others drew closer, it was clear these war ponies died at nearly the same time. Yet one had its mane braided in the Crow fashion for the buffalo hunt. The other horse was marked, neck and rump, in Lakota war colors—its tail, battle ready, tied up in a ball.

First Heyúktan, then the others, stepped forward to count coup by touching the fallen Crow mount. None touched the other horse, the only fallen "Lakota" they could see on a battlefield where any slain Lakota had already been reverently recovered. From here Heyúktan led the others among the ghastly, grotesque, and often mutilated bodies of the Crow.

The buzz of hungry flies. The bloating. The red blood dried to black, caking the earth in great patches. Glassy-eyed faces on every side seemed disconnected from torsos, and broken limbs wrenched in unnatural angles.

Among the rocks and against the base of bunchgrass were bits of hair, brains, entrails.

And everywhere the smell. Not the smell of death. Not yet—but of bile, feces, vomit.

One young warrior, barely older than Heyúktan, lay in what could have been peaceful repose save for a gaping wound to the neck, a partially scalped head, and digits harvested for a likely dried-finger necklace.

"Remember. Touch the Clouds commands us to walk this killing ground without sentiment," said Heyúktan. "He said we must be strong if we invite this adventure. I now understand his words."

They rolled each stiffened body slowly over, in hopes of exposing some small prize. Instead, only more reek of human putrefy—though further on Bear Shield gleaned a leather pouch holding a few Springfield

32

cartridges, and Bad Thunder recovered a quiver of broken arrows, but with useful trader arrowheads attached.

Some bodies, bloating already, had gaping wounds, blasted tissues, jagged bones protruding. Others lay mysteriously unmarked, yet no less dead.

Just then the group was brought to a standstill by a sight that erased any lingering hope of discovering some trace of "glory" on the battle-field—

The lifeless young Crow mother was on her back, her infant at the breast, pinned there by a constellation of Lakota arrows.

"No quarter given. None expected." To generations of Lakota and Crow children, this mantra was oft repeated, never questioned. Heyúktan swallowed hard and fought back tears.

Pretty Bird and White Shell were now crying softly without bothering to wipe tear-stained cheeks. And imploring the others to retreat with them to camp.

Bear Shield and Bad Thunder took halting steps toward the awful scene, perhaps coveting the arrows. Heyúktan nodded to the girls so as to assure them that the adventure was ending. Then he spoke: "Touch The Clouds warned us of this moment. Still, let us pause, and not run homeward as so many fearful rabbits. It will smell of defeat. Let us walk the reflective walk back to camp."

They turned north, walking a deliberately meandering path that helped keep a distance from the more grotesque bodies.

The now somber mood turned quickly to high alert as they ascended one of the low river bluffs. Heyúktan had spotted movement just ahead.

Still below the gently curved rim of the bluff, Heyúktan and party crouched low while straining to see who, or what, was coming their way.

Was it Crow warriors returning to claim their dead?

Wolves or coyotes come to scavenge the dead?

But then the intruder's barely visible craniums revealed a trademark ridge of hair on otherwise shaved heads. Pawnee!

Also traditional enemies of the Lakota, the Pawnee ranged south and east of the Black Hills. But it was not unheard of to spot raiding parties here on the northwest slopes of the Hills.

The intruders appeared to be apprentice warriors, perhaps only a year or two older than Heyúktan and his companions. Their leader stood out for his red painted forehead with similarly vermillion makeup circling his stiffly roached hair.

Clearly the interlopers too had spotted the Lakota children, reacting in the same cautious, crouching manner.

Time stood stiff as a Sun Dance center pole.

Hunkered behind a spiked yucca plant, Heyúktan briefly regretted earlier events of the day ordaining him the group's leader. Just as quickly, his nimble mind began assessing the situation.

The Pawnee teens had rather expertly found such meager cover as was available. They appeared to number eight, ten at most. By outward appearance eager for a fight, they were close enough to potentially launch lethal arrows.

Heyúktan observed the terrain in three directions for possible escape routes. *My force is small. And with girls of just eight winters, we'll not outrun this true enemy.* Uneasy glances from the twins seemed to confirm what he already believed: fighting these older boys would be as foolish as fleeing.

Heyúktan's glance fell to the western horizon, and the peculiar summer sight of sun dogs shimmering to either side of a reddish sun.

A good omen, Heyúktan thought.

Stillness reigned on both sides, but presently the Pawnee's movements suggested a willingness to press the issue. So Heyúktan used common hand signals to tell the younger children to remain partially concealed, even as he motioned Bear Shield and Bad Thunder forward.

"The three of us need not, should not hide," he whispered, "for in seeing us the Pawnee may believe the others are as old or older. We must be tricksters, appearing other than who we are. So string your bows, and notch one arrow."

Even as he said this, Heyŭktan knew the twins carried only the short bows of younger boys, tipped with "bird point" arrowheads meant only for practice in hunting small birds.

Fate, though, had intervened days earlier when Heyŭktan received the manly full-sized bow from Spotted Eagle.

A verdant breeze brushed all cheeks, bringing wisps of fog and haze up from the river flats. With it a resolve began to rise in Heyŭktan's breast. Everything, blades of grass, grains of sand, became sharp and clear. As if he was born to this hour.

It was to be life's seminal moment. Even for a youth who had entered his world a little too late to ever be a great warrior, or mighty hunter, or all-seeing scout of the people.

"Arise," said his heart, then his head.

With mists blowing round his ankles Heyŭktan whispered to his companions, "Now is come our salvation." He uncoiled from a crouch to stand at full height. Big for his age, carrying the now-strung long bow, one might mistake Heyŭktan for an unconcerned, unafraid young warrior.

Within range of arrows, this boldness smacked to the Pawnee of one expecting mounted reinforcements. Or was it the display of a madman, or a contrarian, or did he represent something altogether different?

The sun and its guardian sundogs hung as if anchored to the lip of a western skyline. Heyŭktan's form hummed with confidence, all eyes on him now. He looked north before pointing to the south, making the motion to "come forward" as if signaling some unseen army behind him.

The crimson-headed Pawnee youth rose up on one knee. Without taking his eyes off this brazen Lakota, he reached back to pull an arrow from his quiver. Then came hesitation as he noted the two crouching figures behind Heyúktan. All three were notching arrows into bow strings. "Am I seeing three warriors? How many more crouch just beyond the rim of the hill?" thought the crimson-headed one.

The Pawnee leader did not hesitate, scrambling downhill towards the southeast, towards the tribe's ancestral heartland. Presumably towards the out-of-sight warriors of his tribe. The others followed in disorderly retreat.

For the relieved Lakota youngsters, built-up tension flowed from their heads and hearts down into their feet and the ground—for now they were walking, then running towards camp. Stringing out in the fashion of prancing fawns or wild foals.

Heyúktan kept to a walking pace . . . occasionally glancing over his shoulder even as the others hurried ahead upon spying their people's black-topped tipis.

Entering camp, the group shouted to any who might listen, "We crouch in danger, but he stands tall for us. Heyúktan rises up like the mighty bear. He stands his ground. He stands for us!"

Even six decades later, Bad Thunder spoke almost reverently of this day: "It was as though the spirit of *Canopus* (creator) came to rest for a moment on Heyúktan. A grace was upon him."

Word spread—Who stands for them? Heyúktan stands for them.

In this hour the arc of his life was set.

So it was that the family and friends of Heyúktan began almost at once to organize a naming ceremony. Heyúktan, all agreed, had today named himself for all time.

In the gloaming Heyŭktan's father Elk Robe, Grandfather Santee Man and *hunka* uncles individually counseled with him. "In two sleeps," they had all told him, "we cannot, will not, ever again call you Heyŭktan. This may feel strange, but such thoughts will last for only a moon or two."

Heyŭktan spent the balance of the evening illumined by the amber glow of his mother's cooking fire. Repeatedly looking at his hands, touching his face, wondering at his newness, at a loftier path now visible. The path of both opportunity and peril.

Next day, beneath a white-hot sun sliding in cloudlessness towards evening, all gathered at the central fire of the Eat No Dogs. It was to be a naming ceremony, with Heyŭktan's family promising a buffalo hump feast and a give-away to honor their eldest son—the quiet one who had by actions, not words, stated his case for admission to Lakota manhood.

Elk Robe officiated at the brief but dignified ceremonials. His voice rising, not in volume, but in majesty. Then a hawkish gaze in the direction of his eldest, "There is a moment, perhaps only once in a lifetime, when a person must either stand up or remain out of sight. That moment has come."

Across the fire sat a cluster of Heyŭktan's former tormentors, most now sitting as admirers. Among them perched the glum-faced Shirt Of Bones, and to his left Skunk.

When it came time for the bestowing, Heyŭktan was surprised and a little awed to have High Backbone step forward to retell the story of the face-off with the Pawnee. He ended with these words: "For our people names carry magic. Your only name from this day, your warrior name, will be Nawica Kicijin (Stands For Them). So say your witnesses. So say the people."

Chapter Four

Why Cowboys Walk That Way
1918, then 1861

Cleve put down his splitting axe. He looked up to reckon where the sun floated in the sky, half hoping it was holding still so he could finish cutting a full cord of firewood. But half hoping it was sliding closer to sunset—his only path away from hard labor towards Jessie's warm supper and sleep. One who works sunup to sundown need carry no watch.

At the same hour but miles away, Jessie wiped ruby-chapped hands on her ever more threadbare apron. The day had been as lonely and indistinguishable as the day before, and the day before that. Stepping out the shack's only door, she inhaled just as the great prairie exhaled its elemental loneliness.

Shadows served as her clock, and they said hours to go before sunset. Hours to go until the brief welcome company of another adult. She'd endured over three years in the badlands and the windswept melancholy of it all, mostly invisible to men, was growing.

Today as she often did, Jessie reread letters from her sisters. They would understand. For only they had lived both in verdant Iowa and arid Dakota. Only they knew what it meant to lose the tree-lined fields, whitewashed fences, rolling meadows, tidy farms, and charmed villages of early sisterhood.

Looking out the small kitchen window, she wondered, "Is this what I signed up for?" Still, one must keep up appearances. So after rereading each letter, twice, she took up her fountain pen to write what she did not believe: "Oh sister, I'm sure it will get better. When we prove up on this homestead we'll sell and move to California. Petaluma or Thousand

Oaks or some such place. Don't they sound lovely? Cleve promised me. It's our dream. I just hope he doesn't fall too deeply into this rough cowboy life." She paused to shoo a fly away from the table.

"We arrived from Tripp County with 33 head of livestock, counting the milk cow. Our brand will therefore be a rather plain-spoken "33." Cleve's already had the blacksmith in Norris fashion the branding iron, with a flat top to the "3" as everyone says this makes it harder for rustlers to alter the brand.

I was allowed to bring my fine saddle mare, Ginger. I so debated bringing my side-saddle, too. I'm glad I didn't. The country here is rough and so I ride as men do. In any event there's no one to disapprove, and Cleve does not care a whit. Riding astride is much more fun.* But for the most part, sister, life here in the pioneer West seems always about some future dream. Never the present, which can be so harsh. Always next year, next year, next year. I have resolved to believe in the man separate from the man's dream. I will say this sister, Cleve is not overly influenced by others. He is his own man."

She put down her fountain pen, hesitated, then added a P.S.: "Here in Dakota especially, but in Iowa too, isn't a woman's life always bent to fit the arc of the man's life?" Tall, painfully thin, Jessie sealed the envelope and turned to her endless rural chores: Tomorrow was laundry day, where a large cast iron tub over wood coals required homemade soap fashioned from beef tallow and lye (having run out of both last month she resorted to the local soapweed). Jessie completed those preparations, then onto piles of sewing, to thirsty vegetables calling from

---

* In 1899, 1903 or 1910 a proper young lady did not ride astride. It was impractical given the long, heavy skirts and considered indecent by norms of modesty. Hence the need for a sidesaddle. But times were changing, so in the badlands Jessie Berry rode Ginger cowboy-style— a much enjoyed weekly pleasure.

the garden to critters needing water and feed hauled. Her dark eyes and long neck bestowed a sort of racehorse beauty that was even then stumbling towards a premature and shadowy middle age.

Cleve too had found the struggle of homesteading tougher than expected. The couple lived without mail service, or telephone, or electricity, or running water, or any indoor plumbing or toilet. Their drafty tarpaper shack was hand-built by Cleve, and he was no carpenter. It stood exposed and uninsulated, and within the thin walls heating and cooking were strictly by firewood.

1886 had been Cleve's birth year. Babies born that year were the last American generation to assume their world would be powered by horses, never mind the passing fad of horseless carriages. But by 1918 the horse was no longer center stage. Except in pockets of the still-frontierlike West. Pockets like the Cedar Butte country.

*****

This morning, like most mornings, Cleve had been up before the sun. Jessie and the babies could sleep a little longer while he fired the squatty cookstove with split cedar logs. Jessie would then make an outsized breakfast to fuel Cleve's twelve-hour workday.

She watched Cleve rush through flapjacks and eggs, but as always, his kiss on the cheek to thank her. Time to catch and saddle the right horse, a choice depending on his job. Today he needed a horse surefooted and fit enough to scale the highest reaches of the butte in pursuit of the last wolf in the territory.

The horse for the job—a newly acquired and rather hot blooded one among his geldings—leggy, sable-colored and called Jug on account of his ample head. A natural cutting horse with a deep bottom.

Across Prairie Dog Flats and into the rough country they advanced. Any old cow puncher spotting the pair would have said, "That man can sit a horse." Rifle in the scabbard, and a $4 Oneida Wolf Trap tied on the pommel, the pair entered the jumbled badland buttresses holding high the flattop of Cedar Butte. The initial big draw, just now bathed in the sun's first frail rays, quickly tapered to a lightly worn cow trail leading ever higher.

Cleve trotted Jug into the draw, reining him towards the impossibly steep, narrow trail to the tabletop. To gain the crest, he must first throw his heart up there—then the horse would follow.

Closer now and without being asked, he felt the horse gather beneath him, take the bit, and by blood and muscle rise like a tidal wave, sweeping to the top on gravity-defying lunges.

Cleve coveted this explosion of energy—the crux of life it seemed—nature's exclamation point. To him it was the moment a thousand wild geese launch as one from water to air—the twinkling when coursing dogs are let slip—the instant rival bull buffalo vault to collide suspended. For horsemen this is that moment, the electric jolt of energy that welds rider to steed, exposing for but an instant the full brawn of the beast.

From the top Cleve sat the horse, for Jug had earned a blow. Up here Cleve enjoyed a forty-mile uninterrupted line of sight, taking in most of the Cedar Butte-Pine Ridge-Black Pipe Creek country—that province where the moonscape of the badlands crashes against and finally succumbs to the Great Plains. Hoodoos, canyons, mesa formations, and gumbo walls. A land of many hiding places where steep, narrow trails beckon horses and cattle but forbid wagons and motor vehicles.

Partly because of these constraints, this borderland of the two big reservations was and still is a haven of plainsman traditionalism. Here the cow pony never quite yielded to the pickup truck or any other machine. *Just as it should be,* thought Cleve as he reached down to stroke Jug's neck. He'd need this horse tomorrow. For it was November, the start of South Dakota's frightful winter. With it came a cold weather job dreaded by man and beast. Cleve's livestock required one good daily drink of water, made impossible by creeks and stock dams frozen over. Each morning 900 thirsty cows lined up at dams across the spread, knowing their rancher would come.

Armed only with a single bit axe to chop through thick ice, Cleve daily alternated among his strongest saddle horses for the bone-chilling circuit of six or seven far-flung dams. On such frigid mornings, a mount could be more easily bridled and saddled if offered a few kindnesses—first a little oats, then Cleve grasped the icy steel bit in his bare hand to warm it up before asking his horse to open its mouth for the bridling.

Thus commenced the long race to beat back frostbite, exhaustion, and the dangers of working alone. But not really alone. The right horse could be a lifesaver. As Cleve finished chopping the ice on the last dam, he thought back to a similar wintry scene when he first learned the right horse can rescue a life.

It was Christmas, time for a little holiday trip. At just twelve, Cleve was surprised and proud to have received permission to drive the big team . . . pulling the sledded hay rig over four miles of whiteness to Uncle Zeke's ranch house beside Dry Creek. Sisters Elva and Dude were bundled in layers of wool and scarf for this cousins outing.

The December sky was fair, but with scattered clouds grazing across winter's deep blue dome . . . not a day to make a grownup worry about bad weather. And five inches of snow on the ground would be no problem for such a heavy team.

On departure, the team belied their girth by coltishly high-stepping on account of the chill air. Cleve's father smiled to see Cleve standing more than sitting on the high wagon seat, his full weight needed to manage the reins. James Baxter Berry's smile and wave assured Cleve he was handling King and Ol' Clancy just fine.

The sisters sat on bales of hay behind the high seat. The trio's cross-country trip was uneventful. Arriving a little earlier than expected and watching Uncle Zeke lead the team to warm stables, the children were soon enjoying games and picture books, sipping hot cider, and later downing a steaming lunch of beef soup with dumplings.

When it came time to re-hitch the still-harnessed team to the rig, Uncle Zeke helped. Oddly, a few snowflakes were now dancing in the air. The sky was gray but not dark.

"Get to goin', youngsters. Do not tarry." The lumbering hay rig lurched out of the yard, as if pushed by the now sharp wind. The tip of Cleve's nose and his cheeks felt the bite of dropping mercury.

When barely a mile north of Zeke's, the blizzard of 1898 dealt Nebraska a bare-knuckles wallop. A horizontal wall of snow pellets arrived as the wind shifted to the northeast.

White everywhere. No up. No down. In minutes Cleve could see only the muscular snow-covered rumps of King and Ol' Clancy.

Then it happened. The right sleigh runner dropped suddenly into some ditch or streamlet hidden in tall grass. Hopelessly stuck. Worse yet, Cleve could see upon climbing down that King and Ol' Clancy had broken part of the double-tree in their lunging efforts to free the wagon. Still worse, all sleigh tracks were now covered in white, obscuring directions back to Zeke's or homeward.

Children don't often see their own mortality. But as each looked by turn at the other's tearless, wide-eyed face, the youngsters saw it and felt it.

Then through howling winds and rising panic rose a voice calm and certain. Their father—"If ever stranded in a blizzard or fog, put your faith in the horse to find its way home. They have powers we humans do not."

Though closer to Uncle Zeke's place, Cleve knew the horses would "home" through the storm in but one location: their own corral and stables.

Leaving horse collars and harnesses in place, and racing against numbing fingers, Cleve disconnected traces and reins so as to give the horses "their head" in the blinding snow.

Without being asked, sisters pitched in to unhook the tugs from the curled iron ends of the singletrees. Then with a leg up from Cleve, they boosted up to ride double on King. Cleve clamored up on Ol' Clancy.

With a gravitas befitting the moment, the lumbering horses began trotting a wide circle 'round the wagon as if still harnessed side-by-side. Once, twice, three times with heads high and nostrils flaring so as to divine from the very air the direction home.

Then—sure as homing pigeons—they were off, churning through the whiteness like equestrian statues come alive. The children clung tight to mane and harness, trusting this best chance at deliverance.

The whiteout muffled every noise save the dull thud of hoofbeats on frozen ground. Beneath arched necks the big team pumped out steam-like breath.

At length Ol' Clancy pulled up as though there were an obstacle in his path. Half a step behind, King did the same. Through snow-crusted eyes the children could at first see nothing—but then glimpsed the obstacle. The horses had stopped directly in front of the familiar barn-yard pump.

They were home. When wrapped in quilts before a high fire, the three exchanged teary-eyed glances more knowing than their tender years would imply.

Human and horse sense would save yet another Berry life sixty years later:

It was a fine spring day. Heads and tails high in that manner of beasts fresh off the winter range, a dozen shaggy horses thundering towards an open corral gate. The gate was held open by Cleve and beside him was his visiting daughter, Marian, and her toddler son. They stood to witness this galloping spectacle.

Then with a child's bad timing, Marian's wee boy darted into the path of the horses. As Marian shrieked and moved to save the child, Cleve grabbed her arm. In that moment the horses neatly sidestepped the unsuspecting child as they thundered into the corral.

After closing the corral gate, and with his grandson safely back in Marian's arms, Cleve explained why he'd grabbed her arm so forcefully, "Honey, those big critters are spooky from not being ridden in months. But horses naturally avoid hitting anything to trip 'em up, living or not. If you'd bolted out to save Johnny, the confusion would've shied one or more horses into running over your baby."

The close call got Cleve and Marian to talking horses as they walked slowly back to the house on the narrow trail between two stock dams. Having put Johnny down for a nap, Marian joined her father at the kitchen table where they continued the conversation over the day's third cup of coffee.

"Yeah, devotion to horses runs deep in our people. Even choosing love of horses over personal safety, even unto last breaths. You know how your Grampa Iddings died. But do you know what killed my Gramps William Preston?"

Marian looked up sharply from her coffee, "Grampa Iddings, sure. But no one ever told me about Great-Grampa." Cleve stood to warm up his coffee before continuing.

"Well, then here ya go. It was 1874. Grampa was in his mid-50s, returning home from working a claim. To get home he'd had to drive his team and wagon over that damn frozen Verdigree. It's a tributary of the Niobrara River."

"My dad remembered the day well—gray and chilly even for a late winter's day. Chilly enough to give confidence that the Verdigree River would be frozen safe and solid."

"Halfway across, it happened. A kaboom like a cannon shot. The ice collapsed, and instantly horses and half the wagon were in icy waters.

"It took the full efforts of Willian Preston Berry and two bystanders to save his panicked horses. Must have been a frightful scene, great chunks of ice—dreadful dangerous for those people and those half-mad horses."

"Somehow Gramps saved those animals. But then he had no choice but a long, wet, cold ride home in the dark. Saw to his team's needs in the barn, naturally, before stripping off his wet clothes. Took sick of course. I think it was just a few days before he was dead. Death certificate says death was by acute inflammatory rheumatism. The family always said it was death by love of horses."

Cleve looked across at Marian before looking down at yet another work-related series of nicks and cuts to his calloused hands. She left to attend to Johnny, then crying out from the upstairs bedroom.

Sitting alone now, another recollection of the Gramps he never met bubbling up, this one from fifty years past—the afternoon little Cleve entered his father's bedroom, unbidden, to find a dusty field Bible in a cigar box under the bed.

The first page of the ragged Bible made it clear this was Grampa William Preston's own, perhaps the one he took into battle in the Mexican War, or maybe the War Between the States. On that page, below his name and in his own hand, was written this: "See page 514." Cleve had flipped straight to that page, where Grampa'd used what must have been a crude pencil to circle this short passage in the Book of Job:

"Hast thou not given the horse strength?

Hast thou not clothed his neck with thunder?

He swalloweth the ground with fierceness and rage . . ."

Later as Cleve trod the narrow path between two stock dams separating his barn and house, thoughts drifted from Grandpa William to that other family member who died for love of horses: father-in-law Joe Iddings.

Cleve never much liked Joe. But he allowed that the old man was one hell of a judge of horseflesh. This talent started early: When a teenage illness rendered Joe unfit for hard labor, he learned to make a living primarily as a horse trader. He bought low and sold high, his practiced eye always seeing the lame horse that would recover, the gaunt horse that could be fattened, the wild horse that could be gentled.

The remount quartermaster at Fort Robinson, with whom Joe did plenty of business, once said, "If you tied every horse Joe Iddings has bought or sold head to tail, they'd damn near circle the globe!"

Cleve had been to the Winner, S.D. Livestock Sale Barn many times. Particularly for the horse sales. But not that summer day in 1946 when his cantankerous father-in-law, frail and eighty-four, spied a stiff-legged two-year-old filly he fancied. Interested in possibly purchasing the callow horse, he could not resist climbing aboard. When Joe Iddings was bucked off, the injuries led to his death.

Next day Cleve looked up with a smile to see Stands For Them examining a horse he did not recognize beside the water trough. The man's big hands passed lightly over each of the horses' four legs, pausing here and there to stroke twice over some joint, sinew, or muscle of interest.

As Cleve watched, it struck him that here stood an Indian of that last generation to carry the deep skills of aboriginal horsemanship. Cleve approached the pair. Together, wordlessly, the men assessed the animal's merits. Theirs was becoming a companionship wonderfully lacking in words, but also in obligation—no blood ties, no business ties. Tied not by someone else's marriage or race or language or any other thread. Mutual love of horses they had, but best was these things they did not have.

Both knew that of all the horses a man might own or ride, always there was the recollection of one's first horse.

For Stands For Them it was a morn when he awoke to the smell of Eat No Dog fires simmering breakfasts of rabbit meat and wild onion.

Five-year-old Heyúktan stood in dawn's mustard light, as enshrined in memory. The rays of sun filtered through a wall of cottonwoods to alternately conceal and reveal his father leading a chestnut foal with a white blaze down the nose. His first horse!

In a brief private family ceremony at once joyous and solemn, Elk Robe handed the lead rope to wide-eyed Heyúktan.

For the rest of the morning, Elk Robe led the mounted Heyúktan and pony in ever tighter circles—first steps towards the fine art of Lakota horsemanship. He showed his little boy how to rub one's body smell into the nostrils of a foal so the animal would forever carry the signature odor of her owner. He taught Heyúktan to pass hands gently over every part of the animal's body—the ritual calming that over time convinced the creature that certain two-leggeds meant no harm.

All the while Elk Robe suppressed a smile, for he wished Heyúktan to know the gravity of horse ownership. Heyúktan would henceforth be responsible for seeing that the foal had clean water, proper pasture, exercise, and daily human contact. All of this in preparation for that moon when riding lessons might begin.

"One day, perhaps next summer, you will join the bigger boys in village horse races. You and I have often watched and cheered these races," said Elk Robe.

"And if you are very patient and very lucky, this little horse may grow up to be a buffalo runner. But only steeds brave enough and well-trained enough to gallop in among stampeding buffalo will carry this name." Elk Robe did not burden his son with further details, but in the rare instance when such an admired equine was sold, it commanded twenty or even thirty common horses in trade.

By midday Heyúktan's new pony was staked beside the family tipi, but even then lessons continued when Elk Robe and son sat cross-legged beside the cooking fire. "Heyúktan, listen closely to the Lakota way of the horse. Our people are supreme riders in both war and on the hunt. Each horse is of high value, being our swift legs in war and our escape from prairie fires. When all hunting fails, horse sacrifices its very flesh to our empty stomachs."

"We Lakota came late to acquire *sunka wakan*. We rightly call ourselves the Horse Nation, but our enemies the Crow and Shoshone came by horses first. And even now they have more horses. You know I own this number of horses." He flashed ten fingers twice. "But a Crow headman of my status will have forty or more!"

Hesitating, Elk Robe stirred the red-hot coals with a stick. He hated to acknowledge a Lakota field of inferiority, but he did so now to impress on Heyúktan that each and every horse was important to the *oyate*.

Turning towards Heyúktan's new mare and gesturing, Elk Robe said, "Your animal was bred and born here. This is a good thing. Slowly our tribe learns these skills. Even so we gain most new horses, new blood stock, in the old manly ways—by capturing wild mustangs in the Sand

Hills. Or by horse raids that you will soon join—a double goodness to gain horses at the expense of our enemies."

Horse Raiding

By the Frost-in-Tipi moon of his sixteenth winter, Stands For Them rightly considered himself among the elite riders of the Miniconjou Lakota. He'd first garnered glances of admiration in the impromptu horse races among village boys. Bareback, with only a cord of uncured leather looped over his mount's lower jaw. Bent to the horse's neck, his long black hair matching the mane and tail of his horse in streaming horizontal. Usually winning. For though Stands For Them didn't always ride the swiftest animal, when he asked, his mount answered.

Many were his horse mentors. But the elder Two Lance, of a Cheyenne father and Comanche grandmother, had shared with him the deepest secrets of a great rider:

"Learn," Two Lance said stern faced, "that a horse naturally moves away from pressure. Apply the pressing of your legs alone to steer the animal." Two Lance would then mount his fine roan Sha' hinska, being yet limber enough to demonstrate this skill, returning to his pupil with a sliding stop and dismount in one clean motion. In time, Stands For Them too could ride with legs only, hands free to wield a hunting weapon.

Two Lance was, however, too old to demonstrate the prowess of a mounted warrior. But by carefully listening, toward summer's end Stands For Them could be seen galloping a steed, then hooking a heel over the back and grabbing a handful of mane. To village observers he thus seemingly disappeared, dropping to the side to give an enemy nothing to shoot at.

In their last lesson together Two Lance revealed the secrets of a horse stealer. He showed how by rubbing one's body with sage and then lightly putting a hand over the nose of a nervous Crow or Pawnee animal, Stands For Them could manifest a quieting down, a standing still, a becoming undetectable even to the noses and ears of enemy camp dogs. These were the death-defying skills of one who would be a horse stealer.

This last day spent with Two Lance inspired Stands For Them to later pose lofty questions to his father. "Where did the first camp dogs come from?" Elk Robe answered that all dogs were once wolves. "But then where did horses come from?" pressed Stands For Them.

To this holy mystery, Elk Robe could bring no good answer. But after some thought Elk Robe offered this: "I have only known a world with horses, but when I was little, in one of the more pitiful little tents in my winter village there sat an ancient one who yet carried faint memory of days before horses."

"Her name was Forest Woman, and she was as small and wrinkled as a winter plum. She talked of how hard life was before *Shunka Wakan*. She spoke of a people always on the march to avoid enemies and follow game. The oldest and youngest all must walk, and all must carry back-breaking burdens."

"One day Forest Woman surprised us all by saying life before *Shunka Wakan* was in some ways less fearful. In those ancient days, she said, an enemy raiding party could not appear with such lightning speed. She spoke of how the horse created uncertainty. And wealth, and from this came greed and war."

Stands For Them listened spellbound to these stories of a once new creature so special that the Lakota called it *Shunka Wakan*, loosely translated as "holy dog' or "God's dog."

He learned that time and space changed when the first Lakota mounted a horse. That distant ridge was no longer a half day's walk away. The stampeding buffalo no longer out of reach.

He closed his eyes to imagine the Winter of Much Buffalo Meat, the year his father said scouts reported seeing a new kind of animal ridden by the U.S. Cavalry: American horses that towered over the sturdy little Lakota ponies. The people gave these outsized animals a special name: *sunka wakan Milahanska*, "Holy Dog of the Long Knives."

After Stands For Them's horse racing years, there followed a summer of training unbroken horses. It was a time when Stands For Them's hands and gaze and words spoken and unspoken spun an irresistible aura. An aura telling any wild horse he approached that it did not belong to itself anymore.

Near the end of that summer, Stands For Them had accumulated ten animals. Two runners—these for the buffalo and antelope hunts. One war horse. A wife's mount, though he had no wife. Two ponies for packing his small tipi, the bundles, the dried meat. One gentle general-purpose horse that could, for example, carry two or three children on its back. And then as usual a pair of horses in training, beasts soon available for trading or as gift horses. His herd gave Stands For Them a certain status if not quite a swagger, the latter seemingly out of reach for one so sickly in boyhood. He aspired to but one further thing equine—acquiring or training a proper scout's horse.

Sleepy-eyed, Stands For Them could hear a predawn commotion around his tipi—meaning surely that he was invited to join a teenage group trying their hand at acquiring horses in the old manly ways. They had caught wild horses before, this group. When not out hunting, Stands For Them had often joined them.

Easily the best place to find the wild ones—the vast Sand Hills. So any time the Eat No Dogs were near the Sand Hills, Good Thunder, Red Claw, Smoke and Feather would be mounted up and trotting around Stands For Them's tipi before even first light streaked the east.

Stands For Them completed the team, and soon they gathered at the village exit and looked to their member most experienced for final instructions.

"Now," Feather leaned forward and pointed towards the Sandhills, "remember that success comes most easily when we can surprise the stallion, and separate him from his mares. When bedlam reigns, we shall surely herd a few of the circling mares into a box canyon!"

On this adventure all were disappointed, turning homeward with only a buckskin mare and a yearling dun stallion gained. For their riding skills or perhaps just luck in the chase, Smoke was awarded the mare and Good Thunder the young stallion.

On the return trek, Stands For Them and Good Thunder spied the tracks of a three-legged antelope, a fourth leg broken and dragging. Such an easy harvest elicited a quick glance one to the other, saying they must together pursue. This they did as Good Thunder left his young stallion with Feather. The tracking was so easy they could advance at a trot.

Cresting a low ridge and entering a long valley, the pair saw no antelope. But in a flash they were startled by a dozen Pawnee warriors, whipping their ponies, closing fast. To which the Lakotas spun around, leaning into their mounts and asking for speed. What felt briefly like a game of tag quickly became a dead serious horse race. Galloping side by side, Stands For Them shouted advice. He then slowed slightly so as to lure the pursuers up a side creek, over a divide and back to the main creek—where Good Thunder and his more rested cayuse pony waited to taunt the enemy into pursuing him as Stands For Them darted into a thick cedar grove. The fast-tiring Pawnee horses were no match for Good Thunder's coal black gelding. The gambit, the coyote's trick, had somehow worked. Reunited, the Lakota youths each touched a trembling hand to heart so as to consider themselves henceforth as *kolas*, a thing more connected than biological brothers, a pact obligating each to give his life for the other if needed.

Grateful for Stands For Them's quick thinking, Good Thunder would brook no protest in gifting his new kola with the dun yearling stallion. Stands For Them named him after the whirlwind, and realized with such a stallion he might truly dream of becoming a scout, a truth teller of the people.

Chapter Five

The Truth Teller
1874

By the summer of 1874, many bands spent part of every year near one of the agencies. Even traditionalists like the Elk Robe tiyospaye. More bluecoats arrived daily at Red Cloud and Spotted Tail Agencies. Rumors traveled from tipi to tipi: "This growing army will surely confiscate all Lakota ponies."

Elk Robe considered the worrisome hearsay. Should his entire tiyospaye join sons Stands For Them and Stealing Horses who had spent the previous summer off the reservation with High Backbone and fellow Eat No Dogs? There to roam the tribe's last dependable hunting grounds—between the Powder River and the Little Bighorn. On those grasslands even now hunters occasionally found large buffalo herds.

Protective of the tiyospaye's rather large horse herd, Elk Robe came to believe the rumors were likely true—General Sherman had in fact ordered a dismounting program, knowing that Indian "infantry" was less of a threat than Indian "cavalry." Even so, Elk Robe carefully weighed the high cost of leading his people on the tiresome 20-day trek away from the Red Cloud Agency, around the sacred Black Hills, and into the treeless buffalo country.

Elk Robe had in recent years inclined towards peace. But in this season he was weighing defiance, a moving away from the agencies and joining the buffalo hunters, the traditional and even militant branches of the Lakota.

On a warm but windy late spring morning, he gathered the adult males of the tiyospaye, knowing that each man harbored pros and cons about breaking for the north.

After preliminary pools of silence and a contemplative passing of the sacred pipe, Elk Robe signed for those assembled to speak their heart. Some spoke at length. Some merely pointed north or to the ground at their feet as their mute vote. After considering all of this, Elk Robe stood to announce his intentions. He understood that any individual or family was free to follow his lead . . . or not.

"The hunting grounds, and traditions, are calling. I choose to go."

On this day all but three chose similarly, and preparations began immediately for a stealthy predawn departure from the boundaries of Red Cloud Agency.

Stands For Them and Stealing Horses were joyous at the news, for the alternative was traveling alone to the Powder River, and only then meeting up with High Backbone. But this year their father, their band's *naca*, would join his sons in the north.

Taking a break on a fallen cottonwood near his tipi, father watched the subtle uptick in activity that to the outsider appeared ordinary, pedestrian. From his seat, Elk Robe could just see the Eat No Dogs horses grazing the riverbank grasses near the agency buildings. He knew them by the colors, many being a distinct buckskin, and many others with great spots on their flanks. The horses and their watchful young herdsmen spread across the still verdant flats just below the pine-studded and chalky badland cliffs so common to the upper White River basin.

As he did every evening, Elk Robe walked out to meet the boys as they brought in the most prized horses to be picketed near each owner's tipi. It was his chance to check the spring fattening of the animals after what had been a snowbound winter.

This week, just as the week before that, Elk Robe frowned—for his band's hundred ponies were still a bit lean for the long Powder River trek. But earlier that same day had come further urgency to a quick departure—the arrival of still more bluecoats. Too many soldiers. They had set about erecting a camp of sorts, a fortification soon to be renamed Fort Robinson.

As they had last summer, Stands For Them and Stealing Horses planned to ride side by side most all the way to the hunting grounds. But instead of riding as hunters, this year the boys rode as formal scouts, ahead of father's tiyospaye.

A scout's need for total alertness meant little time for easy conversation, the exception being mealtime. So with all made ready for a morning departure, the boys were more talkative than usual over the evening's venison roast. They spoke of this year's burden of responsibility, yes, but agreed it was better to be moving north with the big family. It meant a summer of less hunger, more horses.

"Pass me that piece of meat. No, the big one," said Stealing Horses, as the boys shared the bounty of a deer they'd stumbled upon just that morning. "This is good, but I look forward to *pte* tongue or *pte* hump, as you surely do," said Stands For Them. His mouth full, Stealing Horses merely nodded.

The young men smiled across the fire, self-satisfied. Then, gazing off to the north, Stealing Horses mentioned his eagerness to again see the mystical warrior. The unconventional war chief first named Curly but now known as Crazy Horse. "Big brother, do you recall the time and place when you first laid eyes on the strange one?"

As was custom the brothers used the name "Crazy Horse" sparingly—for to casually use the name of a hallowed one is to risk that name becoming commonplace.

"I remember as if yesterday. It was at the big camp on the Niobrara, just before the hunt when He Dog touched the white buffalo with his lance. I was not yet old enough to ride on the hunt, my duty being to mind the fresh buffalo horses. Still, this *pte* pursuit filled me with big dreams."

"Your stomach may remember those lean days. The hunt was not successful. So there was idleness allowing me to sit the middle branch of a rustling-leaf tree with other boys. Below us appeared a group of young warriors mingling near the central fire. The youngest seemed twenty winters, the oldest not thirty. Stealing Horses, I tell you all were men in their fighting prime. They walked and talked in that relaxed, convincing way of young men full of their own power."

"As boys our gaze naturally followed all such fighting men. But I was surprised when my eyes would not leave one of the less impressive, standing apart from the group. He wore no feathers in his hair, no hint of war paint, no scalplock fringe on his tunic. He carried the slenderness of boy-becoming-man in his form, was neither tall nor short. Yet his eyes flashed as does a thunderstorm before the rain."

Stands For Them looked skyward, remembering.

"Grace was on his forehead, in his walk, upon his fingertips. He stood apart for the reason that no other presumed to stand beside him. Yet all vied to be closer than the next. I knew then this can only be the holy warrior, the one that cannot die, cannot lose. Before anyone pointed him out, I thought, *This surely is the one of whom we speak. Of whom everyone speaks.*

"*Tos,*" exclaimed Stealing Horses. "I have seen him more than one hand can count, but the first time . . . you are right, that first time cannot be forgotten."

"It honors us that his mother was Miniconjou. They say he is *Oglala* because he rides to battle with the Oglala. We say he is Miniconjou because on the hunt and in many peaceful summers he lodges among us Miniconjou. Both bands claim him."

"But what does he believe? His thoughts?" Stealing Horses said to no one in particular.

"Our father has often seen him in council and at war society fires—the strange one sits by himself, speaks rarely, and when he does speak it is as a Lakota warrior only. Not as intancan."

"Why does he forsake words?" asked Stealing Horses. Stands For Them nodded, "Because, I am told, he believes silence perfectly balances body, mind, and spirit. Elders say that holy silence is in fact the one true voice of *Wakan*, the great mystery. Next time we share the same camp, watch closely and you see that two, three times a day this strange one walks away, to an alone place among the hills and plants and creatures—they say to find his *wakan*."

Stands For Them paused for a drink of water from the gourd at his side, "This is why he is sometimes called *Chan Ohan* (Walks Among The Trees)."

Stealing Horses nodded, swallowing that last tough piece of meat, then adding with a hint of pride, "He has offered me whispered encouragements. More than once. When I see him at spring reunions, he nods and sometimes asks if I have practiced the firestick and the bow."

"This season he will smile to see us dressed and mounted as scouts," Stands For Them prophesied. "And further, brother, I tell you why he gives of himself to boys who aspire to war paint. Boys like you. He must now be past thirty-five winters, the age when some warriors turn from the fighting path to the priestly or fatherly path. You see this in our Elk Robe, who spends more time with today's peaceful pursuits than yesterday's fierce rides."

"*Nunge Yuza*", Stealing Horses interrupted, "I know before you say it—the strange one has no sons."

"Yes, some believe this is so youth of our age can feel like his sons. Where else can young men turn for both battle advice and spirit advice, from just one mouth?"

Then Stealing Horses smiled the conceited smile that made them both know what came next: "I hope in some tomorrow to go to the one place you cannot follow, big brother."

"I know that place," Stands For Them nodded. "The mystical one's Last Born Society is reserved for second and third-born sons."

Crazy Horse had years before formed an unlikely warrior society of young men who, like himself, were not first-born sons. He had early observed that less favored sons carried a certain boldness into battle, perhaps to prove their worth when compared to privileged first-borns. First-borns like Stands For Them.

"You are yet too young for even that warrior society, little brother. But perhaps next summer, the strange one and his Last Borns will be honored to have a young man of your worth."

The brothers slept well that night, beginning their initial day of travel one hour before their tiyospaye. The first many miles of riding were uneventful before faint disturbances of dust on the trail put both riders on high alert. Stands For Them went to the left, and Stealing Horses to the right, sometimes leading their horses and kneeling to better read the story written in the powdery earth.

Moving. Stopping to view and listen. Moving.

When they came back together, Stands For Them was first to speak, "One of us may need to ride back to the people. As you can see, there are many wasicu trails to *Paha Sapa*. We knew this would be so, as they are crazed for the yellow pebbles. But the signs point to many more than expected. Going both ways. And among them bluecoats."

"I do not see the bluecoat sign," said a mildly puzzled Stealing Horses. That's when Stands For Them motioned his brother over, and pulled him by the sleeve down beside a series of earthen depressions leading northeast.

"Look. These tracks," Stands For Them said, "speak in two ways. The horseshoe shows the back cleats of a remount shoe. And this deeper impression is from a bigger horse. Such a heavy print is made by the large horses the cavalry favors. These marks, little brother, are from bluecoat horses."

Two hours later, the pair found a cottonwood tree just big enough to offer shade, there to share a cold meal of pemmican and dried plums. The band had dared take only minimal food from the agency lest their departure be exposed. Hunger could not be far off.

The brothers then discussed another of the day's challenges—the search for water. Not for the people, as pouch and gourd canteens held enough, but for the horses. So they resolved to watch especially for swallows—the bird that must have water for its mud nests and mosquito diet. Watching also for certain willows that so dependably reveal a water source.

With a growing sense of his own prowess Stands For Them considered these skills rather trifling. His focus of late was to gain experience as the people's navigator. To a people without the compass, map, or road there was highest acclaim for the scout who could navigate across hundreds of miles of open country. Stands For Them sought this honor.

Finishing the light fare, Stands For Them spoke admiringly of father's mental map of the 100,000 square miles of Lakota homeland. He spoke of those vast tracts where Elk Robe's grasp of the terrain was complete, and of those fewer areas where Elk Robe would travel with less confidence. "I can picture many but not all of the rivers and mountains," Stands For Them said with a sigh while idly scratching lines in the dust. Lines that Stealing Horses instantly recognized as the parallel rivers White Earth, Cheyenne, and Niobrara. "Still, I will be many years gathering such knowledge as father has gained."

He wondered aloud what he and his brother had often privately considered, "Do you and I best serve the oyate as scouts? I turn over in my head the other paths. Perhaps I could be a great hunter. Or perhaps the other roads—healer, holy man, weapons craftsman, horse herder or horse gentler, story-teller . . . and of course warrior."

Stealing Horses listened while cleaning his teeth with a sharpened twig, then tossing it, "If I cannot be a great scout then I wish to become *akicita*, the watchman of the hunts and the battles, the enforcer of our rules." Stands For Them smiled at his little brother, for both knew that to be *akicita* was not something one chose, but rather the choice of an august council of elders.

But it was the life of a scout that Stands For Them presently coveted. Scouts were called the truth-tellers, their first obligation to tell the tribe precisely and unwaveringly what was out there—the game, the enemy camps, the landscape, the water resources, the trails. The bad with the good. "Wolves of the people," grandfather had often said.

So, on this trip Stands For Them practiced the higher skills of tribal scout—he'd been trained, for example, to use saliva to moisten his nostrils, heightening his sense of smell so that breezes might bring scent-news of buffalo, or thunderstorms, or distant prairie fires. That next morning, with nostrils sufficiently awakened, he detected humidity carried on the winds to lead them to a much-needed water source.

They used rocks to point the trailing tiyospaye to the water. Now back on their horses, in imitation of wolves, the brothers made a habit of looking back from whence they came, so as to recognize on their return the buttes, the canyons, the lone trees—"bread crumbs" of a safe return, and a safeguard in case of being followed. The day warm enough for the pair to ride nearly naked, breechcloths only, it being said that "great scouts discard the robe to expose more skin to the world's every invisible touch."

As they rode side by side now, Stands For Them missed few opportunities to school his brother, "Just like wolves, brother, it is possible to smell the buffalo or antelope though we cannot yet see the creatures. And like the wolf, one must eat often of the flesh of the intended prey to have any hope of also smelling it. Here, brother, is another skill. In hungry winter months, drink much water before you seek night rest. This will force you to rise at the first hint of light—the best time to scan the horizon for that faint cloud formed by distant damp breath of a thousand buffalo."

On this day they continued to ride close so as to converse, but henceforth the brothers often rode apart. They were entering a realm where the Crow or Shoshone might be encountered. Safer to ride separated, in the alert way, and often beyond sight of each other. Yet by means of howls mimicking coyotes, or signal mirrors, or by watching the intuitive ears and eyes of one's horse, the brother knew where the other rode.

The seventh day dawned drizzly and overcast, but not so wet as to compromise equine footing. The brothers had learned by now that riding as scouts was hard, for if the band traveled twenty-five miles between sleeps, Stands For Them and Stealing Horses would be expected to ride nearly twice that distance, exploring and scouting left and right of the tiyospaye's more direct line of travel. Only rarely could they spend nights with family, more often dozing under the stars to provide a sort of early warning system. Two other scouts performed similar security to the rear of the group.

Despite such hardship, scouts enjoyed one modest daily pleasure— their mounts were always among the best available to the band.

Stands For Them's scout horse was the coltish mustang dun he'd caught in the Sand Hills, inches taller now than most Indian ponies, muscular in a rangy sort of way. Whirlwind offered alertness without skittishness.

Together Stands For Them and Whirlwind moved through tall grass far to the left of Stealing Horses, rimming a river bluff to gain commanding views up and down the floodplain. Stands For Them occasionally glimpsed Stealing Horses on the opposite bluff as both riders held a high trot, a horse's natural and tireless gait. Ceaselessly the young scouts scanned the horizon for game, for fire, for enemies.

As they consumed the prairie in this way, Stands For Them leaned over Whirlwind's neck with an encouraging stroke across those strapping, churning shoulders. By this touch the equine life force passed through Stands For Them's hand and into his own body. Mysteriously the previously separate thoughts of man and beast, the instincts and movements too, melted together. As the miles piled up, two creatures approached oneness.

Where the sun showed itself briefly, there came a narrowing of the valley floor. This brought the brothers closer. It was here that they crossed the spore of what looked to Stealing Horses like deer. It was, said Stands For Them with a shout, a small herd of elk. He then briefly instructed little brother on how to tell the difference, how to use the prints to estimate the herd size, their speed and direction of travel, even how long it had been since they passed.

"The wasicu have their reading leaves, which are said to yield mountains of knowledge. We Lakota do not have such books, yet we "read" in the ways I just showed you. Ways that no wasicu can fully understand." Stealing Horses considered this for a moment, then said, "Remember when grandfather once said today's Lakota are not the trackers that his father was?"

"Grandfather spoke the truth. He said when Lakotas received our greatest gift, and elevated ourselves onto the back of *Sunka Wakan*, they were no longer very close to the ground. So yes, our horseback tracking skills may not rival those of the ancients on foot."

Resuming their separate but parallel travel, the brothers moved steadily northwest. Then Stands For Them's peripheral vision caught a flicker of unexpected motion in his brother's direction. Stealing Horses was acting as if he'd encountered something out of the ordinary. Some danger.

Stands For Them felt a similar quiver of muscle through *his* horse's withers, followed by a snort, Whirlwind sensing approaching horses long before frail human senses. But did unknown horses mean the passage of traditional enemies—Pawnee, Crow, maybe Shoshone?

It was worse. Stealing Horses raised a sign language; both arms held heavenward. It signifying the double-track all white man needed for their heavy wagons. This message told Stands For Them that they were upon another of the Thieves' Roads to the Black Hills, the newly constructed Cheyenne-Deadwood Trail.

Moving forward, Stands For Them was soon upon these same fresh double wagon tracks cutting cleanly through tall grasses. Bent grasses to either side of the trail told the tale of a wagon train that had only recently passed northward.

The brothers did not cross the trail but turned to ride towards each other. Soon they were huddled together, heads lowered, brows furrowed, to discuss this invasion.

Stands For Them was deliberate in his examination. "This scar on our prairie is from the new seizers of *Paha Sapa*. The dried horse and oxen scat tell of many, many wagons moving here. If we wait but a short time, we'll surely see more white-top wagons." With this Stealing Horses pointed to the southern horizon like he meant it: "Hau, you are a truth teller brother. See it? Far off, a lumbering white-top wagon is visible."

"Our *tiyaspaye* must cross this Thieves' Road with caution," said Stands For Them. "One of us will stay to watch the road from safe hiding. The other rides back to alert the people."

Quick glances at the respective condition of their horses showed Stands For Them's mount fresher for the long roundtrip ride back to Elk Robe. Both nodded, Stands For Them bounded up onto his light wood-framed buckskin saddle and rode off. Stealing Horses found a suitable hiding place.

A prairie breeze set their world of grass in motion. Stealing Horses pulled a buffalo robe round his shoulders, settling into his nook hidden by a copse of junipers but offering views of passing rigs. Remembering as he did that wherever a man rests, for an hour or a day, that place should become the center of all.

Meantime Stands For Them rode fast and steady, hoping to back-track to his people while they paused for midday meals. Sooner than expected, he topped a ridge to see below the tiyospaye circled up to rest. One small cooking fire burned. All eyes lifted to Stands For Them as Whirlwind picked his way down the ridge.

Upon handing the reins to a waiting cousin, Stands For Them moved immediately to his father's side. He knelt before Elk Robe in the obliga-tory posture of all returning scouts.

Then rising, he said, "*Naca*, you know that wasicus crawl over our *Paha Sapa* in search of the yellow rock. But today I report to you their numbers are even greater than rumored. The Thieves' Road has ruts telling of many, many wagon trains."

Others could not hear this conversation of eldest son and father. But all could see the band's calmest young man, Stands For Them, gesturing in ways that must mean trouble lay head.

Considering his son's blunt description of the situation to the west, Elk Robe said, "Our small band must suffer neither trouble nor delay on our journey to the hunting grounds. Food is running short. Tell Stealing Horses we cross the Thieves' Road tonight after dark."

Stands For Them knew the answer, but asked anyway, "May I stay for a warm meal before returning to Stealing Horses?"

A stone-faced Elk Robe turned away briefly, returning to hand his now-mounted son a purse of dried pemmican. Barely enough for one, but meant for two. Stands For Them tied the purse to his pommel and awaited a father's final words.

Elk Robe's words, even to his sons, were not exactly commands. Yet only a fool would disregard his judgements. Now in his early forties, Elk Robe was of the age where a man considered putting down the warrior's lance and picking up the peace pipe. With one foot in each world, Elk Robe commanded high respect in his tiyospaye.

Before dispatching his son to the northwest, Elk Robe motioned for quiet from those nearby. His eyes looked over the heads of the people to scan the circled horizon, then followed the sky clear to its zenith. All the while his nostrils flared, as if gathering some property from the air.

Stands For Them's face tightened as he waited, fearful that father might ask a more experienced man to accompany him. Or replace him. Instead, Elk Robe gave an encouraging stroke to the neck of Whirlwind, his way of affirming his eldest son.

"When you are safely beyond the Thieves' Road and have located a proper campsite for all of us, I ask you to then make the hunter's kill."

"Fresh meat will cheer us," he continued. "The wasicu have ruined this country for the big hunts of old, but I have seen ravens so perhaps small herds of elk and buffalo are grazing now in some valley to the west. Remember, the raven follows the wolf, because wolf follows the buffalo."

"But Father, I may not find the animals in this big country."

A smile pushed high cheekbones still higher: "Know this my son: yesterday a runner brought wondrous news—the ancient Sans Arc shaman Wolf Soldier is but a day behind us, traveling by fast horse with his grandson."

No one had to explain this good news to Stands For Them. All knew stories of the grizzled Wolf Soldier, including his redemptive power of summoning the herds during lean times. For it was said, "The best young scouts bring the people to the herds. Ah, but the best old scouts bring the herds to the people."

Buoyed by the news and a solemn nod from his father, Stands For Them rode back to the hiding place of his brother. He had to ask Whirlwind only once to hold the high pace. His cayuse was born to run long and hard. But even the toughest horse can come up lame. When two miles east of Stealing Horse's hiding place, Whirlwind picked up a stone bruise on the hard bottom of Antelope Creek. Stands For Them immediately dismounted, forced to walk his lame horse up to his brother's hiding place.

To assure Stealing Horses that it was he who approached, Stands For Them retrieved a small trade mirror from his saddle and used the setting sun to flash a signal of assurance to Stealing Horses, who returned a like signal indicating the coast was clear.

Stealing Horses was happy to see him, and for the present Stands For Them withheld the bad news about his horse. The tired younger brother had kept awake using the old trick of putting pebbles between his toes.

"Father asks us to position ourselves to know all things of this valley . . . to know when to cross so that no wasicu will see our band. To know where to make night camp when we have safely crossed the Thieves' Road. To know where we might find fresh meat tomorrow."

Stands For Them then shared the good news. "Father believes Wolf Soldier will soon join the band." They squatted round the deliberately tiny fire, slowly chewing pemmican strips so as to make less seem like more. The conversation turned to those presumed powers of Wolf Soldier. Stealing Horses admitted doubts about Wolf Soldier's alleged power to conjure big game.

"Even so, my brother," Stands For Them countered, "who has not thought of calling a dog, but before making a sound the animal comes, as if just thinking makes for calling? Who can say this same power, in greater force, does not belong to Wolf Soldier?"

As Stealing Horses considered this prospect, Stands For Them retreated to check on his lame horse. He then urged the animal up to the hiding place. On seeing a brother's alarmed expression, he explained their further troubles. "For the present Whirlwind can travel only slowly. Yet Father says we must reach Mule Creek in two sleeps."

Just then the distant white puffs of another wagon train topped a far horizon, prompting Stands For Them to continue with urgent matters at hand: "With only one sound horse and two men and much ground to cover, we must travel by the old way. This trick some say was passed to our tribe from the Spanish, or the mountain men. Grandfather said it came from our Cheyenne allies."

"What trick do you speak of?" Stealing Horses moved from sitting to a crouching position.

"Listen carefully. I shall leave Whirlwind tied where he is and place four rocks on our trail to this spot so that father's other scouts will surely find him. Then the women can bring him along more slowly with the children's ponies." Then in hushed tones inviting undivided attention, Stands For Them explained how they must travel. Soon the brothers were on their feet , discarding burdensome supplies including all remaining food—preparing to travel light and fast.

Stands For Them checked again that Stealing Horses understood how to proceed before mounting his brother's paint, and heading west at a gallop. As instructed, Stealing Horses ran after, though he could not keep up. When Stands For Them had covered a distance that would surely tire any runner, he stopped, picketed the horse, and he himself commenced running westward. In time, an exhausted Stealing Horses came running forward to mount the now-rested horse. While the horse surged forward, the rider Stealing Horses had a chance to catch his breath. Presently he overtook Stands For Them and kept riding a suitable distance ahead, there to picket the horse and again become the runner.

In this way the threesome advanced, each receiving rest when most needed. Hooves and moccasin feet were cooled by night air, wetted by the dew of first light, dried by the heat of late morn. Such rapid progress would mean time to fulfill Elk Robe's instruction: "Find a secure campsite. Collect firewood of the ash tree, so that cooking fires will make little smoke. Locate and then attempt to procure meat for our pots."

When entering the broad basin of Mule Creek, the scouts slowed so as to absorb the prairie, seeking that one campsite that might win father's approving nod. Here they turned to another old scout trick—look to the bent grass showing where animals bed down, as the four-leggeds unfailingly find the most sheltered place in any landscape. Advancing on a promising grove of cottonwoods populating the base of a south-facing hill, Stands For Them found many pressed-grass circles indicating last night's sleeping spot of deer.

Anticipating the band's arrival later that day, Stands For Them and Stealing Horses looked squarely at each other as if asking who'd assume the favored task of seeking game—and who must do the woman's work of setting up camp, dragging in firewood, carrying rocks for tenting spots and for rimming fireplaces.

Stands For Them asserted a first-born's prerogative as he sprang to the stirrup and turned the paint to the south. His puffed-up chest and flexing jaw muscles were of a predator sure of success. Then over his shoulder he shouted back, "The hungry wolf is the best hunter."

Soon he found the vantage point of a high ridge, a fine place to see the game his father had hoped for in this valley. On hearing the faintest sound on this cloudless day, he dismounted to press his ear to a prairie dog hole, confirming and even roughly pinpointing the rumbling hooves of some unseen buffalo herd. Trailing the great beasts would surely be some antelope.

On returning to the campsite, he was surprised to not yet see his *tiyosapye* but pleased to note that brother had worked hard at preparations. With a thud he let slip a still-warm antelope carcass from across his lap.

With all things ready for the anticipated arrival of the tiyospaye, the boys built the smallest of fires to sup on roast antelope. They sat in silence until a midnight breeze carried with it a distant baying. Wide-eyed, the brothers grunted—for on such a moonless night a howl might or might not be a wolf, or a Pawnee, or a Crow.

Chapter Six

Niobrara Winter, Cowboy's Crucible
1899-1902

Cleve shuffled from foot to foot as he stood with fellow graduating eighth graders to recite the Pledge of Allegiance.

Then a man he'd never seen before handed him his eighth-grade diploma. Not a trifling thing for a fourteen-year-old boy in rural America in 1899. It was the end of education for most, since a lad would by this age be needed year-round on his parents' farm or ranch.

At the coffee hour following graduation, his father confirmed Cleve's short-term future: "For this summer, son, you'll be needed in the fields. But first I have a project."

Six days spent in the dim tack room of father's barn, oiling six double sets of harness gave Cleve a chance to consider if he really coveted the rural life. That's when it struck him, perhaps he'd enjoy being a shopkeeper, like old Mr. Fitzpatrick.

So in just two weeks, with father's grudging approval, Cleve had enrolled in the business "college" in O'Neill, Nebraska. But despite a modest knack for business ways, Cleve soon cooled to the tedium and indoor nature of number reckoning. The business school experiment lasted five months. Now growing into a young man's body, Cleve began searching for a more robust young man's job.

Months later, a scribbled postcard came from brother Tom saying he might find temporary work in one of the last open range roundups . . . the 1902 Rosebud Roundup was set to collect 40,000 government cattle from grasslands both on and off the reservations. Cleve wondered if his green cowboy skills would measure up. Maybe he'd get lucky and snag one of the roundup's full-time drover positions. But not many teens were hired as roundup hands. That's because a top hand was expected to show up for work with a string of ten good mounts.

Cleve had a horse alright, a pretty good one. But just one. After O'Neill he'd found the odd work as a hand on ranches clustered south of the reservation line, mostly for just room and board . . . not the going cowboy rate of a dollar a day.

Less than twenty-four hours after reading Tom's steely postcard, Cleve was on his way. Riding through an all-day rain. If moisture wasn't at such a premium on the Great Plains, it would have felt like bad luck.

Leaning into sideways pellets of rain, Cleve rode into his brother's temporary camp straddling the reservation line. Alas, Tom was not there. Only Shorty, the camp's dependably ornery cook.

Shaking out a thoroughly wet felt hat, then adjusting the brim to better divert rain from his face and collar, Cleve dismounted, "Reckon you're Shorty. Do you know when Tom will be back?"

"No idea," said Shorty without looking up and between spits of chew. Not stopping for an instant in his roping down of the chuck wagon's canvas bonnet.

Nor did he offer Cleve shelter from the elements. Nor, for that matter, did he seem inclined to direct this skinny kid to the wagon boss's tent.

After an awkward few minutes in the rain, Cleve resolved to picket his horse and figure which of a dozen tents was his brother's.

Poking his head into one wall tent after another, Cleve at length spotted a cot he recognized as Tom's. That's when he heard a familiar "hooray" from the other side of the tent—Tom just dismounting his soaked and lathered roan gelding.

Seven years Cleve's senior, Tom knew why Cleve was in camp. Without bothering to shake hands, he offered little brother a short-term job, not as "wrangler", the minimum position Cleve had anticipated, but as assistant wrangler. As wagon boss Tom could make such minor hires without consulting the top roundup boss.

"Well," Cleve said as he considered the offer while kicking his boots together so as to dislodge clumps of mud, "assistant wrangler don't sound all that grand. But I guess I'll take it." With a vaguely arrogant smile, big brother invited little brother into his tent—there they sat on opposite ends of the cot so as to school Cleve on the workings of a roundup outfit: "Listen close, Cleve, cuz here's where you fit: Everyone answers to the big roundup or trail boss. He's in charge of all the crews. We call 'em wagons, eight, no nine of 'em total. I'd suggest you not so much as look at this big boss. His righthand man is known as the ramrod. Then comes the nine guys called wagon bosses. That's me."

"The cook is also high rankin', as you'll soon learn. Don't mess with Shorty.

Then comes the lead night hawk. This guy's a top hand who with one or two helpers can manage the herd whilst the rest of us sleep. Cook and night hawk are about the same rank, if the grub is edible."

"Next come the working drovers, 'tween twelve and sixteen per wagon.

At rock bottom, Cleve," he said with a wink, "is wrangler . . . and hell, you're even below that. Wrangler, as you know, cares for each cowboy's horse string—hobbling 'em so they can graze, corralling 'em in rope corrals, catching and even saddling 'em when requested."

A wrangler's low rank was perhaps best summed up years later in an account that Cleve chanced upon in a regional history book, quoting a cowhand on this very same roundup—part Indian and working cowboy, James Burnette, who said when interviewed, "The wrangler was usually a stupid cowhand, or a broken-down one or a punk or halfwit or screwball or something of that sort."

If James Burnette had such contempt for wranglers, he neatly hid it that summer by showing tenderfoot Cleve certain considerations. He cottoned to Cleve because he knew the lad's brother-in-law George Lamoureaux, also a mixed blood, part French-Canadian, part Sicangu Lakota. Burnette showed Cleve tricks that even the Oklahoma and Texas cow punchers didn't know. Like how to direct a horse more with one's legs, less with the reins.

Cleve couldn't help notice—many mixed-blood and a few full-blood Lakotas were finding work as cowboys. He knew it made sense—they were natural horsemen, plus well-suited by skin tone and habit to working under a blazing sun.

Cleve began learning his duties next morning, and soon found that "assistant wrangler" was more of a camp go-fer. Yet he accepted it, for this felt like his chance to observe one of the Old West's last big round-ups.

Indeed, those few weeks with the 1902 roundup would be Cleve's sole glimpse at what once was: the fenceless, boundless High Plains. Then, but never again, could a horseman ride for 60, 80, or more miles without opening a gate, without coming to a fence, crossing a road, or seeing a house. A decade hence, when Cleve first met Stands For Them, he saw in the old man someone who surely once knew the fenceless Northern Plains in its totality. Cleve envied that.

But any romance of a roundup quickly faded to tedium. There were 186 horses in the remuda. For Cleve this meant each had to be watered, fed a small ration of oats, then at various times fitted with hobbles and allowed to graze on the green grasses of summer.

One chilly evening Cleve found his familiar place, alone on his warbag, to collect and clean the crew's many iron picket pins. Each cowboy needed a number of pins to picket horses when away from the main camp's rope corrals. Tonight, as always, he did this chore while alternately chowing down supper.

Tired from ten working hours under the sun, Cleve was startled by a figure suddenly standing above him. It was his brother, ordering him into the dark to work the herd as one of two night hawks.

Without complaint, for after all it was a rare chance to ride, Cleve finished the remaining pork and beans, saddled up, and rode out for the 8 p.m. to 2:30 a.m. shift.

On this moonless night of gusty wind and distant lightning, he and the other night hawker worked hard to keep restless cattle out of the bramble. The other nighthawk? Cleve never knew his real name but others called him Banjo, long-haired, leathery, maybe 45. He'd come north on the Goodnight-Loving Trail, moving longhorns. The pair rode 'round the herd in opposite direction so as to meet twice on each circuit. Near the end of their shift Banjo said, "Well son, on nights like this I could tell ya what we used to do back in the 80s. It was a little harsh . . . but . . ."

"I'm all ears."

"Them longhorns back in the day were like wild animals. Hard to keep 'em out of the brush. So, we'd watch to see which were the boss cows. Then we'd catch up two or three of those old cows and "eyeball" 'em."

"What's that!?"

"Not pretty! We'd head and heel 'em to the ground, then cut the top eyelids off. Them boss cows then instinctively stayed clear of the thorny brush . . . to protect their eyes. When the boss cows stay in the open, so do the others. Tough on the leader cow, but most times they wouldn't go blind or crazy till we got 'em to the slaughterhouse."

Cleve was learning, accepting. This cattle business sometimes had room for kindness towards animals but was just as likely to offer cruelty. Whichever led to the greater profit.

After three weeks with the 1902 Roundup, he returned for a spell to help his parents. There a melancholy crept in, caught as he was between father's dull farm work, and more attractive but hard-to-find cowboy jobs.

The letter was sitting on his bunk bed when he came in from evening chores. A rare letter from older sister Hattie. She who had daringly married George, the handsome part Indian man, back in 1891.

But as Hattie's letter explained, George was absent. With winter approaching, Hattie was worried. As was his habit, George had ridden the stock train to Omaha to sell all his yearlings. He was likely on a weeks-long bender. Sure, he had disappeared for weeks or months on other occasions—the full pockets of stockyard cash a temptation to hit the road. He would in time return.

But what if George did not return by winter, who would tend the foundation stock of the Lamoureaux ranch? Who would "ride line" on the cattle and horses, a necessity in what was still partly unfenced open range? Hattie feared the family stock would drift away when pushed by icy northwest winds.

Without next year's breeding stock, the Lamoureaux's faced ruin.

Hattie fought the idea of pulling her sons out of school. They were good students and had only recently learned to stand up to the taunts of "half-breed." Taken out of school, would they ever return? So, she sat down to write to her younger brother by the yellowish light of a kerosene lamp.

"Dear Little Brother . . ." Cleve read by similar yellowish light, "I have a great favor to ask." After describing the tough circumstances, she laid out her thin proposal for the coming winter: "I cannot imagine that our stock will survive even an average winter if we fail to move them to places with best grass. You know those places, Cleve, better than me. And open water, you will know how to find it.

"I can't find help as so many young men in this country look down on the tough cowboy life. They're all bent on farming the river bottoms, or shopkeeping. And with Fort Niobrara having closed, you know, the hangers-on have drifted back East."

"Even if I could find someone, I can't even pay hired-hand wages. Your "pay," Cleve, will be from the stock that makes it through winter. Come spring you get at least two heifers. I figure this may help with your dream of one day starting your own ranch. I reckon you have plans for this winter, brother. But my desperation falls to you.

"I write this knowing it will be unbearably lonely up there, with just a tent for cover. Those river bluffs seem to get all the worst gales. The valleys are less windy. But George says the low places drift up with snow by midwinter. You probably know this.

"If you agree, it will mean staying with the cattle until the first grass greens up in late March. Then you can bring 'em back home, as we'll have enough nearby graze for the herd.

"Please write back, or just ride over here if your answer is yes. I have $1.75 you can have, and some supplies packed and ready here on the ranch.

Love, your big sister Hattie"

So he rode.

It was nearly dark when Cleve topped the low rise southwest of the Lamroueaux ranch. He had hoped to arrive earlier, but slick gumbo roads made the going tough.

Hattie parted the calico kitchen curtains to peek at the setting sun. That's when she saw only a bobbing cowboy hat. Then shoulders. Then the hands, so easy on the reins, gentle on the bit.

Before she recognized the rider, she recognized the horse. A fine-looking horse leading a second horse, steam rising from both. Instantly her eyes were shining, then brimming to the lids. It really was Cleve—rising to her distress, taking up the lonely winter watch.

Having spied their uncle on the low rise, those outdoorsy Lamoureaux boys came running from all corners.

Cleve reined up at a hitching post by the unpainted Lamoureaux barn. He proceeded straightaway to unsaddle and rub down the horses, as his sister stepped lively to stoke the fire with two split cedar logs, sliding the remains of that evening's meal to the center of the cook stove.

"I've eaten," were his first words after closing the creaky front door.

"Okay. I'll put this in the root cellar. Warm it up for breakfast. You're here for breakfast?" hands in supplication at her heart.

"Yes Hattie, got your letter. I'm here for the job."

"God bless. I thought as much when I saw you riding in so deliberate, and leading that bay with the bedroll pack. Made me tear up a little."

When Cleve turned from hanging his coat on the peg, Hattie couldn't resist an awkward big sister hug. Cleve looked around for a chair, then roughhoused a bit with his nephews.

As the boys retreated to homework and whittling, Cleve accepted a cup of coffee as Hattie turned to the practical, the matter-of-fact.

"Most of the cattle are two-year-olds, Cleve. Forty-nine head, 'bout five are steers and maybe thirty bred heifers and the rest open heifers. They're already up on the bluffs in a little corral. Hungry and thirsty, but they'll be okay til tomorrow. Neighbor helped us move 'em up there early yesterday."

"When you ride out, you'll need to trail the twelve longhorn-cross critters that're out behind the barn. And our two saddle horses, you'll need 'em as remounts. There's only enough hay and graze down here to keep the draft team."

"Okay then," said Cleve even as he thought to himself, *one rider trailing twenty head of stock. I could do that. But the mix of horses and cattle . . . that could be tricky.*

Hattie's curious expression begged a response—"Well, it should be fine as long as tomorrow ain't real windy," offered Cleve. "Your boy Charles can work stock. Before school can he help trail 'em out for the first ten miles or so?"

"Sure. Then will you just trail 'em up the mail stage road to the bluffs allotment from there?"

"Yup. Been a while since I've been to that "bluffs" allotment. What can you tell me?"

"Rolling," said Hattie. "It's a lot like the country above the old fort. Not much for firewood—just a few cottonwoods low down, scattered pines 'n cedars higher. Good views up and down the Niobrara valley. You might be able to just see the lights of Valentine on a moonless night. It's open range of course. You knew that, right?"

Cleve nodded as he peered into a now tepid coffee cup.

"They claim the wind blows the snow off them bluffs. We'll pray for that, and for decent winter graze. But if we get a blizzard like in '99, I don't know what you'll do."

"I'll manage."

"I reckon you will. Before I forget, those sacks by the door are for you. Sugar, navy beans, some hard tack, jerky."

"What's in the little tin box?"

"Oh, that's your surprise. For when it gets rough. Tell ya this much, couple 'a chocolate squares and a little Bull Durham. George must'a forgot he had it in the dresser. Guess you still smoke roll-your-own's," she said with assurance. "And here's that little bit of cash for when you need to resupply. It's all we have until I get more egg money."

She returned to the stove for a moment, then added, "You could see wolves. Most have been trapped or shot out or driven up into Dakota. Do you have a gun?"

"Just Dad's old Springfield. But I have a near-full box of cartridges."

"Rest of what I got for you is piled by the barn door: A canvas tent, oats, a small oil-burning tent stove. Plenty of rope for setting up corrals, or to hobble the horses at night—whatever you think best. Heard say if you keep just one or two horses tied up nearby and have water and a little hay or oats handy, them other horses will not wander far."

"Almost forgot, that old buffalo robe is from George's grandmother, *Huntkalutawin*. She musta had it up at Old Ft. Laramie or even before. You know the story, that's where she met George's grandpapa, the trader James Bordeaux. That robe'll be a great comfort. Heavy and warm."

The room's suddenly hazy air meant Hattie's kitchen table lamp needed wick trimming. That could wait until daylight but provided the boys a welcome excuse for trading those last pages of homework for bedtime.

The morning dawned clear and breezy, with a rim of ice on water both indoors and out. Before leaving for school, Cleve's nephews helped him load the tent, stove and supplies onto the backs of those horses least likely to buck.

Charles helped Cleve move the herd as far as the mail stage road. He then galloped off to school, little cakes of snow flying up behind.

With a wave of his hat, Cleve turned to the task of pushing the critters those final miles to winter pasture. Such was the sweeping nature of the country that Cleve needed to open only two gates.

"This is it?" thought Cleve on reaching the bluffs area. More wind-swept and desolate than he was remembering. Even so, he found a suitable place to pitch the tent.

Cleve settled reasonably into this lonely life, owing to three weeks under "Indian summer" skies. Then winter set in. As cold and snowy days piled up, Cleve came to regret not having brought a dog with him—for the companionship and for help with heeling the stock.

By mid-December, Cleve was searching the skies for a suitably mild day to ride into Valentine to resupply. But cold wind and deep snow persisted. He could only ration the food and wait. Long nights, short sunless days and isolation made Cleve feel he was going loco—a self-imposed definition of toughness his only anchor.

Cleve thought he'd done a pretty good job of keeping track of the days, his knife scratching one "x" per day onto the tin lid of the "surprise" box Hattie had sent along. How else could one know which of a string of depressingly similar days was Christmas? For only then would he open the little box.

But there came a day he could not remember: "Damn. Was it this morning that I made the 'x', or yesterday?"

Finally, the unseen Black Hills cooked up a toasty chinook wind that ate the snow cover in just one morning, signaling his day to resupply.

So he rode into Valentine, seeing here and there that people were taking down the paper Christmas ornaments. He had missed the big day altogether.

The Valentine shopkeeper dropped his chin to eyeball the scruffy, wind-chapped young man before him. Likely doubting he could have money to buy anything.

"I'll take this axe, please, and that little tea pot, sir. And this box of kitchen matches too." Cleve dug the silver dollar and change out of his pants pockets. His saddle horse was tied up in front of the store, and though he would have liked to buy a couple more "camping" necessities, there wasn't room in the saddle bags—not with the potatoes, hard tack, and flour procured earlier down at the general store.

"On my next trip to town," he promised his horse, for by now he was accustomed to talking to critters, "I'll get me some salt bacon, green coffee, maybe navy beans. And an apple for you."

Yet on this the day after Christmas, Cleve's next trip to town was eleven weeks away . . . on the other side of winter's toughest times. Cleve knew these would be weeks of endurance, of dreary routine, of summoning the stubbornness of Scots-Irish ancestors.

"Up before dawn" was the unhappiest part of these fifty days, as deep cold rousted Cleve from his cot an hour or even two before the gloaming. In darkness he'd fumble with matches to reignite fire in the wee tent stove, only to retreat under cold covers until frost was dripping off the inside tent walls. Then he'd sit hunched beside the stove's thin warmth until bands of light edged the eastern sky. Never really warm. Never really dry. Wears on a man.

Next chore was to thaw out the "starter" needed for sourdough pancakes. In time he learned a way to slowly thaw the always frozen potatoes, so as to have 'em ready for breakfast: Just take two or three spuds to bed. And don't forget to slide those iron-stiff boots close to the fire to soften them, but not so close as to toast the leather.

Then it was out into the elements. With his best horse saddled, Cleve rode out to bring in the other horses, one of which he would select for his remount for later in the day.

A little hard tack and jerky in the pocket would suffice for lunch. He'd need to be on the open range most of the day "riding line" on the cattle. Some mornings the beeves would be in one big bunch, maybe even within sight of the tent. Most days they would have drifted before

the wind, following creeks and sometimes breaking into smaller bunch-
es.

Riding to the highest point, a chalky hill with a view clear up and
down the Niobrara, Cleve looked for the cattle. If not seen, they'd most
likely be in one of three or four favored coulees snaking towards the
river.

In the early weeks Cleve studiously tallied the cattle to make sure
none were missing. But soon enough he knew the various critters on
sight, and likewise knew which were missing without counting. They'd
become individuals to him, their quirks, grass preferences, fraternization
habits all known.

Long winter nights offered the chance to study the sky. But then he'd
always studied the heavens. For Father had often warned that the frontiersman who could not divine the next day's weather was a failed man.

"Mark my words son," said James Baxter from beneath a walrus
mustache, "study the evening sky. That'll help choose whether to mend
fence or cut firewood or move cattle or haul hay. Helps to begin a day
when necessary tools, supplies, and proper horses are made handy the
night before."

If the darkest part of winter is December and January, for a cattleman
the dreariest is surely late February to late March, when wet ground,
damp air, and high winds conspire to make winter feel endless. So it was
for Cleve.

On one snowy March evening, Cleve sat on the edge of his cot and
buried his chapped face in equally chapped hands for the longest time.

The life of a shopkeeper suddenly did not look so bad. *But damn it
all, I've seen the way a rancher walks among other men, weather-
creased face frozen in a smile, gaze on something far off, something big.
Never saw that look on a shopkeeper's face.*

True spring did come, if haltingly. All but one of the livestock were eventually brought back to his sister's homestead, along with eight bouncy new calves.

In the last mile to Hattie and George's ranch, Cleve thought of what he'd most missed over the long winter: to sleep again in a real bed. To soak in a hot bath. To resume those long rides to area dances. Wooden-floored little establishments where he might hope for another dance with Gussy Slaughter. Or maybe those doe-eyed Iddings sisters.

As he closed the cedar rail corral gate, Cleve turned for the house, looking thinner but otherwise about the same. On the outside.

On the inside he was becoming a plainsman—living in the open, from horseback going armed and ready, if necessary, to guard his life by his own grit. Calling no man master.

Chapter Seven

Dark Angels on Rosebud Creek
1876

Well before dawn of what would become "the other Little Big Horn", young men in both the Cheyenne and Lakota camps awoke to the call of camp criers. Their high-pitched bellows were plain enough: "Today on Rosebud Creek the smell of war is in the air."

One young man was sleeping the deep dream sleep, and did not hear the camp cryer. He was dreaming of the day earlier that year when lovely Tall Woman had shyly presented him with gaily beaded moccasins. Before the eyes of both families gathered for a feast, her handmade gift was the customary way for a young woman to signal her acceptance of a marriage proposal. In the dream as in life, the recipient had only to put them on to instantly enter marital union . . . as Stands For Them did without hesitation. This simplest of all Lakota ceremonies, the marriage rite required only that he provide a modest dowry apt for his station in life—one horse and some venison.

This dream on Rosebud Creek was interrupted by the bride's touch to Stands For Them's forehead. He opened his eyes slowly, sat up, touched his head as she had, feeling one side of his hair free flowing, the other side neatly braided and covered in otter fur. It reminded him that he faced a weighty decision. Like on each previous horse raid, each battle, Stands For Them and every other Lakota man stood alone, free to dress for war. Just as free to stay in camp.

Had not even the greatest war chiefs sometimes chosen to remain in camp? Was there not wisdom in some warriors remaining to guard women, children, elders? Such were his thoughts, as he did not want to go.

Yes, a warrior might choose to retire from a fight if sensing his "medicine" was bad, if his war horse was ailing, or if he sided that day with "treaty" or "agency" relatives.

Stands For Them considered the dust motes in the air, the cozy smell of the buffalo sleeping robes, the urge to return to sleep. He felt Tall Woman's warm gaze on the back of his head and turned to look. Her face still warm with sleep. She was as ever beautiful, fragile, elegant. Her chipped front tooth showed as she smiled. That made Stands For Them smile, for it came from her flattening of porcupine quills for his regalia.

"Only you can decide," she said. "Remember no less than *Tasunka Witco*, the Horse that is Crazy, even he chooses each time—sometimes he picks up the war club, sometimes he leaves it in the tipi."

Stands For Them thought of all this while turning to search for the leather pouch containing his spirit bundle, only to see it held at arm's length by Tall Woman. Her unspoken intention surely the same as his— that he open the holy bundle, pray over its contents, and thus determine if this day held the necessary potency to protect him.

He would pray in the young man way. For while elders pray for inner enlightenment, prophecy or healing, young men seek spiritual inspiration only to gain an edge in battle, or horse raids, or the hunt. Stands For Them was no different—he must know if the medicine was with him today. Or not.

So beside the ashes of last night's tipi fire, he carefully placed totems holding deep meaning: an eagle bone whistle, a beautiful spear point fashioned by one of the last stone knappers, the blindingly brilliant feather of a snowy owl, a cord rope woven from buffalo hair, a tousle of sweet grass and sage bundled tight. All were connected to Stands For Them's vision quest of five years ago. Sweeping cupped hands over the articles and facing skyward, Stands For Them chanted a prayer song and closed his eyes in hopes of direction, inspiration.

He thought back to the springtime day when his people arrived at the hunting grounds. Joy of so many reunions had been tempered by news from the agencies: Any native who failed to return to their assigned reservation in three moons would be considered a "hostile." To be dealt with henceforth by the military. The strong rumor said further that hostiles would suffer their horses to confiscation.

For young men of a certain age, such as Stands For Them, it was the season to consider one's store of courage. Society seemed to offer only a black and white choice—either risk the hero's death, or live a meaningless life.

Of the few skirmishes he'd been in, plus horse stealing raids and enemies encountered while hunting, all had been against other Indian tribes. But now loomed a battle against the Long Knives . . . a test of a different magnitude—against cannons, trained fighters, and modern rifles.

In recent nights the beat of war drums thumped for hours. It was during this time that a gnawing self-doubt led Stands For Them to the tipi of uncle Black Coyote. Now forty winters and a minor chief, Black Coyote had in recent years earned the title of war counselor as well.

He stood nearly a foot shorter than Stands For Them but had a sturdy air demanding attention if not respect. He was missing his right eye, the result not of battle but of a stray arrow launched by a fellow antelope hunter many summers past.

Black Coyote had somehow divined the arrival of his nephew, and stood beside the tipi entrance as darkness fell. Together they smoked, sitting cross-legged in reflective silence. At length the host spoke. "Your eyes say you carry a burden. I am honored to be sought out, and to smoke together. This tipi is the place to put down burdens." He smoothed the front of his buckskin shirt.

Encouraged thus to speak, Stands For Them handed the pipe back to Black Coyote, straightened himself. "Uncle, I do not know if I will be able to defend this great nation in ways bringing honor to my father, my people. I have courage, but is it big enough?"

Black Coyote smiled as he made a gesture of supplication to Father Sky, and then looked more past his guest, then at him. "We know your story. Your very name tells us that you will stand up for this nation."

After letting the words simmer in silence, uncle added "Bravery is a strange thing. It manifests in the doing, not in the thinking. Courage need not be big on a peaceful day. It is a seed that sprouts when needed, so watch for it to rise up as needed on your fateful tomorrow."

Stands For Them nodded and gazed into his hands.

Then came what Stands For Them took for Black Coyote's closing words: "The mighty oak sleeps in the acorn. The great eagle awaits flight inside the fragile egg."

More words tumbled out, more than Stands For Them had ever heard from Black Coyote: "Remember, the truly great Lakota warrior wants first to understand the enemy. This is why we remind young fighters of the mystic power in touching the enemy with the coup stick. A thing separate from the act of killing.

"As you come to understand the enemy, you may even come to admire him. See how we revere the buffalo and the antelope, our reverence reaching its zenith even as we bring them to ground. This is our secret. It is why we are, man for man, better hunters then the wasicu. We can become better warriors when remembering that our fight is not for coins or for some faraway Great White Father. We fight for the nearby tipis containing our babies, our wives, our old ones."

With this, Black Coyote returned the pipe to its otter-fur case—thus signaling that his young guest was free to go if he did not have further questions. He did not.

Now, on this morning, Stands For Them was calmed by the remembered words of Black Coyote.

After holding the snowy owl feather above his head for some minutes, Stands For Them opened his eyes and announced to Tall Woman the declaration she both feared and desired: He would take his place with the warriors.

Camp noises were rising. Dogs barking and little boys whooping and hollering as they scrambled to gather war horses. Hawkish chants rose from distant tipis.

Stands For Them moved quickly to assemble the infrequently-used items of his weapons kit: a single-shot Spencer trapdoor carbine, his bow and arrows, a sheathed trade knife, and a war club. He poked his head out of the tipi flap to ask a passing horse herder to fetch his war mount.

All the while, Tall Woman remained seated and facing away from the tipi entrance, singing just loud enough for Stands For Them to hear these words: "*Hoka hey, hoka hey, hoka hey*"—take courage, let's do this, advance. Her words sent blood flushing through his temples, up and down his arms. In ancient Indian fashion, he acknowledged by not acknowledging.

The air throughout the Eat No Dogs camp hummed with tension, like a tightened bowstring. How could it not? Clusters of young warriors were already goading their mounts to a full gallop, a practice meant to bring horses to their natural "second wind" before the battle. Most had unbraided their hair as a sign of war.

Stands For Them now stood and walked through the tipi flap. He wore only a breechcloth, a bear claw necklace and a single eagle feather in his hair. Weapons and shield were propped outside the tipi.

He lacked but three things: First, the coveted "glance" each warrior wished for from his stands-beside-him woman. Tall Woman followed into the open air to be seen by all beside her husband. Their eyes met in a gaze packed tight with meaning.

The other items lacking were more obvious. Wasicu called it "war" paint, the seemingly chaotic colors and symbols adorning a warrior's face and body, and his horse as well.

But to a Lakota fighter like Stands For Them, the painted symbols were more personal and familial than martial. Symbols representing awareness gained from vision quests, from the trances of the Sun Dance. Stands For Them knew that going to battle without these painted symbols meant *Wakan Tanka* would find him unrecognizable . . . and thus unprotected.

He saw two young warriors still lacking paint lining up at Snowy Owl's tent. Snowy Owl was in those days too old for war, but not too old to deftly mix paints and apply requested designs.

Stands For Them had prepared for full battle only once before. Even so, Snowy Owl needed no prompt to recall this tall young man's vivid designs and symbols—blue lightning bolts on forearms, sacred whirlwind symbols on cheeks, the unusual turtle symbol on his chest. The latter a symbol typically associated with the feminine, but not for Stands For Them. It had come to him in a vision dream, and for both dance and battle he wore the emblem unapologetically.

Finished with those ahead of him, Snowy Owl began applying Stands For Them's body art intently, wasting no motion. In minutes the tall one was ready to join the others, having acquired the holy paint and other minimal finery—hoping for victory but dressed for death.

Only the painting of his horse remained. He did this himself: white strips on the forelegs, a red circle around both searching ears. Then a stick man on each side of the withers, signaling that this horse runs for the man who today stands for others. Finally, he dipped his right hand in dark blue paint and placed his palm print on the right rump. Surely now *Wakan Tanka* could not fail to know the identity of both man and horse.

The crowning touch was to paint yellow rings around each equine eye, meant to endow this war horse with supernatural vision.

Decorating of horse complete, Stands For Them performed the final step: the unbraiding of the left side of his hair. Flowing jet-black below the shoulders, this signaled to all a man ready for war.

Now that all was prepared, he simply stood beside his horse, blowing his breath near the animal's nostrils, alternately rubbing his own limbs and then those of the horse against the early chill. He and the other warriors would be mostly naked for a reason— no cape or warbonnet meant less chance of frightening these most spirited of mounts . . . and no leggings meant a touch of skin-to-horsehide—the most connected way to ride.

After mounting, he positioned himself in a nervous grouping that included *kola* Good Thunder on his right and a childhood friend whom he'd not seen in years, War Eagle, on his left. Tall and lithe like Stands For Them, he once asked Stands For Them to show him how to mount a horse with a running vault—two hands on the rump. Nearby rode Good Weasel on a fine sorrel. Good Weasel had been a childhood tormentor of Stands For Them, though the pair now shared the odd admiration that can sprout from discord.

Close behind rode Stealing Horses, not yet worthy of the front row of warriors but at sixteen something more than an apprentice warrior. Looming among Stands For Them's challenges for the day would be keeping this little brother safe.

All waited for High Backbone. Then without fanfare he was among them, astride a spotted pony pirouetting in quick-hoofed circles. High Backbone was now twenty-nine winters: warrior in prime, and a war chief too. None could fail to notice his large veins among a crowd of muscles on forearms and upper arms and across a bronze chest.

Employing glances and hand signals only, High Backbone made stern adjustment to the three dozen assembled. In this formation they started for the main gathering grounds—as arranged the potentially reckless newcomers were positioned behind or beside more experienced, more calculating warriors. Stands For Them glanced over at Good Thunder's high forehead sloping to heavy brows over hawkish eyes—the effect was a fierceness not fully deserved, yet picture perfect for the moment.

Soon the Eat No Dogs contingent was on the flats between the villages of Spotted Eagle and Crazy Horse. Armed men were gathering like blackbirds, and a palpable energy piled in as would hailstones. Sometimes Stands For Them needed a second take, but here and there he found familiar faces behind war paint among the Sans Arc, the Hunkpapa, the Sicangu, and the Oglala.

Each man was astride his very best horse. Each horse's tail tied in the tight bundle signaling war, for in close combat no mounted warrior would want an enemy to grab the tail to possibly unbalance his horse. Then there came a line of warriors riding hard, having started from the farthest villages. Their horses glistened with sweat, and many a young man leaned over to smear this lather on his hands, hence on his face and arms and legs—thus adopting some of the horse's power for himself.

They rode like men impatient, so that others scrambled to make room. Out front galloped the dauntless Red Thunder, holding aloft an eagle-feathered lance. The sight visibly stirred Stands For Them and many others, for it served as a battle flag equal to the strange tri-colored banner of the cavalry.

There came among this force a riderless white horse, head high, red-rimmed eyes blazing a wildness. Untethered but prancing close by the other ponies. "Behold Tasunka Wakan," Stand For Them whispered to his brother. As quickly as seen, the Spirit Horse was lost in the growing maelstrom of warriors.

The sun crept above the horizon, but it's rays carried no warmth. What warmth there was seemed to hang in the visible breath of hundreds of men and animals united in common crusade. Among the growing horde were occasional knots of allied Cheyenne warriors, easily identified by distinct paint and feather arrangements.

Stands For Them leaned over to Good Thunder to ask, "Are we waiting for a command from *TaSunka Witco* (Crazy Horse)?"

Good Thunder answered without taking his eyes off of the horizon, "Kola, I do not know, but I saw him briefly when we approached this gathering ground."

"No, Crazy Horse rode in darkness up the valley" War Eagle interrupted, "He and his warrior society did not sleep. They launch the battle at first light. We are the rear guard. The final wave. Listen and we may hear the roar of guns even now."

Stands For Them nodded. He returned his gaze again and again to High Backbone. For it was this Miniconjou leader who would tell his several dozen warriors when to move out, when to fight, when to retreat.

For High Backbone, Crazy Horse's closest friend among his mother's people, carried with him this sixth sense—he knew what Crazy Horse planned even without hearing him, he knew where Crazy Horse rode even without seeing him.

Stands For Them's heart was steady, calm. *Odd*, he thought, *for today I might die. And I will assuredly ride side by side with death.*

Then it happened. A signal, a yelp. Warriors began riding into first light in groups of 30, 100 or 200. High Backbone's slight nod put the Eat No Dogs in motion, but at a slightly different line of travel. Stands For Them worried at first that communication between the groups was not strong enough. But then occasional "wolf" howls told disparate units they were traveling connected and in the right direction. The distant echo of cannon further confirmed.

Stands For Them saw a knot of warriors advancing on foot, and caught Good Thunder's eye, who nodded. "These are mostly Oglala, and a few Sicangu. Grandfather calls them the boastful ones, going to battle afoot because they are so confident of riding home on a fine cavalry horse." Stands For Them responded with a smile, for had he not done the same thing once or twice when leading a horse raiding party?

Advancing up the valley, all were heartened by the sight of women of their tribe on high knolls, standing before small blazes, some holding torches aloft, all offering tremolos to stir the men to bravery. Reminding them that in defeat men risked returning to a home camp of burned tipis. Stands For Them thought he saw half-sister White Bird. The women looked down on what for them were the sons of light soon to battle the sons of darkness.

The line of march was windless but cold, with only high emotions and warm bodies of horses to keep men tolerably comfortable. Shafts of rosy light continued to paint the eastern horizon as Stands For Them felt energy rise in both tribesmen and war horses.

Bridging a low divide, Stands For Them could now hear individual rifle shots from the daring mounted ambush of General Crook's sprawling campsite along Rosebud Creek.

Everyone dismounted, leaving horses in the care of Stealing Horses, and climbed a low but sufficiently protective ridge. Here, Stands For Them knew, he'd see the battle. Here, he'd better grasp what was to come. What he saw were many tents in orderly fashion where the soldiers among them scurried like insects. These men were part of a three-pronged offensive: Crook, Custer, and Terry, meant to subdue or annihilate the free-roaming Lakota.

From the ridge top Stands For Them saw yet more chaos. Lakota and Cheyenne warriors were making high risk sprints into the maelstrom, some turning to daringly gallop parallel to army lines.

Certain soldiers were still rushing out of their tents. Some were half dressed, but all were armed. Bullets and arrows in equal numbers fairly jumped through the smoky haze. Color and light and movement were everywhere: it took a moment for his eyes to absorb it all. Horse raids and buffalo hunts had never been as intense, as deadly, as confusing. He struggled to regain his center.

The Eat No Dogs group settled to their reserve position on the ridge just beyond rifle range from the main fight, there to watch wave on wave of mounted Lakota warriors rushing forward. In these charges, the warriors rode bunched together so as to whip each other's horses, making even the thought of retreat impossible.

Through it all, Stealing Horses remained at the base of the ridge, obedient but impatient while holding the group's mounts. He could not see the battle, nor even his brother or the others at the ridge top.

Stands For Them and his group could only wait for the eagle bone whistle—their signal to enter the battle as reinforcements. They watched in slack-mouthed awe as the latest wave of Lakota and Cheyenne warriors seemed on the verge of overwhelming the unprepared soldiers. Perhaps their wave would not even be called to battle.

But at the seminal moment, two swarms of unknown Indians in full war regalia appeared unexpectedly on the opposite ridge. As they galloped downhill, it became apparent to Stands For Them that these were mortal enemies of the Lakota—Crow, Shoshone and Arikaree army scouts. Known by all as the "army wolves", their ferocity in defending the shell-shocked soldiers was enough to turn the tide . . . to narrowly deny the hostiles a victory greater even than the coming triumph on the Little Big Horn.

The smell of human and horse blood filled the air, causing many a steed to recoil. But the best war horses plunged onward. Many fell, being the bigger targets—shrieking, kicking, thrashing about.

Stands For Them and his party watched spellbound, none bothering to conceal their position as it seemed well beyond rifle range. This feeling of being mere observers ended sharply when a bullet pinged off a nearby rock and whistled overhead. Then another. Something grazed Stands For Them's cheek and shoulder, raising red welts and a shallow wound. Whether a bullet fragment or flying piece of rock, he never knew.

Stands For Them and the others scrambled for better cover.

"It must be someone we cannot see."

"Perhaps a Shoshone scout."

"Perhaps a wasicu fighter."

Just then the fusillade stopped.

War Eagle rose up slightly, to better survey the surreal pageant below. He ducked as a bullet pinged off the boulder on which his arm rested. Sparks flew as more bullets hit the hard gravel against which the men pressed their chests.

Then a dull thud, as if a heavy stone had landed nearby. Stands For Them wiped something from his face, then heard a groan from War Eagle. With muted horror Stands For Them looked at his hand to see bits of bone and bloody flesh. Not his own.

In the same instant War Eagle touched his hand to his face. His finger tracing a gaping entrance wound. Now he rolled on his back to face the sky, hands clinched in fists. Struggling to suppress a wail, struggling to be worthy of his sudden, irrevocable fate as a martyred warrior. His look was astonishment—could this so soon be his dying day?

War Eagle moved a trembling hand from wound to crisscrossed cartridge belt, down to sheathed knife, then to his rifle stock, as though this inventory somehow still mattered.

Stands For Them crawled to his side with whispered encouragement. "Brother, be brave of heart."

War Eagle gave only the slightest nod, when above the din rose the screech of the eagle bone whistle calling the Eat No Dogs to action. In ragged fashion they moved down the ridge. All but Stands For Them and Good Thunder—they stayed with their wounded comrade. Knowing he would die soon, but not alone.

Careful to keep a low profile, the pair positioned themselves to carry War Eagle down to the relative safety of the horses. Just then a flight of arrows zipped over and through their position. One arrow grazed Good Thunder's arched back before pounding into War Eagle's thigh.

Now all three could see it: The quivering arrow's feather pattern. It was the arrow of a Crow scout. "*Kangi!*" War Eagle spat out the word as if it were a bite of rotted meat.

At the temporary shelter of a rock outcrop Stands For Them felt the dread having risen in his chest dissolve into a steadiness. Then came the anger of a man who would avenge War Eagle's mortal wounds. He settled himself flat on his stomach and began pouring much of his store of ammunition towards the enemy scouts among the boulder field. When bullets ran low, he let fly an arrow or two, but winds and distance were too great.

Stands For Them and Good Thunder now half-pulled, half-carried War Eagle's barely breathing form down to the position of the astonished Stealing Horses. "Yes, this is what war looks like," said his big brother's eyes.

Stands For Them looked back up the ridge at the Crow and Shoshone scouts and a handful of infantrymen now taking up his former position.

This threat from above added urgency in getting to the shelter of a nearby cottonwood grove. Stands For Them bent down to help lift War Eagle to a riding position, but in that moment he knew it would not be necessary. His old friend's eyes showed only white. So they draped War Eagle's body over the horse as bullets pockmarked the ground around them.

It was time for a mounted sprint to the cover of the grove. The young men made it. Not so all the horses—War Eagle's mount was felled in a hail of Crow bullets just as they reached the safety of the grove. There it lay—a heaving, dying but still breathing mass of flesh, hooves slowly thrashing the air for the next hour.

War Eagle's lifeless body was hopelessly pinned under the horse. No equine mercy killing was possible as long as there was hope that the animal might yet rise.

The horse would not rise. The body could not be returned to War Eagle's family, another arrow of pain piercing hearts.

During these surreal hours Stands For Them watched proudly the actions of his little brother, the model young warrior. Holding horses when need be, bravely running odd errands for water or ammunition. And now relishing the chance to return fire when the group gained a covered position in the cottonwoods.

Stands For Them and Good Thunder mounted and prepared to retake the ridge. Stands For Them looked down at his brother in such a way that Stealing Horses knew instantly his moment had come. He would replace the fallen War Eagle. He sprang to the stirrup.

Riding at full gallop, the trio snapped across the open ground without incident and soon caught up to their original group. High Backbone had directed the Miniconjous, now including the Eat No Dog sub-band, to assault a hilltop to the southwest presently containing nests of both Shoshone scouts and army infantrymen.

Stands For Them scrambled forward, calling out to those ahead to allow the trio to catch up. All were soon reunited, on their stomachs, and just beyond the line of enemy fire.

The Miniconjous leaned into the gritty work of staying low, zigzagging through sagebrush and boulders in hopes of retaking the hilltop. Stands For Them kept an eye on Stealing Horses as they advanced under moderate fire. With a cry of pain Good Weasel, so close beside Stealing Horses, took a flesh wound in the arm. He struggled to stop the bleeding, forcing his retreat to the horses. The others soon topped the now largely undefended hilltop, where they took a breather and observed the central battle still unfolding below.

By midday it seemed to fighters on all sides that the tide of battle was tilting to the soldiers. Into the no-man's-land between the combatants rode a knot of seemingly fearless Cheyenne fighters, plunging down and across shallow Rosebud Creek. They did not wish to play a subordinate role to their Sioux kinsmen. At first it looked to be a headlong charge into the federal lines, but at the last instant riders peeled left and right to show off the horsemanship for which their tribe was rightly famous.

But one rider, Comes In Sight, continued to ride recklessly exposed straight at the troops. The cavalry marksmen did not miss, one bullet tearing through the meaty part of Comes In Sight's right thigh. Another piercing his shoulder. A quick grab for the pony's mane failed, and he bounced to the ground where he was unable to rise.

Next his horse was shot, tumbling slow motion in a cloud of dust. Like other horses dropped by munitions meant only to kill a man, the animal would thrash and snort and suffer as fighting continued.

Stands For Them and Good Thunder noticed a rescue rider approaching the fallen Comes In Sight. He was crippled but very much alive, and raised an arm in supplication to this rider. Only seconds earlier his fate seemed sealed. But now the fighting abruptly stopped—soldiers and Indians alike watched in disbelief as the rescue rider thundered ever closer.

Amazement turned to grudging admiration for those who could see the rescue rider to be Buffalo Calf Road Woman, Comes In Sight's sister. Barely slowing, she leaned down to assist in scooping her brother onto the horse's rump, returning safely to the native lines. Then the queer spectacle of both sides standing to cheer.

The scene took Stands For Them's breath away. The Cheyenne were one of the rare tribes to allow women into combat. Known as the "man-ly-hearted women", they often fought to avenge a martyred husband. But not Buffalo Calf Road Woman. She entered the battlefield that day to fight alongside her brother. One week later, she would be the only woman warrior at the Battle of the Little Big Horn.

The dramatic rescue galvanized Cheyennes and Lakotas alike. See-ing the others take heart, Good Thunder, Stands For Them, and their small group moved below the ridge's lower rock outcropping seeking optimal shooting positions. Pushing the advantage.

Just then a tall, thin, dark-skinned Oglala warrior unknown to Stands For Them moved up beside him. Out of breath, the man wore the fiend-ish smile of exhilaration not uncommon to the day. As bullets pinged off the rock ledge above his head, the Oglala looked at Stands For Them and whispered a saying common among warriors of the High Plains: "A brave man dies but once, a coward many times." He vanished ghostlike into the dust storm of combat. Never seen again.

But his words stayed with Stands For Them. He would not be a cow-ard. He was now feeling some of the madness of battle. Quivering like an arrow on a pulled bow string, he moved to a more exposed position, darting up a narrow draw. There he chanced upon a gravely wounded enemy. Lying flat on his back, seemingly unable to move but fully conscious, the Arikaree scout's fingers were mere inches from his carbine.

This young man met Stands For Them's gaze with a look that seemed to say, "Do what you will, what you must."

Yet the scene gave Stands For Them pause.

Had not the Lakota occasionally befriended the Arikaree people, those strange planters by the big river? Had not he entered their sad little village once or twice to trade buffalo robes for corn? Were this man a Shoshone or Crow, Stands For Them would dispatch him with relish. But should he kill one already so helpless? Could he do this in the way one might kill a tethered dog meant for the feast?

"The Lakota warrior is hard-hearted." The maxim was part of his earliest memories. There was tellingly no word for "mercy" in the Lakota tongue.

Ignoring the maxim, Stands For Them would save a bullet and instead take the man's water and his ammunition belt and proceed in crouching fashion up the draw.

For the rest of his life, Stands For Them wondered if anyone had seen him take the soft-hearted path in that surreal hour.

At gully's end, Stands For Them found a rim of earth less than a rifle shot from federal troops. Firing with the forlorn Arikaree's stolen ammunition, he surprised himself when two enemy horses, both with riders, tumbled to the ground at his volley of bullets. One was a jet-black officer's horse, pirouetting in a failed effort to untangle quivering legs. The weight of that horse crushed its hapless rider lifeless.

Had he really made this kill? Stands For Them hesitated before dashing across the open ground between himself and the dead bluecoat. He touched the twisted leg and tall black boot of the officer with the butt of his rifle. Though not certain he'd made the kill, there was yet great honor for whomever was first to touch a fallen enemy. He retreated to a tangle of fallen trees.

Having thus counted a first coup in full view of his tribesmen, Stands For Them 'officially' gained a war record.

When a galloping patrol of bluecoats found his position, Stands For Them was pinned down for twenty minutes as whizzing bullets kicked up dirt clods left and right. Two nearby pockets of allies, one Cheyenne and the other Lakota, provided lifesaving cover for Stands For Them's careful retreat. He glimpsed the mounted Crazy Horse among those Lakotas.

The Battle of the Rosebud was now being fought under a blazing afternoon sun. Too tired to be afraid, Stands For Them now felt only the thirst, hunger, exhausted nerves and that strange banality of extended fighting and killing. Through eyes red from dust and black powder, he saw neither winners nor losers. Indeed, the battle was devolving into a see-saw affair where neither side could claim full victory.

Here and there among the bluecoats Stands For Them saw a very odd sight—bottles consumed, bottles shared. A surprising number of the enlisted men, especially veterans of the Civil War, believed in the power of liquor to dull the panic of battle. Most also carried a cord with which to use a toe to discharge their own rifle in suicide, preferable to the surety of eviscerating torture awaiting captives of the Lakotas.

With the battle at stalemate, General Crook ordered a tactical retreat to the south. It was enough for Crazy Horse, who with a simple wave of his feathered lance withdrew the larger portion of warriors under his influence.

In their turn lesser war chiefs, both Sioux and Cheyenne, embraced the chance to claim a partial victory. When Stands For Them and Stealing Horses saw High Backbone dismount to untie his horse's tail from the knotted war position to the free-flowing peace style, they did likewise and began moving downstream towards the village.

Thoughts turned to celebrating the day's many courageous deeds. Certainly there would be a feast. Stands For Them mused that he might be included among the honored warriors, many of whom would in pantomime relive the day's acts of distinction.

With thoughts both heavy and joyful, the brothers and their rump contingent moved north at a brisk trot, navigating the divide between two small creeks before dipping into a tree-dotted valley promising the most direct path to camp. One among them must shoulder the burden of telling War Eagle's wife and mother that he would not be coming home. Each wondered who that would be.

Hugging the left bank and rounding a curve between the bluff and a high cutbank, they abruptly and unexpectedly came upon three mounted bluecoats and a like number of Shoshone scouts, one leading a riderless and bloodstained horse. In a flash, both parties pulled their weapons and dismounted—for rare was the man who could shoot accurately from the swaying back of a horse.

The Lakotas were first to fire, but without visible effect.

Immediately came a return volley from the government men. A slug tore through the jaw of Stealing Horse's mount, sending this favored animal spinning and kicking over the cutbank and into the shallow creek.

Though Stealing Horses had been holding the reins, he nimbly sidestepped the half ton of beast as it fell past him to its muddy grave. Stands For Them searched his brother's face but saw no hint of panic.

There followed a pause of stunned inaction, time enough for both parties to reload their carbines, then a scramble as all combatants sought better cover. Together Stands For Them and Stealing Horses dropped over the edge of the cutbank. Their feet found a ledge of soft rock providing foothold.

Bursts of gunfire and silent-killer arrows kept all pinned down. The Lakotas enjoyed seemingly better cover and line of fire. Even so, a volley of federal bullets sliced through the air above and between the brothers.

In silence that followed, nervous bobbing heads of the small government force betrayed their interest in finding a safe exit from the standoff.

Suddenly Stands For Them noticed a scarlet stream pumping down the neck and bare chest of his brother. Though seeming not to acknowledge his wound, Stealing Horse's breathing was swift, shallow, labored.

"Are you badly hurt?"

No response. Stealing Horse's gaze was steady on the enemy. But a sharp nudge from big brother elicited a dismissive wave of the left hand that seemed to say "I'm okay" . . . even as his right hand let go the rifle to press firmly over a seeping wound to the neck.

The bullet shattering his horse's jaw had nicked the young man's carotid artery.

Stands For Them realized there could be no way to stem this spurting flow of blood. He'd surely failed to safely guide little brother through his first major battle.

Stands For Them's heart cried out even as he crawled closer to offer small encouragements. So close now, he could not ignore a bubbly red froth dripping from Stealing Horses' nose . . . and color draining from the handsome young face and form he'd always considered a better version of himself.

Sorrow welled up in him. He put his head next to his brother's. Conveyed tender words by whisper. Listened to his brother's softly chanted death song.

Soon the soil of the cutbank was soaked in a creeping deep crimson. And before the brothers knew it, the time for words had passed. But then Stealing Horses shuddered, lifting his head and chest inches off the ground. Stands For Them brought his ear close to his brother's mouth.

"You were the boy Curved Horn, who then became the man who Stands For Us. So I ask you, do I at least die the warrior's death?"

The older locked eyes with the younger.

"More, even, than just a warrior. Today you stand tallest for our oyate. When the sun rises tomorrow and ever after, the name Stealing Horses will be among the martyrs."

Before the younger one could move his lips, life slipped away.

So did the enemy.

For Stands For Them it seemed only moments earlier his mind was fully on returning to camp, where the welts on his cheek and shoulder would show where the wings of death had brushed by. To dance and feast in celebration of his coups and his brother's first battle.

These thoughts now far distant, Stands For Them tied his brother's still warm body onto his own horse. This doleful act drained any lingering glory of 'lance and shield'. Instead, he foresaw the women of his tiyospaye wailing mournful tremelos, and he resolved tonight to eat a cold meal far from the excitement of the bonfire feast and victory dance.

If such a withdrawal appealed, back in camp Stands For Them's rank as the eldest son of a headman grieving a warrior son's death would mandate his presence, however reluctantly, at the bonfire.

Entering his tipi, Stands For Them saw Tall Woman already sick with the news of Stealing Horses. He insisted she speak her grief as she washed paint from his face and body, then brought him a simple antelope-skin shirt and matching trousers. Dressed thus, he turned to her, offered a sad smile, and made the slow walk to the bonfire alone. His grief hung in the chest and throat so as to make breathing almost painful.

At the fire Stands For Them's bowed head and slumped shoulders made obvious his grieving status. He'd found a place to sit cross-legged in the third row. From there, he had a clear view of his father's position in the first row.

Stands For Them anxiously scanned the blanket-draped women milling about at the fire's furthest circle, hoping not to see a relative for reasons just then beginning to dawn on him.

Only those in the first three rows might expect to smoke from the sacred pipe. A rumor raced round the fire saying tonight they would smoke from the fine mountain mahogany pipe belonging to Elk Robe . . . a way of honoring this older warrior and headman who balanced the grief of death with the pride at a son's ultimate sacrifice for the nation.

All fell silent when Elk Robe pulled from a long doeskin bag the *chanupa,* the sacred pipe, its bowl a fine-grained red pipestone. The wooden stem featured a raised spiraling ridge, as a vine might entwine a branch, but in this case meant to represent the dervish or sacred whirlwind.

Elk Robe intently cradled the pipe on fingertips, holding it at arm's length towards the four cardinal directions. Then up towards Father Sky and down towards Mother Earth, before lighting the *Cansasa*, a tobacco of the inner bark of sacred Red Willow. All knew the smoke they saw carried the people's various prayers aloft. Elk Robe inhaled deeply before passing the pipe forward.

Eyes half closed, Stands For Them felt the pipe coming clockwise or sunwise round the circle. Closer and closer. Before long it was in the calloused hands of the old man they called Medicine Blanket. Next, there was a tingle as Stands For Them touched the wooden stem. And he felt many eyes on him for indeed today he was *wasigla*—one grieving a family death. Upon touching the mouthpiece, he again closed his eyes.

This sacrament was for Stands For Them as it had always been—a calming pool amid life's stormy waters. He found he could close his eyes, tilt his head back, breathe deeply. He could think of Stealing Horses in a way that for just these moments did not ache.

Having passed the pipe and fully opening his eyes, Stands For Them immediately spotted Good Thunder across the fire. He summoned his kola to take the now empty spot to his left side.

The pipe eventually returning to Elk Robe's ample hands—where with deep dignity he again lifted it that the smoke might ascend to brush the face of Father Sky, even as his bare feet were squarely planted on Mother Earth. As this sacred ceremony ended, a din returned to the assembled.

Stands For Them leaned over to share a confidence one dared expose to perhaps only one person. His words barely audible: ". . . Good Thunder, I am now heavy with the killing. My war medicine falls away."

This most unusual admission for a young Lakota man elicited a mere knowing nod from Good Thunder.

As kolas, they owed each other their lives in battle, if called upon. It was a bond even deeper than a brother's common blood. So deep that even darkest secrets could be safely shared.

Good Thunder chose a long silence as a way of telling Stands For Them that nothing would change between them. Then at length he said, "You are Stand For Them. Everyone knows your story—you stand for your people. I confess my stomach for the killing rises and falls as well."

Stands For Them nodded. Such was the dilemma of the era. Native societies demanded each male be two persons—the village man was expected to be slow to anger, patient with children, generous, putting the needs of others first. But in war and on horse raids, society demanded this same man be utterly ruthless when encountering enemies, even women, children, and the elderly.

Neither Good Thunder nor Stands For Them could know that their generation would be the last to shoulder the incongruity of village man vs. warpath man.

Stands For Them looked around to make sure others weren't listening—then to his kola: "I learned two things from today's battle: first that I lack the hard heart of a killer, but neither is mine the heart of a coward." It was all he could think to say. The day had been long. He was tired in body, and in heart. He would stand for his people, whatever that meant.

People moved closer to the fire to better hear the telling and re-telling of events from the day's battle. The stars came out strong against an indigo sky. There were whispers of a revenge attack from the soldiers, so certain warriors left to take up sentinel positions in the darkness.

More Lakota women gathered at the edges of the circle, many of them in their finery, from lovely shawls to near-white deerskin dresses decorated with scores of prized elk teeth. Celebrating the return of most sons, brothers, husbands.

The appearance of so many women moved High Backbone to rise and make his way to the special oratory place by the fire. The crowd hushed. "Horse nation, I ask you to move your gaze away from me and other orators. Rather, rest your eyes on those whose bodies bring us generation after generation of warriors—our true power, the Lakota women. Look on their shining faces, for there you will see a vision of a victory far greater than what we witnessed today on the Rosebud. "

The women beamed. The men smiled and nodded, secure in their status as males but appreciating how High Backbone acknowledged the womanly glue holding every piece of Lakota society in place.

But keen observers noted a different group of women standing to one side, their dress the calico of everyday, their hair disheveled and missing great chunks. On calves and forearms blood had dried from self-inflicted wounds. One new widow, barely old enough to be a bride, had chopped off a finger. She stood unsteadily, held up by a pair of older females.

At first Stands For Them was relieved to not see among these grieving ones any from his tiyospaye. Surely they would be there, to honor Stealing Horse's memory. But he could not see them, until Good Thunder pointed to the right and there they were, the tear-stained faces of Stands For Them's mother Sitting Bird and sisters Eagle Lodge and Worships The Earth.

With vague dread Stands For Them noted now the short, measured steps of mother and daughters as they began moving among the seated men, searching. Stands For Them's mother passed not far away as she made her way towards a warrior in the first row. His sisters followed. Many watched as Sitting Bird laid her right hand upon the head of Iron Nation. By ancient ritual she thus designated Iron Nation to avenge the death of her son Stealing Horses.

She had chosen wisely. Lean, big-boned, dark-skinned and accomplished in all the arts of war, Iron Nation gave a nod without looking up—signaling a willingness to be the avenger and thus square the account for his cousin Stealing Horses.

He understood that the man selected should feel an urgency: for a mother must grieve a martyred son for however many months or years it took Iron Nation to avenge the death by presenting her with a fresh enemy scalp.

A similar scene played out not far away as Worships The Earth laid a trembling hand upon the head of veteran warrior Greets With Fire.

Stands For Them looked away from the scene, and then down at his well-muscled arms and ample chest. Why, he wondered, did he feel both relieved and ashamed to not feel the touch of mother or sister for the avenging?

Next morning as Stands For Them stepped from his small tipi, this time with Tall Woman at his side, the bright sunshine on his cheeks seeming to mock his mood. Through a sleepless night he'd accepted this anguish of losing a brother so close in age and outlook as to be a lifelong wound. Tall Woman said like his physical wounds, this wound might one day scar over. He said impossible.

Chapter Eight

The Bloody Little Bighorn
1876-1877

The Battle of the Rosebud was over. Stands For Them's heart was hard, but his head had cleared.

He knew General Crook's troops had retreated in ragtag fashion. He knew native scouts reported no other bluecoats close by. He knew the Lakota and Cheyenne elders felt safe in moving a short distance westward to the meandering Greasy Grass River. A stream the wasicu called the Little Big Horn. He knew all this. He did not know why war still hung in the air.

Many others felt the coming storm as well. This is why all seven council fires of the Lakota gathered close. And those dependable allies, the Cheyenne and Arapaho. It would be the last great gathering of Northern Plains tribes, and Stands For Them could feel the energy. He overheard groups of threes and fours considering the rare might of the encampment, and how long before the soldiers returned.

Stands For Them's thoughts were on yet darker matters, the burial of a brother. After the events on the Rosebud, there had been no time to lay to rest Stealing Horses. His body had been brought along, draped over the back of his second favorite horse. Now summer temperatures made it incumbent on the family to bid farewell to the body.

Even before pitching their new camp, Elk Robe's tiyospaye began sad preparations. The older women, aunts mostly, washed blood and dirt off the now stiff body before rubbing pallid skin with the aromatic and sacred fringed sage. Then littlest sister, Walks Behind, was given the honor of bringing forward a fine and neatly folded Hudson Bay 4 Point blanket. This was the red robe, Stealing Horse's death shroud.

At an invisible signal, people began winding their way towards one of the few Eat No Dogs tipis erected, that of Elk Robe himself. Inside, the ceremonial body washing had concluded.

An uncle stepped forward leading Stealing Horse's childhood pony Star Runner. With the blanket-wrapped body carefully secured across the back of the little horse, Elk Robe was handed the lead rope. He took time to calm this horse made momentarily skittish at the smell of death.

The father then raised his right hand high before starting at a dignified pace towards a prominent cottonwood tree partially obscured by a nearby hill. It was a sufficiently prudent distance given the season's ever warmer weather. All followed Elk Robe, slowing their pace to match his.

As the party, nearly a hundred total, moved along it seemed custom would reign, in that the only eulogy would be private prayers and soft songs murmured by individuals.

But as he advanced, Stands For Them considered the prospects of a "graveside" ceremony of sorts. Sometimes a brother to the fallen one would be asked to step forward, to speak. Walking immediately behind Star Runner, this prospect further clouded his already slate grey mood.

The selected tree rounded into view. It possessed one very stout horizontal branch, substitute for the preferred high scaffold—for during wartime there was neither time nor materials for construction of a scaffold.

When the cortege neared the tree, at about that distance which a small boy can shoot an arrow, Elk Robe again raised his right hand high above his head.

Stopping and turning around, his gaze met Stands For Them's. He held out the buffalo-hair lead rope so that this living son might lead his fallen brother and horse the final distance. In his father's steely eyes there was a further message—one Stands For Them had been dreading.

Stands For Them took a deep breath and stepped forward. He ran his hand along the rump and withers of the horse, being careful not to touch his brother's body even as he reassured the animal. Star Runner quivered, lifted a rear hoof. Stands For Them gazed into the animal's dark sparkling eye as his throat tightened. This would not be easy. So much of life was suddenly not easy.

He took the rope firmly in hand, feeling both a bit of pride at being thus singled out, and a heavy-heartedness. For by clasping the rope, he had agreed to perform the funereal ritual accorded certain martyrs, that of killing the departed's favorite living horse . . . so that together man and steed might travel the spirit road.

Arriving under the tree, Stands For Them dropped the lead rope— that signal to every well-behaved horse to simply stand still. He then helped his father and uncles secure Stealing Horse's body to the tree limb. Difficult for both doers and watchers, still the effort was not without a tender grace.

When they were done, and had stepped back, a great uncle and mentor of Stealing Horse came forward. This was the old one called Bloody Mouth. Small in stature, his muscles on arms and throat were like braided ropes.

Bloody Mouth, known to be poor with horses, was otherwise steeped in Lakota lore, legend, and scouting skills. He was the kind of person whose failures at romance and male bravado made him all the better at what was left to him. He was that rare exception: a Lakota male without war record who was yet greatly respected.

Bloody Mouth squinted at the blazing sunset and began a short message to Stealing Horses . . . through sign language, so as not to break the code of silence. Though the meaning was difficult to interpret, Stands For Them gleaned the following from the old man's flowing motion of hands and arms: "This northern place feels far from those camps Stealing Horses loved most—the verdant bivouacs on the White and Niobrara Rivers. But this is a good tree, and his was a good death."

When the old man's hands returned to his side, all eyes turned to Stands For Them.

Taking a long breath and stepping forward, Stands For Them extended a knowing hand to hold the obedient Star Runner by a clump of his long-flowing mane.

Anyone selected to perform this ritual could choose how to dispatch the animal.

Stands For Them had seen it done the modern way, with a bullet. He thought this too violent, since it caused a thrashing and unpredictably dangerous death. In his experience, a single bullet was often insufficient while a second bullet was near impossible to administer. He chose instead the old way, the mostly painless method of using his sharp knife to open Star Runner's large jugular vein.

This he did so deftly that hardly anyone noticed. The horse reared up only a little, then stood trembling ever so slightly. In a minute or two it was as though the roan were falling asleep. Lowered head, swaying body, life draining bit by bit. Now Star Runner was on his knees. Now on his side. Lastly the big head disappeared into the season's tall grass.

Stands For Them looked downward, seeming to concentrate on cleaning off his knife and in hopes none would notice his glistening eyes. After a brief silence the assembled turned as one towards camp, confident now that a young man and his horse were together again.

When back at his tipi, Stands For Them felt the heaviness of his brother's death lifting, if only slightly. But it was replaced by a vague restlessness that sent him out among the horse herd for solace in the spaces between the beasts. In time he found his best horse, Whirlwind, and was soon riding bareback using only a makeshift hackamore. He went where his horse wished to go, wandering among the various camps strung out along the Greasy Grass River—first among his own people, then past the mighty Sicangu, next the mystical Oglala, the generous *Itazipco*, the resourceful *Sinapse*. In time he dismounted to walk beyond these allied tribes to the fires of the Cheyenne and Arapaho. Remounting, he could not help noting the increasing stream of new arrivals—some from scattered hunting camps but most from the agencies. It seemed in that hour, the hour when the sun goes to sleep, that every Indian of the plains was gathering in the great camp.

Stands For Them rode up onto a small bluff, more of a mound, from which he considered this human spectacle at sunset. People walking from one camp to another looked up at this man and a horse that seemed to share what should have been the rider's sadness only.

Shadows quickly covered most everything—but being astride a tall horse on a hillock, Stands For Them's face alone shined bright copper as the sun's last rays framed head and hair. To the sun he offered a final goodbye to his brother.

In darkness Stands For Them found his way back at his own modest tipi, composed of just eleven buffalo hides. Not far from the imposing sixteen-hide tipi of his parents.

Tall Woman was away. So he entered the parent tipi, where he saw only his mother. She was quietly applying colored quills to a pair of soft new moccasins. The death of Stealing Horses had created a rare opportunity for Stands For Them to seek comfort from her presence, her words. Today, burial day, a young Lakota male and his mother would be permitted more than superficial pleasantries.

Stands For Them took a position opposite his mother, and quietly observed her work until she looked up. He could see fresh cuts on her arms and her hands, the public show of grief. Dried blood on the dirt floor of the tipi suggested that beneath her skirt she had done the same to her calves and thighs. Sitting Bird was forty years old, but missing teeth and a sunken mouth made her look older. Her eyes had been drained of tears by days of mourning Stealing Horse's death. He thought he saw a new fierceness, for she was now and forever mother to a dead warrior. Through it all a sad loveliness shone, that same loveliness in male form that Stands For Them cast.

Taking care not to make eye contact, she said "My son, I watched with pride today as you bravely delivered your brother's horse onto the spirit road. I know these days have been the hardest of your life, and the same may be true for your father. He and I do not speak of such things."

A long silence allowed camp sounds to drift in—dogs growling over broken bones, horses nickering softly, keening women beside some distant shroud.

He had not spoken, had not planned to speak. Then words of self-doubt came tumbling: "The very courage that allowed me to earn my name so many years ago, or to enter fields of battle, or to slip into the enemy village on a horse raid—this courage no longer comes to me as does the rising sun. Perhaps you know this. Perhaps this is why at the big fire you chose another to provide the revenge scalps that will help you move past the mourning."

Sitting Bird looked up, her face at first startled then softened in considering her Nawica Kicijin—her young man of many hearts—the brave heart, but also hearts curious, kind, devoted, mindful, merciful. She put her quillwork down. "Nawica Kicijin, even though your father is a war chief and may have hoped the same for you, we soon must step into a new world. It is a step that cannot be avoided. In this new world you will be a leader, perhaps renowned. In any case, your people will need you to be a peace chief. The need for war chiefs is passing away."

At this she reached into a nearby satchel and produced something saved since her childhood—an eagle wing with leather handle decorated with quills and beads dyed in the favored colors of her grandfather, a

Miniconjou leader among that era's peace faction. Without comment she placed the mighty wing and beadwork at the feet of her son.

Stands For Them offered gratitude in the form of a nod and smile, and watched as mother put her quillwork away and began preparing the evening meal. He could see the full moon had risen, so Stands For Them stood up in that nimble way of all athletes, ducking out the flap to resume his anxious wanderings among the various camps.

Soon he was walking beside the many cooking fires of the big Hunkpapa contingent, hoping to see one or more of this band's vaunted war chiefs. Perhaps he'd run into Gall. Or Rain-in-the-Face. Or maybe even Sitting Bull himself.

Seeing no one of note, he instead squatted down to find some distraction among a rollicking pile of puppies, picking up first one and then another of the fawn-colored balls of energy.

The hush of evening descending over the great camp was shortly shattered by runners excitedly loping from one campfire to the next. Stands For Them moved to within earshot of the messengers. "Have you heard? Listen all. *Tatonka Iyothanka* has had a great dream! A prophecy to elevate the oyate!"

In this way the news of the prophetic dream spread beyond the Hunkpapa fires to all seven council fires of the Lakota nation, and even to Cheyenne and Arapaho tipis.

"This great dream has come to *Tatonka Iyothanka*, the Bull that Sits, but it belongs to all the people. His vision is of soldiers falling out of the sky."

Each listener would interpret the dream for themselves. Stands For Them considered: *The dream surely foretells a great victory.*

He was caught up in excitement swirling like bonfire smoke up and down the valley. In this tribal fervor he saw himself, perhaps for the last time, applying his war paint to self and horse.

Arriving back at his tiyospaye, Stands For Them was lifted to see his family gathered 'round a larger than normal fire. Such a fire signaled an evening of storytelling, or maybe even feasting. A backrest had been saved for him beside his father, who had just begun speaking.

"I remember only one Lakota summer gathering equal in numbers to this great camp. It was a few years before Nawica Kicijin came to this world—both events beside *Mato Paha*. Open wide your eyes, young ones, for you'll not again see a camp as vast as today's—too many people, too many horses, god's beasts in such numbers quickly eat all the grass."

Heads nodded agreement.

"There is more," he continued as he rose to move among the gathered. "So many people also scare away the wild game making for poor hunting. This encampment must break up in two sleeps—three at most. We of the Eat No Dogs will follow High Backbone, of course. I will counsel him to move westward towards the Snow-in-Summer mountains."

This feeding of so many horses was becoming a dark cloud over every headman. So, following a hearty meal of dog stew, Elk Robe called aside his oldest son and the like-aged nephew White Shield, intent on solving the puzzle of feeding their hundred horses for another day.

Placing meaty hands on their shoulders, Elk Robe lowered his brow, "I have been told that green grass can be found north of here, where the rivers meet. I ask you to leave only the eight best war horses here, and at dawn take all the rest to this grassland. Stay with them until you are sent for."

By dint of a nod and glance, the young men acknowledged the instructions and committed to meet here at first light. Parting, they spoke of Elk Robe's disquieting order to leave the war horses in camp.

When predawn arrived, sleepy-eyed Stands For Them stumbled to the cold fire to discover White Shield was nowhere to be found. Stands For Them went back to his tipi, disgusted but not surprised. How would his people survive with men so slow and unreliable?

He brought forward and saddled a favored cutting horse, Running Walk, then sat waiting in his tipi to avoid the morning's light rain. Half an hour later came a horse nicker and a scratching at the tipi flap.

Stands For Them looked at Tall Woman and shrugged his disappointment at the late start. In time they'd gathered up the horse herd. As they rode White Shield rambled on about this and that. The horses were cooperative, perhaps sensing they were being guided from the camp's close-cropped stubble to more lush pasture.

Some miles north of the great camp the young men and horses came to the green meadows Elk Robe had predicted. Dismounting, Stands For Them hobbled three lead mares. The young men could then relax, knowing the greater herd would not wander far.

Together they found a suitable hillside from which to sit and observe. When seated, Stands For Them produced Tall Woman's parfleche, containing pemmican, a handful of June berries, and a few fresh tubers. The sun had cooked away the rainclouds. They began thus to share both warmth and food.

But Stands For Them could not ignore a tingling in fingers and toes, swiveling his head often to look downstream.

"Is it the Long Knives?" asked White Shield.

Stands For Them shook his head, "Where we sit may feel like the Lakota nation. But just two years ago, the Crow summer camp was right here on the banks of the Greasy Grass. Their lodges even now are close by on the Yellowstone River. They hunt north of the Yellowstone most days, but would not hesitate to enter this valley. To take our horses, or our lives."

Even so, a climbing sun relaxed body then mind—and Stands For Them was soon as languid as White Shield. Each had come prepared, dressed in light deerskin loincloth and shirt, armed with bow and arrow, and beside Stands For Them the Springfield carbine that only days before had belonged to Stealing Horses.

Stands For Them's comments on the Crow prompted White Shield to ask about a rumor. One regarding his own tiyospaye. "Stands For Them, speak to your father's strange words at the council of headmen on the Powder River?"

Feeling no need to defend his father, yet having heard all manner of rumor, he carefully gathered up words, "My friend, you did not hear Elk Robe's speech at that council fire. Nor did I. But it is a rare thing for Elk Robe to speak publicly, so later that day I begged him to repeat his oration. Here is what he said:"

" 'The Crow are our ancestral enemies and I have fought against them, but there are tribesmen far greater than me who now see these horsemen as possible allies in our fight against the Long Knives. We have debated whether or not the Lakota should hunt north of the Bighorn Mountains. Soon we will vote. I will raise my stick in favor of staying to the south. Why you ask? Because an enemy that is hungry is more dangerous, more warlike. This season our war is with the mighty blue-coats. So let the Crow have their traditional hunting grounds. With full bellies, they may join us in defending these last hunting grounds.' "

Stands For Them looked skyward. "You see, White Shield, my father did not call for friendship with the Crow, only that we wisely choose our enemies and our battles." White Shield seemed satisfied in this answer.

With the grass now sufficiently dry, White Shield reclined full length on the ground. Stands For Them was careful to first put down his saddle blanket before propping himself on an elbow—the habit of one con-cerned with appearance. It showed in his dance attire, his war paint, his everyday tendencies. The first born son of a headman, and now almost twenty winters, he could afford to ignore the sniping of those who called him vain.

Breezes carried off the sky's last cloud. Stands For Them looked up from the herd to what he at first mistook for an eagle. But no. It was the black body and naked red head of a vulture. Wings motionless, it soared southward. Then he saw another. Then a group of four. All riding the thermals, all spiraling southward.

Wide-eyed, he looked at White Shield, then back at the birds—the scout in Stands For Them knew this aerial show contained a veiled message.

Together they observed as still more vultures appeared on the horizon and passed overhead.

Stands For Them was first to comment. "Your uncle Elk Robe talks of how different birds bring different news. He says to know where death reigns watch the bird that eats meat but does not kill. The vulture has learned gunfire means either a hunt, or a battle, dead buffalo, dead horses or dead warriors."

White Shield's face flushed with excitement at the thought of events at the great encampment. They stood as one and climbed the ridge for a better view southward. From there they saw a mantle of dust billowing over the Little Bighorn valley.

With the great buffalo herds now gone, such a dust cloud meant but one thing—the battle was joined. "Long Knives has invaded the great encampment. And we are missing it all!"

Stands For Them thought of his family. His odd new ambivalence towards killing was instantly overrun by a desire to defend, to stand up for . . . further fueled by a young man's natural desire to be wherever the action is.

But no matter the pair's urge to join the fight, they dared not bring in the herd without permission of the *akacita*.

Stands For Them made sure White Shield fully understood this before suggesting they take a seat, and a deep breath: "My cousin, you should know of my experience with the *akacita* in times such as these. I have seen them shoot the horse out from under a tribesman who disobeys."

"And remember, if the battle is going badly, fresh horses such as we have will be needed as remounts, or to help our oyate in retreat." Even as a responsible Stands For Them spoke these responsible words, his heart yearned to be at the defense of his wife, mother and remaining siblings.

The young men moved to catch and mount their personal horses. Reading each other's minds, they compromised by moving some miles closer but not too close. To a high hill known as Eagle's Nest. From there they hoped to hear the gunfire, know the tide of battle. All the while keeping the herd safely in reserve.

How could they know that for a lifetime the pair would explain, over and over, how they somehow missed the greatest victory of the Lakotas or any other Indian nation. Never mind that they were simply doing their duty for the tiyospaye.

Stands For Them nervously took the hobbles off the lead mares. But rounding up the balance of the herd required expert horsemanship, for the animals resisted departure from such succulent grasses.

As the men and horses moved ever closer to the dust cloud, there were audible cracks of gunfire in ever more sporadic patterns suggesting a tapering of the fight. The horses, both ridden and herded, held heads and tails high. Prancing now as if they too felt energy from the battlefield.

The pair held their herd briefly on a terrace above the river before succumbing to the magnetism of what lay below.

Approaching the north end of the great camp, Stands For Them saw occasional smoldering signs of what had surely been a terrible conflict. Here an upside down cavalry saddle, the cinch ripped in half but otherwise undamaged. There a camp dog, shot through the head. Then coming into view, in a side ravine, a great circle of dead horses and humans in blue jackets. Among them walked Lakota women and children, sifting through the dead for useable items.

Stands For Them looked over at White Shield, incredulous. "This must have been a great, no, the greatest Lakota victory."

Stands For Them deftly guided the herd into a simple rope corral with only a bit of help from White Shield. Having thus secured the herd, and their mounts, Stands For Them and White Shield proceeded on foot.

Among the Lakota council fires was a nation unsure how to observe such an outsized victory. Singing, dancing, and feasting at every hand, overlaid with a sense of the stunned. So many young women pirouetting below still-dripping scalps given by a husband or suitor. Even the camp dogs were wagging their tails, anticipating the scraps from such confusion and feasting.

Here and there were islands of sadness, even horror. The family of Comes Flying, a Miniconjou youth near Stands For Them's age and well-known to him, were wailing and keening beside the youth's blanket-covered body. Further on, the ground was covered with the wounded and dying, each attended by a family member or medicine man.

Stands For Them stopped in front of the tipi of the family of War Eagle. There he kneeled as a way of honoring the comrade who'd died beside him days earlier on Rosebud Creek. Stands For Them was surprised to be joined in kneeling by Little Big Man, Crazy Horse's crafty lieutenant. From his waist hung two fresh wasicu scalps.

Not all wailing was from mourners—near the dance bonfire sat two prisoners, one a boyish and bruised but very much alive 7th cavalry private, the other Bloody Knife, Custer's favorite scout. Both had been stripped, bound, and were enduring the torture of certain young warriors each brandishing burning sticks. Men made cruel by a cruel life.

Things were going especially bad for Bloody Knife, son of a Hunkpapa Sioux father and an *Arikaree* mother.

Having no tradition of fair treatment of prisoners, there could be no mercy for either man. Theirs would be a long night without a sunrise. The dark art of Lakota torture was practiced by few, but condoned by many. Yet as Stands For Them walked past, trying not to look, he hoped that before first light some respected elder might approach the tormentors and with a simple hand motion declare "Enough of this loud suffering. Grant them death."

After strolling the length of the great camp, Stands For Them and White Shield returned to the Miniconjou tipis and approached the central fire of the Eat No Dogs. They found a great feast underway, lit by a blaze leaping ten feet in the air.

Stands For Them and White Shield were greeted with both cheers and jeers, for they had missed this most celebrated of all battles. Then to anyone who would listen, "We were close. We could see it, smell it, hear it. We would have joined the fight. But our duty was with the horse herd."

Drum circles were forming, singers were warming up their voices. Shouts arose for Stands For Them to go to his tipi and dress for the dancing, as even now he was among the best dancers of the Eat No Dogs. Never mind that he'd missed the fight!

Elk Robe had quietly taken a place of honor not far from High Backbone, the Eat No Dogs intancan who again on this day distinguished himself in battle. Even at a distance Stands For Them could feel his father's warm gaze, declaring that he'd done well to protect the horse herd, and should feel no shame in joining the dance.

Not convinced he should presume to dance a victory dance, Stands For Them instead found a seat beside his father. There to spend a quiet hour simply observing.

Despite air so thick with the smell of victory, Elk Robe felt the need to remind his first born of a sobering truth: "The Long Knives will now hunt us as never before. We won today, son. We will not win tomorrow." Then turning his face away, "You and White Shield did well. You've given us what we most need tomorrow: well-fed, well-rested horses to stay ahead of vengeful soldiers." Father and son sat straight-faced for a time absorbing this new state of affairs. But the smiles returned, for tonight was a night to celebrate.

Finally yielding to occasional encouragements, Stands For Them retired to his small tipi to change. Tall Woman followed to assist. He emerged wearing a beaded loincloth, copper bells on ankles and knees, a hair-fringed war shirt, and a headdress of roached horsehair framed by twin eagle feathers. Soon the pounding rhythms entered the bone, turning Stands For Them's dancing into a prayer. Flickering silhouettes thrown by the fire reminded the tall one that he was dancing with the ancestors.

By morning Elk Robe's prediction was a sentiment on every tongue. "The great encampment must break up—go in many directions." Further urgency came when Arapaho scouts brought news that General Terry's mighty cavalry and mounted infantry advanced from the north. The small Arapaho village was first to leave. What direction they took no one could bother to note.

The Cheyenne headman Dull Knife seemed poised to follow next. But in fact the Oglala bands were next to leave, having most urgently rolled up their heavy tipi skins. The various bands acted independently, some returning to the relative safety of the reservations, others vanishing into the Snow-in-Summer mountains. Elk Robe's people were rumored to be bound for the headwaters of the Little Powder River.

All morning the three hundred souls of the Eat No Dogs moved with no waisted motion in packing up. Such swirls of activity made it unclear which tiyospayes might follow High Backbone's lead, which would return to the reservation, and which would pivot north to join Sitting Bull's race towards Canada.

As the three factions departed north, east and south, there came a high-pitched whining among certain camp dogs. For while some trotted off unhesitatingly behind a favored master or mistress, others whimpered, dashing here and there as if baffled by this fracturing of their human and canine pack.

*****

Thus began months of moving, dodging, and rarely resting. Stands For Them never got this winter of 1876-77 completely out of his head ... the worst season of his life. The rigors of this snow season his elders had predicted, for the elk had come off the mountains earlier than normal, and tribal ponies had grown their shaggiest winter coats. But none fully predicted the resolve of a vengeful wasicu army.

It was a season when the twin eagle feathers in Stands For Them's hair announced his pride in a tiyospaye refusing to return to the reservations. The consequence of such pride would be hunger for many in the tiyospaye.

The Elk Robe family fared better than some, for in a landscape devoid of buffalo, Stands For Them had a knack for pinching the odd deer or antelope. Such stealth, however, required that he hunt alone. So on the first morning of the Moon of Popping Trees, Stands For Them emerged from his tipi dressed for the solo hunt. He asked a young cousin to fetch and stake his preferred hunting horse, Tashunka Ska.

But on this morning as he prepared to depart, a bent figure followed him, shaking her finger and clucking her tongue. She the village weather woman, the aged Bird On Nest. Deep wrinkles and a toothless smile suggested she was not long for this world. But still plucky, Bird on Nest had for decades honed skills at forecasting storms. She conjured her prophesy each morning by sitting before a uniquely smokey little fire, there to observe the smoke's behavior. On this day she saw the smoke weave and billow in roller coaster fashion. The smoke was her simple yet effective barometer, foretelling the unstable air preceding a storm. So she shared this message: "Stay in camp young man, or you risk being stranded in a blizzard."

Stands For Them nodded but didn't break stride as he walked to un-stake Tashunka Ska. He made quick adjustment to the saddle, then rode forth on his hunt. Resolved, for just that morning he'd heard still more cries of young children with empty stomachs.

As he rode, the morning was unremarkable as to weather or game. But by midday the sun was abruptly obscured, and a mild breeze steadily blowing the horse's tail between its hind legs switched to a biting headwind. When ice pellets began peppering Stands For Them's face he turned back, having procured but a single jack rabbit.

His retreat to camp came too late. In minutes the air was white on white. Then the ground was white and the horizon gone. In two hours the snow on the flats was up to his horse's knees—in the gullies sometimes past the saddle cinch.

For horse lover Stands For Them there came a terrible choice—find a bit of shelter in the dim hope of surviving the night. Or, urge the mount ever onward through heavy wet snow to the point where the animal plays out . . . in this way getting close enough to camp that he might plod the last few miles. He knew the equine mind will give when asked, up to and even past the threshold of death.

The wind pinched Stands For Them's cheeks as he paused to consider. But there was no choice—the storm too fierce—his sole chance of survival to urge Tashunka Ska ever onward.

The inevitable came when his fine horse foundered on the twelfth valiant mile.

After dismounting Stands For Them urged the animal up onto wobbly legs and into a pocket-sized cottonwood grove. The horse again collapsed as Stands For Them tied him loosely to a trunk. Numbing fingers stripped bark from the cottonwoods, making a pile of this emergency food within reach of the horse.

As the storm grew still more furious, Stands For Them surrendered any hope of the horse surviving the blizzard to be retrieved in fair weather. Nor would Tashunka Ska regain strength, pull free of his intentionally loose mooring, and trot back to the village. So Stands For Them bent down to take the animal's large head in his arms. To caress the forehead and neck, to blow the master's breath into Tashunka Ska's quivering nostrils.

Now in near darkness and through swirling snowfall, Stands For Them set off plunging through drifts. He banked on a thin instinct for where the village would be. Feeling the land more than seeing it, he used every sense and all his tricks. At one point he felt completely lost, then oriented by noting branches of a small tree searching the sun's direction.

His hair and face plastered with snow, Stands For Them staggered into camp to collapse against the flap of his mother's tipi.

This winter continued to spread a pallor. The Eat No Dogs managed to find enough food to survive but never to satisfy. They conserved energy by retreating to stout animal-hide tipis and staying sometimes all day under ample buffalo robes.

One midwinter day Stands For Them was gathering firewood, normally a woman's task, when he looked up to see a line of hunched figures coming from the west. It was the Cheyenne band of Chief Dull Knife, ousted from their Bighorn Mountains camp. They had been overrun, scattered, and all possessions had been put to the torch in a surprise attack by the bluecoats.

These homeless ones filing past Stands For Them were of all ages, wearing few clothes, and possessing few horses and no shelter of any kind. They arrived rightly believing the Lakotas would share what they could. Stands For Them offered a horse, two buffalo robes, and what little he could spare of dried meat. But Dull Knife's people would spend the balance of winter huddled in the most miserable of makeshift shelters, begging with blackened fingers through the season.

Near the end of winter, Stands For Them witnessed the desperate attempt of a Cheyenne mother to save a badly chilled infant. The mother herself was bone chilled. Her fire's meager warmth snatched by high winds had left but one last-gasp act remained to restore her infant's body temperature.

She cried out for a Cheyenne boy of ten, perhaps her son, to find the weakest pony from the tribe's very few, one that would likely not survive winter. This boy enlisted an older male to help kill and disembowel the creature. Then into this warm, damp cavity with trembling arms the mother placed her mute, seemingly frozen but still-breathing baby. In minutes the blue little one was crying.

Stands For Them never knew if the baby lived or died. But the scene planted in him a seed soon sprouting with knowledge that it is futile to confront the wasicu war machine.

Chapter Nine

The Rambling Years
1907

Cleve needed a job.

The right job might be a grubstake, a first step towards his dream of one day owning a ranch. The streets of Valentine pulsed with rumors that more reservation land would soon open to homesteading. Grizzled contrarians always adding, "This just might be the last chance to homestead."

Hence he unfolded the March 15 *Valentine Democrat* to "Help Wanted." The broadsheet covered most of the cafe table he sat at. "Hiring young men, willing and strong, to join our threshing crew. Hiring this spring for wheat harvest in Oklahoma and north Texas. Those hired will follow the harvest season north. Employment to Nebraska or the Dakotas. Inquire in person at offices of Meyer & Bleem, Amarillo, Texas."

Trouble was, how would a broke guy get to Texas? The answer was to ride the rails.

So Cleve took a deep breath, and jumped his first slow-moving boxcar leaving the freight yards of Atkinson, Nebraska. Feeling very alone and not sure when or if he'd ever see his beloved Niobrara valley again. He soon learned how to leap frog from this train to that, choosing those heading south. Asking other hobos about the train schedules, the risks. *Odd,* he thought, *I was the shy one as a little boy, the one watching four older brothers take the big chances. Now it's my turn.*

In the vast yards of Omaha, he sat beside a rawboned drifter, a Civil War veteran, who shared hard earned advice, "Stay hidden by day sonny, then aim to jump the moving boxcar of a night train. That way you'll avoid the rail yard bulls. They got billy clubs that'll knock you silly. Somevm' have guns, too."

Cleve spent the next two nights slow cruising through Nebraska in cold, empty boxcars. His duffle containing only two shirts, and his wallet only two dollars. On the third night he jumped a car blessedly half full of hay bales. Cozy, heat-producing hay bales, but still empty of human company. There was some company in the steady din of the great engine as it blustered and rumbled and pounded across prairie and over wooden bridges spanning broad, brown rivers.

Somewhere in Kansas, Cleve found a sunny seat at the open door of a fast-moving boxcar to witness a green spectacle. For the roll of the calendar towards springtime was compounded as the train hurtled southward into an increasingly vernal world.

The effect was hypnotic—in one long day Cleve traveled from winter to spring, as if riding a leafy, blossomy wave. Into old age he would recall this day ". . . when summer rose up like a bear out of hibernation."

Lonely travel remained the norm. But to Cleve's surprise, on the seventh night the boxcar he jumped held plenty of company. In darkness and judging only by counting voices, he figured there must be a dozen fellow vagabonds. The banter revealed each to be a solitary traveler. In spite of or because of this, a comradeship swiftly formed. Darkness left Cleve with little to do but listen.

As conversation waned, the man who Cleve unrolled his bedroll beside started up with a Jew's harp while also singing sad songs. He had a most beautiful baritone voice. By 2 a.m. his music was lullaby to an audience that one by one began snoring. When the music man fell asleep the clickety-clack of the tracks took up a similar cadence for Cleve.

At first light he opened his eyes, rolled over, and was taken aback by the ebony skin of the man sleeping beside him. It was the music man.

At his next chance to walk into a post office, Cleve scribbled a post-card home. It said in part, "Somewhere in Kansas or Oklahoma my boxcar had in it the first negro I ever saw. He filled that damn boxcar with the best damn song."

Two more days hiding from the yard bulls, two more night trains and Cleve was on the muddy streets of Amarillo. He had no trouble finding the offices of Meyer & Bleem in an alley off Main Street. They looked Cleve up and down, then helped him catch on with a 'binder crew', a traveling team of men using pitchforks to lift hefty wheat bundles into the thresher. Within 24 hours he was a member of a rawboned crew of sorts as they followed the ripening grains northward. But there would be no grub stake, with wages much lower than expected.

Cleve looked on the ever-changing crews of shadowy young drifters, wondering if he was really any different. Months later, work ran out in a whistle-stop below the South Dakota-North Dakota border. The foreman simply said, "That's it, boys," and walked off. Cleve found himself standing beside a gravel road, with two bits in his pocket. He stuck his thumb out towards Nebraska.

How he'd both hated and loved this vagabond year. For the rest of his days a train whistle, near or far, would bring up the travel itch borne of that season.

Back in Nebraska, Cleve found short term ranch hand work while silently cursing his birth order. For the eldest son was presumed heir of a father's property, and he felt squeezed towards a hired hand's life, working always on someone else's place.

So it was with interest that Cleve overheard his sisters discuss a letter having arrived to their father from cousin Dane, who'd moved up to Red Deer, Alberta. Dane had joined outliers of the Berry clan in a territory of Western Canada that in 1908 was like the American West of 1880; fenceless, broad areas still unmapped, railroads just creeping in.

Two months later another message from Dane, this time a postcard addressed to Cleve. "There are jobs up here, cousin. Pretty good jobs going begging."

Cleve resolved to see this last frontier for himself. Maybe see actual snow-capped mountains, a first for this Nebraska boy. He packed a duffle, sold both his horses, and headed north by a herky-jerky combination of trains, freight wagons, foot power, stagecoach, and even a hitched ride with the proud owner of a 1903 Stearns horseless carriage.

Such traveling days were hard, bumpy, hunger-filled, but he was carried along by the excitement of entering a new nation. Still, there were days when Cleve had to push back the loneliness of solo travel, and the nagging feeling that he'd never again see his boyhood haunts on the Niobrara River valley, or his family.

When finally he arrived at the border, Cleve was disappointed to find, well, nothing. Not a "Welcome to Canada" sign, not even a barbed wire fence, just a foot-tall boundary stone alongside a dirt road, with "U.S." faintly engraved on the south side.

An hour north of the border the landscape seemed to swell with bucolic freshness that at once surprised and pleased Cleve. Pressing north of rollicking and ramshackle Calgary, the occasional roadside farms he passed were now spaced further and further apart. He could sense, though not quite see, the looming Rocky Mountains. Here Cleve could begin to feel how different the rangeland was from his native Nebraska. Here he could feel on his skin that clean but harsh beauty of the Far North.

He spent a couple days in Balzac, there to have the rare pleasure of a short conversation in a mercantile with a bonneted Canadian lassie. Smitten by her face so easy on the eyes and the sweetness of a shy smile, he would pass her once more before leaving town. She met his gaze. But

Cleve lacked the courage and the means to offer anything more than a lopsided grin and a tip of his hat.

Another day of travel and then finally, from the back of a hay wagon he turned his head and there it was. Red Deer—a clapboard sort of town without a single example of brick-built respectability. Cleve failed to see any "Help Wanted" signs in any shop windows. In fact, one of the windows to the little post office was busted out. It appeared as a "boom town" for which the boom had expired.

Asking around, he discovered it was but a short walk to the modest home of Dane and his new wife. Dane's place sat just west of what passed for a downtown. The house sat unpainted and unremarkable in every way, with a yard full of chickens, two goats, and a bony milk cow. The day had retreated to cold, misty and overcast, typical early spring in Alberta.

Dane met him at the door. Auburn-haired, on the meaty side for a Berry, an affable smile.

"Cleve, when I wrote your dad and then you, it really seemed like everyone around here was hiring. The granary, the freighters, the farm equipment dealers. Felt like overnight it all moved west. I know this ain't what you expected."

"I'll stay on a couple of days, if that's okay. Maybe ask around for work," Cleve shrugged to cover his disappointment. "Will see what other travelers are talking about, and then decide which way I'll head. Probably west."

After gazing around the yard and house, he added, "I'm happy to help with chores. Looks like you've got firewood needs splitting."

Later at the supper table, "When I passed through Calgary there was some talk about your new railroads. What can you tell me?"

"Well, the Canadian Pacific line is done. But rails for the Canadian Northern Railway been laid only as far as Edmonton. Might be work west of there."

And so it was that Cleve split three cords of firewood in two days, then grabbed his knapsack and was once again on the dusty road, with still no snow-capped mountains glimpsed. A hundred miles to Edmonton. Farmsteads grew still further apart, looking more like trading posts. A vast, bleak land it had become, indifferent to but mirroring Cleve's slumping morale. It was feeling like his last roll of the dice.

Then, when it seemed the country could not get more plain and windswept, Cleve saw what he assumed to be Edmonton. It was to be the northernmost wedge of agrarian North America, a place waiting for new strains of wheat to match a sufficiently warm but painfully short growing season.

Cleve knew that beyond Edmonton one could hope to make a living only by fur trapping, or trading with the Cree people. He'd reached the end of the line in his quest for employment.

As Cleve entered Edmonton he found it even less appealing than Red Deer. Here, too, his American money was coveted, so that two dimes bought him a fine lunch. Then it was straight away to the office of the Canadian Northern RR, just a large canvas tent with wooden floor.

"No, young man. We are certainly not hiring for graders or tracklayers. This railroad won't push on over the mountains for some years," said the bespectacled hiring agent before rubbing his forehead and fishing for a handkerchief. "Even if we were hiring gangs now, didn't they tell you?—Canadian citizens get preference. Sounds to me like you're born and bred Yankee, right?"

"Well, that's right." Cleve put his hands in his trouser pockets, and as he turned to exit by ducking under the tent flap he heard the agent telling the next in line to try the adjoining tent of Brewster Company.

Cleve straightened his hat and wondered why he hadn't been similarly informed. Feeling now not just far from home but homeless, he gloomily entered the neighboring tent.

Brewster Company was indeed looking for a few men, mostly accomplished horsemen. Horsemen to support the railroad survey crews just then piercing the mighty Rockies west of tiny Fitzhugh. The Brewster agent interviewing Cleve did not ask about citizenship.

"Can you rope?" "Yes." "Can you trim hooves and shoe a horse if need be?" "Yes" "Can you wrangle the crow-hopping mule or horse?" "Yes" "Are you easily unhorsed?" "No."

The twenty-year-old horseman was hired on the spot. He tipped his hat, feeling a little more hopeful, and happy to be away from both tents, for he never much liked standing in front of the kind of men who half hide behind a desk. Smooth-handed, tight-collared men.

He spent just one night in Edmonton before joining three other new hires in leading the survey crew's empty packtrain westward.

Because the stony conditions required more pack mules than pack horses, Cleve was now a muleskinner. Not sure he liked the handle. But in time he came to admire mules for their sturdy doggedness. He took the job and its rough summons in his stride.

It would be two hundred miles from Edmonton to the foothills of Cleve's longed-for snowcapped mountains.

Finally, before him was the collection of shacks that was Fitzhugh, later to be renamed Jasper. Cleve was assigned a cot in a crowded and windowless upstairs room of the Fitzhugh Hotel. From downstairs there drifted up the smell of cheap cigars and moonshine whiskey. Then came two days of further familiarizing himself with the peccadilloes of big mules, climbing atop each to see which might buck. Examining each for soundness. Then moving out in Cleve's favorite direction: Westward.

Every morning North America's answer to the Alps towered impossibly higher, to Cleve's eyes the peaks and glaciers seeming to float in the crystalline air.

These were unexpectedly pleasurable days, for the trail was still smooth enough to accommodate freight wagons. This meant wagon teamsters moved most gear, leaving Cleve and the other muleskinners to proceed with a nearly empty packtrain. On passing the last ranch before the mountains, the route narrowed to a single track. Here Cleve bent to the task of unloading the freight wagons, for from this point everything needed to cross the Rockies must be balanced on the backs of the mules.

As he fumbled with the many straps of a pannier, Cleve felt an unwashed hand on his shoulder. It was the senior muleskinner. "Son, you don't need to move quite so fast. We live by a saying, "Pack slow, travel fast." The adage was reinforced when two weeks later a pannier too hastily secured by someone else came loose. Both mule and cargo toppled over a cliff, the failed effort to save both bringing the outfit to a half day halt.

Each day now Cleve learned about, and from, his mules. Stronger, pound for pound, than horses, the mules nonetheless questioned his every command. Each morning, Cleve's icy fingers fastened strings of bells to the pack harness of every fifth mule—for it was claimed the rhythmic chiming created a working cadence for the animals.

Of the twenty-four men on the crew, twenty-three were to Cleve not fully trustworthy. Father's apt farewell advice came to mind, "Son, crossing from the frontier to the womanless wilderness will mean the men around you will be mostly unsavory." The sole exception was the wide-eyed apprentice surveyor Jack Dundee. Born and raised in Toronto, he and Cleve saw themselves as outsiders and founded a thin friendship on that basis.

The higher the packtrain ventured, the less traveled the trail—though here and there was faint evidence of the passage of Indians. Cleve urged his charges deeper among the darkly forested summits. At times there came a hot feeling on his neck, as if the Blackfoot or Cree were spying on his party. The wonder of these mountains became a reverence on the day he saw caribou in the morning, and moose at sunset.

Progress was slow. On a good day twenty miles sunup to sundown. That was all the men and ninety animals could hope to cover, given the need to gather the horses and mules, harness and check each hoof of each animal, then balance and secure each 260 lb. load. Just before dark the boss surveyor would raise his hand high, Cleve's signal to unload the panniers and picket each animal to graze its dinner.

He watched as Jack Dundee little by little showed signs of mental breakdown caused by extreme isolation in the wilderness. In those days folks called it 'prairie madness.' Once or twice Cleve offered small encouragements, which Jack seemed not to hear.

Cleve's age and recent hire put him at the bottom of the pecking order. So he was not surprised when the boss surveyor tabbed him to escort the now thoroughly disoriented Jake Dundee 180 miles back to civilization. It was, as Cleve later told it, ". . . pretty damn hairy for the first sixty miles. But the closer we got to Edmonton, I'll be damned if he didn't start to regain his sanity." They learned from each other, Jack learning that Cleve was slow to form opinions and much more inclined to listen than to talk. Cleve learning that "loco" is not a brand a man wears forever, but rather a thing that can fade. Leaving Dundee in the care of an employee at the Brewster tent in Edmonton, Cleve turned his horse immediately back towards the mountains.

No sooner was he reunited with the survey crew than there came another odd event. It was the coldest morning in weeks, and as Cleve secured a pack on the outfit's biggest horse, the blue roan, it just blew up. Bucked right through the cook fire and stomped vacant but still warm bedrolls.

Cleve minimized the damage by hanging onto the lead rope for dear life. But it cost him a deep rope burn on his left hand. Looking at the wound he saw rope fiber and animal hair mixed with blood, but his only first aid was lye soap and cold water with a dirty bandana for a bandage.

Within thirty-six hours Cleve's hand and arm swelled as though filled with hot water, red streaks snaking from fingers to shoulder. So again, the boss ordered his young wrangler to ride east, this time to the nearest doctor in Edmonton.

Inexplicably the boss sent his young muleskinner alone, though Cleve was already weak and in pain. "Hell, Cleve, if I send someone with you, that means I'm three men down, counting Dundee. Just can't do that. But go ahead and take your pick of the horses." Cleve's mount of choice was a stout chestnut mare with a trace of mustang blood. The hands called her Molly. Cleve and Molly departed that hour.

Cleve felt his strength might fail, so he pushed hard for two days and nights simply getting out of the mountains. By the time he was on the prairie, Cleve found it hard to rise from his bedroll and saddle the horse, what with only one good arm. While passing the lonely ranch known locally as Midpoint, Cleve was not sure he could stay in the saddle as he choked down a lump that was part panic, part despair.

Twice he fell off. Twice Molly stood faithfully by her fallen rider until he conjured the strength to remount. It was Molly more than Cleve who navigated to the threadbare and lonely Hunsted Ranch.

The pair arrived as light was failing, and cold rain falling. The barn door was open, and that's where Molly delivered her half-conscious rider.

Cleve was more carried than led to the house by rancher Hans. His wife, Gudrun, promptly began caring as best she could for this fevered stranger. Cleve remembered only snippets of that longest night—a feeble amber light from the kerosene lamp, the wick trimmed to suggest the couple was low on everything. A spitting wind howled nonstop over a low tarpaper roof. And always, the rancher's wife sitting beside Cleve and dripping warm water on his infected arm. At some point deep in the night he heard her say to her husband, "I'm afraid this nice young man is not going to make it."

But Cleve did make it, and by late morning felt just well enough to resume his ride. Before he ducked under the low door header Gudrun offered an awkward hug and a sack smelling of fresh bread and marmalade.

As his right leg swung up and over Molly's rump and into that leather cradle of his saddle, his world, Cleve imagined he just might survive this scarlet infection.

When safely beyond the gaze of Hans and Gudrun, Cleve felt a wave of emotion overtake his customary Scots-Irish stoicism. Tears streamed down his cheeks, a feeling of sweet sadness. It was for him the purest of emotions.

Ever after, Cleve counted the experience as ". . . the night the ranch wife saved my life."

He found the one doctor in Edmonton and within two days was fit to turn Molly westward to rejoin the survey crew. Cleve spent the rest of September and October with the crew before returning to Nebraska. He arrived back in Valentine with cash in hand but the furrowed brow of one still far short of a grubstake. Yet within a few weeks the harder memories of all the tumbleweeding gave way to that itch for the open road.

As it were, years later he sat sharing a smoke with Stands For Them and learning by sign language and gesture that the old man had himself come of age in Canada. Stands For Them brightened at the memory.

Their eyes met briefly, eyes that for both seemed always searching some remembered horizon.

Chapter Ten

Wyoming Cow Puncher
1910

That Niobrara winter in the tent could have soured Cleve on the cowboy life. Instead it oddly galvanized, confirmed. Thus, the telegram had Cleve smiling, then feverishly packing before the springtime sun was down.

This telegram had been hand delivered to the Nebraska ranch of brother-in-law George Lamoureaux. From Uncle Charlie in Wyoming, saying he had work for a good cowboy. He of course meant Cleve.

Two days later, Cleve was riding west. Leading his second-best saddle horse to pack in his outfit. Traveling light, he carried but an 8'x 6' canvas tarp as shelter from the rain, and minimal trailside food: dried soda biscuits, jerky, frijoles, four pickled eggs, and a jar of sorghum molasses.

He urged the horses on the three-day segment of the ride to Rapid City, weaving through the moonscape of the Big Badlands. He would have liked to make it in two days, but spring rains and even a little snow made for slow going. Then he rode up through the villages of Piedmont, Sturgis, and Spearfish, skirting the northeastern slope of the Black Hills.

Cleve could have gotten to Crook County, Wyoming more swiftly by train. But on rereading Uncle Charlie's telegram there was the hint that he'd best bring his own good horses.

Passing Spearfish and rounding Crow Peak, Cleve entered a stretch of road where traffic, be it wagon or car, was uncommon.

A methodical three hours brought Cleve nearly twenty miles deep into Crook County, Wyoming. Uphill and down he urged his horses to a trot as a way to cover six miles each hour.

This cross-country ride under open skies dwelt in Cleve's memory always—for you see 1910 was the year of an especially brilliant Halley's Comet. During his ride, planet earth passed through the comet's tail. "The Apocalypse" screamed headlines of the day. But Cleve was utterly devoid of hysteria . . . so from horseback and at prairie campfires he simply enjoyed his front row seat on the century's great celestial spectacle. He never saw a better fireworks show.

The road now led westward towards Sundance, perhaps twenty miles ahead. But Cleve was growing concerned, knowing the importance of not missing the unmarked trail forking north off the Sundance Road. He rummaged about in his vest pocket for the telegrammed directions: "Watch for a big dead cottonwood at my junction. There'll be an old eagle's nest high up. Take this trail north."

More hours in the saddle, each reminding Cleve that any glamour in overland horseback travel fades away after about 150 miles. He found himself looking forlornly around and then down at his rather pathetic net worth of secondhand gear and a couple horses. No sweetheart in sight, landless, zero prospects for a job if Uncle Charlie can't offer one.

Then, blessedly, there it was. Though the eagle's nest was unoccupied and in disrepair, this surely was the right tree. Cleve neck reined his horses north and was soon cresting a series of wide horizons with renewed enthusiasm.

Even as he scanned the bottomlands for Uncle Charlie's ranch, Cleve was falling a bit in love with the seemingly endless, fresh air country of northeast Wyoming. It was a vision of what cattle country should be, dotted with imposing buttes, pine clad ridges, shortgrass tablelands, and surprisingly lush creekside meadows.

Using a bandana to wipe sweat from his neck and the band of his hat, Cleve held a fist to the declining sun. It told him that by riding hard he had just enough time to make the ranch and avoid yet another night of camping in the open. His horses met the call, and just before sundown Cleve found himself on a bluff overlooking ranch buildings neatly fitting Uncle Charlie's telegrammed description.

The structures all low slung and spread horizontal—and so many of 'em—made the ranch look like a small military outpost. Three-sided loafing sheds for cattle, more for horses, a calving shed looking more like a granary, a chicken coop big as a small house, and a large white-washed barn.

Excepting the big barn and modest frame house with a shady front porch, every building was fashioned from rough lumber—yellow pine cut and milled from the distantly visible Bear Lodge Mountains. A tall windmill plumbed the steady winds just behind that big barn. Wildflowers sprouted here and there. No garden was visible.

Reckoning Charlie would still be working, Cleve rode past the ranch house and up to the open door of what looked like the smithy shack. And there he was—hammering rusted nails out of a set of old horseshoes. Wearing a flat brimmed felt "boss" hat, a half-buttoned blue work shirt and short chaps fit for either roundups, or like today, blacksmith duties.

Charlie greeted his nephew with a hearty hug. "Well, by golly you made it. You just drop your gear in the bunkhouse later, but first let's get your animals grained and brushed down."

As they walked together towards the stables, each leading one horse, Charlie had a chance to size Cleve up. Though he had a number of dependable cowhands in the outfit, Charlie was seriously in need of a ramrod.

He happily noted Cleve's jeans—sure sign that the wearer was a working cowboy, the pants were shiny with a hard-earned patina of sweat, bovine blood, tallow, manure, wagon axle grease, mud and horse hoof oil. Cowhands often did not bother to wash real work pants, for when sufficiently grimy, the garments were nearly waterproof. And rough enough in the rear to be a handy surface on which to strike a match.

Charlie also noted Cleve's buttoned vest, the angle and brim of his hat. Both were of a style then favored by northern cow punchers. And then there was his nephew's fine saddle horse. For even in 1910 Charlie still believed one could judge a man by the horse he rode.

Charlie told Cleve he'd be hired on at $1 a day, plus room and board, with a possible two bit raise down the line. They shook on the deal. An inch or two shorter than Cleve, Charlie delivered a handshake backed by a leathery body built for the rigors of ranch work. And a mind that would help Cleve learn the best tricks to turn-of-the-century ranching.

The first trick was to circumvent Abe Lincoln's homestead act, so ill-suited to the American West: For while railroads made millions by transporting homesteaders and their plows, Charlie knew a homestead-er's allotment, 160 or at best 320 acres, was too small to sustain a farm family on the West's poor soils and low moisture.

Cleve both watched and listened—learning that the patient small rancher could become a big rancher by waiting out the other homestead-ers. Most were destined to go broke, to "starve out", forced to sell their dream for sometimes a dollar an acre.

As light faded Cleve took a perch on the highest rung of the corral as cowboys came in from all points, their fifteen-hour workday precisely matching available daylight. He could easily guess where each hand was from by the man's hat or on closer examination by his horse tack. Cleve was happy to note three or four cowboys up from Texas, each nestled in the deep seat of a Mexican or charro saddle—high pommel in front and high cantle in back.

Cleve spent a restless night on a lumpy mattress and was up before the sun for his first day of Wyoming ranching. By day two he'd met every one of the other summer ranch hands. Some were marginal characters to be mostly avoided or ignored. Others he'd quickly count as friends. Among the latter was Cord Wallace: weather beaten, rawboned as a colt and with a haystack of sandy hair that seemed odd on a veteran Cleve figured must be pushing fifty. Maybe older. After all, Wallace's campfire tall tales contained just enough hard fact to convince listeners he'd ridden north in 1886 on the last great cattle drive up from Texas.

It was also common knowledge that Wallace once spent a year in jail for stealing a horse, putting the skedaddle to that dime novel myth that horse theft was always a hanging offense. "Sure," Wallace later explained to Cleve, "I had a big string of horses and there happened to be one or two with the wrong brand that mixed themselves in with mine. Horses'll do that, and I sure intended to return 'em. Live long enough and the same'll happen to any cow man. Includin' you."

For his part, Wallace figured Cleve must be a fellow Scots-Irishman, adding to his tendency to vouch for the hardworking young cowhand.

When moving cattle that long hot summer, the pattern was always the same: Cord Wallace would be named trail boss, whereupon he'd tab Cleve as his "ramrod," second in command.

One Wyoming roundup stood tall among Cleve's old-age memories. It was the fall of 1911, and Charlie needed to gather every fat calf and steer to be trailed to the railhead at Aladdin, Wyoming. From there the long ride in cattle cars would take 'em to the great stockyards at Omaha where Charlie arranged for an agent to meet the shipment.

First task, round up all the cattle on the ranch and on the leased grazing parcels on adjacent federal open range. Then, cut out the critters bound for market, while separating unbranded mavericks and those animals with neighbors' brands to be kindly returned. It would then take four days to trail the market cattle to the railhead.

This undertaking required all of Charlie's several hands, and even temporary hires from among the cowboys on neighboring ranches. Twenty-eight riders in all.

Charlie would take personal charge. He and Cleve discussed often the many important elements of the operation. "Cleve, I'll want you to ride point most days. But not on the first day . . . those mighty young boys riding drag and swing will need your advice. And the last day— That's when I'll need you to ride ahead to make sure things at the railhead are in order."

"Sure will. I reckon you mean making sure the big loading pen gate is open, right?"

"That, yes. But also see that the yard boss knows how many head, the exact count, we'll be bringing in. And then find a flat, dry place for us all to set up camp. All the other outfits are shipping 'bout this time, so they may beat you to it."

"For now, Cleve, make sure all riders know we'll start by setting up the remuda corral at the high point of Hawk Ridge. That's where every-one should gather early."

On the appointed morning, cowboys could be seen riding in from ranches on all points of the compass. A few were there a full hour before first light, lining up on the ridge, facing a vast primitive basin to the west.

Each man had brought a string of horses to ride. Ten head was a typ-ical roundup string: one night horse, three good cutting horses (at least one doubling as a roping horse) and six long-winded circle horses for the hard business of gathering the cattle.

As men and horses gathered, there grew a low hum of wildness to the scene—an invincibility wrought from the gathering of so many male bodies astride so many tons of horse muscle steaming in the crisp air.

None present doubted that here stood, pound for pound, God's strongest creatures carrying God's smartest creatures.

As revealed by predawn streaks of light, cowboys were now adjusting their reins and headgear, checking their cinches, re-looping their lariats, and flexing lean bodies against the leather curves of cantle and pommel. Everything at the ready, a spring coiled energy was building and would not uncoil until the horses moved out.

Cowboys looked up and down the line. Staring back were suntanned faces much like their own. Fueled by bacon and cigarettes and jet-black coffee—so alert, so ready for action that one could be forgiven for imagining he heard a bugle call.

It is that moment known only when twenty-five or more mounted souls unite for common purpose. The instant before the saber charge.

Men feel it. Horses feel it.

Uncle Charlie stands in his stirrups to give final orders by voice and gesture. At his signal they ride out like Cossacks, Mongols, Scythians. Moving as a cresting wave.

There is something in the scene that harkens back to the Lakota's great galloping buffalo surround. Or the 'Charge of the Light Brigade'.

For the rest of Cleve's life, this memory burns bright. It is the end of an age.

On this his third Wyoming trail drive, Cleve asked Cord Wallace's advice on mastering the art of selecting the Judas steer. Cord answered, "Carefully watch cattle as they meander down the trail or move to water, and in time you'll identify a steer which the other animals naturally follow. This is your Judas steer, trusted by other cattle but a betrayer too as that's the animal that will lead the others to slaughter."

Cleve leaned forward in the saddle to better hear Cord explain the odd worth of this animal—"At the end of the trail, whether rail stockyards or slaughterhouse, see how we maneuver the Judas so as to lead the other cattle to their fate with damn little hassle. Hell, a top Judas steer might even be spared slaughter so Charlie can use 'em to lead cattle on the next roundup. Especially if he's also a good swimmer. On crossing a high river, Cleve, you'll appreciate having one critter willing to dive in. The others'll always follow."

By this last Wyoming trail drive, Cleve was hoping to gaze on something all the locals said he had to see. Devil's Tower. So, Cleve used his roundup lunch hour one day to ride for a high hill off to the southwest. There he figured he might see this odd landmark that Teddy Roosevelt had only a few years prior tabbed as America's first national monument.

Though the Tower was nearly five miles away, there he could see it floating on the skyline. Looking for all the world like the stump of some colossal pine.

He had skipped lunch not only to see this sight. It was also a welcome respite from some tormenting he'd recently endured from a drover hired just eight days earlier by Uncle Charlie.

Curley they called him, for out of his felt hat tumbled long corkscrews of inky black hair. Curley was ten years Cleve's senior, and half a head taller. Part Mescalero others murmured, and hailing from Durango, Colorado, Curley had arrived with a string of horses carrying no fewer than nine different brands. Word of mouth had proceeded him—Curley was not a man to be crossed.

From his nine horses, Curley most often saddled up one of three dapple gray Andalusians, warm-bloods capable of enduring any rider's horse handling . . . the demanding rider, even the cruel rider. One day Cleve saw Curley kick the camp dog hard enough to lift the animal in the air. Thereafter the little yellow dog limped and whined at the rear of the moving herd until one day disappearing.

Just why this man started picking on Cleve no one could say. But at meals and before bedtime Curley baited Cleve with his comments, his looming presence, and occasionally even his foot-long Bowie knife. This made even the other cowboys uncomfortable—for in it hovered something darker than a common bully's harassment.

Cleve was in many ways an unlikely victim for Curley's taunts. Of average height and scrappy build, the twenty-four-year-old Cleve was skilled at riding, cutting, calf roping, and branding. He was in those days moving through life with a quiet confidence. Other drovers noticed. Most liked him.

But then a bully like Curley does not always pick the most likely mark.

"Just mebby the bad blood started that first day Curley joined this outfit," Cleve confided to a younger hand named Wesley who'd asked about the hazing. "On that morning, Curley and I and four others were sent out to head off a bunch of steers that broke free the night before. I figured Uncle Charlie'd want me to take charge since I knew the country. So, once we hit the creek divide that's just what I did, sending three men down the east side of Dry Creek. Then I motioned Curley and Al Fellows to follow me down the west bank. We could see the tracks of them steers, looking to be about three hours ahead."

Wesley, curious on how *not* to get on Curley's bad side, was all ears.

"Now maybe Curley didn't like me calling the shots. Maybe he thought we took too long to bring those beeves in. But by golly we did get all of 'em in."

More perplexed than fearful, Cleve mined his father's examples and words on how to handle a tormentor. He knew such situations often called for more of a psychological than a physical solution. "Hold your peace. Then find just the right time and place to send a message," were Papa's words.

Bringing in the remuda one evening he made a point of riding up beside Charlie to gain an uncle's counsel. After hearing the situation, and mulling options in his head, Charlie reined in his horse to behold this concerned nephew who he thought of more as a son.

Reaching back into his saddlebag, Charlie said, "This is what I suggest." He pulled out a well-oiled six shooter, but on seeing Cleve's double take he quickly added, "It's not what you think, young man."

"I'll allow as how Curley is a rough customer, and generally bad for morale. Still, I just can't afford to fire anyone at this point in the drive. Too damn many cattle. And I know you're not asking me to do that."

"But here's what you might wanna do, Cleve. Tomorrow noon you come in for grub a little early. Get your plate plum full, then take this gun, loaded or not, and slip it under your plate. Have the handle just peek out a little from under your plate, real close to your right hand."

"Then what, Uncle?"

"Well, nothing really," Charlie said, smiling. "You'll see."

Cleve tossed and turned till dawn. Sure, he thought, a bluff might work on a schoolyard bully. But Curley was no schoolboy. Peering from his bedroll at first light, Cleve came to a rather wobbly decision: Trust of Charlie and distrust of Curley were of equal weight, but the tightness of throat would not abate so he would gamble on an uncle's scheme.

A morning of gathering and moving cows had been uneventful as Cleve rode up to the chuck wagon a tad early, got his grub, and sat down cross-legged in his accustomed place. On his tin plate was a bigger-than-usual pile of pinto beans, the choicest piece of beef from the midday fire, two sourdough biscuits with marmalade . . . and on the ground in front of him steamed a black coffee. Balanced on his dusty denim-clad legs just below the plate was Uncle Charlie's barely visible Colt .45.

Shortly came the sight and sound of other riders converging on the chuck wagon. Cleve looked for Curley, did not see him yet, then reckoned on whether the big man would be armed himself. Other than the certainty of his Bowie knife, that is.

It did seem likely that somewhere under Curley's boot-length duster lurked a holstered gun . . . but by 1910 sidearms had gone out of fashion with most cowboys, for on roundup or trail drive a gun had proven unnecessary weight.

Just then Cleve's eye caught movement on the northwest ridgeline—a glint of silver from a rider coming hard. Too far away to identify the rider, except by his horse's thrashing head. For Curley rode his horses on fear by reining with a brutish Spanish bit. This type of spiked bridle iron had few advocates here on the Northern Plains. The bit hinted that Curley may indeed have been a vaquero from south of the Rio Grande, though none had dared ask about his past.

Presently horse and rider approached the hitching rope in the showy, sideways, single-footed fashion of Andalusians.

Curley dismounted with a grunt and used a boot to slide a water bucket within reach of his sweat-soaked horse. He then made a bow-legged amble over to the coffee pot, filled his plate, and sat down facing Cleve, not four feet away. Cleve only pretended to eat, his throat too tight to swallow, but by degrees he felt himself rising to the moment.

The tension was palpable for all, since none knew when today's tormenting would begin—perhaps immediately, perhaps as plates were licked clean. A bully culture of fear hinged on unpredictability.

Apparently deciding it would be sooner than later, Curley ignored his food in favor of sizing up Cleve from head to toe. But then his gaze moved to the plate, pausing at what looked like a pearl gun handle peeking out. He glanced away briefly, then back to whatever that was under the plate—a thing too damn close to the young man's right hand.

Then he looked up into Cleve's emotionless face . . . a countenance that might or might not be holding the winning poker hand.

And that was the end of it. Horns clipped, Curley looked down, commenced picking at his food, and never so much as looked at Cleve again.

For his part, Cleve carefully slid the revolver into the side pocket of his jacket. There the weapon stayed. Out of sight, its work done. He discreetly returned it to Uncle Charlie that night—after all, no one need know who really owned the pearl-handled Colt .45. While doing so, Cleve caught Uncle Charlie's twinkling eye, theirs a brief but ageless connection any father and son would envy.

Chapter Eleven

Crossing the Medicine Line
1877

After such jubilation on the Little Big Horn, the various Lakota bands scattered, some melting into the mountains, others taking familiar trails back to reservation life, still others hesitating. By the Sore Eyes Moon among the non-reservation camps a message circulated that neither distance nor logic could smother: "We must join Crazy Horse. He carries our magic. He preaches that one more victory will secure the Powder River hunting grounds for seven generations."

Many among the Eat No Dogs wavered. Notable among them was Elk Robe. His *tiospaye* was not large, eight lodges containing some sixty people. But his influence was considerable, thanks to a reputation as a headman willing to weigh both sides. A headman who might smoke the peace pipe one day, then on another the war pipe.

After hearing all the rumors and opinions, Elk Robe called together his remaining sons, a half-brother and four male nephews: including High Shield and Living Bear. Together they would consider whether Elk Robe's warriors would join Crazy Horse in tying up the tails of their horses . . . or instead slip away in the night for the long journey to the reservations.

Elk Robe was naturally first to speak. "I hear many rumors from the agencies, saying those returning are forced to surrender all horses and guns. And winter rations have already been reduced. At yesterday's big council fire, good and strong men rose to speak of the futility of fighting the wasicu. Their iron horses and great smoking river boats now deliver 100 fighters to every one of ours."

There followed a long silence, broken when Elk Robe reminded each man that he was free to choose the war path or the road of peace. But time was short—Crazy Horse was calling for a morning attack on the garrison beneath Wolf Mountain. By turns many rose to give their views. Stands For Them did not. When discussion waned, Elk Robe retired to his tipi with Stands For Them, there to discuss merits of those paths available.

At supper fires word circulated: Elk Robe would recommend his people neither retreat to the agencies, nor join Crazy Horse in the coming battle. Instead, Elk Robe and certain of his warriors would stake the middle ground—forming a home guard protecting the camp's vulnerable noncombatants left behind even as many men of warrior age streamed south to do battle.

The next morning Elk Robe's men, Stands For Them included, picketed war horses nearby and had weapons handy. Vigilance their keynote, they anxiously watched the falling snow all day, and wondered at the outcome of the battle beneath the visible and towering Wolf Mountain.

By midafternoon here they came, one group of warriors after another with their shoulders and the rumps of their horses covered in blizzard-plastered snow. They were greeted by women with high tremolos of joy. But not all women. Some were doomed to launch wails of grief upon seeing their loved one's horse either rider-less or carrying the red-shrouded burden.

One of the warriors riding past did a double take on seeing Stands For Them and dismounted to warm himself at the flames of the Eat No Dogs fire. An accomplice on many a horse raid with Stands For Them, Comes Alone was the middle son of a Cheyenne mother and a Lakota father. He took a seat close to the fire, knowing he'd be welcome always among the allied peoples of either tribe.

Broad chested and with a rather haughty face set atop the neck of a bull, Comes Alone looked every inch a warrior—though still too young to have many war honors to his credit. Yet he was eager to share with Stands For Them his witness to the battlefield.

First he described that place where the forces met, a valley surrounded by foothills peaks. He had been among a group of Cheyenne nearing the main battlefield by way of a plain, then unexpectedly caught in an army crossfire. As he spoke, the enthusiasm in his voice drew a circle of listeners closer around him. He had seen two horses shot out from under Crazy Horse, the mystic warrior unhurt and unfazed. He described acts of singular bravery and terrible cowardice on both sides.

Then Comes Alone summed it up. "The blizzard was the only winner at Wolf Mountain. But something is now clear that was not clear—this wasicu army can fight even during winter's harshest moon."

In coming days there would be many councils among the Hunkpapas, the Miniconjou, the Oglala, the Sans Arcs gathered here. In the end all agreed, "The time to gather together had come and gone. It was time to scatter."

Certain bands of Miniconjou and Sans Arc headed east to accept lean government rations at the reservations. Some of the Oglala followed Crazy Horse towards his beloved Niobrara River country. With the cavalry closing the noose, Sitting Bull and his Hunkpapas had earlier chosen Canada.

Bull Dog, Spotted Eagle and Sitting Bull had spoken fondly of *Unci Maskoce*, the Grandmother's Land. They trusted the royal queen across the great waters, felt her red-coated police would provide sanctuary. Best of all, U.S. soldiers could not follow them into this land.

The Eat No Dogs had not yet chosen. Surely the Eat No Dogs band would do as they had always done, reach consensus, then move together towards a new home. But Stands For Them sensed a coming rupture.

He hoped a morning conversation with his father would hold answers, but Elk Robe was nowhere to be found. Unknown to Stands For Them, High Backbone had declared a council of all Eat No Dogs headmen. On arriving Stands For Them knew he could not participate, but he could observe. He took up a respectfully distant seat as the big bellies assembled. For unknown reasons, Black Shield was not present. his absence elevating High Backbone to the position of highest influence.

After all had prayerfully smoked the holy pipe, High Backbone rose and dropped the blanket from his shoulders. Perhaps he was overly warm from his place of honor so near the fire. Perhaps he simply wished all to see the two new wounds on his torso. His left hand held the long wooden handle of a stone battle club so easily that it seemed part of the man himself.

"Oh wise *nacas* of the Eat No Dogs. We fought hard at Rosebud Creek and here at Wolf Mountain. But it was our victory at the Greasy Grass bringing both joy and bitterness to the mouth, for it means the Long Knives will punish us again and again." At this he reached down for a handful of dirt, throwing it in the air in an age-old act of defiance. But then his demeanor shifted—

"We will soon have many decisions to make. Choose wisely for your tiyospaye. Crazy Horse wavers. Sitting Bull sends word south that we should leave this sacred space and move to Grandmother's Land. His runners speak of a prairie where large herds of buffalo still roam."

High Backbone then pointedly frowned at two or three headmen, Elk Robe not among them, saying, "Others talk of returning to the agencies, where there may be safe haven and rations. But will our fine ponies be confiscated if we return? What are we to think?"

"Bull Dog and Red Leaf say the Wazhazha will continue the fight for these hunting grounds. They say ten winters ago Red Cloud showed us that winning a war with the wasicu is not impossible."

This recollection brought grunts of approval from every throat. Nearly all present had taken up the lance during Red Cloud's War—history's only war in which Native Americans claimed full victory over the whites.

High Backbone's mood changed yet again; his habit for maintaining the full attention of any audience. "I believe we now face an army with numbers greater than the hairs on my head. In recent years I've parleyed with Colonel Miles. I believe he speaks with straight tongue when saying we'll be treated fairly at his fortress on the Tongue River. Some say we might even receive a white man's pay to fight the Nez Perce and the Crow."

Here he paused, drawing himself up to best show his bullish chest and arms, pointing to his many battle scars, then setting the war club at his feet. His way of reminding everyone that he was first in battle, but could also be first in peace.

Then in a resolute voice, "Who will follow me to the mouth of the Tongue River?" sounding more like a challenge than a question. When none immediately responded, with imperious bearing High Backbone stepped away from the council fire.

With this the Eat No Dogs council's uneasy mood flowed to every tipi of a band never again to know full unity. By next morning all three hundred souls of the Eat No Dogs were busy with departure preparations. In the swirl of activity, it was unclear which tiyospayes would follow High Backbone's lead, which would return to the reservation, and which would pivot north to join Sitting Bull.

Yet as shadows shortened it became clearer—Fewer than a dozen members of the Eat No Dogs band would join High Backbone in his tactical "surrender" to Miles at Tongue River Cantonment. A somber Stands For Them noted departure of this small group while packing his own possessions. He watched as his father exchanged stormy last words with High Backbone. This told Stands For Them his tiyospaye would join those traditionalists making a break for Grandmother's Land. He was pleased.

Next morning Stands For Them was up early, stirred by thoughts of purposeful movement after days of idleness and delighted to be one of those scouts to help the band dodge the noose thrown down by the bluecoats. He led his people to the safest ford of the Yellowstone River. Once across, the day unfolded in a spirit of adventure worthy of the Grandmother's Land and freedom.

When sufficiently out front, Stands For Them rolled a leg over his simple native saddle, straightened his back and swiveled to observe the line of march. Even from a distance he could see his tiyospaye's animal members, canine and equine, also felt the energy of this day.

Fair weather made for fast travel in what was an exhilarating cross-country sprint for Elk Robe's people. Lively steps were made still livelier by not knowing if bluecoats were in pursuit.

Stands For Them was happy when his tiyospaye arrived at Medicine Rocks with daylight remaining. For he was eager to again see the mysterious petroglyphs of the mighty rocks. Hobbling his horse and turning it loose to graze, Stands For Them walked up among the outcroppings so lavishly adorned with symbols. There to marvel.

Created untold generations before his people moved westward unto the high plains, the meaning of these petroglyphs was mostly lost to the ages. Yet some elders offered faint recollection of the symbols' stories. So, Stands For Them came to know a little and wonder a lot, about pinwheel spirals, petroglyphs of long extinct beasts, levitating godlike beings—clearly not his people's gods.

Some believed these petroglyphs changed from season to season without human intervention, the changes predicting future events. No such epiphany came to the elders at this evening's campsite, only the urgency to rise early and make haste for the border.

The following morning Elk Robe called his scouts to the central fire for final instructions. He asked his son and Good Thunder to ride as the rear guard. The pair started the day riding side by side and spoke as always of the celebrated Medicine Line but also other matters large and small. From time to time, when winds were favorable, they dismounted to torch the prairie behind them. The scorched earth meant to rob possible pursuers of graze, and make tracking more difficult.

Having remounted, Stands For Them caught Good Thunder's attention by reining his horse closer. "Kola, I believe in this trip to Grandmother's Land, long and risky though it is. We are all tired of eating the stringy meat of the timid little wasicu steers. In the north, runners tell us, the noble buffalo still roams."

The laconic Good Thunder brightened, "Surely you are right. In ten sleeps you and I will again feast on the hump of our brother the buffalo."

And so, they proceeded until one crisp clear morning when it was starting to feel like they'd never reach this promised land. Elk Robe finished the last mouthfuls of a cold breakfast before summoning Long Soldier. He asked the young man to ride up on a nearby high hill, for only Long Soldier had been across the border before. Upon his return Long Soldier reported to Elk Robe that the border would be just over the horizon.

On hearing this, Stands For Them walked to a smaller hill to gaze northward. The distant rolling prairie seemed no different than the land he stood on. Nothing to say this land was America, and that land just ahead was a place the bluecoats could not enter, and redcoats would reportedly offer the hand of friendship.

A dry stack stone boundary monument was the goal, peeking above waving rye grasses. Placed but three years earlier by the first survey crew to formally mark this longest land border in the world—a belated formal dividing of the 100-year-old United States and the barely ten-year-old Dominion of Canada. A rare marker on the mostly invisible Medicine Line.

Soon the band was marching in joyous anticipation. The elation was short-lived. With Grandmother's Land just two miles away, Stands For Them and Good Thunder came riding hard from between two hills, and pulled up alongside Elk Robe. Both smelled of dust and horse sweat.

Good Thunder spoke loud enough that all might hear. "*Naca*, we have seen bluecoats in our tracks. They move at a fast trot. You may see their haze on the horizon even now." Before Elk Robe's lips could form the obvious question, Good Thunder answered: "No, they did not see us. But they surely move as though they have calculated our line of march."

Elk Robe pondered for but a moment, then turned in the saddle so as to gain the attention of all followers. While some had been walking, at his hand gesture everyone jumped up behind other mounted ones or found a sitting place on a travois.

Then as Stands For Them gestured excitedly towards the south, nearly everyone swiveled in their saddles and squinted at the austral rim. A faint plume of dust was visible. And out of it, barely visible, mounted men. Coming fast.

"*Mita Kuyepi!*" Elk Robe shouted so as to gain every ear. "Proceed with haste towards the Medicine Line, but together. We must not string out, so I ask those with faster horses to bring up the rear."

With roars from the men and tremolos from the women rising above the yelping dogs, off they all went, trotting, then galloping for the border. Some looking back in fear, for cavalry horses were bigger, faster when sprinting. All could see the distance between the bluecoats and the natives shrinking. Desperation lit the faces of those women whose laboring horses dragged travois piled with tipi poles and children.

On came the cavalry. On rode the natives, furiously urging their mounts forward by whip, voice, and heel.

Now Elk Robe could see that leading the cavalry were a group of four Crow scouts. Ancestral enemies turned mercenaries. This was too much. With a sweeping motion of his arm, he directed three young men to turn back, to use weapons to slow the pursuers.

Stands For Them, Many Horses, and Good Thunder reined their mounts round, rode back south a short distance, and took out their firearms. This temporarily slowed the oncoming Crow and bluecoats, it being difficult to fumble for their own firearms at a full gallop.

Soon shots filled the air, one whizzing by Stands For Them's ear. He and the others returned fire. But only a few shots. With bullets still flying over their heads, this rear guard in mortal danger rode hard to catch up to the others. To cross the magic line, Stands For Them and his mount, as if forged together, threw themselves into each stride.

It was just enough. As Stands For Them looked ahead, he could see the main band was surely across the line. In short order Stands For Them, Many Horses, and Good Thunder joined then.

Slowing to a clip-clop pace, and leaning forward to stroke Whirlwind's lathered withers, Stands For Them caught the glance and half-smile of Good Thunder. In this moment the kolas had the same thought, one the elders had always preached: "Over distance sturdy Indian ponies will outlast heavier and initially faster cavalry horses."

Looking back, all could see that the soldiers had reined up. But the Crow scouts were citizens of neither nation and unrestrained by international borders. They rode right across the border with bravado. Small in numbers, these army Crow scouts soon slowed to a trot, then to a walk, hurling insults as they turned back.

Stands For Them and the other scouts were now talking among themselves. Had they been sufficiently brave? Had one of their shots grazed the arm of a Bluecoat? Many Horses thought so.

The band could now safely relax, make reassuring eye contact with loved ones, breathe deeply. The band continued northward for another mile. Then, by simply reining in his horse, Elk Robe signaled that here all should dismount, form a prayer circle.

Elk Robe uprooted a nearby sage plant, rubbed his hands on the aromatic leaves, then passed open hands lightly over his head and hair.

Facing south, where all prayer begins, Elk Robe raised his arms in supplication. He offered similar thanks to the five remaining directions: east, north, west, Mother Earth and Father Sky. All were in the circle now, watching Elk Robe's face, hoping to see in his beatific expression the sacred center. Stands For Them memorized his father's every move, then listened: "Brothers, sisters—we have been spared yet again. In this way *Wakan Tanka* reminds us to continue to walk the Lakota path, the path of warriors, mothers of warriors, hunters, scouts. Not the path that wasicu would have us trod, of those who put seeds in the ground and then sit and wait."

Then he called Stands For Them, Good Thunder and Many Horses forward, instructing them to ride ahead to find a suitable camping site before darkness.

Soon women were gathering cones and dry branches from the few pines clinging to ridgetops, children were playing, men were smiling to know here they might again join the big buffalo hunts of old.

Chapter Twelve

Ghosts of the Buffalo

1916, then 1878

It was a fair-weather fencing day beneath a feeble midday sun. Cleve was just close enough to head home for lunch—a rare chance for a hot meal, shelter from never-ending wind, welcome company of wife and first born. Having seen her husband and horse coming from afar, Jessie stoked the wood stove to warm up last night's leftovers.

The morning's gales were so tiresome for Jessie. She hated few things more than wind without rain. It shook their tarpaper shack in a daily reminder of Cleve's poor carpentry skills. As she looked up occasionally from the stove, something struck her as strange. *What is that white thing draped over the saddle horn?* As Cleve reined up at the hitching post, Jessie saw now that he had picked yet another buffalo skull, this one bigger than the others, complete with widespread shiny black horns.

When Cleve first laid eyes on this land, it had been three decades since the last buffalo herd crossed Cedar Butte. Yet phantoms of the buffalo were close-at-hand—perhaps just up the next ravine. Buffalo wallows still caught spring rains. Older tree trunks rubbed shiny by the great beasts. Certain badland passes requiring single-file passage, deeply sculpted by numberless buffalo hooves long before settlers' cattle and horse herds.

And bleached buffalo bones still caught morning sunlight among native buffalo grass, the turf that mimics the curly hair of its namesake. Eastern fertilizer companies were eager for the prairie's vast bone phosphorous resource. Cleve had collected buffalo bones in Nebraska for spending money. Locally farmers supplemented meager harvests by tossing bones into buckboard wagons. When a wagon was full, it fetched one silver dollar at the railhead in Belvidere.

A more practical echo was Jessie and Cleve's wonderfully warm buffalo robe. Since they didn't yet own a motor vehicle, this wooly robe kept the family snug in winter travel by buggy or sleigh. As he folded the robe following such a trip, Cleve wondered what buffalo tales old Stands For Them could tell. So many tales to share, if only they'd spoken the same language. He resolved to enlist a young Lakota to act as translator should such an opportunity arise.

Just that day Stands For Them had trudged nearly to the top of Cedar Butte in pursuit of *Wagmu l'eju ta*, the holy wild gourd, when he chanced upon a ghostly bleached buffalo skull. This prompted a day-dream of his last buffalo hunt so many seasons ago in Canada.

Grandmother Land was like nothing he or his people had known. Could he see farther? Was the sky really a deeper blue? Did the air and zephyrs rearranging that air carry mysteries of the rumored "always frozen land?"

He remembered life there as initially quite easy. Food was no prob-lem, with game plentiful and the Blackfeet and Cree eager to trade with the strangers from the south. The royal government was even willing to provide some rations.

But as late summer turned to winter with no fall to speak of, hunger walked the village of Spotted Eagle, where Elk Robe and Stands For Them often erected their tipis. A few of the elderly and infirm had died. Some families had even taken to boiling and eating the corners of their tipis.

Then one fine morning a pair of scouts, one Cheyenne and the other Lakota, rode into camp in a manner that made clear what they'd discov-ered: *Tatonka*!

Stands For Them was braiding a new leather rope but put it down when hearing the news. He walked straightaway to where the best horses were picketed and found his stout buffalo runner in that standing-yet-sleeping way of the species. Stands For Them quietly approached his *Honska-Tahteh* (Long Wind).

At his "*Kiktayo!*" the horse perked its ears forward. Stands For Them undid the hobbles, mounted bareback, and rode out to greet the sun. Putting his mind right by spending moments on a ridge top would invite a bountiful hunt.

Back in the village excitement spread from tipi to tipi as more people learned the details—buffalo had been sighted on the broad plain between Wood Mountain and Cypress Hills. Stands For Them smiled as he dismounted and prepared for the hunt.

Now nearing fifty winters, Elk Robe was no longer expected to join so vigorous a task as a buffalo hunt. He would depend on his sons to fill the near empty parfleche bags with dried meat.

Stands For Them retrieved his short bow and trade point arrows. He mounted, drew back his shoulders, and inhaled that crispness of a Canadian morning. It was time to join the group of thirty equally adrenalized hunters, most veterans of many a hunt . . . but among them three or four wide-eyed youth on their first hunt.

How could they or anyone know that today would be the last great buffalo hunt in Grandmother's Land. Indeed, one of the last of all times.

Stripped to the waist, Stands For Them drew glances from the youngest hunters. Now in his mid-twenties, he was at his peak of strength and coordination, and fully accomplished in Lakota skills of horsemanship, marksmanship, hunt strategy.

Just as many eyes cast admiring glances at Stands For Them's *Honska-Tahteh*—a piebald mustang. Although gentled Spanish Barbs were favored as war ponies, for the buffalo hunt most Plains Indians preferred

167

captured mustangs. Having grown up grazing alongside buffalo, wild horses had no fear of the great beasts and would gallop close enough to a buffalo's side so a hunter's arrow could find the vulnerable kill spot.

By now women and older children leading pack horses stood ready to come when called—theirs was in many ways the bigger job—butchering and transporting carcasses and hides. Only when the killing had commenced would they march out of the village. Armed with skinning knives and fleshing stones, and with poles and lines to immediately begin to jerk and dry the meat.

One of the teen hunters, perhaps seeking a way to settle his nerves but unsure about approaching a veteran hunter, rode up beside one veteran hunter he felt certain would not rebuff him. Stands For Them.

They exchanged the typical sideways-glance greeting of male Lakotas. After a polite minute of wordlessness, Stands For Them offered what he sensed the boy was seeking—someone to prepare him for what the hunt would bring. "Hawk Dog, there are many ways to hunt *tatonka*. Today you will join the hunt we call a surround."

As they talked, still more riders arrived. Only two summers previous Hawk Dog had been among the "wild children." These preteens had been content to enter the field only after the killing. Wait until sundown, when young calves came into the open, hungrily seeking their fallen mothers. Then the wild children would have their mock hunt, and lasso the calves or drive them into camp.

Now his only family a grandmother, and feeling manhood coming, he hung on Stands For Them's words—"We shall take up positions all 'round, forming a large circle well back from the herd . . . so far away that neither our sight nor scent will alarm them." The boy kept his eyes on the still empty horizon but offered a solemn nod.

"When you are in position, watch carefully for a blanket signal from Spotted Eagle. If you cannot see him, the signal will be relayed through other blankets. On this signal we begin to circle the herd, riding in the 'stars moving' direction."

"As the circle tightens, you will see the head of this or that *tatanka* rising. Others will continue grazing. When the herd starts to mill and walk, we trot. As the herd starts to trot, we gallop. All will soon be in motion. Think of it as the whirlwind."

Now both Stands For Them and Hawk Dog urged their horses forward—for an *akicita* had arrived to order each hunter a bit closer to the unseen herd. Hawk Dog made sure to match his horse's pace to that of Stands For Them's, happy to hear any additional instructions that might be offered.

"As the circle constricts, Hawk Dog, you'll see the milling beasts with heads high, eyes rimmed with white, wanting to stampede. As we tighten our noose, you must look for those animals on the edge. They will try to break away from the trap. Do not be too eager. The one buffalo you are destined to kill will present itself to you . . . will offer itself to you. Recognize this beast as today's surest chance for you to achieve a kill."

Hawk Dog glanced down at both his rusty carbine in hand, and his quiver of arrows tied with bow to the saddle. Stands For Them saw the question rising in the boy's tight throat, "Use the bow first, the fire stick later. Your arrow feather colors will put your family name on this first kill. You dare not stop to claim it otherwise."

"Aim your arrow to avoid ribs but angled towards lungs and heart. If the animal stumbles, go on to the next target. Leave the first one to bleed and fall where your women folk can find it and begin their butchering. If you lack a person to butcher, my family will help."

"You might not make a second kill—the force of the herd cannot be contained. As beasts scatter, you must choose a possible second kill.

When I was your age, I was advised to ignore the glory of killing a big bull. Hard to kill. Meat tough."

Hawk Dog's otherwise smooth forehead wrinkled with both concentration and apprehension.

"Ride instead after a young cow or yearling bull. Success in a second kill depends on your riding skill and the endurance of your buffalo runner."

Knowledge received, Hawk Dog stroked his horse's withers, smiled his appreciation, and scanned a horizon still yielding no sign of the prize. As the two parted, for riding close would not do, Stands For Them heartened the boy by shouting, "At sunset we feast on buffalo." Hawk Dog appreciated every word, for Stands For Them rarely spoke in the fashion of falling leaves.

Distantly now the herd came into view. They appeared as ants on an anthill. Shortly several more stone-faced *akicita* whipped their horses up and down the lines, their warnings insuring that no overly eager hunter would break rank to spook the herd.

Stands For Them and others began the surround in earnest, first walking then trotting. As the riders put the circle in motion, Stands For Them and others could see the individual buffalo milling, some only just sensing danger. As did each horse. As did each man.

The maelstrom threw creature against creature. As happens on all big hunts, Stands For Them lost himself in the excitement. He seized on a yearling bull that presented itself to him. Steering *Honska-Tahteh* with his knees only, Stands For Them tired the bull by goading it with his fleet horse. Soon he was close enough for a kill shot.

His aim was true. The bull bellowed once, took two faltering strides, then tumbled head over heels. From horseback Stands For Them shot a second arrow. The coup de grâce.

His arrows, banded in green and yellow, told the soon-to-arrive women that here was an animal to be rendered by Elk Robe's tiyospaye. Lowering his head briefly, Stands For Them prayed this fallen animal might have good travel to the animal spirit world.

Because Stands For Them was hungry, he then dismounted to slit open the hide at a point where he could with effort retrieve the warm liver. He ate the delicacy while flavoring it with the bile of the gallbladder.

As the sun angled downward Hawk Dog could be seen on foot beside his kill, a yearling cow. Up beside him rode Good Thunder. Here was Hawk Dog's chance to ask a question he'd dared not ask Stands For Them directly: "Your kola pursues the buffalo as though he were one of them. I see by the blue-dyed feather in his hair that he claims membership in a society. Is it a warrior society or a hunter society?"

Good Thunder smiled kindly at the naive question, and used a left hand to reveal his own small blue-dyed feather hidden in his locks. Similar to Stands For Them's, but trimmed differently.

"My hunter skills are not worthy of Stands For Them's society, but I am among the Tonkela Dog Soldiers sect. A warrior society. As you see, the feathers we wear are not the same. Stands For Them rides with *Ska' Yuhas*. Just last summer he was honored to join the *Ska' Yuhas* because he always brings home the meat." For two years now, Stands For Them had been a *Ska' Yuhas*—the distinguished hunter society. Perhaps not as prestigious as the top warrior societies, yet an honorable body.

In coming weeks the Canada fugitives enjoyed the fruits of this last old-time buffalo hunt—first the feasting, then packing full the stores of pemmican and dried meat, finally the tanning of so many hides.

During one feast in brief ceremonies, Stands For Them and Good Thunder each stepped forward to make Hawk Dog a *hunka* nephew. A good thing for all, for in a kinship society more relatives meant more allies, more resources. Becoming a relative was not exclusively a matter of biology, but of negotiation. Or in the case of Hawk Dog, charity.

The fires all around were bigger now, with snow season beginning. The winters here so much harsher than in their homeland, Stands For Them, Good Thunder, and Hawk Dog enjoyed full stomachs even as they dreaded the coming moons of chill and darkness. It would be a winter such as Stands For Them could not have imagined. Then a summer with rapidly thinning buffalo herds, the animals too scattered, too spooky to hunt. Then another equally brutal winter.

Stands For Them rubbed his gloved hands together vigorously but failed to restore feeling. The gathering of firewood had always been a woman's task. But in this second winter of extreme conditions, Stands For Them and other young men were recruited to assist.

Modern axes and saws improved gathering efficiency, yet such was the weather that staying tolerably warm plus cooking food meant that a day's required firewood precisely equaled a day's wood gathering.

Disgusted, Stands For Them put a hand in each armpit to restore feeling. When he spat, he noted the cracking sound of spittle snap-freezing before it hit the ground. Minus 49 degrees on the white man's thermometer.

By the late-arriving spring of 1879, buffalo herds thinned to the point where even small hunts were impossible. The Canadian government was weary of providing rations to the Lakota. And resident tribes, the Black-foot, Cree, Assiniboine, and the mixed-race Métis grew resentful of the newcomers.

So four of the six thousand Lakota refugees turned southward, homeward. Elk Robe had approved delicate inquiries concerning the possibility of surrender. But if so, where and when? He summoned his eldest son to discuss the matter.

"Let us weigh this decision carefully, son. Our people have been promised amnesty. There now seems no future here. Terrible winter cold, buffalo gone, rations ended." Stands For Them nodded. On these subjects he knew more than his father. "Those who precede us say we will live only temporarily in bluecoat camps, and in a later season will be taken by boat down the great river. We must choose from one of several military encampments for our surrender."

Elk Robe considered this for a moment. "Perhaps we should choose Fort Buford. It is close, just three sleeps south of the Medicine Line."

"Father, I propose we make the longer trip to Tongue River Cantonment," Stands For Them replied. "A familiar route and a distance we must travel anyway to again see our homeland. Spotted Eagle and many of our brethren in the Sans Arc are rumored to choose such a surrender to Bear Coat (Col. Nelson Miles). Our own High Backbone is camped there and scouting for Bear Coat."

Stands For Them looked carefully into his father's long face seeking possible agreement or some idea of what tomorrow would bring. Elk Robe instead retreated to a copse of ash trees for an hour's meditation. He returned with a flourish of instructions to tiyospaye members, and an appreciative nod to Stands For Them.

So it was that the tiyospaye retraced their long journey of two years earlier. Commencing under a crescent moon setting, the tiyospaye arrived at the mouth of Tongue River on the Yellowstone beneath a full moon rising. They were met by twenty mounted bluecoats who asked Elk Robe to erect tipis within the designated internment zone, an area of ten square miles surrounding the former cantonment recently renamed Fort Keogh.

Father and son rode out to survey possible campsites. Others of the tiyospaye waited at the Yellowstone River crossing.

"Where in this zone may we best erect our lodges?" Elk Robe wondered aloud as he turned in his saddle toward his eldest son. Stands For Them frowned as he considered the question—he feared his father would opt to join those few Eat No Dogs who had remained with High Backbone to serve as army scouts. This group had for two years pitched their tents just outside the walls of the fort.

Upon returning to the tiyospaye, father and son dismounted, found a suitable log, and bent heads together in discussion.

In twenty minutes, the pair came forward and with gestures indicated the tiyospaye would not camp near the fort, but rather as far away as permissible near the Spotted Eagle village. This was of course the Spotted Eagle who had some years earlier presented Heyúktan with his first long bow. His village hugged a river bottom affording level ground, towering cottonwoods.

At Elk Robe's command, his big family moved out. As they advanced, Stands For Them was saddened to see Spotted Eagle's village. These *Itazipacola* people had always been the ones with cleanest tipis, the most glossy-coated ponies, the fullest stores of dried meat. But spreading before him was a ragtag encampment better suited to prisoners of war. Which sadly is what they were. The tipis were smallish, spotted with grease and dirt, most of dingy canvas rather than buffalo hides . . . and all lacked any colorful imagery. The tipi poles were short and frail by Lakota standards.

Stands For Them dismounted. He began to arrange his possessions on frosted ground, observing a few *Itazipacola* men idly shuffling from one tipi to another. Nearby were two women scraping and curing buffalo hides strung on seven-foot square wooden frames. Surely these were hides brought from beyond the Medicine Line, for buffalo were all but gone in America.

So began Stands For Them's dreary year of sitting, waiting. The government had assured all who'd voluntarily returned from Canada that at some future date they would be transported closer to the old homelands. Young men were allowed to leave for short hunting trips. On one such trip, Stands For Them detoured to visit the cutbank where Stealing Horses had died.

On that bleak creek bottom he fashioned a temporary memorial to his brother: a three-foot-tall cairn of stones. With head thrown back and eyes glistening, Stands For Them raised a howl to wind and clouds.

As Stands For Them returned to camp, he hopscotched the stones of a nameless creek, aided by moonbeams sparkling the water. His moccasins were soon soaked by beads of dew clinging to the season's tall grass. He chose an unadvised shortcut home, skirting the backside of the fort's officer's quarters. One such brick structure brought him up short, curtains pulled back and windows open to the night breeze revealed wonders within. In this interior bathed by bright gas wall lamps, he saw a young woman seated at an upright piano, small hands moving quickly to make unexplainably bright sounds. Beside her a blonde-headed girl of perhaps ten winters played a violin. The portal to another room revealed a great cook stove, its pots steaming. Opposite the piano a stone fireplace towered over a woven rug on which sprawled a staghound as if sunbathing.

Stands For Them blinked once, twice, then turned from the scene with a frown. *All strange,* he thought, *A dog sleeping inside, for what purpose if it cannot bark the approach of strangers? Tonight this dog sleeps warmer and dryer than me and my people.*

In the spring of 1880, word came that all natives detained near Fort Keogh would be moved by steamboat down the Yellowstone and Missouri Rivers to Fort Yates, Dakota Territory. Even Sitting Bull would be transported in this way.

Weeks later the *Itazipacola* people and also Elk Robe's band were herded beneath a tattered American flag. A blonde-haired and well-mounted officer read from a wind-whipped proclamation. His mixed-breed interpreter stood beside him and translated. "You are all to be ready to board a steamboat in six sleeps. Each person may take no more than two bundles onboard. The bundles together must weigh less than the person. Limit of one tipi per ten people. No dogs will be allowed onboard, save for one small favorite dog per tiyospaye."

Thus began long hours for Elk Robe's wives selecting those limited possessions to be taken onboard. Then carefully bundling those possessions. And killing most camp dogs, to be rendered into dog stew or dried for later consumption. They preferred a fairly humane method of dispatching a dog unchanged for ten thousand years: A rope looped over the dog's neck, the ends of which were then pulled by two women until the animal fainted and expired.

As Stands For Them watched this sad spectacle, he wondered what would be done with the family's tall piles of buffalo hides. And of even more concern, what would become of his beloved horses? Surely they could not board the steamboat.

As the appointed morning approached, Stands For Them considered the rumors of horse confiscations, and jailings—He knew this gossip, true or not, fueled other young men to consider alternatives to boarding the steamer. Some of his peers spoke of stealing off with a handful of horses, bow and arrows, and riding out to join those few hostile bands still roaming in pursuit of game. He considered such a life for he and Tall Woman. But census takers were always counting, and bluecoats were always nearby.

On the day before the steamboat was to depart, Stands For Them and Tall Woman busied themselves in carrying family items towards the landing. There he was approached by a member of a different group of adventurous young men. Theirs was a more concrete way to avoid the drudgery of the slow boat ride.

"Stands For Them," shouted Black Buffalo from across what only yesterday had been the last central fire. "You have been asked to join the tribe's young horsemen volunteering to help the army solve their big problem—how to honor the Great Father's surrender promise that our horses will not be confiscated." His voice boomed with confidence.

"Yes," said Stands For Them, "we have been promised our horses . . . yet many wonder how this is possible. Surely such large animals cannot be transported on the boats that make fire. Tell me more of what you know."

Black Buffalo stepped closer, lowering his head as though sharing a deep secret with Stands For Them—"Our entire horse herd will be driven overland to the new Miniconjou and Sans Arc agency by the great river. It is a mighty distance, perhaps fourteen sleeps. Bear Coat and the other officers ask us to provide trustworthy herdsmen. There will be only three or four bluecoats to escort us."

Then that breathiness that comes from emotion entered Black Buffalo's throat—"This may be our last great adventure. We will live off the land. We will ride our best horses and encourage the rest through open country. We will again see our heartland. You must come."

Stands For Them was taken aback. His father must have known of this grand plan for the horses, and yet he'd not told his sons. Stands For Them kept quiet the rest of the day, busying himself with the tiyospaye's preparations for a morning departure. He glanced up now and then at Elk Robe's inscrutable face for what he hoped would be instruction on whether to travel with the steamboat or the horse herd.

Some families had insisted that their sons help drive the great horse herd eastward, perhaps to watch over certain prized ponies. Perhaps to better lay claim to those horses when all reached Fort Yates.

If Elk Robe harbored some knowledge of what might happen to his family's now smaller herd of forty-three horses, he gave no hint. How could he be so non-committal when it came to his tiyospaye's involvement in the great horse drive? Sitting far back from the evening fire, and then through a sleepless night, Stands For Them weighed his options.

When a rosy red sun finally crested, the killdeers of the shoreline and the birds of the bushes were oddly silent, invisible. As seemingly was the whole Yellowstone River valley. Just then the steamboat whistle blasted. In the old days the camp crier would have awakened all. But this was a new world, with powerful new machines. Stands For Them felt in that moment his duty was to board with the others.

Like an anthill stirred by a stick, the village came alive with natives scurrying this way and that. The best prepared were dragging their last neatly tied bundles and tipis towards the landing. A bottleneck formed at the water's edge as adults and children, all but the smallest balancing hefty bundles, converged on the single wooden gang plank connecting shore to steamboat. Indecipherable to those boarding, faded black paint spelled out the vessel's name on the prow: *General Sherman*.

His big head high above the crowd, a heavily laden Stands For Them waited to board. Then back to shore, then again across the plank carrying much of his families' possessions; four trips required. With his people and trappings on board, Stands For Them made one last trip ashore—to stuff his little camp dog in a burlap sack, this being the only way dogs were allowed onboard. But a few dogs that had escaped the stew pot in recent evenings would be left sitting expectantly on shore, to fend for themselves.

Stands For Them paused at the waterline. Before boarding for the last time, he looked around at this wild land, at this loveliest of all western river bottoms . . . then stepped onto the gang plank. In that moment he could feel himself crossing over—never again the free-roaming nomad, forever now an agency Indian, a ward of the American government. There settled upon his forehead an inescapable sense of having outlived his world almost before he entered it.

It was a feeling heavy on many native brows that morn. The ache that foreshadows a conscious sense of sadness. Even the land, the very earth, exhaled with this sorrow, much as the land does every fall with the leaving of the birds. Mournful howls rose from a trio of skinny dogs onshore.

A faint counter-note to this grim song could also be heard, in the form of hearts beating a little faster—the pulse of possibilities humans feel when making a new home.

Having climbed to the second deck, Stands For Them gazed longing-ly at those several Lakota young men on the bluff just above the river. He could see them all, mostly bachelor volunteers. Horsemen who even then were gathering up the scattered horses to form a great herd of Miniconjou ponies to be driven cross country to the Missouri River. The nearness of so many horses came to Stands For Them by nostril as much as eye—the riverine air damp with the smell of equine dung.

By squinting Stands For Them could occasionally spot Good Thun-der among the circling riders. Stands For Them regretted that he was not riding beside his kola. But had not his father, by his very silence, sig-naled that he would need the tiyospaye's protector on this trip and especially when the steamship arrived in unfamiliar territory?

Stands For Them moved to the third deck where members of his family were making ready for the long boat ride. The crew and military would occupy the lower deck cabins, Indians sequestered to the open, smoky upper decks. Elk Robe stood at the General Sherman's port side rail, where he was approached by a clearly concerned High Backbone.

"There is trouble with one of the young Sans Arc riders assigned to the long overland horse drive. Yellow Lance was caught stealing pemmican from the fort's warehouse. He sits even now in the blockhouse."

"The Eat No Dogs are requested to offer a rider to replace Yellow Lance. I feel the rumble of the fire magic of this boat, so we must act quickly. Can you spare a young man from your tiyospaye?"

Elk Robe did not hesitate. He nodded to High Backbone—then prowled the upper deck to find his firstborn, conveniently the best horseman he knew.

"Stands For Them, there is urgent need for a replacement rider for those herding the horses overland. We Eat No Dogs have been asked to provide this new rider. I wish that you be that rider."

The news made Stands For Them smile and lift his chin as though hearing some distant call. He found eye contact with Tall Woman, and her nod sealed the deal. He quickly gathered those few items he would need for the ride. Surely this was the tribe's last high adventure: guiding the great herd across sweeping vistas, down the valley of the Yellowstone River, over the divide leading to the Little Missouri River, down the Cannonball River. In a twinkling he was back on land.

Whirlwind's head shot up as Stands For Them whistled him in from the herd. Shortly Stands For Them was mounted and helping Good Thunder and others haze a thousand horses eastward.

Even when out of sight of the river, the riders could hear the whistle blasts of the *General Sherman* signaling its departure. In coming days Good Thunder and Stands For Them would often lead the way, for the Little Missouri country had always been the center of their band's hunting grounds.

At night they helped split the herd into two groups, to be positioned on opposite sides of the encampment. In this way, the random horse to escape the night guards of one herd would likely wander to the other herd. The soldiers kept to themselves, mere observers of the undertaking. Stands For Them was assigned night duty every third night. On one such night the air was cool, the wind high, the sky moonless. He set about reassuring a restless herd.

A large curve in the Little Missouri River provided a broad natural corral of sorts. Stands For Them took up the worrisome downstream position, riding back and forth, using his baritone voice to calm the herd. Flashes of initially soundless lightning illuminated towering clouds on the western horizon.

The first crash of thunder sent a shudder through the herd, a wave of nerves rolling visibly from critter to critter. In the incandescence of lightning flashes, Stands For Them could see other riders looking his way, seeking leadership in keeping the herd together. The thunder had awakened camp, sending three additional riders to Stands For Them's side. Welcome reinforcements indeed, but what to do?

"Let them move," said Stands For Them. His horseman's intuition was to not restrict the horses to the creekside flats. Their nervousness needed an outlet, so the young men spread out to let the animals trot to-and-fro. They held tight to only a few of the older, steadier horses, anchors for the herd.

As quickly as the thunderstorm rumbled eastward, the old lead mares, then the stallions, then the entire herd quieted to where most everyone could return to sleep.

Next morning, everyone helped to push the herd up out of the river valley and on towards the green pastures and watering holes of the Cave Hills near today's South Dakota/North Dakota border. For Stands For Them it was a landscape of genial ghosts and faded summers past. Happy to see these rolling hills, sad to know he would never see them again.

From here the plan was to move north by northeast to *Wakpa Mazawakhan Thanka*, the Cannonball River. This river valley would be a natural funnel eastward to Fort Yates.

But within hours, the big plan was in disarray. For a rare fog bank descended, and would not lift—The kind of fog where it was difficult to keep track of the herd. Or even to ride safely, or to venture afar on foot on this high featureless plain between rivers.

It was disorienting. There was nothing to do but pitch camp. And wait.

At length the natives assembled to consider if it would still be possible to arrive at Fort Yates on time. And if so, which way was which? The fog thicker than ever.

Many were those who spoke with anxious tongues. But not Stands For Them. He was calm, quiet, as though carrying a happy secret. His answer to the puzzle of which way to proceed would hinge on one of the last skeins of the migrating snow geese winging northward.

At length, Stands For Them moved close to the central fire, paused, reached down for the colored stick giving the holder the right to speak. Then straightening to the fullness of his notable height: "It is late spring. The great high-flying birds must answer the call of the North. They have no choice. So, this evening I bid us not to talk, but to listen. If we hear the honking pass overhead, though in darkness we'll not see the 'V', our ears will follow the sound trailing north. Then at first light, fog or no fog, we can confidently proceed eastward to our destination."

Stands For Them was immediately challenged when one of his childhood rivals among the Eat No Dogs, Charging Wolf, rose with a disdainful look. Charging Wolf, the short tempered, short statured, long winded one. But tonight he simply spat out a few ill-considered words as all eyes swiveled to his place at the fire—"You ask us to ride after a flock of mindless birds. I say simply wait until the fog lifts and we are guided by the far wiser sun or stars."

Stands For Them paused until every eye had returned to his aristocratic face. "We are expected to meet our people at Fort Yates when they depart the fire boat. The appointed day is just four sleeps away. To do this we must depart soon. As to my words, more powerful still are these words of the ancestors. They remind us that each four-legged and each winged, no matter how humble, has wisdom. Of the great geese it is said their wingbeats and heartbeats never fail, their flight always certain."

Charging Wolf offered a sneer, but no retort.

And so that night many remained alert to the sounds of the firmament. As if by revelation in the darkest hour before dawn, faint honking cries of unseen birds grew louder overhead and then softer in a direction that could only be true north. Their high-altitude cries to each other marking the ancestral, invisible highway of air.

It was the signal to saddle up and gather the herd. They traversed the last 150 miles in mostly fair weather. Only a single horse was lost, a small paint mare that became separated from the herd and was pulled down by wolves.

At last below them was the fort. The steamboat with its cargo of families had arrived only hours earlier. Into this festive atmosphere with high-pitched cries, Stands For Them and the others galloped the great herd down the high Missouri bluffs and onto the parade grounds of Fort Yates. Their tails up, so many horses made a fine spectacle.

Elk Robe, High Backbone, Spotted Eagle and many other headmen quickly dressed in finery and vied for positions of honor in welcoming the herd and the herdsmen. But absent was Sitting Bull. He and others of the Hunkpapa had been sent further down river to serve unknown terms as prisoners of war at Fort Randall.

Before the festivities and feasting were even fully under way, the soldiers insisted that all new arrivals line up. To be counted and assigned new homes on the reservation. For two hours Elk Robe and his *tiyospaya* waited as others before them gave brief family histories to a pair of businesslike junior officers and a half-breed interpreter at a rough wooden table. The officer with a great red beard seemed in charge.

When Elk Robe's turn came, he answered the interpreter's questions without once looking at the officers. "What are the names of your children, oldest sons first?"

"Stands For Them, our martyred Stealing Horses, Thunder's Son, One Who Kills An Enemy."

The bearded one raised an eyebrow; for a father having sons with particularly bold or militant names was significant. He jotted a brief notation beside Elk Robe's name: "Possible Troublemaker."

The Eat No Dogs of High Backbone, reunited with Elk Robe's tiyospaye, were sent to the Cherry Creek area of Cheyenne River Reservation. Before leaving Fort Yates, each father of each family must stand before an agent at another small table—there to learn how many horses he may take to Cherry Creek. Despite the earlier pledge, all but two of Elk Robe's ponies are confiscated with only promises of future compensation. The rumors had been true. Stands For Them questioned the purpose in driving all those horses across the treeless 500 miles. But he never questioned the adventure.

Cherry Creek, as it turns out, was a fine location for the tribesmen like the Eat No Dogs, folks like Stands For Them—far enough away from Fort Yates, Fort Bennett, and the "uncivilizing" influences of the Missouri River's liquor and goods trading cartels. Far enough away to retain a more traditional lifestyle.

Stands For Them knew these first months of reservation life were not a great time to hope for a larger family. But it was the ordained time. So with great interest, Stands For Them observed Tall Woman's sickness and wan smiles most mornings, and then her whispered news that she was with child.

As the time of birth drew near, Stands For Them saw less and less of Tall Woman. Older women watched her carefully. In small ways they blocked his access to her. On a chill evening in the Moon of Popping Trees, she came to him holding a fine baby boy.

Both Tall Woman and Stands For Them believed that before a baby comes to this earth, she/he looks upon all peoples and chooses the proper mother and father. For this reason, they felt blessed to have this spirit being appear in their lives. Come summer, Stands For Them's outsized hands fumbled a bit before holding up to father sky his naked and unnamed baby. The parents on this day chose a daring name exalting the once mighty Sioux country even as that might slipped away: Nation (Oyate).

Tall Woman did as her grandmother advised, using only the sing-song word "ahhou, ahhou" when comforting their baby. Stands For Them asked why. Tall Woman instructed: "Because this is the only sound a newborn recognizes. 'Ahhou' is the one word that belongs to infants."

In the first years on Cherry Creek, Elk Robe and Stands For Them, like most everyone, continued to live in tipis. Even on the reservation a tiyospaye might move camp every couple of weeks, if only a short distance. Such a mobile existence had always made sense, bringing a fresh campsite free of trash, renewed opportunity for firewood, game, unharvested berries and wild turnips, new grass for the ponies.

Then came the day when it all started changing for Stands For Them, who was splitting firewood for his parents. He watched as Elk Robe was approached by the reservation's agent and two Indian policemen. Moving closer, he was able to overhear the conversation. "You must now live in government-built log cabins. No exceptions." For Stands For Them another cultural blow. Still, no one could stop a Lakota from setting up a bright, breezy tipi beside the required cabin.

Six months later, the farm boss darkened Elk Robe's cabin door. Word had circulated among the farm bosses—Elk Robe did not believe in plowing the earth and had similarly discouraged all fifty-nine persons within his tiyospaye. No cornfields sowed. No gardens planted. Instead, Elk Robe sent his daughters to harvest native tubers, and his sons on horseback to those far-flung valleys where game still wandered.

The farm boss stepped through the threshold, and behind him came the young half-breed Jacque Bordeaux as translator. The farm boss ignored Elk Robe's gesture to be seated. Then through Jacque, "I have come to both ask a question, and to give your big family some bad news."

At this Sitting Bird and Tall Woman, with wee Nation on her back, slipped through the door and into the tipi. Elk Robe motioned Stands For Them to come closer.

"The question is this—why would you refuse the chance to grow more food? We give you tools, seeds, training?"

Elk Robe stood motionless, betraying no emotion, employing the Indian craft of looking neither at nor away from his guests.

The farm boss pressed for an answer, punctuated by a single step forward . . . a step he knew would cross the invisible line surrounding every Lakota male of a certain age and status.

Elk Robe's reaction again was no reaction, though Stands For Them took a forward step to match.

"I will speak for our leader of few words," Stands For Them said, his look challenging Bordeaux to translate truthfully. "We admonish our children to place their feet in such a way that the soil is not disturbed. We do this to leave no track, and because we know the faces of future generations are looking up at us from beneath the ground. For earth is the mother of all, not to be ripped or plowed."

The farm boss pretended to weigh Stands For Them's words, then began a litany of the consequences of not farming.

Stands For Them didn't bother to listen to the translation, instead thinking back to those seasons when he first tasted the satisfying brotherhood of organized hunts. Oh, how poorly the lonely task of farming compared.

Awkward silence followed, across which Elk Robe and Stands For Them exchanged solemn glances.

Then the farm boss's verdict: "This tiyospaye will have rations reduced." He and Bordeaux stepped up into the buggy and departed.

A curious few filtered back inside, waiting for a sign from Elk Robe. When at length he turned to survey the roomful, he spoke not a word but instead nodded towards the horse pasture with a smile.

His message was clear only to his sons—this tiyospaye would not bow to the threat of annuities reduction . . . not when young men like Stands For Them and Thunder's Son could still ride fine horses up the river in pursuit of deer, antelope, perhaps even one of the few remaining buffalo.

Nation was three now, and so full of life, and was in fact life itself for his father. So it was with great astonishment one morning that Stands For Them watched a tear-stained Tall Woman walk towards him carrying their barely breathing child. It was called by some the White Plague, by others tuberculosis, or consumption. For the Lakota it was *chagusica*, the cough that kills. Tall Woman held Nation throughout the four days of his illness, never sleeping, never bothering to dry her tears.

When the boy died, it was for Stands For Them as if the sky were ripped open. Sunshine became a mocking version of darkness. All happiness disappeared from the beginning of the world to the end of time.

No one was surprised as weeks passed to see Tall Woman eating less, sleeping less, developing her own deep-chest cough. Her behavior, at first simply listless, became increasingly strange. Near the end she spoke only of her burial, her reunion with Nation. Stands For Them was helpless to save her, that lovely but lifeless arm across his chest as he awoke one morn.

The death of Stealing Horses had been brutally hard, life altering, the end of innocence. But these twin deaths, within the dreary confines of his cabin on Cherry Creek, should have destroyed Stands For Them. He retreated to his tipi, where none dared disturb him, to burn through the sorrow.

How could his heart keep beating instead of bursting? How could breath flow when he took no interest in breathing, nor food, nor water, nor sleep?

But true to his name, five days later he willed himself to stand. It seemed to Stands For Them that he stood with no help from heart or muscle or bone. He stood against the truth that even time would not dent this coupled grief. When he stepped from the tipi, the village saw that future losses, and there would be many, could only further ennoble the man. They watched as he walked often to treeless places, where the emptiness there called to the emptiness in himself—Twin chasms offering a bittersweet balance.

It was the winter of deepest sadness, finally yielded to muted spring. Growing with the grasses was a sense for Stands For Them that he must seek a new land—something untried, untainted.

These were days of free movement between the reservations in Dakota Territory. Stands For Them began making horseback trips from Cheyenne River Reservation to Rosebud Reservation. There he could visit friends from the buffalo days in Canada. Men like Bull Dog from the mystical Wazhazha band living along Black Pipe Creek.

Here in the south people noticed the tall and melancholy figure by stages moving more freely. Making short trips to hidden hunting camps, standing at the outer edges of powwow circles. They noted that here he could smoke the pipe with his kola Good Thunder, who had the prior year moved south to be among his father's clan.

One remembered day, Stands For Them and Good Thunder lingered until they were the last two at a powwow site, walking among the bent but still green grass so recently pressed by tipis and dancing feet. It was a chance for Stands For Them to share just a little of the shuttering loss of wife Tall Woman and toddler Nation. And of his all too empty feeling life on the banks of Cherry Creek.

At Good Thunder's gentle urging, Stands For Them found a bit of healing by reciting Tall Woman's many virtues as a wife, and Nation's unlimited appetite for mischief. Good Thunder thought of other things that might lighten the shadow that darkened Stands For Them's face: "Perhaps you would be happier here along Black Pipe Creek among the Wazhazha. It is a place far from any agency, where tradition is even stronger than at Cherry Creek. Come next moon, when there will be a great Sun Dance. Only the Wazhazha would dare perform this forbidden ceremony. And only here so far from wasicu eyes is it possible. It may be the last Sun Dance with the piercings, the full sacrifice."

Side by side now, the pair shielded their eyes against a late afternoon sun to take in the valley and its surrounding promontories. Sweeping his right arm from horizon to horizon, Good Thunder continued his persuasions. "Here, Stands For Them, are mesas and buttes and badlands fit for vision quests. Here are hidden forested slopes where the sacred cedar, pine, and mighty cottonwood stand together like mute armies."

Indeed, the panorama was its own testament. Wisdom of silence descended as the pair sought out a shaded log upon which to sit.

Here Stands For Them meditated on Good Thunder's words. Finishing the deft rolling of a cigarette, Stands For Them turned to Good Thunder: "I will step forward as an initiate in this Sun Dance. If I prove worthy of the Sun Dance's sacrifice of flesh, this is my sign to leave the waters of Cheyenne River and Cherry Creek. Leave the Eat No Dogs band of my birth."

The next day, Stands For Them returned to Cherry Creek, retrieved his few personal possessions, and bid a stoical farewell of sorts to his clan. That same day he was riding south with plans to move temporarily into Good Thunder's loggie while preparing for the Sun Dance. Such preparations must be thorough—fasting, prayers, meditations in anticipation of a vision, then the sweat lodge for spiritual purification.

At night, Stands For Them wondered if he would prove worthy of this act of communal self-sacrifice: chest piercings with bone pegs at the end of ropes tied to the high fork of a ritually harvested cottonwood tree. To be suspended in the air. To suffer. To jerk free, tearing muscle and skin. But in a short two weeks, ready or not, the summer solstice arrived—this the appointed time for all Sun Dances. Seven young men stepped forward into morning sunshine to invite the self-mutilation of the ceremony, Stands For Them among them.

Sharp wooden pegs plunged into pectoral muscles, attaching each participant by ropes to the sacred tree. At some hidden signal the tribe's drummers began a slow, rhythmic drumbeat that would last all day.

Stands For Them kept his gaze firmly on the sun while reciting prayers. All the while he pulled backwards against his tethers, still on his feet and inwardly hoping that by day's end these efforts would free him with a tearing of flesh.

Just before sundown, Stands For Them, by now in a trance, became only the second of the participants to ask to be hoisted birdlike into the air in the agony that might tear him free. He was in that moment lifted out of himself by divine powers, briefly seeing a shimmering world where the loss of Tall Woman and little Nation was understandable.

How he ended up on the ground he never knew. As Good Thunder and Holy Bear bent to tend his wounds, Stands For Them had sensations to last a lifetime—that he had once more earned his name, that only by shedding blood for the people might he transcend personal grief.

Later that night the people feted Stands For Them for his transfiguration at the pole. There was a large fire, and feasting. But no dancing. Stands For Them was warmly greeted by the venerable Wazhazha chieftains Red Leaf and Lip. Then came Bull Dog, who suggested the young Miniconjou remain in the valley of Black Pipe Creek. This was the invitation Stands For Them so needed. He would stay.

Within four months Elk Robe, wives Sitting Bird and White Mountain, and five siblings followed the oldest son south, donning his same hope of better prospects among the Wazhazha. Stands For Them had agreed to come north to help the relatives on the journey to Rosebud. As he passed the place where Black Pipe Creek flows into the White River, he chanced upon an old man driving a two-horse wagon. The kind of rig the government was issuing to Indians. It was Jerome Black Bear, the blind one. The one whom many people talked of, but whom few had met.

Stands For Them dismounted and watched with appreciation as Black Bear guided his team down a steep and winding stretch of road. It was clear to Stands For Them that Black Bear was perceiving the landscape from the wagon seat, feeling what his animals were seeing through the reins connecting his hands with the headstalls.

When safely on the bottomland, Black Bear stopped to wipe his forehead and asked in a loud voice who was watching him. Stands For Them stepped forward to introduce himself. They exchanged names, lineage, then the reservation's obligatory list of common relatives. Stands For Them would have liked to ask but did not: can you harness the team without help, are your horses especially tractable and gentle, as though they know you are blind?

Black Bear offered Stands For Them a cigarette, made earnest small talk, then began to satisfy the curiosity of any new acquaintance:

"I have been blind since my third winter. Today I only faintly remember the difference between light and darkness. But I am fine here in the darkness. I cannot see the world around me, but I'm able all the better to see those truths that are veiled. The sacred mysteries."

To which Stands For Them asked what for him was the smaller but more practical mystery: "I see that you are returning from the Running Bird village. How do you know which of the many trails to follow?"

"Oh, my new friend, this is not difficult. I know where things are. Look, and you will see that now I point at a large cottonwood. Am I correct?"

"Yes."

"And while I must be more alert when traveling to a destination, when time to go home I can depend on the horses. They always know where home is. Sometimes I even nap a bit on the way home. And on days like today the warmth of the sun on my face, high or low, reveals the direction I travel and whether sundown be near or far." He cocked his head and smiled. "Darkness brings other gifts: I can tell a woman's beauty by her voice alone. Do not ask how. In Owl Canyon I can shout at the stone cliffs so that the returning echos paint for me a clear picture of the canyon."

Stands For Them offered the old man a drink from his canteen, said he hoped they'd meet again, and urged his horse towards Cherry Creek. But before he'd gone five paces, Black Bear called Stands For Them back: "Young man, because we may never meet again I ask you to look into my sunken eyes. Now remember that blind eyes, even so, see in dreams the brightest lights—likewise things you see with your eyes closed will be your true and lasting visions."

Chapter Thirteen

Wounded Knee
War Pipe, Peace Pipe
1890

The years since 1885 passed one much like another, victims each to the monotony of reservation life.

1890 was to be different. Yet for a year so tumultuous, 1890 started gently enough. In the season's *Istawicayazan Wi*, the Moon of Sore Eyes, there was bare ground on the banks of Black Pipe Creek. Weather almost balmy—what cowboys in coming years would call an "open winter."

A season when Stands For Them could venture into the canyons of both Cedar Butte and Pine Ridge, where he found only light dustings of snow making game tracking and harvesting almost easy. On one providential day he returned with two deer, a porcupine, and three rabbits. Another day people came out to see draped over the back of his horse a fine antelope, and three fat prairie chickens.

But then too much snow came. Deep enough to keep the hunter at home. And soon the larder of the single man Stands For Them, and his parents, and his extended family, grew thin to the point of famine.

With empty stomachs but now a spark of hope the Elk Robe tiyospaye received news—agents would distribute the reduced and delayed winter rations on the morning after the first crescent of the Moon When Ducks Come Back. On the appointed day, Stands For Them approached the beef issue station astride his best horse, riding beside his father and mother as they bumped along on their government-issue wagon.

He had come to help his parents lift a month's worth of freshly butchered beef, flour, fatback, biscuits. Reduced rations meant more room in the wagon box than usual, enough for their portion plus his.

Ahead he saw scores of Lakota wagons already lined up, blocking the road to the issue station and snaking for nearly half a mile. All patiently waited in order of their arrival.

The son and parents took their place, hunkered down. When his horse had relaxed to the head-down pose, Stands For Them curled his left leg and foot 'round the horn of his well-worn J.G. Read saddle—the most comfortable way to sit a spell on such a heavy working saddle.

Fully settled, Stands For Them heard the jingle and grind of another wagon pulling up behind. As he turned 'round, his eyes widening slightly at the sight of Pute', otherwise known as Chief Lip, firmly holding the reins from the wagon seat. Sitting cross-legged behind the venerable intancan were two of his three wives.

Others also noted the new arrival, sending a visible ripple of turning heads up the long line—and steadily one teamster after another pulled his wagon to the side of the road. It was a silent invitation to old Chief Lip to take a place near the front, apropos of his rank as the great intancan and spiritual torchbearer of the Wazhazha.

By pretending not to notice, instead dismounting to check the harness of his spotted horse team, Lip both accepted the honor and declined the invite in humbleness befitting a peace chief. He would maintain his position at the end of the long line.

Many knew that Chief Lip was presently both troubled and animated by the gathering storm clouds of the Ghost Dance uprising.

Later with rations loaded and horses reined north, Stands For Them rode closer to his parent's wagon so as to invite conversation. Only after passing Parmelee did father and mother look his way. "Tell me father, why does a Wazhazha such as Lip not choose sides?"

"He can walk on the old man's middle ground, the contemplative ground. You however will need to choose sides. Your Wazhazha neighbor Short Bull is a leader of this new thing, and he will see that there are no young man neutrals in our valley."

It had been one year since a Nevada Paiute named Wovoka had a vision during a total solar eclipse—the message strange and beautiful enough to sweep across the American West, carried only by voices and reaching even as far as the Dakotas. Curiosity drove Short Bull and Kicking Bear to make the long journey to Wovoka's home. Reaching Nevada later in summer, they sat at Wovoka's feet to hear his vision: "If you as devotees will do a certain ritual dance, the Lakota and other native people will be united with deceased relatives, the buffalo will return, and the white man will simply disappear."

His words carried echoes of both native and Biblical prophecy. Headlines proclaimed the Messiah Craze. Short Bull and Kicking Bear returned from their pilgrimage as true believers, becoming the leading apostles of this new faith for a desperate Lakota nation.

Many Lakotas quickly joined the movement—abandoning their meager homes and possessions, some by give-away and some by fire. It was as though the people, their lives suspended when forced onto the reservations, awoke as one to the promise of a red-skinned messiah. Such desperate hopefulness touched even the undecideds like Stands For Them. Even the doubters.

President Benjamin Harrison's response was to order the largest military mobilization since the Civil War. But this wasn't an uprising— Most ghost dancers did not want a fight. They wanted only to be left alone to worship the Great Spirit in a new way. To await their savior, their Red Messiah. Flocking to "hostile" encampments in remote areas of the reservations: Pass Creek, Black Pipe Creek . . . or deep within

Badlands, where desperate factions sought a last stand, a final fortress for the Lakota nation.

There Short Bull and his followers found such a natural citadel at the impregnable Stronghold Table. A virtual island in the sky, this mesa connected to the much larger Cuny Table by a land bridge as narrow and defensible as the Strait of Thermopylae. Here the ghost dancers dug trenches where a handful of riflemen might repel hundreds. Here at the Stronghold the ghost dancers would briefly occupy their "sanctum sanctorum."

Even before this tumult, Stands For Them was struggling to firm up his philosophy for surviving reservation life. He was influenced in equal measure by those few Lakota who prospered in the white man's econo-my, and by staunch traditionalists and oldfangled spiritualists such as the aging Red Leaf of Black Pipe Creek and casual acquaintances like Short Bull of nearby Pass Creek.

Undersized and sharp-featured, Short Bull was a minor medicine man ten years older than Stands For Them. A mystic Wazhazha, Short Bull was known as a prophetic man walking life's spirit path.

Stands For Them felt he owed the movement some respect—for was not Kicking Bear of his mother clan, the Miniconjou, and Short Bull of his adoptive Wazhazha. But one part of the new religion he considered old, dead magic—the part about the muslin "ghost" shirts rendering the wearer bullet proof.

Yet other of Wovoka's promises touched Stands For Them deeply—a beautiful vision of the passing away of the present sad world ruled by the wasicu, and with it the idle life of the reservation . . . then the coming of a new world with buffalo and antelope and no fences, no bluecoats. Life lived once again from the back of a horse.

All Saints Eve, 1890 found Stands For Them eking out a living at one of the few jobs available, albeit perfectly suited to his love of horses—freight wagon teamster between Valentine, Nebraska and the Rosebud Agency. For this reason, he would miss a notable gathering near his old neighborhood: Short Bull, he heard, was calling all new believers together at the Red Leaf camp on Black Pipe Creek.

On this day Short Bull delivered what would become the key sermon for the new religion. Here his apocalyptic words vaulted Short Bull past Kicking Bear to become the uncontested high priest of the movement . . . if only for a few months.

Accounts of Short Bull's sermon raced by word-of-mouth across the reservations and to the ears of the undecideds such as Stands For Them. The short address was preserved for history in a later official report penned by Major General Miles—

"My friends and relatives. I will soon start this thing in running order. I have told you this new world would come to pass in two seasons, but since the wasicu are interfering so much, I advance the time from what my Father above told me to do. The time will be shorter . . ."

". . . Now there will be a tree sprout up, and there all the members of our religion and the tribe must gather together. That will be the place we will see our dead or ghost relations. But before this time, we must dance the balance of this moon, at the end of which the earth will shiver very hard. Whenever this thing occurs, I will start the divine wind to blow . . ."

". . . Now we must gather at Pass Creek, where the tree is presently sprouting. There we will be among our ghost relations. You must not take any earthly things with you. Then the men must take off all their clothing, and the women must do the same. No one shall be ashamed of exposing their persons . . . You must not be afraid of anything. The guns are the only things we are afraid of, but they belong to our Father in Heaven. He will see they do no harm . . . I will now raise my left hand up to my Father and close what he has said to you through me."

The oration had reached Stands For Them's ears in an hour when the setting moon and rising sun faced each other. Next day, after an uneasy night's sleep and light breakfast, Stands For Them looked up from his doorstep perch to see a lone rider approaching. Stands For Them was neither alarmed nor surprised, for many an acquaintance had taken to dropping by his cabin to try recruiting him to the Messiah Craze. Young men like Morning Star. Of unassuming appearance but a quivering intensity, Morning Star sometimes wore his ghost shirt when visiting Stands For Them. Not today, though. Today he wore a calico shirt and dungaree pants as he took a seat beside Stands For Them, rolled a cigarette, and lit it before telling Stands For Them of the preceding evening spent with none other than Short Bull.

"Short Bull calls Wovoka the most holy man he ever met!" Morning Star's keenness showed in his deep-set eyes, set in a rather round and meaty face. "This new world will have buffalo and antelope again, and native peoples can return to the old ways."

Even as he spoke, Morning Star saw in his body language that Stands For Them would likely not join the ghost dancers. Yet the visitor persevered.

"The new world will be possible through the power of the Christ, who this time comes to *our* people. When he came so long ago to the wasicu, they hanged him on a tree. We will do better."

Taking a long draw from the cigarette but then flinging it aside, Morning Star turned to his friend, "But this new age comes only if we dance the dance." Stands For Them praised an eyebrow and looked down at his folded hands, wishing he had more belief in this attractive vision. So he said nothing.

Morning Star hailed from the hamlets lining Pass Creek, not far from Short Bull's loggie. Short Bull's status had risen high, some even whispering that he was the Red Messiah.

When Short Bull proclaimed the cosmic tree would sprout on Pass Creek, it drew so many to gather near his home. To await the new age. For many it seemed right and proper that redemption would arrive first in this Wazhazha village.

Two days later at Morning Star's invitation, Stands For Them joined him for a ride over the low divide separating Black Pipe Creek from Pass Creek. He was, if nothing else, curious to see this great Ghost Dance encampment near Short Bull's cabin. Besides, a trip to Pass Creek was a pilgrimage—for there one could sit beside holy medicine bundles reputed to bring prophecy and potency. Stands For Them remembered that Crazy Horse and Sitting Bull had in earlier years made this same pilgrimage.

As the young men topped the divide, there below was a sight from bygone days, stretching northward on either side of the creek sat nearly a thousand tipis. Even from afar, Stands For Them could hear the plaintive song of the Ghost Dance. Smoke from a thousand campfires cast the scene in surreal amber light.

Morning Star reined up, turned in the saddle, and raised his left hand, "Behold the valley where the new Indian world will emerge."

Intrigued, mesmerized even by the vibrancy of the place, Stands For Them proceeded some distance before reining in his suddenly nervous horse at the edge of the great camp. He sat motionless in the saddle for so long that Morning Star finally shook his head in frustration, riding on alone among the tipis and ultimately to his own cabin.

Stands For Them thought back on Short Bull's words, "Now there will be a tree sprout up, and . . . that will be the place we will see our dead or ghost relations." Stands For Them knew the tree to be a mere symbol of the new nation, but in spite of himself gazed among tipis that he might see a young tree sprouting.

A while longer he sat, knowing in the bone this would be his last view of such a gathering of free-nation Lakota tipis. At length he turned his horse around for the ride back to Black Pipe Creek and home. He felt the rumblings of a big decision.

There came a blue-sky day when Stands For Them did not have freighting duties, so he coiled a lariat over his shoulder and set out for his parent's cabin to continue a chore that had occupied free time for weeks—to gentle a green horse that Elk Robe had received at a give-away ceremony the previous summer. Elk Robe hoped to use the little sorrel as both a saddle horse and wagon horse. But the animal, high spirited and untrained, needed the touch of a man like Stands For Them. Elk Robe had named this horse Little Scout.

Upon reaching the Elk Robe cabin, Stands For Them did not stop to greet his parents. He walked in his rolling, long-stride gait straight for the corral. Once inside his every motion slowed—for Little Scout, though less wary, was still not drawn to this tall human. So for nearly an hour, Stands For Them stood quietly near the horse. Nothing else.

In those days a lot of cowboys, some Indians too, figured a horse wasn't "broke" until the man beat the spirit out of the creature. Not so with Stands For Them. He meant first to gain the animal's trust. All training flowed from that trust. It was the old slow way.

After the hour of just standing, he rubbed the horse from head to tail with a gunny sack, sometimes mimicking the action of putting a saddle blanket in place. Fifteen minutes later he loosely tied a placid Little Scout to the corral fence and climbed aboard. Bareback. Just sitting.

The day's lesson complete, Stands For Them now sought council of his father on how to handle pressure mounting on those young men who'd not yet chosen sides.

Many of Stands For Them's peers were inviting the holy baptismal water to be sprinkled on their heads, indicating they would not be joining the ghost dancers. It was a path Stands For Them was considering, though he could not expect his father to follow.

On seeing his son darken the threshold, Elk Robe gave a chuckle and pulled the cabin's single chair close beside a cast iron stove's remnant heat from noontime cooking. His son did the same with a tree stump stool. Only yesterday Elk Robe had passed his beloved son on the road. They'd simply nodded then, but father noted Stands For Them's formal dress. Now he inquired, "I saw yesterday that you again joined those Lakotas hearing stories of the white man's god who came to live among men. Do not assume I think this a bad thing, my son. Any spirit road is a good road. And perhaps there comes a day when the wisdom of our old spirit ways and these new spirit ways come together."

Elk Robe leaned away from Stands For Them to ask Sitting Bird if she might retrieve his holy pipe and his pittance of remaining tobacco. The men then sat and smoked sparingly, wordlessly.

At length, Elk Robe recited the names of some long dead ancestors, melodious names that Stands For Them recalled hearing as a small boy: "Rolling Thunder, Rattling Leaves, Walks Among the Stars, Daughter of the Moon, Holy Standing Buffalo." When father said these were relatives from seven generations before, Stands For Them knew his father was asking him to view the present 1890 turmoil as part of a much bigger picture. Elk Robe ended his wisdoms by speaking that old Lakota adage: "Remember that you are connected to peoples of seven generations past. But here is the trick: your obligation is to conduct yourself in ways that leave a good world for the seventh generation to come. Think always of the seventh generation coming so as to walk in goodness."

On this day the son kept private his thoughts, so as to show a special honoring of his father's words. With a respectful smile he stood, presented his mother with a package of dried meat, and walked out the door.

Stands For Them was surprised to hear his father following him out-side. Elk Robe beckoned his son to join in taking in the grand view of this valley rimmed with badlands and tabletops. He used his long arm to point out the many landmarks, then sent his son off with this benediction: "Remember the God of the Black Book comes to his children only indoors, in those white wooden buildings. Not a bad thing. But better is our temple—whole earth and sky, our holy water not dammed in a font but moving freely in every river, every stream, every raindrop."

For reasons well known yet deeply personal, Elk Robe would not himself ever be baptized. His first pillar of recalcitrance towards the wasicu religion: Elk Robe was a traditional headman with more than one wife, a thing he had always seen as charitable in a world where husbands often died young. Indeed, there was societal obligation to take as second wife the widow of a fallen brother, or displaced sisters of one's first wife.

On the short ride home, Stands For Them mulled his options. The polygamy ban presented no obstacle to a man of Stands For Them's age, his generation having largely renounced the old custom of plural wives. But what of the strange expectation that the newly baptized should cut their long braids, put on white man's clothes, and pull on the white man's heavy shoes? These physical changes, especially the short hair, were meant to show outwardly that a Lakota convert was inwardly reborn. Even so, to cut his waist-long raven-black hair? Stands For Them resolved that he could not do this. *Why should I,* he thought, *when the Jesus of this new religion wore long hair?*

As daylight increased so did the drumbeats of the new creed sweeping the reservations. Perhaps because of this, Stands For Them was often drawn to the quiet halls of the little Episcopalian chapel. There to find calm counsel from "White Robe" Father Aaron Blelark.

Plus Father Aaron spoke fluent Lakota, with which he offered a basic and native-friendly version of Christianity. Some he hoped would consider baptism. But most days Stands For Them listened inattentively, his gaze on the Niobrara Cross hanging round Father's neck.

Ah, the famed Niobrara Cross. Stands For Them pondered its symbolism, for it was as much a circle as a cross. At the ends of the four arms of the silver-plated cross were four tipis, each surmounted by a tiny cross. Four!—the holy number. On this day as they often did, Stands For Them and Brings Three White Horses stayed behind to hold and examine this icon that they saw as comingling the two religions.

Father Aaron considered the pair natural leaders among the valley's young men. So, he paid them special attention and on this day brought forth a very large Bible so as to invite these illiterates to select any verse by pointing. There seemed always to be a touch of magic in it for all involved. He would read the selected verse in English, translate it to Lakota, then offer the verse's deeper meaning. Brings Three White Horses went first, smiling, closing his eyes, and pointing.

Next was Stands For Them, and he selected a page very near the end of the big black book, closed his eyes, and pointed to a verse. Father Aaron read the verse in English, hesitated, then translated words he hoped would not send either young man from his church to the Ghost Dance camps: Revelations 21:1 "Then I saw a new heaven and a new earth, for the first heaven and the first earth had passed away."

There followed a hollow silence. The Lakota pair exchanged glances that said they were thinking the same thing: "Perhaps Short Bull and Kicking Bear are right. Perhaps Wovoka's strange new religion is this promised new world. For we see its roots even here in the white man's sacred book." Father Aaron closed the Bible, smiled, cleared his throat, and mentioned again the coming ceremony, should they choose to be baptized.

With this, Stands For Them rose from his bench and motioned his friend to follow. The other Lakota men had already departed the treeless chapel grounds leaving just two horses standing patiently, at the back fence, their big heads swinging 'round to watch as the men approached. Stands For Them had tied his animal head to tail, the swooshing tail of one horse shooing biting flies from the face of the other.

Having mounted his horse, Stands For Them bid Brings Three White Horses join him in riding together in conversation. For was now not the moment to make the big decision together—be baptized, or join the ghost dancers?

Brings Three White Horses could see on his friend's face visible doubts about baptism. Adjusting the cinch on his saddle without dismounting, Brings Three White Horses said, "Remember many mighty Lakota leaders have touched a knee to the ground for this new God. Red Cloud himself was baptized in the very year you moved south to this reservation."

Ducking his chin and pretending to examine his horse's headstall, Brings Three White Horses added that White Robes like Father Aaron were more willing to look the other way when a Lakota initiate retained bits and pieces of the old spiritual and social customs . . . at least when compared to the Jesuits.

Stands For Them gave his friend a stern look that said, *You do not know my mind*, but then relaxed his manner. "I am bothered by that passage I pointed to in our lesson. I wait for a dream, or an admonition by some holy sage among our people." They rode in thought. Each gave his mount its "head." This allowed for relaxed contemplation at a steady clip-clop pace.

Stands For Them rolling a Bull Durham, eyes on the roll, then briefly on his friend. "Do you believe Father Aaron will approve if we as

Christians still dance our dances at *wacipi* and sometimes don the buckskin and feathers that many wasicu holy men call heathen?"

When no answer came, weighty topics yielded to small talk peppering the last miles to their nearly adjacent homes. By the time he had turned his horse loose in its small pasture, Stands For Them had made up his mind about baptism.

As one moon slid to the next, soldiers bivouacked in ever greater numbers at both Pine Ridge and Rosebud agencies, and on Cheyenne River and south of Rapid City.

Stands For Them remained, publicly at least, a man in the space between. Watching, listening. And sometimes, as on this day, just riding—the rhythmic cadence of a striding horse a meditative sanctuary. In this way he came upon three charred cabins where Simms Creek flows into Black Pipe Creek, the blackened logs still smoking. He knew these acts of arson to be perpetrated by both factions as a message to the other side. Ghost dancers even torched their own government-issued loggies as acts of defiance. An act that said, "For me there is no turning back."

On the appointed day, Stands For Them rode alone towards Father Aaron's chapel to at long last take the holy water on his head. Hopeful but not sure if Brings Three White Horses would be there.

He arrived late. The fifteen people assembled were waiting patiently, for how could they proceed when one of three slated for baptism was missing. Stands For Them smiled to see Brings Three White Horses. The other initiate was the young woman White Blanket up from the Red Leaf village.

Stands For Them raised no eyebrow when entering, punctuality not being a pillar of native life. He took an open seat of honor on a bench near the altar, facing the tiny congregation. Those able sang two simple, memorized hymns in English, "River of Jordan" and "The Old Rugged Cross." Then came Father Aaron's short sermon in the Lakota tongue.

Next the baptismal ceremony, much of it inscrutable to Stands For Them. But not the part where he was asked to share his new Christian first name. With Aaron's help he'd chosen from an acceptable list . . . one he thought sounded important, maybe even dignified. Henceforth thirty-three-year-old Stands For Them would be known on documents and in census listings as James Stands For Them. Brings Three White Horses assumed a similarly biblical name in Levi. Neither young man ever once used "Levi" or "James" when addressing each other, preferring instead their original, singular, meaningful names.

When the water was three times poured on Stands For Them's head, it ran in rivulets down the long, black strands to form a dozen tiny puddles on the rough wood-plank floor. For true to his promise, Father Aaron had not asked the men to cut their hair short.

When the cold water soaked into his warm scalp—when Stands For Them considered himself fully baptized—no dove fluttered down on a beam of light. No heavenly voice murmured. But he did feel quietly spoken for, a part of some big new mystery.

To seal the ceremony, Father Aaron handed the doe-eyed White Blanket a *Certificate of Baptism,* for she had attended Carlisle Indian School and thus commanded a bit of written and spoken English. Then he turned to the two illiterates. With a flourish from his vestment pocket, he brought forth two baptismal medallions. Small shiny versions of his own Niobrara Cross. Stands For Them would keep this medallion in his medicine bag for a lifetime.

Stepping from the chapel into brilliant sunshine, Stands For Them and Brings Three White Horses departed afoot, leading their horses on the old trader's road passing through shrubby trees just behind St. Thomas Episcopal Church. The better to talk over this new reality.

Leaf-filtered sunbeams were pleasantly warm, the air moist and flush with late spring's meld of earthen smells. Having taken the holy water, both felt better prepared for yet another big decision coming.

Brings Three White Horses had been first to ask the question many weeks earlier: "Which of our brothers shall we join? Whether on this side or that, we will need to take up the lance. For only the young man who makes no stand is damned."

Pressing practicality fueled today's rolling discussion, for both faced the imminent end to their current jobs. And there seemed zero prospect of earning support for a family if they joined the Ghost Dance camps. Brings Three White Horses was set to complete his ninth month as custodian of the new Black Pipe Indian Day School. He faced a summer layoff, with no guarantee of a rehiring. Stands For Them had parlayed his charm with horses into short-term teamster contracts with the freight company running weekly wagon trains from the Valentine, Nebraska railhead to Rosebud Agency. It paid $2 for each week's eighty-two-mile roundtrip. That contract was likely to expire, for the huge army presence was now moving their own supplies.

Then came news of a novel and intriguing job prospect: "You have heard," offered Stands For Them, "that because of Ghost Dance troubles, boss soldiers at Fort Niobrara and Rosebud Camp are seeking those Lakotas who were scouts in the old days. Good Thunder says they seek men of our age, strong and still young but old enough to remember the scouting skills from when we were *Pte Oyate*, the buffalo nation. Ah, but those who sign up will make no friends among the ghost dancers. And can scouts make enough for families, and for tobacco, and coffee too?"

Neither offered to guess what scout enlistees might earn. Days later they were pleased to learn scout privates would pocket $10 a month.

Brings Three White Horses then uttered the name *Chat-Ka*. Meant to remind both that theirs was a complicated world and scraping together a living required trade-offs. Both knew the story of Chat-Ka, an acquaintance of their youth who some years before had joined as a 7th Cavalry scout to better support his family. Discharged from his service mere weeks before the troubles of 1876, Chat-Ka then joined the free Lakota before the Battle of the Rosebud. He would also fight with the "hostiles" and against his old 7th Cavalry comrades at the Little Big Horn, there to die a martyr.

The pair proceeded down the road in that slow, silent cadence of two souls pondering one question: *Are we any different from Chat-Ka— ready to use warrior skills for defense and support of the oyate, in whatever way best supports our family?*

Both missed the strut of their pre-reservation roles. Both felt they might reclaim some favor by returning to their first role as scouts. By today's baptism, they'd entered space where this adventure seemed possible.

Stands For Them was poised, and yet he hesitated—would being an army scout make him no better than those who wore the blue uniforms? He wondered, turning to his friend, "I have seen something sad in the Lakota police, and the native soldiers—in their ill-fitting uniforms, their straight lines, their long hair clipped and lying on the ground. Living sometimes in barracks far from family."

Brings Three White Horses finished rolling yet another cigarette before speaking, "My friend, it will not be as you describe, should we join as scouts. The Army Indian Scout is allowed to be on his own horse, his hair streaming long in the wind, or in braids. He can live at home or with friends. Indian Scout clothing need not be so different from hunting or warring garments of old. They say our obligation can be short, as short as thirty sleeps."

Coming to a shady curve in the trail, Stands For Them paused, looking up at the horizon as though seeing something for the first time.

"Brings Three White Horses, if we choose to return as scouts then we will show the young ones our old Lakota ways are not dead. We will be real persons again."

Level, unblinking gazes signaled two men reaching the same conclusion at the same instant. "Yes, let us do this. Let us recite again those warriors who served as army scouts before us." Brings Three White Horses proceeded to count on his fingers:

"Gall. High Backbone, Chat-ka. Yes, even Crazy Horse. His clan says he jumped at the chance to ride as an army scout against the Nez Perce. And comrade warriors Red Bear, Buffalo Ancestor, White Cloud, and Bloody Knife." Stands For Them thought back to the 1870s when he and his father considered native army scouts as mercenaries, traitors even. But this was 1890, and now most Lakota had softened their position on scouts who rode for the army. These days many saw Indian Army Scouts as *akicita*—protectors of the people.

The pair continued to walk the old trail and discuss many forces tugging on them from both sides. Still, as light faded to night, Stands For Them smiled to have finally chosen, to see his arrow of life let fly from the bow. Better to have made this choice with another. They would be cheered, also condemned, but all would know these two chose together.

Stands For Them now had only days to enjoy the wages and solitude of his twice weekly duty as a teamster from Rosebud to the railhead at Valentine, Nebraska. He would as always hope to work with horses, but might be stuck with ornery mules or bellowing oxen. Each return trip with loaded wagon covered forty-one miles and required one or two nights of camping under the stars. Discussions round those campfires always returned to the zeitgeist of 1890—the Ghost Dance movement. Men of all allegiances, and no allegiances, could be found among the teamsters—even Short Bull himself. On this second-to-last trip, Stands For Them sat quietly, having not yet gone public with his decision.

Word had come among the freighters that Bear Dog and Eagle Man, both Wazhazha men with war records, had announced as enlistees in the army scouts. "The army seeks always to recruit top warriors as scouts; thereby turning old enemies into friends," said someone ironically smiling from the opposite side of the fire, "so we should not be surprised to learn this of Eagle Man and Bear Dog."

Next morning, home again, Stands For Them stepped from his front door and looked across the valley where he could just make out the adult sons of his neighbor, the venerable Bull Dog. He could not at first discern their feverish activity. But on closer examination they appeared to gather lances and guns and sizable bundles onto a shared pack horse. Once on their saddle horses, the pair rode westward at a high trot. Their dress and direction of travel suggested persons traveling to join the Stronghold hostiles. They were only a little younger than Stands For Them. He knew them. Not well, but well enough to admire their fierce Lakota patriotism.

Stands For Them was ready to publicly take sides, and wished to do so in the old, hard way by announcing first to a leader who would not agree. Perhaps this was his chance.

So it was that Stands For Them walked across the valley floodplain and knocked on Bull Dog's thick wooden door. If he could tell this Wazhazha headman and leader of the Canada renegades, and say it with pride, surely he could tell anyone.

Bull Dog was sitting on the cabin's lone chair, sharpening a hunting knife. His loud grunt invited Stands For Them to enter. But with no place for a visitor to sit other than Bull Dog's unkept bed, they wordlessly moved outside to sit on opposite ends of a fallen log. Somewhat surprised to see his neighbor paying a visit, Bull Dog was first to speak. "Stands For Them, I admire your father and I remember you as a great provider for our people in the Grandmother's Land. You stood first among all hunters."

Then, with a wry smile and before Stands For Them could utter a word, "You come today to tell me, and all the valley, that you will ride with the Army Scouts. It is a noble thing to tell me first. I will not scold or judge, but I tell you what I just told my sons—*Above all, protect the oyate.* That is all I have to say." With this he returned to his knife sharpening.

Having uttered not a word, but seeing no need to, Stands For Them took this as his summons to leave. Of course, he neither sought nor expected a blessing from this elder of the Crow Dog faction, one whose sons were entering the fight on the other side. But had not Bull Dog's manner hinted at a grudging acceptance of Stands For Them's right to make such a decision? Every man his own master—the Lakota way.

News of Stands For Them's meeting with Bull Dog drifted like puffy cottonwood seeds across the valley of the Black Pipe.

Next morning Stands For Them rose from his pallet to share his intentions with his tiyospaye, though most of them already knew—Stands For Them would accept the army rifle, joining the next enlistment call-up with Brings Three White Horses, Eagle Man, and Bear Dog.

Stands For Them, with but two days remaining on his teamster contract, proceeded next morning by horseback to Rosebud Agency and hence to Valentine.

Before picking up his assignment, Stands For Them was surprised and a little alarmed to see the depot and rail yards bustling with trains arriving one after the other. Down the ramps came war horses, cannons, troop tents, ammunition; not the standard annuities bound for Rosebud.

As he waited just outside the freight office, Stands For Them was approached by Philip Wells, a mixed-breed Sioux who often served as an interpreter for the army. The two men had developed a cordiality in recent years.

What Wells told Stands For Them on that dusty street corner sat as an unwelcome guest on the tall one's shoulder for many days. "I tell you, these trains are only part of the army being assembled to war with the ghost dancers. They are coming from all four directions."

On parting Stands For Them nodded in thanks, "Your words do not make me fear for myself. They do make me anxious for my oyate." Twenty minutes later Stands For Them finally heard his name called, and was relieved not to be named a whip man behind the plodding but powerful twenty-oxen yokes. Today he was assigned the somewhat speedier six-mule hitch, requiring him to ride the near-side wheel mule.

Stands For Them's team made good progress until descending to Minnechaduza Creek where a young freighter stood with hands on hips, his oxen train and wagon mud mired. Stands For Them knew the oxen capable of pulling the wagon out if motivated by a certain sound. So he dismounted to retrieve a bullwhip from the sidebox, uncoiled the whip, then snaking it through the air where the crack of it was as a rifle shot. The oxen heaved to and pulled the wagon out.

Stands For Them arrived at Rosebud's long dark stable early on the second evening. He and a stablemate dispensed rations of grain to each mule, then began removing and hanging the harness.

Stands For Them turned from hanging the last heavy draft harness to confront none other than Short Bull, so recently a teamster himself. Behind Short Bull skulked and muttered a trio of formidable stone-faced native men.

Stands For Them and Short Bull acted as two Lakotas are obliged to act when on opposite sides of an issue—each signaling hostility in subtle ways that to the outsider looked like indifference.

Neither spoke a word until Short Bull, spinning on a heel, said over his shoulder "You have news from Valentine. Others wish to know what you know. Wait to hear from me."

Short Bull's enigmatic words hung in the air as Stands For Them returned to the day's remaining duties. He was soon joined by fellow freighter Red Fish. Of a Wazhazha mother and Sans Arc father, the nimble undersized Red Fish was as confident with draft animals as he was awkward with people.

Together they hurried to oil the harness, turn the mules out to pasture, and wash down their mud-splattered wagons. Working quickly might mean just enough daylight to ride up to their home communities north of Rosebud Agency.

On the ride Red Fish was oddly chatty, apparently inspired by what they'd encountered at the railhead. As Stands For Them listened, he found himself back at the depot, watching the detraining U.S. 9th Cavalry in its spit'n'polish glory: Cavalrymen, officers, freshly oiled saddles, army horses sporting bold "U.S." brands, Gatling guns, various wagons—a din punctuated by bugles blowing and train whistles screaming. Red Fish shared rumors that had not reached Stands For Them's ears, "The 9th has orders to arrest all Ghost Dance leadership. Their biggest goal—capture Short Bull."

They rode at a trot through the amber light of the day's old age. Arriving in Parmelee, they stopped at the Red Fish cabin where Stands For Them stayed for late dinner before remounting to ride by moonlight to Black Pipe Creek and home. Sleep came swiftly when at last Stands For Them settled into his narrow cot.

Next morning, Stands For Them was awakened by someone shaking the foot of his bed. It was Keeps the Mountain, a fellow freighter, dressed as always in wasicu clothes—dungarees, a flannel shirt, heavy boots ill-suited to native horsemanship. Keeps the Mountain was of medium height, with lightly muscled limbs offering locomotion any antelope would envy. With narrow shoulders, reclusive personality, and piercing eyes, it surprised no one that he was second cousin to Crazy Horse. Keeps the Mountain would surely have made a fine warrior, but being five years Stands For Them's junior, he'd missed those last chances for battle honors in the '70s.

Stands For Them quickly dressed and joined his visitor on the east-facing doorstep to let sunbeams warm them up. Before conversation Stands For Them roused himself, entered the cabin, and returned with steaming coffee in dented tin cups. When settled, Stands For Them turned to look past his guest, in this way inviting the younger who apparently had something to share.

Keeps The Mountain fiddled with the frayed cuff of his shirt, then looked skyward, "We are requested to smoke the pipe at Red Leaf's Ghost Dance encampment, for those gathered demand news from Valentine and Rosebud. And who better than freight teamsters? This comes from Red Leaf himself. And Short Bull too." Then as if to explain, "I am but the messenger. I am, like you, a man in between." Stands For Them was surprised that Keeps The Mountain had not heard of his choice to ride with the army scouts.

Keeps The Mountain looked down at his cup of coffee, "This request we dare not ignore." Stands For Them offered nothing at the obvious, instead slapping hands on knees and rising with a grunt to prepare his horse for the short journey to Red Leaf's camp.

As they rode south, Stands For Them admitted mild foreboding at this meeting. "Yes, he wants our information, but does Short Bull want more? I saw him yesterday. He surely knows Brings Three White Horses and I show interest in joining the army scouts."

It was midmorning when they arrived at Red Leaf Camp. As was custom, they stopped at the cabin of the aged Red Leaf to pay respects and leave a small pouch of tobacco. They then surveyed the surroundings. Many small cabins and a few tipis. Keep The Mountain noticed but one tendril of smoke signaling what must be Short Bull's summer tipi. Stands For Them scratched at the tipi flap to announce their arrival.

The pair waited. Shortly came a cough inviting them to stoop to enter the murky interior.

Standing erect, neither could at first see much of anything. But vision was not necessary to feel a tent full of bodies and vague tensions.

Keep The Mountain spied two vacant places 'round the little fire, opposite the place of honor where Short Bull was tap, tap, tapping tobacco into the bowl of a long pipe.

Lowering himself to the ground using crossed legs only, Stands For Them could see this was no peace pipe. The beadwork and sashes signaled that today they would smoke the pipe of war.

The elfin Short Bull looked out at the world through hooded eyes. His features those of a sparrow hawk, a trademark bearing of dignity further amplified by recent Ghost Dance notoriety.

Short Bull lit the pipe. He lowered his head in what all assumed to be prayer, lips moving without sound. Then he held the pipe up to Father Sky, before finally drawing a single puff and starting the pipe around the circle. Minutes passed as each in turn held the pipe reverently and inhaled/exhaled, smoke rising from each private invocation.

At length this formerly minor medicine man of the Wazhazha reclaimed the pipe, replacing it in the antler holder, then smiled fatherlike in the direction of Keeps The Mountain. But though his gaze fell on the younger man, his question was for Stands For Them:

"Son of Elk Robe, bring us what news you will of the iron horse, of Valentine, of Rosebud."

Through hazy air Short Bull then shifted his gaze to Stands For Them as if looking at a tree stump. *He must know I soon saddle up as an army scout—in his eyes I ride with the enemy*, thought Stands For Them. Whatever his opinion of Nawica Kicijin, Short Bull tilted his head, ears eager for new information. Stands For Them had the floor.

And so he began: "Red Fish and I come just yesterday from the long straight lines of the iron horse, delivering soldiers to Valentine station as geese land on springtime lakes, one flock after another. These wasicu are armed with guns bigger than ours, they unload tall horses, much food. And they come to encircle the ghost dancers, to confront them. But first they will try to arrest you."

Then the ill-mannered words he suddenly realized he must say, risking the enmity of a tipi full of less than friendly men, and the wrath of Short Bull—

"For the sake of our people, you can turn yourself in now. Else they'll fire on us all. They will treat you no worse than they treated *Sinte-Gleska* so many years ago."

At these words, Keeps The Mountain put both hands on the ground as if to rise but did not, his eyes darting around the circle—Stands For Them had surely offended his Crow Dog-leaning hosts by invoking the name of the once briefly imprisoned and now martyred Chief Spotted Tail (*Sinte-Gleska*) of the peace-leaning branch of the Sicangu.

To Keeps The Mountain's relief, Short Bull sat motionless, his palms in the placid heavenward position. He even murmured in apparent appreciation of Stands For Them's frank assessment of the situation. At length he picked up the pipe, cradling it in the crook of his arm, before addressing the assembled:

"It is as son of Elk Robe says; many Long Knives come. I will call my people together on these waters and also on Pass Creek, and tell them to move forward to the safety of Pine Ridge Agency. Red Cloud will see that they are protected." He did not say if he would turn himself in. Silence fell as the south wind could be heard to shift northeast. With it came a staccato of heavy raindrops on the tipi canvas.

When next he spoke Short Bull raised his voice further, to be heard over the weather, "I will stay here alone. I do not want my people to have any trouble on my account. I tell them what I tell you today—I want nothing but what is right for me and my family. My brother White Thunder and my cousin Thumb have been killed for jealousy and now they want me. Go on, I will stay here; if they want to kill me, they are welcome."

Thus Short Bull ended the council and dismissed the young teamsters, who backed out of the tipi flap in a gesture of respect that seemed prudent.

Despite Stands For Them's prediction, the soldiers did not come, but instead massed on the reservation borders. Stands For Them had only repeated the prevailing opinion among teamsters, but ever after Short Bull would blame this son of Elk Robe for bringing ". . . blasphemy and lies" to that Red Leaf council. Yet Stands For Them was for Short Bull merely a minor player among men the ghost dancers called the tellers of the big lie. Short Bull often called them out by name, for they counseled against joining the Ghost Dance: American Horse, Charging Thunder, Spotted Horse, Fast Thunder, and Good Back.

As Stands For Them and Keeps The Mountain rode north from Red Leaf camp, they fell into a stilted conversation further complicated by a misty headwind. "These men in council do not know what to think of me," offered Keeps The Mountain. "I am young and unaffiliated and my family is not powerful. But surely you saw your bold words draw long faces on High Shield, and Broken Face, Burning Breast, and even Plenty Wolves. They are formidable, and you will need to watch out for them."

Stands For Them reflected on this, then explained his decision to challenge the higher-ranking Short Bull. "We are both Wazhazha, him by birth, I by adoption. So like it or not, we are brothers. I spoke as I did to protect the Wazhazha band."

Upon reaching one of few places on the trail sheltered by trees, they dismounted to offer their mounts the waters of a little spring. Each rolled a smoke using corn husks, cigarette papers being too dear. Stands For Them broke a long silence: "Keeps the Mountain, I live now without fear or regret. Have I not hung suspended from my own flesh on the Sun Dance tree, as sacrifice for the nation? Do I not have a war record? Have I not earned the right to support my tiyospaye by standing as an army scout? Our mission will be to save lives, not end lives. You may join the ghost dancers tomorrow. Or you may ride with me as a scout one day. The path of honor is a forked trail."

The pair remounted to proceed home on separate dirt trails. In gathering darkness a sliver of moon popped in and out of clouds. The Moon of the Rutting Deer.

November brought bold headlines to South Dakota broadsheets:

November 13 – "President Benjamin Harrison Authorizes War Department to Suppress 'Indian outbreak' "

November 20 – "More 9th Cavalry "Buffalo Soldiers" Arrive at Rosebud Agency"

November 26 – "Vaunted 7th Cavalry arrives at Pine Ridge Agency"

November 27 – "Mysterious False Messiah Appears at Pine Ridge"

People of all persuasions were anxious, twitching like a finger resting on the trigger of a loaded gun. In early December there came a knock at Stands For Them's door. "You are to report in two days to the red and blue tent, the new scouts' tent, there among the white tents of the big army garrison at Rosebud Agency."

When this call-up came, he needed only minutes to fetch his few possessions, for they were neatly arranged by the door. It took longer to catch his chosen horse for the coming hard riding of scout duty. Tokala was the gelding's name, for he moved like a big fox. Gelded as an older colt, Tokala retained a splash of stallion spirit.

Later that day Stands For Them could be seen trotting down the Red Road in the direction of Rosebud. He rode with straight back and high head, hoping to present to others the surety of his decision. He'd received a favored assignment: riding in an all-Lakota patrol of six scouts.

The day's travel was fair by early winter norms, but foul in the soul of every Lakota—for as Stands For Them journeyed along the Red Road towards the army garrison, he heard calamitous news. At first he saw only the distressed faces of fast-moving messengers, some on foot, some mounted. Finally he waylaid one of them: "What big news do you carry? I must know."

"Have you not heard? The wasicu and their Indian police murder Sitting Bull, merely on rumor that he supports the ghost dancers."

Only yesterday, so said the messenger, someone unwisely determined that Indian police could best secure Sitting Bull's peaceful arrest. The great intancan agreed to go to jail placidly, asking only that his specially trained dapple grey horse (a gift from Buffalo Bill following Sitting Bull's stint with the Wild West Show) be saddled and brought forward as dignified transportation.

Three times on the road to Rosebud, Stands For Them reined in Tokala to sit quietly in the saddle as another breathless tribesman retold the terrible story. Three times he listened in stunned silence to such details as were known, summarized best by the old camp crier Holy Door of the Ring Thunder settlement: "At the last minute, Sitting Bull's followers resisted. The old warrior and several others on both sides lost their lives among bullets. No one knows who shot first. But this is fair and true, the chief's white horse showed real magic. Oh, the wasicu claim the animal merely responded to gunfire, his cue to do tricks at the Wild West Show. But these were not tricks. Our people, police, and the dancers, saw it and all believe it—Sitting Bull's soul jumping from his fallen body into that of his spirit horse."

Stands For Them reached down from his saddle seat to give the old man a twist of tobacco for his telling of the story. "Thank you Holy Door. This day is bad medicine for all Lakotas."

His mind wrestled with, then with effort chased away new doubts as to his present course of action.

All this commotion slowed Stands For Them's progress so that as darkness fell he was obliged to sleep with friends near Ghost Hawk Lake. He accepted that this risked a late arrival to dawn's mustering in by the red and blue tent.

Next morning Stands For Them was indeed a bit late in joining his fellow scouts on their first day of action. Dismounting Tokala, Stands For Them rounded the corner of the Rosebud Agency grainery to find four of his fellow patrol members mounted and patiently waiting.

With relief he learned they were not waiting for him, but for One Feather, expected any minute with the day's orders. Before joining them, Stands For Them took a moment to contemplate these four horsemen whom he'd soon ride into the struggle beside: Thunder Hawk he'd known the longest, hunting partners all those many years ago in Canada, and even before.

Thunder Hawk was astride a fine black horse, and unlike the others wore his hair short in the wasicu style, the result of his prior brief stint in the U.S. Army's experimental all-Indian regular troop. A flannel scarf half covered a neck scar earned at the Little Big Horn. He appeared happy to be joining a patrol with the freedom to wear a mix of Indian and military garb. For him this meant an army-issue wool overcoat against the cold but also visible Lakota trappings—knee-high beaded moccasins, a bone pipe choker, fur-lined buckskin gloves, and a buffalo fur cap.

Beside him was Bear Dog, who had like Stands For Them taken refuge in Grandmother's Land. Relaxed and confident aboard his red horse—the broad-faced Bear Dog's unbraided hair fell black and thick to his waist, and among the locks was attached a lone eagle feather. Sewn haphazardly onto his right sleeve was a crossed arrows patch, which just that year had been authorized as the Indian scout insignia.

Little could Bear Dog imagine that 100 years later, when the Indian scouts were no more, this same crossed arrows insignia would be adopted by the U.S. Army Special Forces.

Leaning his right arm over the neck of his pale horse, the dour Eagle Man seemed underdressed for the clime. His army-issue overcoat was tied behind the saddle, leaving him clad in just a muslin shirt lavishly trimmed with long scalp locks, a brightly beaded wool scarf 'round his neck. His long hair was wrapped, not braided, using heavy red trade cloth. Nothing about him would tip off the casual observer that Eagle Man was either army scout or ghost dancing hostile. Yet any adult

Lakota would somehow know at a glance. Eagle Man was warrior to the core. It showed in his downturned mouth, his stony unblinking gaze. And like many a Lakota in this season of trouble, he might as easily have sided with the hostiles as with the "friendlies." Such a tendency to flexible allegiances ran deep in Eagle Man's tiyospaye. For you see, Eagle Man was nephew to Chat-Ka.

Last among the four horsemen lined up before Stands For Them was Brings Three White Horses. Lately he was often seen on a coltish buckskin, but today was astride the aging yet worthy former war pony Heavenly Runner, a pure white gelding. Brings Three White Horses looked snug in his army-issue fur cap and overcoat. From the side pocket of that coat protruded a small medicine bundle. Like most recruited scouts he still trusted the power of a medicine bundle, choosing to carry such a bundle into scout duty just as in the war parties of the 1870s.

Thus the five waited on that chill December dawn for One Feather, and the morning's orders.

Smiles emerged all around when at length One Feather trotted up on his fine little pony balancing a pot of steaming coffee at arm's length. Several pouches of Bull Durham roll-your-own protruding from a shirt pocket.

One Feather was the youngest member of the patrol, having attended Carlisle Indian School in Pennsylvania for one lonely winter of his youth. There he'd been forbidden to speak his mother tongue, instead learning some of the white man's strange, thick-tongue language. So despite his youth, bilingualism vaulted One Feather to a position as interpreter and titular patrol leader.

He motioned his new comrades to gather round for coffee and tobac-co, and to hear the day's orders as given by their new superior, Captain Shafter. Together they moved to the side of a nearby building sheltered from the wind but still in the sun, there to squat down and hear what One

Feather had to say. With so little breeze Stands For Them could take one of the little cotton pouches of Bull Durham and roll himself a cigarette. In one motion he struck the match and closed the sack by pulling on the yellow string with his teeth.

When everyone had either a coffee or roll-your-own, One Feather began, "We are told to ride northwest until seeing the village of Red Leaf. Our orders are to patrol but not enter this village and detain any ghost dancers who seek to cross Black Pipe Creek in the direction of the Stronghold."

"We are to detain hostiles only when their intentions are clear. Better that we are seen as the calming ones. Mediators between many factions." One Feather then showed off the piece of paper containing written orders of the day's assignment. Though none could read it, the paper carried authority, including the official name of their unit stamped at the top of the page: U.S. Army Rosebud Indian Scout Patrol No. 8.

Murmured conversation followed, ending with hurried swigs of coffee. At some unseen signal the six rose as one, moving to stand by the horses. Some rechecked their saddle and bridle. Stands For Them mounted straightaway. The patrol was soon moving from walk to trot and into the maelstrom of history.

Each had his private justification in riding forth. A couple desperately needed a scout's $10 monthly wage. Some had a score to settle with one or more ghost dancers. None would consider themselves as soldiers of fortune. And the six shared a common thread: They held at least grudging admiration for the defiant love of the old ways uniting the ghost dancers.

Today as on every day they'd hope not to see Governor Mellette's haphazard cowboy militia, the so-called Home Guard—a force said to carry "shoot first" orders when spotting any Indians on the move.

Icy winds whistled through badland spires. By midmorning the patrol overtook eight fellow Indians traveling, some by foot and some by thin horse. Their line of march was to Stands For Them inconclusive—were they moving towards one of many hostile encampments, or simply towards a safer place. His palms down motion signaled to others that tact would be needed.

As planned, one unarmed member of the patrol, this time Eagle Man, rode forward. He offered to build a fire and share what food, coffee, and tobacco could be spared. Only after the travelers agreed and a fire crackled did the rest of the patrol join the circle. Small talk followed. But when all eyes finally turned to the tall one, he gave assurances and the offer of an escort. Deep-throated Stands For Them excelled at this role. And today the travelers gladly accepted an escort to the tiny village of Hisle.

In time the patrol settled into a routine—Up before dawn, men and horses at the Rosebud flagpole for bugle call by 7:30, then came the patrol assignment requiring a one to three-hour ride from the cantonment. During such rides, Stands For Them and One Feather had grown adept at scanning the horizon for dust clouds, revealing those encampments with ghost dancers—the dust created by so many dancing feet.

As the season of long nights deepened, daily assignments became almost routine. Then a noteworthy exception. Out after dark and riding the banks of Black Pipe Creek, the patrollers eyes were drawn to a strange light on distant Medicine Butte. What they saw could be neither the Northern Lights, nor lanterns, nor fire, for the top of the butte was glowing blue. The six simply sat on their mounts and observed the spectacle in reverent silence, roused to continue home finally by chill night air. None discussed the light, not then, not ever. Each content with the mystery of it.

There finally came a day when the assignment was not routine. Captain Shafter, leader of all Rosebud army scout units, asked One Feather to translate for his comrades the latest intelligence report—

"Groups of young natives are moving westward from the village of Bad Nation and southward along the Cherry Creek Road connecting Cheyenne River Reservation. We believe they move to join the growing hostile camps further west. We are asked to turn them back, and take prisoners only when necessary." Finished, One Feather looked back at the captain for more words to translate:

"The army asks this patrol to set a checkpoint on the Red Road west from Bad Nation. Because we will be far from the agency, and many of us have relatives on Black Pipe Creek, we need not return every evening to the cantonment."

Stands For Them smiled at this news. It meant he'd be able to spend a few nights with his beloved tiyospaye—there to feel the warmth of brothers, sisters, aunts and nephews, hunka relatives and chatty elders.

Buoyed by prospects of adventure, the six began a four-hour ride to overnight at the midpoint village of Parmelee, from where they rose early to begin the final leg to the Red Road and the reservation's northern rim. As the patrol neared Cedar Butte, a chinook wind tousled the long manes of each horse and brought midwinter warmth to melt snow . . . and lift human and equine spirits yet higher.

As in the old days, they rode single file to make it difficult for unknown trackers to ascertain the group's size. But unlike the old days, they rode as befits an army unit—openly upon the ridge lines and on high ground to advertise their presence, and to better spot the renegades they sought to turn back.

Approaching Cottonwood Creek, Stands For Them and Brings Three White Horses dismounted to confer over moccasin tracks showing four persons bearing due west. Were they the marks of hostiles trying to get to the Stronghold? After minutes of close examination, Stands For Them settled the matter, "No, these are the tracks of men heading to the Porcupine village, for I recognize the limp of the elder Charging Bear. See? Right here, you will note how he drags the left leg."

Onward they rode. One Feather rode the lead as patrol corporal. Yet it was Eagle Man and Stands For Them, bringing up the rear, who most often formulated plans of action. Today was typical. "You know this Red Road country better than I, Nawica Kicijin, you make choices," said Eagle Man. Indeed, they had reached the heart of Wazhazha country, a place Stands For Them knew better than his own skin. But he waited a respectful time before offering his reply:

"For young men intent on joining the Ghost Dance, riding the bluffs of the White River will be too difficult. And moving towards Wanblee will be a detour. I predict they will move along the Red Road where it approaches Black Pipe Creek. This ancient place, like a funnel, lets creatures easily cross the rough country—a low passage between Hunte Paha to the south and badlands to the north."

"You once spoke of this place," offered Eagle Man. "If memory is true, it was that moment in your boyhood when your tiyospaye confronted the white buffalo herd that in truth was a herd clothed in new snow."

"Hou! That very place, Eagle Man. From there on the Red Road we can question any traveler as necessary. We'll find good cover and firewood for camping, and the distance is short to the villages along Black Pipe Creek." At these words Eagle Man urged his horse forward to ask One Feather to angle more northwesterly so as to connect with the Red Road at the favored place.

As they met the Red Road, a sky filling fast with low clouds brought gloom to a midwinter's late afternoon. The men dismounted to add another layer of clothing. Standing there they could see shod hoof prints of the big cavalry horses—many glances acknowledged the irony that native roads, so carefully chosen for ease of travel, had become avenues of invasion by the army, and would surely one day be avenues of colonization by homesteaders.

One foot in the stirrup, Thunder Hawk's sharp voice and gesture drew his comrade's attention to tiny specks in motion on a far ridge. There, nearly indistinguishable among a grove of cedars: three riders moving west at a steady trot. The trailing rider led a heavily loaded pack horse. At so great a distance it was impossible to make identification—perhaps they were wasicu cowboys—or worse yet, members of the Home Guard.

But sharp-eyed Bear Dog spotted the ageless sign of war. "Tails are tied up," he exclaimed. At these words each man remounted, and drew his rifle from the scabbard. Ten minutes of hard riding brought the patrol close enough to hail the westbound riders. The pursued looked over their shoulders, but kept riding recklessly as do men with so little to lose.

Stands For Them and Eagle Man urged their horses to the front of the group and gave those behind the palms-down signal to slow. Would it not be best to give the travelers a chance to stop for a parlay? Just then it became clear the pursued felt otherwise as they snake-whipped their horses from trot to full gallop.

Now it was horse against horse. Stands For Them's proud-cut Tokala bolted forward, jolting the trailing horses into similar effort. As they cut the distance, it was clear that ponies run fast on grass but even faster on oats. The scout ponies, benefiting from a daily quart of government grain, were literally "feeling their oats."

The hostile trio saw their lead diminishing, so reined up on a hillock to fumble for weapons. Stands For Them heard the whistling through air before he heard the sharp crack of two rifles discharging.

No one was hit. But the scouts stopped too, to better return fire. (On their first day of patrolling, the six had agreed to fire only when first fired upon.)

Distances were long, so whizzing bullets found no flesh. Years later, two of the patrol members claimed they intentionally fired warning shots well over the heads of the hostiles. But not every scout aimed high, for the luckless pack horse crashed to the ground, snow flying and legs thrashing. The lead rope was dropped and the three continued their westerly break at full gallop.

To Stands For Them this looked to be an extended pursuit. But within minutes one of the Ghost Dance ponies was falling behind. The rider urged his mount by heel and lash, but it was no use.

Then a strange scene played out in slow motion, the rider pulling up, throwing his gun to the ground before dismounting, and crossing his arms over his chest as if to say, "You may do with me as you please." With darkness looming, it seemed prudent to allow the other riders to escape. This the patrol did without discussion.

Stands For Them and the others were quick to recognize Red Tomahawk, a man of twenty winters who split his days between the villages of Bad Nation and Red Leaf. Acknowledging he was unarmed, the scouts slid their Springfield rifles back into government-issued leather scabbards.

Red Tomahawk's odd smile was not of one caught in the act. But icy-cold eyes, Ghost Dance leggings, and beneath a heavy coat his ghost shirt all said otherwise. Eagle feathers fluttered from his horse's mane and tail, its rump painted with defiant symbols.

Eagle Man came down off his horse, walked a few paces to pick up Red Tomahawk's rifle, then stepped back to allow private conferral with his comrades.

Stands For Them, coming up on his left side, was first to speak. "We need not embarrass Red Tomahawk by interrogating him, for plainly his horse, his trappings say this one is bound for the hostile camps. But we must act."

Eagle Man's sizable forehead showed creases worthy of a man twice his age. "Yes, we will take him prisoner. These are our orders. That he fired on us does not bother me, and perhaps we could let him go on the promise that he return to Bad Nation. But it grows dark, now past the hour of kindness. What's more, Bear Dog says this Red Tomahawk burned the cabins of two that resisted the Ghost Dance."

"Another storm comes with the dawn. Look at this sky," offered Stands For Them, "It is best for all if we take him back to Rosebud. He will have shelter and food there. Let the wasicu decide if he is to be freed tomorrow, or later."

Not one word was exchanged with Red Tomahawk in the process of taking him into custody—his slightly bowed head the only sign that he was now a prisoner of war.

The scouts showed deference to their prisoner, treating him almost as a fellow warrior while preparing for the trip to Rosebud Agency.

Stands For Them thought now of his own months as a prisoner of sorts at Fort Keogh ten years earlier. At his insistence, the prisoner would not be bound. But Red Tomahawk's horse would be connected by stout rope to one or another of the scout mounts. Against falling temperatures, they bundled Red Tomahawk in the spare Hudson Bay blanket One Feather always carried.

The six, now seven, were soon backtracking on the hallowed Red Road. Bear Dog and One Feather made a short detour to examine the burden of the fallen pack horse. They found the animal prostrate but still drawing shallow breath. Bear Dog administered the coup de grâce with a single shot. They resolved to present Captain Shafter with the pack's contents—small arms, cases of ammunition, winter clothing, pemmican, and two more "bulletproof" muslin ghost shirts.

Ten miles hence the patrol turned south for Parmelee, their waystation for warm meals, beds of straw, and the interrupted sleep that comes from taking turns watching over a prisoner. Brings Three White Horses was by now leading, his pony's eyes and hooves renowned for picking safe passage on moonless nights. All was still but for the iron sound of hoofbeats on frozen ground.

Entering Parmelee, a hamlet of only thirty or so log cabins, the scouts saw but two or three abodes with stove fires still burning. One belonged to the local Indian policeman Darkling. He would surely provide refuge for the night.

Thunder Hawk volunteered for the first and longest watch with the prisoner, as the Thunder Hawk and Red Tomahawk families were closely aligned. In an irony typical of the Sioux, a descendant of Red Tomahawk and a descendant of Thunder Hawk would one day marry to produce a child further binding the families—Loretta Red Tomahawk.

There had been another guest at the Darkling cabin when Patrol #8 arrived, a tall blonde lieutenant of the 9th Cavalry unknown to any of the scouts. At first light he assumed custody of Red Tomahawk, the pair reaching Rosebud before the others.

On the morning of his 27th enlistment day, Stands For Them was feeling settled in his role with Scout Patrol #8 as they rode northward from Rosebud Agency. But come midday, the open country they passed through grew darkly animated by many of the same running and riding messengers who days earlier had carried word of Sitting Bull's murder—though this time their lean forms and sunken faces revealed still deeper shock. Stands For Them asked Bear Dog to intercept the nearest messenger to learn what must be bad news.

As he returned Bear Dog ominously motioned for Stands For Them to come away from the others. By custom Stands For Them must be the first to hear, for only he had relatives among the Miniconjou. "Stands For Them, I must tell you hundreds of Miniconjou women and children, but some warriors too, have been gunned down by the Long Knives at Wounded Knee Creek." Stands For Them's head dropped and his eyes glistened. He would have grown up with many of the murdered. Yet it fell to him now to tell the others.

To his concerned comrades he repeated Bear Dog's words. Then, through trembling lips, "This news will send many neutral *Lakotas* stampeding into the Badlands. To the hidden Ghost Dance camps. We must learn more. Was it a battle, or a massacre? Is this the beginning of a war of extermination on our people of all persuasions?" After brief discussion, the patrol members agreed to follow Stands For Them's lead: to return immediately to Rosebud, to suspend duties . . . for the present at least. Each took separate lodging around Rosebud as usual.

Early next morning the six assembled in an abandoned cabin outside the agency, there to consider options. Bear Dog arrived first, started a fire in the small wood stove and boiled a pot of coffee. When all were present it was Eagle Man who stood up and looked to Stands For Them for a nod that would allow him to proceed. He was straight-backed and sure with his words:

"I had a dream last night," he began. "This dream was somewhat like our waking world. The oyate was in great panic. People fleeing in all directions. Dogs with tails between their legs, horses running through fences, birds scattering. Then I saw a man in white garment. His feet were covered by a low cloud. His right hand was on the head of a small child holding a pipe and small cross. His left arm outstretched downward but with the palm up, as a great bird might hold its wing." Eagle Man paused to test his still-too-hot coffee, looking briefly on the faces around him.

"This dream tells me that it matters less what side of the line we stand on today, but more in what we can do to calm the people. The dream commands that we continue to ride and walk and talk for peace among our tribesmen."

No one else stood to talk. Instead, every head pivoted from Eagle Man to the stony inscrutability of Stands For Them's face. Because he moved not a muscle, all knew that he endorsed the message of the dream. Each would weigh yesterday's news and be free to resign from the army scouts. But all chose to follow Eagle Man's interpretation and Stands For Them's benediction of the dream. For by now each of the six knew the Indian Scouts present at Wounded Knee had scattered at the first shooting. No scout had joined in killing their own people.

In the first days following the terrible news, One Feather's patrol was ordered to stop any Indian parties moving across the open prairie between Wounded Knee Creek and Bear-In-The-Lodge Creek. On Tuesday as the six rode upon iron-hard ground covered here and there with dirty snow, they chanced to cross the very massacre grounds.

At the site of the bloodletting, the military had quickly retrieved all their dead. Three days later, civilian contractors had buried most of the grotesque and frozen Miniconjou corpses in one mass grave. Body on body. Without ceremony. So Patrol No. 8 did not expect to come across bodies.

Because Stands For Them was the only Miniconjou in the patrol, the other scouts did precisely as the tall one did—dismounting to walk forward in the solemn way.

No living soul was visible. Despite thin winter sunshine, there was a murmur of gloom about the place. At the tall one's hand signal, the five held back as he walked alone among piles of blankets and patches of blood-stained snow. Then at his urging they joined him in roaming further among a landscape strewn with burned tipi poles, spent shell casings, odd torn rags of calico clothing, the occasional doll or toy.

Stands For Them led his comrades further along, examining one empty blanket after another, most of a color favored by women. Til at last they came to a ravine where deep within the thicket one blanket seemed not to be empty. Eagle Man stooped to pull back the shroud to expose the hollow-eyed frozen corpse of a girl of perhaps ten winters.

At this Bear Dog led the horses a respectable distance away. Stands For Them turned his face from both the corpse and his comrades. Then together they found a suitable level place on nearby high ground, taking turns to dig a grave in the hard earth with their one short-handled shovel.

From this high point they could see the disturbed earth over the long narrow mass grave, to the edge of which Stands For Them later walked alone. He spent some minutes pacing the length of the trench, back and forth, as if counting his steps. It would be months before he learned all the names, but Nawica Kicijin surely knew that below his feet were the freshly moldering faces of many a childhood friend.

As bitter wind increased, Bear Dog brought forward Stands For Them's horse. He and the others then retreated some distance, wondering what the Miniconjou would say or do.

After another grim scan of the horizon, as if it might hold some faint answer, Stands For Them said, "None can fail to see that this place we walk is no battlefield. This was a place where innocents died. I honor Eagle Man's dream. But have we made a dark mistake in taking up the army scout's rifle? Who dares say those taking up the Ghost Dance rifle are the greater danger to the oyate?"

He spoke now to One Feather and Eagle Man, the three forming the group's loose leadership. "We must know the full story. If you agree, then very soon we ride to the tent of Captain Shafter. We see what he believes happened here, and if he can persuade us that working as scouts can prevent such things from happening."

For a long time no one spoke or moved.

The anxious yipping of some unseen family of coyotes roused all six from the malaise of the place. They ended the day as they'd started it, riding single file at a high trot. Of that place all would surely agree with the later words of Black Elk, "A beautiful dream . . . died there, there in the bloody snow."

Next morning, gathering outside the scout tent on the edge of Rosebud Agency, Stands For Them stood between Captain Shafter and One Feather. It was a chance to report what he'd seen at Wounded Knee, and ask his big question from yesterday which he did through a combination of sign language, doleful expressions, and coarse oral translation by One Feather.

Captain Shafter frowned, weighing the question briefly before answering. "I have heard different accounts of what happened at Wounded Knee Creek," he said. "Your description of the battlefield, and blankets and other personal effects, it is powerful. I can only tell you this—the scout patrols that work for me ride to educate, to reconcile, to pacify. Not to war with their own."

The officer paused, straightening his tunic, playing with his considerable mustache while considering what he might do in a concrete way to reengage these visibly disaffected young men.

Turning to One Feather, he used the simplest, most easily translated words, "One sleep ago word came of a small band of Hunkpapa, mostly frightened women and children. They are huddled on Porcupine Creek now, all former followers of Sitting Bull. Like Big Foot's people, they drifted south, and are now confused, leaderless, and sure their fate will be like those on Wounded Knee Creek. In one sleep, will you ride with me to their camp? Together we may convince them to come in to the agency. It is safer that we do this rather than cavalry."

Wanting but not expecting acquiescence, the captain paused for effect. "No more Wounded Knee sadness in this country. Tomorrow will you ride with me, scouts?"

Two or three nodded in apparent agreement. Thunder Hawk and Bear Dog each brought one hand to the side of their months, signaling to their tribesmen that the captain was leading them as he would dogs. Stands For Them wavered. The six briefly discussed in their tongue before Eagle Man and Stands For Them instructed One Feather what to say to Shafter: "We will ride with you to rescue these refugees, but will from this day ride as members of the Lakota nation and not the army."

Then the six proceeded to that morning's routine assignment within the cantonment; caring for horses. Thunder Hawk was upset to discover his fine black horse had sustained a nasty rump bite from some other horse during the night.

At dawn the next day, Captain Shafter was waiting by the flagpole, as agreed, for Army Indian Scout Patrol No. 8. Stands For Them rode up and by hand sign acknowledged Shafter, then in spite of himself took in the splendor that was a mounted cavalry officer in full winter uniform— long wool double-breasted coat with shoulder scales, open to reveal yellow buttons and braids trimming a stiff-collared tunic, high black spit-polish riding boots over sky-blue trousers, Spanish-type spurs, cavalry hat with brim curled up on one side, a short saber on the left of his slender waist, a holstered Colt-45 on the right. All balanced on an officer's saddle over the withers of a leggy, glossy-black thoroughbred gelding with white blaze.

Soon Patrol No. 8 and the captain were soon urging their mounts towards the big bend of Porcupine Creek. All had expected to find the Hunkpapas straight away. But Stands For Them, first to top the bluff above the bend, saw the previous campsite abandoned. Descending to the floodplain and stirring the campfire ashes, he reported to those following that the fugitives had left eighteen hours earlier.

The traces of the refugees, easily followed at first, led west by northwest. Soon, however, a light snow following cold rain made tracking difficult.

Two hours later the captain and scouts very nearly rode past the new bivouac of the fugitives, for it appeared no more than a trash heap among thickets. Sheets of filthy canvas rigged as pitiful tipis were barely visible among the chokecherry shrubs. Further back were four tiny smokeless fires banked against the cold wind, each flicker surrounded by huddled and blanketed figures of indeterminate age and gender.

Without being asked, five of six scouts held back, leaving the captain and One Feather to approach by slow horse. One Feather carried a makeshift white flag. The captain had been led to believe there might be five men of warrior age, but as they approached, he counted only four, sitting together 'round one of the fires.

Upon seeing the intruders, a pair of rawboned men jumped to their feet in a manner neither friendly nor threatening. The captain and One Feather stopped to display their empty hands. One Feather very slowly dismounted and made the sign for "peace." None could venture what lay under the blankets of these loyalists to the fallen Sitting Bull.

The two on their feet were very young, perhaps not fifteen winters. It was a dangerous age—boys just past the apprentice warrior stage, cocksure and unpredictable, seeking ways to prove their manhood.

Each side sized up the other—The shorter of the Hunkpapa lads, White Wolf, had a proud, careless sneer. To his right was the frowning Young Skunk, a lean youth of tall and soon to be muscled frame. Canceling these demeanors was the simple fact that each was beaten down by bitter cold, hunger, and the desolation of place and season.

Captain Shafter saw the pathetic stragglers as no threat, unlikely to bolt for the Stronghold. Still, he had to consider them free-roaming and armed sympathizers of the martyred Sitting Bull. So he asked One Feather to summon Stands For Them and Eagle Man forward so the four might confer.

With bowed heads, they reached quick consensus that no effort be made to disarm the young men at the first fire—the error of Wounded Knee not to be repeated here.

But there was no agreement on how to proceed. Shafter pointedly deferring. Should the band be taken into protective custody?

In the end, Stands For Them's measured words carried the day— "These people are not fit to travel today. We should leave them what rations and blankets we can spare and come again in one sleep to escort them to the shelter of Rosebud Agency." Looking at the captain, he then said, "But can we promise no soldiers will come with us, and there will be no confiscation of horses?"

Hearing the translated words, Captain Shafter nodded approval. Closer to the fire a three-way discussion followed, where One Feather won acceptance of these terms from White Wolf and Young Skunk. Extra rations and a small government wall tent were left with the Hunkpapas. And after promising to return without soldiers, the patrol was on its way back to the cantonment.

Just as promised, the scouts returned next morning to escort the Hunkpapas to Rosebud agency. The trip was a slow-motion affair, and uneventful, though Stands For Them's sharp eye noted the young warriors concealed sidearms under their blankets.

So it was that members of Scout Unit No. 8 were again able to find some purpose in their duties, if only for a few more days.

The white man's New Year came and went.

The 6th day of 1891 was just another winter day for Lakota scout patrol No. 8, with this exception: Their number was now five. Brings Three White Horses had resigned to return permanently to his tiyospaye on Black Pipe Creek. He'd experienced bad dreams, nightmares really, ever since their day at Wounded Knee. The morning's assignment was to range further west than usual, in hopes of waylaying ghost dance couriers thought to be relaying messages along the corridor formed by Potato Creek.

The patrol saw not a soul on this day until topping a ridge to overtake three women walking against the wind. The oldest among them was Whenona, a medicine woman known to the patrol for her healing powers. The trio, affiliated with no faction, were returning from gathering medicinal plants. Though Whenona could not have seen the wound on Thunder Hawk's horse, she walked behind the animal to place her hand and then a poultice on the gash. The threesome shared fears of the Home Guard, the soldiers, then gratefully accepted escort to their cabin on the slopes of *Waŋblí Hoȟpi Pahá*, the Eagle's Nest Butte.

Thus ended the last action of note for One Feather's scout troop. Two days later their forty-day enlistments expired. Back at Rosebud Agency on the appointed day of mustering out, the five were offered a last chance to re-enlist even though hostilities by all accounts were waning. Following Stands For Them's lead, one after another declined reenlistment. For them Wounded Knee could not be forgotten, or forgiven.

In the first quiet days back in his cabin on the banks of Black Pipe Creek, Stands For Them reflected on all he'd seen and done. Was the Messiah Craze, as certain elders came to believe, the tribe's last desperate attempt to assimilate Christianity into Lakota religion and culture? Was it a big lie, or a thing of beauty?

As a blue winter sunset marked the end of his third day home, Stands For Them was unsure. But he suspected that in some future moon many Lakotas would choose, as he had chosen, to carry both the pipe and the cross. A swelling heart said this was the end of his twenty-year identity as hunter, warrior, scout.

The widowed Stands For Them settled back into mundane reservation life, picking up work here and there, though jobs were scarce. Approaching middle age, he once or twice overheard younger men call him *wakanlica*—philosopher or "one who commands stones." Stands For Them only smiled.

By 1893 Stands For Them made room under his roof for his destitute maternal grandmother. Running Horse Woman lived two more years. And though she could summon her voice only on certain mornings, Running Horse Woman managed to pass along many an ancient tradition to her grandson.

Her stories inspired further resolve to carry the Lakota culture to future generations. But already forces were lining up to oppose those who would carry the traditions. The biggest opposition would come from within Stands For Them's own family.

Chapter Fourteen

Waging Peace
1911

When Stands For Them opened the door, the runner's face spoke of unhappy but not unexpected news—his father Elk Robe was dead.

This messenger was shirtless, copper-skinned and angular in that way of all the Singing Goose boys. Treads The Clouds had come bounding west along the Red Road from Elk Robe's loggie at the head of Cottonwood Creek, all the way to the Stands For Them home.

It was 1911—already a sad year, for the government had taken one final bite out of the once 100,000-square-mile Great Sioux Reservation. Mellette County would be South Dakota's last Indian land opened to homesteaders. Already these scratchers of the ground were rushing in with their flimsy tarpaper shacks and horse-drawn plows, barbed wire fences and sun-scorched little patches of wheat, oats, corn. It thus seemed a logical season for Elk Robe to let himself slip over to the spirit world.

He'd passed old secrets to many a willing listener. But one confidence he'd shared only with Stands For Them: It had happened the previous year as Elk Robe stood unsteadily beside his oldest son in gathering darkness to marvel at the great Flaming Arrow hanging in the west. The wasicu called it Halley's Comet, and claimed it was the same luminescence returning from seventy-six winters earlier.

Elk Robe asked Stands For Them to repeat this claim, then shook his gray head. "If this be possible, then it was seventy-six winters ago that I, a wee boy, first marveled at this same Flaming Arrow. My mother, Pale Antelope, held me up to be bathed in this holy light. She always said the strange blaze meant my life would be long and fruitful."

Shaking his head again and looking at the comet, the aged one told his son that it must be a messenger, sent to comfort an old man who really didn't want to limp through four more seasons of stifling heat, biting cold and meager rations.

"Your grandmother, Pale Antelope, spoke truth when first we saw the night sky's Flaming Arrow, for life *has* been long and fruitful. Tonight we look upon this same brightness, and I believe this a comforting omen that I will soon walk the spirit trail— surely before this moon next year."

By the winter of 1910/11 Elk Robe suffered from a rattling cough, and his arthritis worsened. On especially bad days he would hitch horses to wagon and travel the six miles to find some solace in his son's house. On one such trip, Elk Robe brought with him his splendid ceremonial regalia, crowned with a war bonnet of eagle feathers reaching to the ground. He left it with his son, the only sign that Elk Robe had once been more than what the archivists maintained he was: a minor headman. The Lakota had highly visible leaders like Sitting Bull, Red Cloud, Gall. But they also maintained a shadow leadership, ones like Elk Robe, beyond the reach of government agents, beyond the history books.

With Elk Robe gone Stands For Them found others looking to him now. This rising status was possible precisely because he did not seek celebrity. For any Lakota peace leader, humility was the highest virtue.

But two things more had elevated him. One was of his doing. One was beyond his control:

For so many years a widower, Stands For Them in time found or was found by Cora—small in stature but mighty in devotion to traditional Lakota values. Mightier than himself, he conceded privately. Cora's quick, keen eyes gathered much information from a scene or a stranger and had discerned something lasting in the tall one. She offered her suiter, Stands For Them, the beaded moccasins of the betrothal acceptance. He put them on.

Even on her marriage day, she spent four hours bent to the task of designing and creating purses, pouches, and quilted blankets, all for others. Cora was an Eagle Wolf, making her a member of that Wazhazha subtribe once so powerful and mystical.

With their wedding just hours away, Stands For Them watched her handiwork closely for clues to the Wazhazha way of things. By marrying Cora he would henceforth be Wazhazha and would be expected to know certain things. He had much to learn of the Wazhazha Lakota way of life.

She obliged his curiosity: "Look on this side of the beadwork. You will see here I have included the symbol of the snake, and here on the other side the lines are of water flowing downward. We Wazhazha are connected by these symbols to the underworld. To the mother force that is the cool, damp earth." He watched her hands moving nimbly, soulfully in transforming utilitarian items into something more with her symbol-filled beading.

Not long after this thing of their own doing, this marriage, there came the thing from beyond. It arrived as would a thunderbolt—they were parents of twins. And better yet, twin girls. In Lakota mythology, twin girls were a fortuitous sign indeed, for the first daughter emerging was seen as representing the hunting or meat culture. Cora named her Julia. The second daughter symbolized the vegetative gathering/planting culture. The underworld. Stands For Them named her Myra.

Sire of twin daughters, swift to listen, slow to speak, slow to wrath, a seeker of consensus—this was Stands For Them, to all but his enemies the model peace chief. He became, like his father and grandfather, a contrarian headman, the sort who would say, "Look, the people are going. I must follow them, for I am their leader."

Days before his death, Elk Robe had with trembling hand summoned Stands For Them to his side for what would be a passing of the torch. Others in the room watched intently, but dared not inch close enough to hear their private conversation:

"I know you see, son, that my remaining sunrises are as pebbles in a baby's hand. I wish you to recall that sacred place on the bluffs of the Big River. You know the place, near where you killed your first antelope so long ago. But you do not yet know the secret of that place."

Stands For Them gave a nod to encourage the old man to continue.

"There is a small cave hidden on that river bluff. I wish you to travel there one day, and peer inside. It is so small that only a child could enter, but if you put your head in the opening, you will behold a blue flame that never dies."

Elk Robe could not summon the breath to continue, but in pausing his eyes shone as if he again saw that mysterious place. After a few labored breathes, Elk Robe continued to describe from memory what Lewis and Clark had first reported a century before, the Burning Bluffs of the Missouri River where subterranean coal seams belched smoke but rarely fire.

Stands For Them knew the famed sulfurous place but could recall no one who had seen a cave with such a visible, undying flame. He understood that Elk Robe was asking him to make a pilgrimage.

"Son, my father's mother saw this as the eternal light of *Wakan*. Journey there. And do not share this secret until you are as old as I . . . and then with but one person. Perhaps a son, or a grandson. This will protect the flame." Stands For Them wondered then how he could make such a pilgrimage given that he owned neither automobile nor a horse wagon capable of such a trip.

But today there were more pressing matters, for Elk Robe breathed no more. Stands For Them's eyes glistened but offered up no tears as he bid the children to play outside before calling Cora to his side. "We must consider preparations for Elk Robe's body."

"As you say, Nawica Kicijin." But when she bustled off to retrieve previously cached sacred plants meant to anoint a body, Stands For Them gently called her back. A sliver of amber light brightened the west-facing wall behind his head. "In the morning, my *tawechoo*. Do not trouble yourself now as the sun is setting." Cora knew this to be his way of inviting deeper conversation. So she settled herself at his left hand and asked a question for which she already knew the answer.

"Will you take his name now that he is dead?" A Miniconjou Lakota man sometimes assumed a father's more renowned name, but only after the patriarch was dead.

"No, I will keep my Stands For Them. I feel much power and a big story to my name, and will not put it away." At this the thought of his father's cold, stiff body darkened Stands For Them's face.

Cora took note, and knowing how recollections often soothe, she beckoned her husband to speak of the deceased.

"My earliest memories of father were at winter storytelling. I can see him now. Moving with quick steps 'round the fire but speaking slowly, emphasizing every word in measured cadence forcing listeners to await the next word. His every movement mimicked the action of the story . . . so even those beyond earshot might divine the meaning of his tale.

"Do you remember how he chose words so that every ear at the fire might hear one of three tales hidden in the story? As a boy I understood the simple child's story. Later I could peel that away to reveal the moral meant for young adults. But rarely did I understand the deepest, holiest wisdom, things that made for grunts and smiling nods among the elders." As the couple continued nodding, talking, they moved outside to a place where they could watch the children at play.

"Wakanlica," Cora said, pausing for emphasis—she had never before called him this name reserved for a band's holy philosopher. "You are as of today the bearer of the stories and lessons for the people of this valley."

"Perhaps. But will my memory be strong enough?"

Cora's lopsided smile hinted at what others proclaimed—that her Stands For Them held all five male virtues: bravery in battle, prowess as a hunter, generosity towards widows and orphans, skill as a horseman, and firm knowledge of the sacred ceremonials. Storytelling was among the most valued of sacred ceremonials.

"Your memory will not be found wanting if from this day you stand up and begin to tell the stories. You yourself have said every story connects to some landmark of our nation. Wisdom sits in places. So as you think of certain mountains, and rivers, and paths connecting them, you will surely recall the story relating to each. Your father said the tales reside not in our heads, but are stored on the land. Among our nation everything that must be saved must be said out loud. By one who remembers. You are that one."

"You speak a truth I cannot ignore." With these words, Stands For Them took up his father's legacy.

Elk Robe's wake was to be held on the opposite side of Cedar Butte, some miles from Stands For Them Flats. The Red Road made travel easy for the many on Black Pipe Creek who thus ventured to Cottonwood Creek.

As the years passed, there came a knock on Stands For Them's door. It was his daughter Julia and her new husband Charles Moccasin Face. "Could we move into the little room in the back?" Yes, for the bride always returns with her husband to her birth tiyospaye. Had he not himself initially moved in with the Eagle Wolf clan upon marrying Cora?

The young couple soon had a fine baby boy. Stands For Them could now dream of living long enough to pass his collected wisdoms to little Charles Jr.

It was not to be. Stands For Them's chain of unbearable losses would continue. Charles Jr. died in the week he took his first steps. There being no autopsies available, no one ever knew why. Her baby gone, Julia grew listless, disinterested. She died of the White Death (tuberculosis) four months later during the Hard Moon.

With these dual deaths, Stands For Them occupied ground no parent or grandparent is built to stand on—having outlived every possible heir. Nation, Tall Woman, Myra, Julia, Moccasin Face, others. Most lost to the White Death.

With no male heir, and advancing age meaning no such prospects, Stands For Them resolved that prior to his own passing he must select someone to carry forward Elk Robe's wisdoms. He cast about for this person and saw great early promise in one young relative: a sister's oldest, the nephew Moses Bull Tail.

Moses was almost as tall as his uncle, whom he looked to with reverence in his youth. He was round shouldered, and a meaty face gave him a pinched if not disdainful look. In a reservation world without jobs or the adventures of war, horse stealing, and the hunt, he sometimes saw little option for a young man beyond the pursuit of pleasure.

For Stands For Them time was short. With every passing year more pieces of Lakota culture, art, and religion slipped away. Even the fireside storytelling was fading in most places outside of the Black Pipe Valley. After Elk Robe's passing, his own death no longer seemed so many years off. Doubts grew concerning his choice of a vessel into which he could pour this knowledge.

The old man was sitting on what passed for his front porch. A 1919 Dodge careened past the Stands For Them place eastbound on the Red

Road, trailing a plume of fine dust. The car had caught his attention, for rare was the native person who owned an automobile. The driver, a native Stands For Them did not recognize, was going way too fast. But he could see Bull Tail in the passenger seat, clearly drunk and holding a .22 rifle with which he took shots at nothing in particular. When all was quiet again Cora watched wide-eyed as her dependably mild-mannered peace chief threw his tin coffee cup against the wall, jaw muscles bunching up. Then he unsheathed the knife he wore infrequently, walked to a tree stump, and flung the weapon, quivering, into the stump. Seven decades of indignities on one so dignified—bursting forth.

Oh how Stands For Them had wished this nephew and *hunka* 'son' Bull Tail might have been the chosen vessel. But Bull Tail walked the path of pleasures—liquor, heavy smoking, driving cars faster than the local dirt roads were built for. And what of the rumors of abusive interactions with women? Surely this one had little time and even less inclination for learning the old cultural virtues.

"When I fall," Stands For Them wondered, "who shall I throw the torch to? Who will be strong enough to catch it?" He had honored a father's dying wish by traveling to the Missouri bluffs, where after hours of searching he'd found the tiny cave with the flickering blue flame of Wakan. But whose ears would he pass *this* secret to?

In the seasons following the deaths of Julia and little Moccasin Face, Stands For Them carried grief as he always had, without expectation or even desire that it be taken away. Moreover, the gray curtain made him wish all the more to gift the oyate by selecting a new disciple. Someone to take the place of nephew Bull Tail, by this time languishing in an off-reservation jail. He found his new and unlikely anointed one among the Cottonwood Creek/Running Bird cabins—a brother of the young Singing Goose courier who two decades earlier had brought news of Elk Robe's death.

John Singing Goose was his name. Stands For Them favored the young man for his open face, his earnest ways. Almost fifty years the wakanlica's junior, frail in stature especially beside his towering mentor, John Singing Goose was mild-mannered to the fringes of shyness.

Yet Singing Goose had what Stands For Them sought. He was young enough to carry the stories far into the future. He was humble in spirit, with little chance that ego would compete with the trove he'd carry forward. And in practical terms, he possessed a nearly new wagon pulled by the strongest horse team around.

Early in their friendship, Stands For Them quizzed Singing Goose to ensure he understood the stakes. "We are a people of oral history-keeping. It only takes one inattentive generation to lose these stories which have been faithfully passed on for hundreds of years. The wasicu have tried to create this lost generation by sending our children away to boarding school. Forbidding them to speak our mother tongue."

Singing Goose nodded his understanding.

So it was that Singing Goose became apprentice to an old man praying over the many in need of a steadying presence. At first the pair ministered to families less than an hour away. But as word spread, the old one and Singing Goose ventured further afield—limited only by how far the horses could proceed and then return in the light of one day.

The wagon made steady if slow progress from cabin to cabin. This allowed for much time in conversation and teaching: "Singing Goose, I wish that you look now upon the four reins you use to control the direction and pace of your horse team."

Singing Goose briefly contemplated his hands holding four reins, then brightened, and answered, "Yes, wakanlica, I understand that "four" is the most powerful number for our people."

"Good. But tell me why this is so." Singing Goose looked straight ahead without attempting an answer.

At length Stands For Them spoke, "Consider that all holy things are in sets of four. First the four Lakota classes of gods, though of course all gods merge into one God/mystery that our ancestors discovered as *Wakan Tanka*. Then ponder our four sacred colors. But now look further my son—above this earth are four aspects of light: sun, moon, shooting stars, and standing-still stars. There are four directions, four seasons. Time itself is composed of only four measures—day, night, month, and year. There are four parts to all plants, root, stem, leaf, fruit. We are one of four types of creatures—crawling, flying, four-legged, and two-legged. My life and yours is divided four ways—infancy, childhood, manhood, old age. Also, the maidens that I trust you gaze upon, these young women seek every spring the grama grass bearing four heads. If they find one it is a rare and wonderful sign of romantic luck."

"So, Singing Goose, watch closely—for I carry out daily tasks always in sets of four. You are encouraged to do the same."

Miles later, Stands For Them thought of the deaths young Singing Goose must witness in these rounds, so offered him a paradox: "Why do the dying mourn an earthly future they will miss, yet find me one man who mourns the eternity all of us missed before birth." With this unanswerable, Stands For Them joined his acolyte in silence.

After three miles of riding so, Stands For Them turned to a pupil unsure of why his mentor was today so dogged with lessons, "Let us consider now this road, the Red Road. It may not look like much more than parallel dirt paths. But a well-traveled trail like this, in the center of a once nomadic nation such as ours, is more than it appears. Roads here were also cemeteries, for until recently it was necessary to bury any who died while we traveled. These ancient pathways are also holy cemeteries."

The pair glanced over the horses' heads to see Cleve Berry bent to some labor.

Cleve heard the jingle-jangle of harness and looked up from the brutish task of replacing a gate post to see Singing Goose's wagon rolling west. He'd known Singing Goose first as a lad of sunny disposition—now as a mild-mannered young man said to be wooing the sharp-tongued Belle Pretty Boy. Cleve wondered at the wisdom of such a union.

Cleve had often seen the old man and the young man plying the Red Road side-by-side on Singing Goose's wagon. The cowboy knew only that they seemed always in conversation, and always on some mission. He could not know they were delivering holy plants, laying hands on the sick, comforting the hopeless, surrendering dead babies to the arms of a tree far from official eyes.

One chill dawn, the pair rolled up to the Little Eagle cabin. A tendril of smoke spoke of the meager stove fire within. Of the poverty within.

Before dismounting the wagon, Stands For Them braced Singing Goose for what to expect. "Olivia, youngest daughter of old Little Eagle, lost her baby in childbirth just days ago. And Little Eagle himself is bedridden with a bloody cough that since the baby died has only gotten worse."

Singing Goose nodded grimly, while manhandling the parfleche off the back of the wagon box. They advanced on the cabin side by side. Coming over the threshold, Singing Goose took a seat on a small barrel in the corner, while Stands For Them moved 'round the dimly lit room greeting everyone with a nod and a grave smile. He ended by pulling up a chair beside the bed of old Little Eagle, then inviting Olivia to do the same.

As always Singing Goose marveled at how people leaned into Stands For Them's deep voice and measured motions. He watched with expectation for a moment when something wondrous might happen. But if Singing Goose was a true believer, having seen many rise from their deathbed after Stands For Them's hand passed just above the skin in the area of distress . . . well, Stands For Them himself was not always so sure.

Though he publicly touted the merits of prayer and intercession, Stands For Them was equally sure that many of his famed healings happened on their own. He understood that when patients believed in his medicine, they became partners in a body-mind-spirit healing. The old man never claimed to know more than a sliver of the great mystery. But this was often enough.

All watched as he meticulously unpacked seven items from his sacred bundle—a gourd rattle decorated with beads, a small drum, an eagle bone whistle, a sprig of sage bundled with sweet grass for incense, a small wooden crucifix, and finally an aromatic ointment that filled every nostril.

Singing Goose knew what came next. Carefully arranging the retrieved items on a badger pelt, Stands For Them then paused before dipping into his well-worn medicine bag to retrieve the banded tail of a special animal, one of his totem animals.

Then he began in a firm voice, "Here is the tail of the only four-legged so clean that it washes its food before consuming. A brave creature that is also cunning. We call on this four-legged known as "protector" and "the little doctor," with human-like fists . . . fists that recall the healing hand."

In this way Stands For Them believed he healed not through his human powers but instead channeled the healing spirit of clever raccoon.

Stands For Them then directed the slightest nod Singing Goose's way, signaling the young man to retrieve a bit of food, previously wrapped and placed in the parfleche. The apprentice then took this food around the room for all to see before exiting the cabin. Singing Goose walked with measured steps the short distance to a slow flowing rivulet, where upon a suitable rock he placed the food offering, a beseeching of the raccoon to consider restorative blessings for three souls: old Little Eagle, his grieving daughter, and her lost baby.

Singing Goose reentered the house to a hush. Heads were bowed, then lifted up one by one as a barely audible murmur arose from Stands For Them's throat. But just as thunder rumbles distantly before growing ever louder, the murmur grew to be discernible words. Words to fill the room—More a series of chants, truth be told, a curious mix of the pipe and the cross. Bible parables, Lakota sayings, long ago Caledonian wisdoms. All offered to soothe, to galvanize, to restore.

Stands For Them now turned from the gathering, kneeling beside the bed so that none could see his face. A sound entered the far corner of the room. It seemed more animal than human, and had no discernable source. All gazes went from Stands For Them, to the corner, and back again.

When Stands For Them arose, his eyes had taken on the "far looking" quality. Singing Goose had seen this look many times. He waited, expectant. By this visit's end he saw the sick and forlorn lifting eyelids and chins.

This "praying over" visit, like so many others, lasted more than two hours. Before leaving, Stands For Them touched his hand to the top of Olivia's forehead, then placed her small hands within his. He repeated this gesture upon turning to old Little Eagle. Here the contrast was sharp: though men of nearly like age, Stands For Them's hands—big, strong, leathery—enveloping frail hands covered with parchment-thin skin no longer able to conceal spidery blue-green veins.

It was time for the leaving, which meant a polite refusal of offered gifts—tobacco, or pemmican, perhaps a beaded sash or an eagle feather, and in this case food, these items easily declined. But gifts of a certain magnitude, perhaps a pony, were a problem, for it then became insulting to decline. The items of food offered today were better left for the many hungry mouths of Little Eagle's tiyospaye. At length the pair slipped through the door, so tall and so short, retreated to their wagon and the patient team, then quietly departed.

Wagon wheels were soon creaking and rolling over the hill to the next sadness . . . and the relative quiet provided an opportunity for more lessons. "Singing Goose, you know that our sacred symbol is the circle. Let us look to the four wheels, circles really, supporting this wagon. We spoke of the holy number four recently. See each wheel: See that the iron rims have no beginning, no end. See how most of the wheel is in motion, yet at the very center of each wheel there is a still, calm point."

Singing Goose nodded at the obvious, but his eyes widened at the prospect of a deeper meaning in something so commonplace.

He listened as Stands For Them explained. "Time is something of an illusion when it travels the straight line. But time is closer to the source when traveling in a circle—the sacred hoop. For does nature not present its best spectacles making circles? Witness the sun, the moon, the seasons, the path of a raindrop from cloud to ground to stream to lake, then rising as mist back to the cloud. Is this not a circle?"

The road angled up now, and both horses leaned into the breast collars. After gaining the top of Cedar Butte, Singing Goose glanced up at Stands For Them as if inviting talk. Twenty minutes later he repeated the gaze, to no effect. In due course Stands For Them said: "Singing Goose, silence is the friend that will never betray you."

Within this hoop of time Nawica Kicijin found his influence growing, becoming a nameless entity but certainly something more than *Heyokha Kaga*, the traditional healer.

Seasons slipped by. Singing Goose's wagon wheels turned less often. Stands For Them was past eighty winters now. And even though requests for his ministrations came as often as ever, the body and the weather needed to be just so before he dared dispatch a runner to summon Singing Goose.

He'd sent the runner on this day. Morning sun and a dusting of wet snow met Stands For Them as he opened the door. "Warm enough," he said to a disapproving Cora as he tested the air with a hand. "Warm enough for today's important visits." With breakfast nearly finished, a faint clip-clop grew steadily louder as the Singing Goose horses circled into the yard.

Stands For Them approached the wagon and tried clambering up beside his pupil, but had to wait for a boost from Singing Goose.

When both were settled, the young man shared the rumors then roving up and down the valley. "Words on the wind say there was a special meeting before this recent snow. A secret gathering of old men whose names you know. The people are saying that you, *pejuta wacasa*, will be offered the valley's title of intancan."

Singing Goose's mention of the rumor brought a smile and measured response from Stands For Them. "In recent years, Singing Goose, we have seen our world grow smaller. The chance for greatness in horse raids, scouting, hunting are long gone. With these adventures dead, old ones like me have fewer things to pass to a younger generation."

"I continue, when asked, to offer guidance in the gentler arts. Praying, healing, storytelling. Even so, I believe my name is proposed as intancan not because of my deeds. Rather because I am simply old. If the intancan eagle feather is offered, I will refuse it."

With these words the matter seemed settled, and they rolled up to the home of Brings Three White Horses, around which were gathered the wagons and saddle horses of this old friend's large tiyospaye. Singing Goose commented that it must be the entire extended family of Stands For Them's former comrade from the Army Indian Scouts. The people here did not require healing of a sick one, or any spiritual leadership.

Rather, Brings Three White Horses simply wished his family to experience old-fashioned Lakota storytelling from an old-time storyteller.

As Stands For Them ducked his head through a doorway carpentered for a family of smaller stature, conversations among the twenty assembled ceased. Soon the essential pipe made the rounds. Then people began moving outside and into a wall tent. This tent made a reasonable substitute for the tipi, where in times past winter storytellers so effectively spun their tales. Everyone settled shoulder-to-shoulder in a circle around the weak mustard glow of a kerosene lamp. Someone had placed a pipe on one side of the lamp, and a clothbound New Testament opposite.

Stands For Them lowered himself to a cross-legged position on Mother Earth, his face above the flame, and after minutes of silence he began to recount the great fables. Each tale connected to a specific mountain or river or trail, a place where something happened to the ancestors, good or bad with the lessons timeless. Some ears in the tent had never heard the centuries-old stories Stands For Them told. The bookish cultures would never know what now filled the tent—the spellbinding power of a veteran storyteller in an unlettered society.

With the story-telling winding down, and Stands For Them growing weary, he accepted a question from a plucky young woman, a favored daughter of Brings Three White Horses. "How, wakanlica, might I tap the power of the stories in my dreams? How might one live by the lessons of stories and dreams?"

Stands For Them spoke first from experience, telling of his adolescent dreams of wild horses. "In this way I gained a closeness with the wild *sunka wakan*, and in those days they became my intermediary with the Great Mystery. My only totem animal. You say I am a great horse trainer. Perhaps dreams explain the silent language I murmur with my horses."

"Now for you, your totem creature may change over time and with new dreams but will always be special. Who among you feels close to *wambli*, the greatest of birds?" Three or four heads nodded. "Who among you follows the hawk with your eyes, or the coyote, or the antelope?" Other heads nodded.

"The wingeds and four-leggeds have stayed closer to *Wakan Tanka* than we humans. The right creature can be coaxed to offer a wing or hoof or paw pointing you towards the holy mountain."

Whispers of "Hou" and nodding heads rippled 'round the lamp. Then Stands For Them exposed his fallibility for all to see. His way of inviting others to walk the spirit trail despite their own frailties: "I must tell you that many dreams carry meanings hard for me to understand. Some night visions one will never understand. Take the dream I had just four sleeps ago—In this dream I was living in the small spare loggie near the Singing Goose home. A place I and Cora sought shelter in for a season, three winters past." At this Stands For Them glanced at John Singing Goose, standing in the corner.

"In this strange dream our humble cabin was in pieces on the ground. Then before my eyes each hewn log, in turn, was lifted up by a whirlwind and magically carried to the ranch of my wasicu friend Cleve. When I blinked the cabin was reassembled in this place."

"All this I saw as though I were in the sky. Looking down. I could see beautiful *sunka wakans* being led in and out, in and out. The home for people had become a barn for horses. I have labored to understand this dream. I have failed. But perhaps there is worth in the effort." With this Stands For Them rose to his feet, and all understood that their time with the wakanlica had come to an end. For now.

By 1936 the healing pair and their horse wagon were crowded to the edge of the dirt roads by the grinding of time, and by the occasional automobile. Model A's mostly, but also Hudson coupes, Studebaker roadsters, and Nash sedans.

In a world changing fast, still clusters of Lakota people sent for the pair in times of crisis. Even then Singing Goose hitched up his team, if asked by Stands For Them.

On one such trip it was unusually warm and wind-free, a day encouraging conversation, so Stands For Them shared with Singing Goose his deep frustration at how often he made the two-day trip to the agency only to be told his modest stipend as guaranteed by federal treaty was "not ready at this time."

Then he offered his young teamster the parable of the jackal. Singing Goose understood without being told that the jackal was for them the coyote:

"Here is a story that will help you understand the difference between the old Indian life and today's reservation life. It seemed that the jackal had lived a satisfying life in the foothills for many years. He managed to catch plenty of hares to fill his stomach, and when the hares sometimes grew scarce or hard to catch, well, he could always carefully follow the wolves or the Lakotas or Arapahos and steal scrapes from these large, brainy killers. Perhaps even dining on the leftovers of a big buffalo harvest."

"Then came a day when the jackal's world changed. A new breed of humans entered the land. They brought with them dim-witted and slow-moving beasts known as cattle. These fair-skinned humans and their cattle multiplied and grew fat on the land, but there was far less forage of the hares, so that over time the jackal's main prey grew scarce."

"Into this land of plenty and among the cattle there still trotted the jackal. Meat everywhere, and yet the jackal starved . . . for in this new world the new prey animal was too big, the hunter too small."

The old man paused, and Singing Goose looked at him expectantly.

"Now you see, the sadness is that you and I are become the jackal. Starving in a land of plenty."

As his hands encouraged the team up a small rise, Singing Goose asked Stands For Them how one man can hold so many stories. Stands For Them laughed at the thought, "Ah my young kola, I know only one tent full of stories. You might hear more and different stories from every headman, in every tipi in the Lakota nation."

Unknown to Stands For Them, in a few short seasons he would become the central figure in a story of local notoriety. A story of infirmary, generosity, and healing. A story making the declined intancan honoring a thing of inconsequence.

Chapter Fifteen

Last Wolf in Dakota
1915-1920

Cleve climbed out from under the goose down covers and into the metallic cold of his tottery shack. He lit a match to the potbelly kindling so carefully arranged just seven hours earlier. Then he looked down at Jessie's sleeping face.

Her skin was limpid, relaxed, wrinkle-free. In this light she became again the girl he'd fallen in love with. Then as happened every morning, a gloom crossed that face just as her eyes opened. She pulled the covers over her head.

He turned to put the water to boil for coffee, thought again of how they no longer shared the same dream, and set his jaw to the discomfort of knowing it was his dream that had diverged. She was not loving this raw-boned land. He was losing her to lonely winds, to a malaise sliding to prairie fever.

Today is the day to share my plan, he told himself. *A way of loving her, and the land too.* The house was a little warmer, and the coffee ready. That smell never failed to coax Jessie to the kitchen table.

"Good morning Jessie. How did you sleep?"

"Just so-so."

"I been thinking. I know this ranch life and our lonely spot here makes you miss green Iowa. Your piano recitals. The chautauquas, county fairs, trips to Des Moines."

Mournful wind filled the brief pause as Jessie's gaze moved from Cleve's face to the bleak little shack door that would never, ever lead to such pleasures. "So Jessie, I just think we can make room in here for a piano. Both of us will be better off in a little house filled with music.

Our kids will grow up knowing music. I've looked into it. A Hamilton upright shipped by rail from Chicago. Supposed to be darn near good as a Baldwin, but not so pricey."

"Cleveland, we flat cannot afford that and you know it."

Her gaze, now a stare, was back on Cleve and spoke of financial ruin. Only later would she briefly consider a welcome irony: monthly piano payments might, in running them off this land, be her escape route.

Cleve looked down at his hands, then spilled the rest: "Jessie, I've already done it. Made the down payment, signed the contract, it'll arrive up at Belvidere's railhead on the 30th next month.

A matter settled, yet unsettling for both. "Cleve, you are right that this life has not been what I'd hoped, but I thought I'd hidden my melancholy from you. Is it so obvious?"

"It is." Cleve half smiled.

Here and there Jessie allowed herself some anticipation, in her head hearing melodies of old songs she'd hope to play first. Cleve quietly reduced the herd by three open heifers and worried out loud only to his brothers that he'd overextended.

Everything hung on picking up the 840 lb. piano on the 30th. Even a moderate rain would make the thirty-six-mile roundtrip a near impossibility—turning dirt roads and open pasture crossings into gumbo quagmires. To fail to pick up the piano meant the railroad would slap on a budget-busting per diem storage fee. A double crossing of the Big White River could be treacherous, risking loss of wagon, team, piano.

Jessie and Cleve rose before the sun on the 29th, for the roundtrip to the railhead would be too far for a team and wagon in one day. Cleve would need to camp out overnight.

He returned from the horse barn with bad news and watched as Jessie's face slid from hopeful to troubled. "Babe came up lame this morning. Damn. Must have kicked an upright during the night. Dolly's ready, but I'll have to hitch Duster beside her."

Two horses would be needed to bring the piano in. Cleve had no choice but to harness up the half-broke two-year-old gelding Duster.

"Honey, if the wind stays down and the river don't rise, we just might make it."

With a hug and three sack lunches, Jessie sent Cleve on his way.

That first day the young gelding crow-hopped now and then but was otherwise compliant. For the load was light, the air quiet.

That night Cleve slept little as raindrops drummed the roof of his one-man canvas tent pegged to this sere land where men pray for rain today, only to curse it tomorrow. Next morning, he was at the loading dock to receive the huge box containing the piano. The trip back to the ranch was harrowing, what with slippery roads, the river crossing, and a young horse uninterested in leaning into such a heavy load. Yet Cleve willed the wagon up to the home hitching post. Two neighbors helped in the unloading. That evening an extra kerosene lamp was lit and there descended a welcome lull, a breathing space. Cleve leaned back in his chair and closed his eyes as Jessie played "It's a Long Way to Tipperary."

Weeks later a floppy-eared puppy bounded round and round the big boots of Stands For Them and Cleve, drawing amused smiles from both. If a canine can smile, that puppy was smiling too. As an Indian dog, it carried hints of wolf and coyote in both looks and disposition.

The English word "dog." The Lakota equivalent "*sunka*." This animal Cleve thought a rightful partner of mankind is, Stands For Them thought, a rather slavish and watered-down version of the wolf. His Lakota word for wolf was *Sunkamanitu Thanka*, the "true dog."

Where Cleve grew up, the Niobrara country of north central Nebraska, settlers had hunted out all wolves. So it was in the Canadian Rockies he first saw the fabled creature. Through a narrow opening between aspens one morning two unblinking yellow eyes meet his. Lupinus eyes neither afraid nor threatening. Cleve imagined, incorrectly, that he'd never see another.

By the time Cleve and Jessie homesteaded in 1914 the badlands stood empty of pronghorn antelope, mountain lions, elk, grizzly bears, whitetail and mule deer, eagles, bobcats, a subspecies of bighorn sheep, wild turkeys, and of course the buffalo. All regionally extinct.

There were however a few wolves. Hangers-on. Clever renegades whose great-grandparents hunted buffalo, but whose closer ancestors from the 1880s onward had survived on guile, guts, and much smaller game. Cleve woke deep in that first winter's night to the howl of wolves gathering atop Cedar Butte. He'd not return to sleep, knowing they'd be racing down onto the plain to meet a rising full moon.

White settlement had brought wolves a new food source—cattle and sheep. Slower, dumber versions of the old fare. But when wolves began picking off the occasional calf or chicken it was the beginning of their end. On many a night in the years before 1920 Cleve kept a fast horse saddled in the nearby corral, a loaded Winchester thrust in the scabbard. Ready to give chase at a moment's notice should wolves attack young heifers penned nearby. On evenings when the saddled horse was not called for, he'd drape an old coat over a pitchfork near the heifers, in such a way that wolves might take it for a man.

By 1920 wolves were thought eradicated from South Dakota, and surely from the Cedar Butte country. All but one, ol' Three Toes. This wolf's tracks clearly showing an earlier narrow escape from a trap. Cleve sometimes wondered if it had been one of his nine wolf traps.

The ghostly white Three Toes had outlived every other wolf in the region thanks to a stealthy killing style targeting isolated young cattle, sheep, chickens. Which is why Cleve was so surprised to see Three

Toes, but just once. It was a Sunday morning in April as Cleve balanced a steaming cup of coffee while strolling towards the butte. On topping a rise, there was Three Toes, trotting Cleve's direction and holding a still-kicking jackrabbit by the neck.

Cleve froze—no gun, no horse—nothing to do but look skyward and curse his luck. When his gaze returned to earth, Cleve saw no trace of the cunning animal . . . that is, until he glimpsed a white form loping, impossibly far away. Phantomlike, Three Toes topped the butte, paused for a backwards glance, then melted into the pines.

Cleve and all cowboys of his generation needed no outside expert to tell them their modest ranches couldn't survive side by side with wolves—for the occasional valuable calf killed, but more for the nervous breeding cows stressed to a state of infertility.

So the first Sunday of every month in those years before Three Toes alone remained, Cleve was joined by his brother Tom for an activity part sport, part necessity—finding and eliminating the last wolves in the Cedar Butte country.

On a rare Sunday one or the other might squeeze off a hopeful shot from horseback. At other times they set leg traps. Rarely were these efforts successful.

But in time the brothers learned to condense their wolfing war to pupping season, using one lethal trick: track the mother or sometimes the father wolf back to the birthing den. Once the den was located, they'd return in the morning.

Arriving back at the den at first light, chances were high that both parents would be away searching for food. On this morning's den invasion, the parents appeared to be gone, so Tom took his position just above the entrance. There he stood guard should a parent wolf return, and provided encouragement to Cleve. There was no question but that the more slender little brother must accept the unsavory task of crawling into the den.

In he went, a rope around his waist and trailing back to Tom. With no growl coming from the void, Cleve pushed forward with some confidence that the pups were alone. The air grew fetid, stuffy. Faint claustrophobia rose in his throat, and as always he swallowed it down. The hole was pitch black, smelling of feces and wet hair and a primal odor hard to identify. Faint whines of wolf pups were Cleve's clue of how far back he must still crawl. Every few feet he would strike a match.

With a crude barbed wire tool fashioned to snag the pups, he retrieved squealing balls of fur one at a time. Stuffing them into a gunny sack at his side, with a tug Cleve signaled Tom to pull on the rope that he'd secured to the sack. Coughing with every breath now, Cleve's final act before the more difficult exit was to fling a strychnine-tainted piece of meat into the lair.

The March wind had bitten red patches into Tom's face when Cleve finally backed and squirmed, feet-first, out of the den. "Good work little brother." They both smiled, knowing their adjoining 33 and XX ranches now faced a future containing at least five fewer wolves.

The brothers had an agreement—when the den was on Tom's ranch, he'd dispose of the pups. But this den was on Cleve's property. Which meant he'd be obliged to kill the wolf pups himself.

Hardened to the oft cruel realities of ranch work, Cleve nonetheless had a dog lover's heart. *And surely these creatures in the sack are dogs of a fashion,* he mused.

On this day he took the wolf puppies home. A brief reprieve only, a chance for his young daughters and the bewildered creatures to meet and play a bit outside the homestead shack.

Then, as suppertime neared, with dark duty Cleve returned the pups to the gunny sack. In one more small mercy, Cleve ignored the standard method for disposing of unwanted cat or dog litters; that of putting a rock in the sack and tossing sucklings into a river or pond. No, his coup de grâce was a sharp strike on the bobbing heads with a big hammer. One at a time.

When finished, Cleve washed his hands using Jessie's homemade lard soap. He scrubbed more thoroughly than usual. While scrubbing away he replayed the day's consequential wolfing activity, and how it paled beside a recent memory:

March 1915, the occasion of the brothers' first descent into a wolf den. Jessie had protested to Cleve, "How can you leave me for such risky business? Look at me! I am very pregnant. Your first baby comes any day now, and it will not be an easy birth."

These days, where once he had seen the future in her eyes he some-times saw glassy resignation. Still, he went. "Our ranch business," he said quietly as he gathered up the snare and rope, "is in the balance."

He was lucky that day, then not so lucky. Thirty-six hours later Jessie went into labor. The calendar said "First Day of Spring" even as a fierce blizzard swept across the empty country. Banking on typical weather, Cleve had some weeks prior hatched a plan. Fetch a neighbor woman, and while there use their telephone to call for the doctor. But thirty inches of snow changed everything. Travel was all but impossible. The party telephone line on the edge of the new cluster of settler shacks was down.

Between contractions, Jessie threw Cleve a plaintive stare.

He knew that should the baby not live, he would also lose Jessie to the unbearable loneliness of his place. She'll surely return to Iowa, he thought, and alone I will lose the dream of this ranch.

"I cannot leave her alone for long," Cleve whispered to himself as he sat beside Jessie to consider narrowing options. If panic rose in either of them, they did not give it the power of speech. But creeping fear couldn't be hidden in the expressions. It was common knowledge that birth of a first offspring, whether in human or heifer, was sure to be dangerous and pain filled.

"Tom will help." Cleve squeezed Jessie's hand and started walking fast for the barn, then broke into a wobbly run on high-heeled cowboy boots. In minutes he'd saddled and was riding hard over the three-mile cow trail to Tom's XX Ranch.

Cleve went directly to the barn where he nearly collided with his wide-eyed brother. "The baby is coming," was all the explanation required. In seconds Tom hatched a plan, grabbed his sheepskin coat, and together the men caught and saddled Tom's strapping saddle horse, Bailey, believing this big gelding could handle the deep snow. Cleve returned eastward to Jessie while Tom rode thirteen miles north to the village of Belvidere to bring the woman doctor.

Years later Tom Berry would call it his toughest ride. Snow had drifted so deep in the many draws that horse and rider would leave tracks left and right from the stirrups.

Tom knew it was life-or-death for Jessie and the baby, and no less so for his horse so willing to plunge more than gallop through deep snow-banks. He understood that a horse with a big heart will run itself to death if asked. Bailey was such a horse.

Finally, a knock on the doctor's door; Tom's breathless request, but the doctor would not risk the round trip in such conditions. She did suggest an itinerant doctor in Norris. Tom set his jaw, for Norris lay almost thirty miles to the south.

Backtracking to the XX Ranch should have been easier by following the same hoof prints. Except that the earlier westerly wind, still spitting snow and sleet, was now a headwind. Bailey was yet willing, but an occasional stumble warned of exhaustion.

Pulling his hat low and wrapping a wool scarf in such a way that only his eyes showed, Tom allowed himself but two thoughts, "My sister-in-law and her baby may well die in that cold shack if we can't get better help than what a man can provide. Cleve spoke of lots of blood, the baby may be breach. But I must consider how much more Bailey can endure. I'll be useless afoot."

Loath to ask Bailey to attempt what would be an additional forty-five snow-laden miles roundtrip, he resolved to switch to a fresh mount when back near the XX Ranch.

As he rode, Tom mentally ticked off the available horses, settling on one he deemed up to the task. Springer was not big, but the barrel-chested gray mare had what stockmen called a "good bottom"—the ability to dig deep.

More miles. More blinding snow.

Within five minutes of turning in at his gate, Tom had transferred the saddle from Bailey to Springer, refilled his canteen, and remounted for what was becoming a marathon rescue ride. Over his shoulder he shouted to his ten-year-old son, "Baxter, you rub Bailey down for me, give him two quarts of oats, and keep him in the barn until he's dry."

Reaching under the saddle blanket Tom could feel Springer's freshness as they pressed southward. As luck had it, the phone lines north of Norris were not down, so he stopped at a likely farmhouse four miles short of Norris and from there called the doctor.

"But you must come, Doc. I'll personally guarantee that we get you through the storm safely. No, we can't possibly get a buggy up there. But we'll get you there by saddle horse. This, sir, is a genuine emergency."

But there was no budging the fearful Norris doctor. So Tom thanked the slack-jawed farmer for the use of his phone on the way out the door. Climbing back in the saddle, he was happy to have given Springer a short breather in the farmer's loafing shed. But Tom was increasingly desperate to find help.

There was a last card to play—find a willing midwife. On the way back to the XX Ranch Tom stopped at the Lakota community of Corn Creek. He hoped he would find a school-aged child to translate the predicament, for few adult natives could speak English.

The Holy Bear family seemed a likely place to find such a student. Tom knocked, then entered on hearing a grunt from Moses Holy Bear, who took Tom to the room where all the children slept. There Moses gently woke twelve-year-old Clair Holy Bear. Tom was equally gentle with the little sleepy-head: "Hello Clair. Sorry to bother you. I'm Tom Berry. I need you to explain to your father something about my brother's wife Jessie. You have seen her I'm sure, and she will soon have a baby and needs help from an experienced Lakota woman. Can your family help to find her?"

Soon runners were being sent to this cabin and that, and in less than twenty minutes there came a faint knock on the Holy Bear door. It was one of the village's most experienced midwifes, Maggie Wooden Knife, holding the reins of her little spotted cayuse pony. A middle-aged full-blood with sparkling black-cherry eyes set in a comfortably round yet stately face, Maggie was dressed in her warmest apparel and clutched a hastily gathered assortment of small knives, dried herbs, clean rags, and leather cords: the accoutrement of a traditional Lakota midwife.

With a shake of her head, Maggie indicated to Tom that she would not need his escort to the scene of the labor. She knew well that Cleve and Jessie Berry's tarpaper shack was close by the Red Road . . . and not too far beyond the Stands For Them home.

Her arrival at Cleve's place was heralded as all comings were, by nickering horses, barking dogs, and clucking chickens. On crossing the threshold, Maggie immediately locked eyes with Jessie. Though they'd never met, it was a gaze that carried ten thousand years of mutual recognition, reassurance, sisterhood.

The labor and birth were more difficult, painful, and extended than feared. Yet thanks to the calm, reassuring hands of Maggie Wooden Knife, the long night was not overly fearful for Jessie.

At the dawning there came a scream from Jessie and then a smaller wail from a new life.

But the afterbirth would not come. The midwife was concerned. So with Cleve's help they pressed with their combined strength on Jessie's abdomen. This pummeling yielded no result. In desperation they tried hanging the new mother over the rounded rungs of the foot of their brass bedstead, rocking her back and forth—an agony that finally yielded the placenta. This Maggie promptly carried out of the house to be draped on a low branch of the nearest tree—the ancestral recompense to *Wakan Tanka*.

When Maggie returned, she helped tuck a hand-stitched blanket around the tiny baby girl, then asked by way of signs and bits of English about the baby's name. When the new parents said the given name was to be Marian, but that they did not have a middle name yet, she suggested the Lakota name for a first-born female.

This is how the first wasicu baby of the Black Pipe Valley came to be known as Marian Wynona Berry.

She would forever be a special one to local Lakotas, for all knew the role their community had played: *Waste wiche winchincila,* "the good little white girl," said always with a pat on the head. Natives who did not know her might among themselves simply say *wakanyeja*, a generic term for 'youngster' but which translates more literally as "the child is also holy."

In coming weeks, she became a fat and hale baby, and this greatly lifted spirits in the shack. Most evenings Cleve arrived home uncharacteristically just before sunset, so that he might play with his first born before her early bedtime.

On one occasion as Cleve bounced Marian he said to Jessie, "A homely baby will make a handsome adult," at which both laughed out loud. Jessie countered with, "A baby with big ears will grow up open-hearted and generous." So commenced a back-and-forth game of who could recall more superstitions concerning babies. Some bubbled up from Cleve's Scots-Irish roots, some from Jessie's adolescent years in Iowa:

Cleve: "If a babe is rained upon it will grow up to have freckles."

Jessie: "The first time a baby is taken outdoors, put a silver coin in its hand so that it will always gain riches."

Cleve: "Turn a baby upside down and it will never have liver trouble."

Jessie: "Never wean a baby while fruit trees are in bloom, else it's hair turns grey early."

Cleve: "Swaddle a baby girl in a garment from her father to bring her luck. Dress a baby boy as a baby girl, so as to deceive the boy-seeking devil. Or this one—Don't wash a baby's right hand for months—or you will wash away its good fortunes."

Jessie: "If you wish baby to have curly hair, see that the first person to cut her hair be a person *with* curly hair."

"Well, that last one was pure poppycock," he said, his lopsided grin bringing the exchange to a close. The pair smiled that happy parent smile and leaned back. Jessie balanced a now heavy-eyed Marian on her lap before bringing the child to her bosom.

As Marian grew from babe to toddler to little girl, she'd sometimes fall asleep to differing howls. On her goose down pillow she was learning to differentiate between the baritone bay of wolf, the higher yelp of coyote, and the mundane bark of dog.

Barking dogs made Cleve look up from his task to see Stands For Them slowing his team upon entering the Berry wagon yard. The old man shouted an admonishing "*Shunka!*" to his three dogs who until that moment had silently trotted under the moving shade of the wagon.

While tying up his horses, Stands For Them looked over his right shoulder to see Cleve stretching and tanning hides of coyotes and bobcats on the sunny side of his sod bunkhouse. Cleve set down his work and beckoned Stands For Them to share a smoke under their little shade tree.

There passed before them a small herd of heifers, selectively grazing only those wild grasses presently most succulent. Two of the animals were missing their tails. This was a sign of predation by yearling wolves, who lacking hunting skills often grabbed a cow high on the tail and simply gnawed the appendage off.

They observed these disfigured cattle, Cleve with a frown and Stands For Them with no expression. That each viewed wolves so differently sometimes puzzled Cleve. But then he could not know the old Plains Indian saying that Stands For Them first heard fifty-five winters previous—"The gun that shoots at a wolf or coyote will never shoot straight again."

Indeed, in youth Stands For Them had learned much from observing wolves, then one of two animals on his personal totem of four-leggeds. He adopted the wolfish virtues of stealth, of tenacity, of the hunter's eye, of how endurance trumps both speed and strength. Most of all, the wolf modeled for Stands For Them unfailing loyalty to the group, be it pack or tribe.

For Cleve it was different. The dust around his two most recent livestock deaths contained the signature three-toed paw print. So Cleve and Tom sent word to the neighbors, proposing they unite in hiring the last of the professional wolf hunters. Fred Hanson had recently gained fame in Harding County where his trapping and shooting expertise had entirely cleared that country of wolves. It was twilight for the wolfer profession as by trap, poison, and bullet Hanson hastened his own unemployment.

One look at Hanson, and Cleve was doubly sure they'd picked the right man. Eyes hooded, skin tanned to the mahogany of one perpetually outdoors, Hanson wore a leather jacket with wide lapels. He moved with confidence, and his weather-beaten and outsized cowboy hat completed the picture.

With the nonchalance of old wolfers he'd learned from, Hanson maintained the odd habit of stuffing his loose tobacco and cigarette papers into the same pocket containing unwrapped strychnine crystals, then smoking all day. Yet somehow he woke each morning hale and hearty.

After the hiring, Cleve and Tom followed Hanson on two of his trap-setting forays—Watching as he masterfully set and camouflaged several Original No. 4 wolf traps. They were however not with Hanson when he found the magnificent white Three Toes in one of his traps. The animal had been caught by that paw with the missing toe, and had chewed his leg down to the bone in his desperation to escape.

So ended the life of the last known wolf in South Dakota.

Just as Cleve once knew the ways of wolves, he would in time come to know the animal that most benefited from the grey wolf's eradication—the little prairie wolf, better known as the coyote.

When wolves ruled Cedar Butte, they killed their junior competitor on sight.

But with wolves, bears, and mountain lions gone, the stealthy coyote filled in as apex predator. But the coyote's time of few enemies would not last long.

In the years after World War One there came to South Dakota a curious and ancient way of pursuing the coyote.

No one could say how Cleve and his brothers stumbled upon this peculiar piece of their Scots-Irish heritage, but they grabbed it and never let go: Old World coursing was rather like the English sport of fox hunting. But coursing required larger canines, crossbreeds with mostly greyhound blood, but also some deerhound and a dash of wolfhound.

From Ireland to Arabia, coursing was reserved for nobility and aristocracy—forbidden to the commoner. Those who followed coursing hounds did so on horseback, to better score the dogs in what was sometimes in competition between neighboring estates. In Europe the prey might be hare, or fox, or sometimes roebuck. In America's badlands the prey of choice was the wily coyote.

Cleve became incurably addicted to the chase, a passion second only to ranch work. Jessie would have liked more Sunday afternoons with her husband, but instead she'd pull back the curtain to see him trotting out for Cedar Butte—a pack of thirteen hounds whining with anticipation yet obediently bunched close by the back legs of his best saddle horse.

Man and dogs would scan the horizon in hopes of spotting quarry. When Cleve located an animal suitably positioned to give both prey and pursuers a sporting chance, his sharp whistle and a point of the arm sent the hounds bounding. The chase was on. Horse and rider followed at a gallop, or when blocked by fences or canyons, observed from a rise.

One fair May morning while coursing for coyotes, Cleve was surprised to see the bowed form of Stands For Them slowly climbing a high point on the west shoulder of Cedar Butte. The old man poked at the ground with a roughly fashioned walking stick. *Bent because he is searching, but for what?* mused Cleve.

On this morning Stands For Them sought medicinal plants . . . not for himself but for the oyate. He looked up when he heard the nicker of

Cleve's buckskin mount. Soon the old friends were shaking hands—the hounds milling and whining a short distance away, anxious at this interruption to the hunt.

The sleek chase dogs, coats glistening in the sun, ignored Stands For Them but had eyes locked on Cleve lest he point towards some coyote. The bigger kill dogs were less intense, sitting on haunches or lying about. Stands For Them showed Cleve the single medicinal root in his pouch . . . and shrugged as he held up one finger. He had failed so far to find the coveted Bear with Horns plant, but the long root of the echinacea would make a fine healing tea.

Cleve politely nodded at what he secretly considered just another bit of Indian witchcraft, then held up his own index finger while nodding back at the smallish coyote carcass tied to the saddle's cantle.

Stands For Them's expression was mildly quizzical as he considered the blood speckled wild dog. It was a look that for Cleve harkened back to a discussion years earlier with his sister-in-law, as she surveyed his many coyote pelts. Stretched and nailed to the north side of the barn, they represented a winter's worth of hunting and trapping, and a rare if modest source of cash.

"Cleve, I get why you chase these critters; the furrier gives you some money. But you say you don't really loathe these varmints? Seems like killing and hating ought to go together."

"Dixie, it's hard to explain to a nonhunter. I admired the wolf. Couldn't help but admire their intelligence and tenacity. Now I admire their cousin coyotes."

"How then do you show that love, brother?"

Smiling faintly at her sarcasm, "I show it by sometimes cheering for the coyote. When I turn the dogs loose, there are times when I can get to high ground and watch one coyote outsmart fifteen greyhounds. You might not believe it, but I love that the best."

Stands For Them had once witnessed the more typical end to such a hunt, the cornered coyote outnumbered and outweighed but fighting frantically to the end of a savagely slow and piecemeal death. Even for one as inured to hunting's bloody necessity as Stands For Them, the scene was disturbing.

Stands For Them now had a better look at Cleve's panting and glassy-eyed dogs and wondering at this strangest of all hunting customs. "So many dogs, so much effort for a slender prey that cannot even be eaten," he thought. Stands For Them smiled at parting and resumed his slow climb up the butte in search of the illusive Bear with Horns.

Cleve remounted to ride south, aiming for a divide where he sometimes spotted coyotes. The dogs trotted behind, still breathing heavily from the first kill, a few nursing minor cuts from the coyote's desperate fangs. The cowboy smiled down at his devoted pack, and recalled the only poem he ever heard his father recite:

A man may shake you by the hand
And wish you to the devil,
But when a good dog wags his tail,
You're sure he's on the level.

Chapter Sixteen

Distant Drumbeats
1916

For several days now, when winds blew westerly Cleve cocked an ear. Listening. Listening for the drum beats. Tonight, the winds were especially favorable, and so yes—he could just hear the drums, the otherworldly, high-pitched singing.

This was his signal to saddle up and ride over to the midsummer Corn Creek Wacipi . . . always held at the Stands For Them place. In latter years such gatherings would be called a "powwow." More than just a gathering of dancers, Cleve was coming to understand a wacipi as a place of honorings, prayers, name bestowing, adoptions, ritual giveaways.

This year for sure Cleve would not miss the chance to gift the wacipi, for he had a most expendable steer—one with a bum leg, pinkeye, and a bad cough getting worse. In the current warm weather if the steer died, its meat could not be preserved. The many hungry mouths of a powwow offered a neat, neighborly solution.

But when? When would the dancing start? An open question for many Indian functions. The year before Stands For Them had alerted Cleve to the powwow by signing "tomorrow" as he pointed to a spot in the sky. That spot indicating the sun's position when the powwow might start. The Lakota had no use for time-keeping devices other than this straightforward "sky clock."

This year Cleve waited for the drumming and singing before starting out. Not all drumbeats signaled an event to which he would feel welcome. Certain cadences of drumming and mournful keening told of a

Lakota funeral. Other sounds might signal a private observance such as the Sun Dance.

But today, finally, the winds brought faint echoes of a wacipi. The drumming reminded Cleve that even as homestead shacks popped up across reservations, his particular valley was the center of what remained of the independent Lakota nation.

So Cleve slowly headed west on the Red Road. His steer limped along behind the horse, tethered through a ring in its nose. As he advanced, Cleve heard more clearly the quivering, nasal pitch of the male singers. There was undeniable magic—even for a cowboy—in this quintessential sound of ancient America. In it one could hear a buffalo's bellow, a grizzly's rumblings, distant thunder bouncing off canyon walls, and even for one as secular as Cleve a vague holiness.

He let the harmonics pull him up the Red Road, through the badlands cuts and then finally onto the Stands For Them flats. Here the steer balked at going further, as if sensing his fate. So Cleve disconnected the lead rope and resorted to herding the animal ahead with his horse.

The scores of government-issued rigs pulled up round the Stands For Them house, horses dozing between the traces, and several hastily raised tipis told him this was to be a sizable affair.

Big-bellied men with strangely high-pitched voices sat straining for ever higher octaves at two oval drums. Each sweating singer pounded a similar mesmeric thump, thump, thump with his long drumstick. Cleve could see many human circles besides those around the drums—circles symbolizing no beginning, no end. The dance ground itself was a circle of rough wooden poles supporting a shade structure topped by fresh-cut cedar branches. The dancers orbiting a center pole were themselves ringed by seated male spectators, who in turn were encircled by the shawled womenfolk.

Further back, concentric rows of costumed men squatted in that easy way of all people whose world contains no chairs—arms outstretched as counterweights, each one birdlike in relaxed balance. Yet poised. Ready to rise like the eagles they so revered.

Surveying the circles, Cleve saw faces both foreign and familiar. For among dancers and spectators were young men who only weeks earlier made up the long line of teamsters and their horse-powered mowing rigs he'd hired for the summer hay harvest on the 33 Ranch. *Strange*, he thought, *how much more formidable they look in native attire. Teeth showing. The rims of eyeballs flashing white.* He could see that the assembled were, if only for this hour, transforming from wards of the state to warriors of old.

One of the squaws stepped towards Cleve. He recognized her as a regular at Cedar Butte Store. Smiling broadly, she gestured that she would lead the steer away to be butchered. An eager stripling of no more than fourteen years offered to tie Cleve's gelding close by the other horses.

These powwow grounds were in the middle of James Stands For Them's allotment, close to his foursquare frame house. So naturally all eyes followed when he rose and moved to greet the arriving white man. At his rising, the drumming and singing and adult conversation trailed off. Even the children's laughter ebbed, save for distant hoots from those bigger boys playing rough games in the draw to the south.

First, the white man's handshake. Then words in Stands For Them's native tongue said loud enough for all to hear: "You are most welcome among us. Please sit in this place of honor so as to hear and see our ways. Your gift turns our wacipi into a feast. We honor the life of this four-legged you bring to us."

Cleve understood this welcome—not by words but by gesture, into-nation, the crowd's nodding. Yet the scene held an irony lost on Cleve, if not on Stands For Them or the assembled. For here was the valley's most distinguished native leader, the one who advocated unfailingly for cultural preservation—yet tonight he publicly welcomed one representing the invading culture.

Cleve never did know the story behind his dark-skinned friend's name, but on this day he could see that when James stood up, others sat down.

Earlier he'd spotted the wakanlica's wife Cora, seated and surrounded by several younger women. Cora never missed a chance to pass along the tribe's ancient and beautiful handcrafting skills. The making of beaded moccasins, of soft leather purses, of shields or leggings or quilts or backrests. Each with a symbol sewn in, with meaning enough to animate the article.

With Stands For Them's welcome finished, the late-day sounds returned. Cicadas, whippoorwills, the rustling of nearby tent flaps. Stands For Them ushered Cleve to the honoring place on a nearby log, a good spot to watch both dancing and preparation for the feast. From here Cleve noticed three male arrivals wearing white muslin garments decorated in the manner of ghost shirts.

Though this was 1916, the shirts yet carried a touch of the supernatural in these remote villages of Wazhazha and Sicangu Lakotas.

Cleve watched his host's expression, not knowing that a quarter century earlier Stands For Them considered then declined the more occult Ghost Dance tenants. Even so, tonight the old man was happy to see a Ghost Dance shirt here and there among his many guests. He saw them as counterbalance to the slow death of all things Lakota.

Rivers of cool evening air could now be felt on skin, energizing the drumming and singing to higher in intensity. Cleve saw this mesmeric energy pass like a ripple through the crowd. In spite of himself he felt it too.

Cleve thought now of his people's monthly homesteader dances. These lively events were unknown to the natives, who considered the wasicu a people who moved their bodies only in the ways of work. Even so, there came a day when the visiting Stands For Them saw his friend break into a compact Irish jig, inspired by a melody coming from the Philco radio propped in an open window.

As Cleve settled in, he felt warm if peculiar stares from those nearest him. He sensed also malevolent eyes from a minority wanting little to do with a wasicu, even one bearing gifts. "This wasicu knows he will have a few friends among the Lakota, and a few enemies. He accepts this as the natural order," said Stands For Them when asked later by the youngster White Bull why this white man had been invited to stay.

Cleve's gaze darted among the horned and feathered headdresses, ribbons, the copper bells at knee and ankle, and animal pelts, all in motion. Singing and foot-stomping persisted in flawless unison with the drums. Then he saw a still higher wave of excitement passing through the crowd, as a defeated people on this night at least were feeling again their old powers. The men, so used to standing idle and sullen in the shadows, were transfigured by leaping flames. Lost souls become foot-stomping warriors.

If the moment was not quite hypnotic for Cleve, surely it was for the dancers. The dancing itself had become a prayer. And at the center of each dervish lay a trance-like stillness.

Presently a pause allowed the singers—those hulking men tight 'round the big drum—to refresh themselves with water and a little food. This allowed Cleve to more carefully consider his friend Stands For Them moving among the assembled. Such was his stature that as the odd quarrel or fistfight erupted, Stands For Them would need only walk to stand in the general vicinity of the troublemakers—his mere presence sufficient to restore peace.

The drummers returned to low seats and resumed the beat, their bodies further bronzed by a setting sun red with the false promise that tomorrow could be different.

Cleve was more than once baffled when at some unknowable signal the drums and voices vanished on a single explosive note . . . leaving only deafening silence. The chant might resume in a split second, or after a longer pause—these signals equally undetectable to Cleve.

Just then a dark-skinned colossus, in antelope skin shirt and trousers of the wasicu style, threw his head back to hit an impossibly high note. He held it so long that people followed his gaze skyward perhaps expecting this voice to take physical form.

On the fringes little boys self-consciously practiced certain dances—secretly hoping big dancers might notice, but daring not look. Nearby another knot of males, somewhat older, were passing something unknown amongst themselves. Furtive glances flashed towards Stands For Them and other elders. Center in this group was nephew Bull Tail—this death of traditionalism coming, sadly, from within Stands For Them's own tiyospaye.

Steaming chunks of broiled beef were now being handed out. Cleve watched as male and female elders, the infirm, and the widows were served first. Nearby he saw informal giveaways in progress; blankets, pemmican, and sacks of flour freely offered to needy recipients. He was witnessing the last visages of pure tribalism: when times are fat, all are "rich." When times are lean, all are "poor."

The powwow now entered a more deliberate, more nuanced phase as older men joined the dance. Prominent among the oldsters was Stands For Them, who many considered one of the best "old timey" dancers. As these ancient ones entered the dance arena, younger men gave way.

These elder dancers had neither the flourish nor the athleticism of young dancers. But Cleve watched just as closely, for their eyes seemed focused on glories invisible to others. Their motions measured and precise. Dancers like Stands For Them draped every small gesture with meaning. Here the land of the living was not far removed from the underworld of the ancestors.

Two, three more circling dances were announced and completed. One was reserved for the women, where from the knees up their bodies remained modestly motionless while below stirred light, quick, rhythmic footwork.

Presently leaves whispered that darkness could not be far off. At a drumbeat signal younger women and children withdrew from the dancing grounds. Cleve watched them melt away in twos and threes, no doubt in preparation for bedtime.

Now the younger male dancers returned. Only the still-roaring central fire challenged the gathering darkness. Around it the same prancings that by daylight were to Cleve benign now seemed alien, vaguely ominous. In a visceral way he felt the call to ride home. Politeness, however, required a parting eye contact with his host, a way of saying goodbye before rising to leave. But young and old were now dancing together, and there in flickering light Stands For Them moved as if detached from this world.

Then, as though he suddenly knew, Stands For Them abruptly stopped, walked over and touched fingers to his wasicu friend's shoulder, smiling. A nod towards the cooking fires told Cleve that Stands For Them wished to acknowledge again the donated animal.

Cleve got up stiffly, self-consciously, as one does when he is the foreigner. He offered a shiny coin to the wide-eyed boy who had earlier led his horse away—and who, alert to the departure, stood nearby holding the reins. The passage home was by starlight. No problem, for Cleve was aboard steady Cannonball—an animal whose mental map would find the barn.

In this deliberate way man and beast picked their way home. Night air carried drumming and singing along with them. Other sounds came alive, too; the clip clop of hooves on rocky ground, the hoot of an owl, and a thousand crickets shouting "Here am I."

Presently Cleve and horse approached the one small creek between Stands For Them's place and home, still running high from yesterday's gully washer. In thick darkness Cleve reined up and listened, using a trick for crossing moving water learned in Canada. His teacher, an Assiniboine lad, had said, "Listen and the waters will inform you: a gurgling tells of shallow water running over rocks. Whispering water is deeper, but not too deep for a horse crossing. Beware silent waters, they run deep."

On this night both man and horse heard the gurgling, directing them to a safe ford. Had it been daylight Cleve would use another trick: Look to the old and true buffalo trails, since co-opted by cattle. Or to the wild horse trails. For these traces unerringly lead to the shallowest, safest ford.

Soon horse and rider were up among the cedars, in this hour just ghostly shadows of themselves. Hiding places for who knows what.

As Cleve urged his horse higher, sounds of the powwow faded . . . and the land rose up to him. With it came damp earthen smells and things scurrying among the low plants, and the sixth sense feelings—all these said he was back in a more familiar world, an American world.

But when Cannonball perked his ears, and stopped to lift a high head still higher, Cleve knew man's feeble senses were not reading all this black night held. The big nostrils of his visibly nervous horse had plucked traces of some hidden threat. Perhaps it was simply more Indians, powwow late comers afoot and bound westward on the Red Road. Or maybe a coyote pack.

Odd behavior for Cannonball, thought Cleve, for the extermination of grizzly, buffalo, and wolf meant a man on a big horse had no rivals.

Pressing on, he heard a rustling in the brush fifteen yards away. He could just make out the phantom shape of an adult mountain lion, crouching, tip of long tail twitching, gone in a twinkling.

Shortly Cleve was up on the flats beside his horse barn. Before dismounting, he paused to admire a cloudless firmament that tonight was radiant. Drowsy now, he walked to the shack, exchanging only a few kind words with Jessie as he undressed and climbed into bed beside her.

As always, Cleve was up at first light to kindle the fire in the cook stove, where water was soon boiling for cowboy coffee. As always, he dropped an egg into the simmering coffee, a frontier trick for settling the coffee grounds. How Jessie loved this morning gallantry from Cleve, her chance to linger under goose down blankets, then make breakfast with coffee in hand and without fighting the morning chill.

When Jessie rose, she went straightaway to the corner of the shack which afforded a little privacy. There to wipe the sleep away and examine her face in the small mirror. Hers was a sweet and delicate loveliness that was even then slipping away due to the badlands glare and chaffing winds. Though others thought her a beauty, Jessie had never much fancied her features—in her mind she was too thin, with a neck too long, not to mention her nose. *Oh, to have been born a man,* she thought again and again, *for mirrors are nothing to them.*

She glanced out the tiny south-facing window to see two groups of Indians on the Red Road. One a family in their buckboard heading east, the other group three men afoot and presently milling around. It gave her a shiver, those men, for every girl coming of age in 1890s Iowa knew of the Spirit Lake Massacre and those females taken captive by the natives. Yes, this was a different day. But there was comfort in knowing, this time anyway, that Cleve was home.

Over fried eggs and flapjacks they talked. Jessie tempered her frustration at another late night—knowing that reaching out to the Indians was good business for ranchers dependent on natives willing to lease allotment grazing rights. "Last night you were gone longer than I'd hoped. But I could hear the drums on the west wind. What was it like?"

"They were having a grand time, dancing right there close to the Stands For Them place. Down by the spring near those willows. Maybe two hundred people. They sure liked that tough old steer. Ate the whole damn animal right on the spot. It's like the dancing and singing is their last tie to the old days," Cleve offered between bites.

"Maybe like rodeo is for us?" Jessie's comment eliciting a smile from Cleve.

"Yup," he said, "maybe even more so. Funny thing, I'll bet over half those Indians have been baptized. But they sure weren't singing and dancing to *Amazing Grace*."

He pushed away from the table and made for his felt hat hung by the door. Wondering to himself if the region's rodeos and horse parades and powwows were all destined to pass into history.

Passing or not, always he came back to the outsized cowboy moments. Such moments lasted for only a few precious years, but would stay with Cleve forever—The sharp, metallic screech as heavy hinges on a rodeo chute swung open, the whiplike snap of leather on sweaty horsehide, a thud of hooves shaking the earth, the swoosh of lungs both human and animal exhaling. The explosion of pure energy.

Sure, Cleve had done some bronc busting in his day. Broke a bone or two in the process. Most every young cowboy had tried breaking horses to ride. It was a cowhand's adrenaline-juiced rite of passage. But he'd some years earlier left organized rodeoing to younger men who did not own a ranch to which they must rise next morning.

Yet the arena's magnetism was always there. Eventually he found a rodeo role to precisely fit his character and circumstances—pickup rider for the bareback and saddle bronc events . . . lots of action, ample danger, and in some odd way he loved having responsibility for a buckaroo's life and limb. Considered the best all-around horsemen at a rodeo, pickup riders like Cleve would glide in to rescue roughstock riders from the dangerous animals they rode, then usher the ornery bulls and broncs to the exit. Pickup riders had to be excellent ropers too, often called on to lasso critters posing a danger or unwilling to leave the arena.

A rare long-distance phone call interrupted an otherwise peaceful summer evening on the Berry ranch. Cleve was reading his beloved *Field & Stream* while Jessie dressed wee Marian for bed. Static-filled but audible—"Cleve Berry, this is Hank Pierce. The contestants have voted, and they want you back again as pickup man for this year's Black Hills Roundup. Pay'll be the same as last year, and still no travel allowance. Sorry. But heck, the Lady's Aide will be supplying those free sack lunches again every day. What say?"

Cleve paused only briefly to consider how he'd explain this one to Jessie.

"Well, sure thing I'll do it. You bet. When do you need me there?"

Hanging up the earpiece on the wood box of their crank phone, Cleve figured more than a couple of the nine nosy neighbors on the "party line" already knew his plans for the Roundup . . . so best tell Jessie now before she heard it from others.

Thus he entered the small bedroom and pulled a stool up beside Marian's featherbed, watching for a good spell as Jessie combed the child's hair by kerosene lamp light. "That phone call was the Black Hills Roundup folks—I know the money's only fair, Jessie, but I'm gonna head up to Belle Fourche in a couple weeks. Heck, the contestants voted for me again. Hard to say no."

A wistfulness spread over Jessie's face, and between her eyes the wrinkled knot that always proceeded the pounding. "Didn't we talk about this when you came home last year? You had that nasty horseshoe bruise on your calf. If one of those kicks breaks your leg, Cleveland, or a horse rolls on you, what then? Who's gonna run this ranch? We'll be starved out."

Having no reasonable reply to her logic, he offered only a wan smile by way of declaring the self-evident; he'd already given his word. Cleve looked out the window and up the road, but her eyes locked on his in the glass reflection. In them he saw curtains closing.

Two weeks later, and Cleve is astride his rodeo horse Rex, inhaling the delicious electricity that hangs in the air just before a saddle bronc bursts from the chute—he and fellow pickup man Bill Stanton poised to rescue the bronc buster at the end of what figured to be another wild ride.

Untamed mane flowing and white-rimmed eyes bulging, the bronc Tornado was claimed to be unrideable. But nobody told the seventeen-year-old boy just then sliding onto his back. Jack Pickett, every bit as determined as the quivering animal beneath him, busied himself in wrapping and re-wrapping the rope 'round his right fist.

Pickett was a typical rodeo buckaroo at 5'7", 138 pounds of tightly wrapped muscle and a big-boots swagger, in the arena and on the street.

Man and beast were seemingly all adrenaline, jammed together into that narrow chute. Tornado was in this way forced to tolerate the lean burden on his back, which by equine instinct might as well have been a mountain lion. When the signal came to pull the chute gate open, Tornado was more coiled serpent than horse.

The ride was feral, frenzied, cyclonic—Jack rode well enough to cement his budding local reputation. At the eight-second buzzer, Cleve and Bill raced out of the arena shadows onto either side of the bucking bronc . . . dodging lethal hooves kicking high as a mounted man's head . . . Bill ducking in to release the flank strap pinching the bronc's genitals (the secret to making a bronc buck well). Cleve came riding tight in to offer his torso and horse as a safer dismount option than the dirt . . . and simultaneously pulling up on Tornado's headgear, for no bronc can buck with its head held high.

Bill missed on his first lunging attempt to loosen the flank strap, but not on the second—and Jack's arms lunged for Cleve's torso where he held on for a second or two until his boots felt arena dirt.

As Jack Pickett bow-legged it back to the chutes he gave the slightest tip 'o the hat in response to applause raining down. Perhaps a bit of the ovation was not for Jack, as rodeo insiders knew that contestants risk life and limb for eight seconds once a day, but pickup men like Cleve do it all day long.

Even so, it wasn't danger or human teamwork that brought Cleve back to pickup duties, but rather the strong relationship it engendered between man and horse. Cleve felt blessed to have a rodeo mount like Rex, full of equine alertness, speed, and at fifteen hands just the right size—as no contestant wished to risk dismounting onto a too-short or too-tall horse.

Like all great pickup horses, Rex had the pluck to dodge flying hooves and bump up against crazed bucking broncs. He did this when asked, and often when not asked.

"Spirit before gentleness" was Cleve's favored horse adage. He knew this to also be Stands For Them's favorite sort of horse. What Cleve didn't know is that the qualities of a good pickup horse matched closely the qualities of yesteryear's top Lakota buffalo runner.

At the end of an exhausting if exhilarating day, Cleve unsaddled and carefully curried Rex. Having met his animal's feed and water needs, he placed the saddle against a corral to where the underside served as a makeshift chairback. Bent-legged, he leaned against it with weary but satisfied exhalations. For other than a sprain or two, no contestant had been hurt.

From his low vantage Cleve enjoyed a unique ground-level view of much of the rodeo grounds. Here and there he recognized a face.

In the nearby Indian encampment, a mix of canvas army-style wall tents and traditional tipis, he spied the tall form of Stands For Them in his spotless white buckskin regalia. Topped by a magnificent eagle-feather warbonnet flowing to the ground, he as always attracted attention. From a blue and red ribbon around his neck hung his treasured Presidential Peace Medal. It had been bestowed by some unknown government explorer seventy-six years earlier to Grandfather Santee Man. It carried the profile image of President Millard Fillmore.

Vying to touch the shiny medal were long bronzed fingers of many a young Indian boy. Behind the children stood Kodak-toting white tourists, one group no less starstruck than the other.

Recently Cleve had learned that Stands For Them had taken a "stage name" for these photo opportunities. "White Buffalo", *Ptaysanwee* in Lakota, was this name. And it surely brought forth more 5c and 10c photo requests than did the rather inscrutable name "Stands For Them." He'd once believed as some older warriors had, that this effigy machine might steal one's *nagila*. These days he thought of cameras as a chance for a bit of immortality.

The Black Hills Roundup, 150 miles northwest of Black Pipe Creek, was then one of America's big-time rodeos. But for both Stands For Them and Cleve there was an event much handier and nearly as famous. Frontier Days Rodeo and Powwow in nearby White River was in the 1920s one of the top ten such affairs in all the West. Tom and Cleve Berry were fervent regional promoters of Frontier Days. Tom was first a judge of the riding events, then arena director. For his part, Cleve served as chute boss, and when needed he was more than happy to saddle up as a pickup man.

But the Berry involvement in Frontier Days all came to a turn in 1928. It began the day Cleve's fine young hired hand, Zeb Wilder, asked his boss for permission . . . and a favor.

Zeb was a favorite of Cleve, in certain ways the son he never had. Zeb was lanky, fun-loving, hard-working, happily married to Clara and proud daddy to toddler son Otis. Zeb's reddish-blonde mop more resembling a haystack than a head of hair.

Midway through one hot June day of fence post cutting, Zeb and Cleve sought out a patch of midday shade for a short lunch break. Zeb had dropped the reins of his working horse Tanner, standing patiently as if tied to the ground though in fact the animal was untethered. As the two men contemplated Tanner, Cleve brightened at a thing worth sharing:

"Lately Zeb, I see you picking up most every cowboying skill. That's good. But I want you to know you're only ever gonna be as good as this one thing— trust. Your trust in this here horse is no more, no less, than the horse's trust in you. It's what you see in the top cattle cutting pairs, or a slick roper and his horse. It becomes a dance, a wordless sort of thing."

"Like your wordless times with old Mr. Stands For Them?"

"Yes Zeb, something like that." They drifted into a companionable silence of their own.

Later, between bites of a marmalade sandwich, Zeb asked: "Mr. Berry, do you reckon it would be okay if I signed up to ride in the saddle bronc event at Frontier Days? Word has it that Scotty Philip's boys are trailing their bucking stock down from Fort Pierre, and I think I got a chance of making a little money off them broncs."

"Sure thing. I'd be the last guy to stand in your way. But then you don't hardly need my permission, son." Smiles flashed white on two sunburned faces.

"Well, there's more. Heard tell you used to be about the best pickup rider ever up at Black Hills Roundup. Clara says she'd be a lot more comfortable if you'd agree to be my pickup rider when I compete. Me too."

"Well, I'll be there o' course and will have Rex with me. So why not? Bill Stanton should be around too. He and I usually make up a team."

So it was set. Cleve gave Zeb a week's advance on wages so he could make the entry fee. The days flew by as Zeb worked the ranch's dawn to dusk hours, then in falling light honed his bronc riding skills on an unbroken dun mare that Cleve had sold him for twenty bucks.

By late July Zeb was asking around about the bucking stock to be supplied by the Scotty Philip ranch. For he knew even the wildest broncs behave in predictable ways. One bronc might run more than he bucks. Another might "blow up" right out of the chute. Certain horses spin clockwise. Others always counterclockwise. A dreaded "sunfish" bronc could be expected to kick out with all fours while airborne and twist almost on its side. Hardest to ride might be the cagey bronc known to dip a right shoulder, then unseat the rider by spinning left.

On the Friday morning of Frontier Days, Cleve and Tom Berry held a drawing to see which cowboy got paired with which horse. It is the irony of rodeoing that each cowboy hopes to draw the most dangerous horse, for it gives him the best chance of a high scoring ride.

As chute boss it was Cleve's job to post the random draw on the message board under the grandstand. As he did so he smiled to see Zeb's draw. Later at the board Zeb ran a trembling finger down the list looking for his mount:

Jimmy Chase .... Diablo
Cole Weston .... Last Chance
Beau Black .... Bolt
Zeb Wilder .... High Jinx

Zeb had of course heard of High Jinx, but just the same he proceeded to ask more experienced contestants about the animal. Then he hoofed it over to the rough stock corral to have a firsthand look. With arms folded on top of the corral, and one boot cocked up on a middle rail, Zeb had a good, long gander at the animal.

Then looking over into the arena he saw the backs only of a knot of white-shirted cowboys. One was recognizable for the distinct way he stood—weight on one leg, the elbow akimbo on a flexed hip. It was Cleve.

Zeb's attention returned to the bronc pen, where the advice of veteran cowboys and the sight of his bronc gave him an idea of what he was in for that evening. High Jinx was the biggest critter in the corral. His calico color suggested cayuse bloodlines, but outsized hooves and a jug head hinted at some draft horse genes. Bulging white-rimmed eyes blazed more red than black, and flared nostrils were the size of teacups.

"Here is a horse I can score big points on," thought Zeb as he walked to the camping area where wife and son waited in the shade of the little Wilder tent.

On the way Zeb felt a firm grip on his shoulder, and turned to see Cleve's calm face. "Zeb, by golly, you drew a pretty rank horse in that High Jinx. When the stock contractor handed me the list of eligible saddle broncs, he figured as a pickup rider I'd appreciate some tips on which horses to watch out for."

"What did he say about my ride?"

"He said High Jinx bucks big, high, and honest. So look to find a rhythm. But he said be careful, cuz this bronc is a rare double-kicker. You know what that is?"

"No, Mr. Berry, I sure do not."

"Well son, a double-kicker, when he jumps in the air he can punch the blue yonder like a mule. Thing is, a horse like that might do it twice before coming back to earth. That's a double-kicker. Makes it tough for any cowboy hanging on for dear life."

Zeb considered this as his wry smile concealed a quick succession of thoughts: "Good news, the better to score points, win some prize money, buy another mother cow, get closer to starting my own little spread." The pair then shook hands, knowing they'd not see each other until evening.

Saturday night's rodeo crowd figured to be the biggest in years. The creaky, clapboard grandstand was packed, forcing latecomers to sit and stand on the hoods of motorcars all 'round the low fence bounding the arena.

Cleve kept his promise to Zeb, climbing up into his saddle built especially for a pickup rider. He wore the double-thick "woolie" chaps offering protection against the kicks, head butts, and bites of a wild bronc. To warm up Rex, he spurred him in short galloping bursts across that portion of the arena furthest from the chutes. As area director, Tom Berry supervised aboard his white quarter horse Zephyr.

All eyes were on Beau Black, who had just been bucked off Bolt but managed a clean dismount as he neatly landed on his feet.

That put Zeb next, and he gingerly climbed over the rail and onto the back of the visibly agitated High Jinx. For the occasion Zeb wore a shiny red satin cowboy style shirt, the kind with pearl buttons down the front and at the cuffs. His wife Clara picked up little Otis and rose from her seat on the top grandstand row to have a better look. She had made that shirt from a mail order pattern. She was especially proud of those pearl snaps used in place of buttons.

Meantime, over on the powwow grounds to the west, Stands For Them was observing and enjoying the gentle hypnosis of a lady's Lakota dance, when straight off he arose from his tree stump seat to cup his ear—then to sniff the rising easterly breeze after having wet his nostrils with saliva on a little finger. These were old but true ways of gauging the danger in an evening's air.

The old man wore a concerned look as he moved away from the singing and dancing to a quiet place just beneath the nearby river bluff. There to take the measure of the night. There to hear coyotes howling at a gibbous moon. But alas, the threat he thought he discerned lay in that zone just beyond human sense.

Back in the arena, the metallic screech of heavy hinges signaled a rodeo chute flung wide, then the whip like snap of leather on sweaty horsehide, the thud of hooves shaking the very earth: Zeb and High Jinx burst into the floodlights. Together the fans slid to the edge of their seats.

Jump. Kick. Jump. Kick. Like riding a giant rocking horse, Zeb strained to find the balance point and rhythm needed to stay aboard.

Cleve urged Rex parallel to the bucking High Jinx but at a prudent distance, all the while shielding Zeb from the dangers of wooden and wire fences.

The crowd roared as Zeb spurred the mustang ever higher.

Unnoticed, a cloud obscured the moon and the coyotes fell silent.

Then it happened.

High Jinx bucked high and double kicked. Zeb pitched forward on the second kick, his britches three inches off the saddle, suspended but fighting to reconnect with the horse.

His center of gravity now no longer over the horse, Zeb plummeting headfirst towards the plowed earth of the arena.

But he merely bounced off the ground hard, jerked back by a left boot twisted and pinched in the stirrup.

Every cowboy's dread, the "hang up", turns a bronc from confident bucker to panicked galloping beast dragging some unknown thing. That thing a human body.

Zeb's head bounced off the turf, but he remained conscious; for the moment able to avoid deadly hooves. *Horse turn right*, he willed, *Turn right and I have a chance. Turn left, and I'll go under the pounding hooves.*

Cleve, galloping to the rescue, knew this too. He pushed Rex hard to steer High Jinx into a clockwise circle around the arena. If successful there might be a chance for Zeb. A chance also to grab the bronc's headgear. To slow him down.

That's when a well-meaning chute hand stepped forward with arms held wide in hopes of slowing High Jinx. Screams and groans came from the crowd as the bronc bolted left, dragging Zeb under lethal hooves. The horse thundered on as Zeb passed from a seemingly invincible young man to a rag doll under steam-hammer legs of a 1,200 pound beast.

It was two agonizing minutes before Cleve and Tom together were able to corner High Jinx near the pen gate.

Feverish efforts were made to revive Zeb by the lightly trained medics, the young man so trampled there was nothing to revive. Towards a scene too painful to watch and too compelling not to, the crowd rose as one. Clara rushed down the steps and to her husband's side, holding Otis and screaming a scream where no sound came from her mouth. Zeb's red satin shirt masked the blood on his body, but not on his stoved-in face.

As Clara embraced her dead husband with one arm and balanced little Otis with the other, her hand brushed the pearl snaps on the way to

Zeb's cheek. This ripped the heavens in two, and brought crashing down the sadness too sad to believe. For Clara, for Cleve, for everyone.

Unbidden, rodeo cowboys formed a silent crescent around their fallen confederate, shielding his form from a thousand prying eyes.

Cleve would deal with the images for a lifetime—the violent and public death of his hired hand. A young man steeped in the cowboy lore they both loved. A young family torn apart.

Even so, and despite his own pounding headache and nausea, Cleve was struck by the banality surrounding Zeb's death, of any death. He helped wrap Zeb's still-warm body in a blanket, then joined three others to carry the sad bundle to a 1925 Ford Model-T pickup truck meant to double as an ambulance but serving now as a hearse.

Behind the truck a group of uneasy Lakota men stood with hands folded, drawn by the shouts, the screams. Among them was old Stands For Them, who locked liquid eyes with Cleve for just a moment.

This is the finish of something, Cleve thought. Indeed, the tragedy started a familial ambiguity towards the toll rodeos take on both man and beast . . . lasting a hundred years even onto his still-ranching great-grandchildren. From this day the brothers Berry, heretofore the backbone of White River Frontier Days, distanced themselves from the event's management. At home, they began experimenting with safer, smarter ways of breaking horses.

Old cowboys mulled it over for years: "If he had worn better-fitting boots. If his chute-roosters had rigged the stirrups to hang longer. If his pickup riders could've turned or stopped that bronc."

A decade later at a restaurant in Murdo, Cleve overheard a Kadoka ranch hand, a man who never knew Zeb, recall the 1928 catastrophe— "Well, at least he died the cowboy death, with his boots on." Though Cleve had not yet ordered, he walked over to the table, told the man to shut up, then slammed the door on his way out.

Chapter Seventeen

The Train Whistle Shrieks
1929-1934

Cleve looked up from his morning task of loading refuse on a wagon behind a pair of draft horses. Someone was coming. Someone characteristically raising an arm high in greeting. Always the left arm, "the arm that never sheds blood."

In this way Stands For Them arrived unexpected at the 33 Ranch. Always welcome, never expected. It was the last day in March of 1929. He was hoping Cleve could write a check in advance payment for the winter grazing of cattle on his allotment. That check would be for $10— a rather princely sum given the era and the recipient.

Cleve retreated to the house to find his checkbook and fountain pen, then wrote the check with a meaty hand better suited to throwing a lasso or stretching barbed wire. But today there'd be no time for the usual conclave with Stands For Them under the shade tree.

Folding the check neatly in half and handing it to Stands For Them, Cleve was out the door and headed for the barn . . . he'd noticed Jessie's scribbled note thumbtacked to the back door—"Please take all that winter trash to the family dump. Check the water barrels. I think we're almost out;" She was away collecting eggs; maybe just as well for lately the sadness in her eyes was hard on Cleve. The ranch was growing bigger each year now, sometimes by a thousand acres or more—this made for the ascendency of Cleve's dream, and the slow death of Jessie's hopes for a California life. Yet the less her rather dreary life resembled her dream, the more dedicated she was to its magic. She had not quite given up.

Each homesteader or rancher of this era needed a trash heap. For there was no organized trash removal. The Berry dump, as was typical, sat at the bottom of a cutbank, just beyond sight and smell of the house.

With a nod to his old friend, Cleve climbed aboard the box wagon piled high with butcher bones, an old mattress, broken windows, what seemed like a thousand tin cans, and the rusty reservoir of a kerosene lamp. A wrist snap to the reins and the team was headed for the dump. Curious about this strange process, Stands For Them followed on foot. The dump came into view at that break where badlands formations interrupted the prairie sod. From here the arid land rolled lunar-like northward out of sight.

Arriving at the rim, Cleve coaxed his team into a slick half-circle backing maneuver to bring the rear gate of the wagon just above the dump. As he began shoveling trash over the edge, Cleve paused to acknowledge Stands For Them's curiosity.

"Yes," said Cleve, motioning Stands For Them to join him in the wagon box—his way of allowing that one man's trash might be another's treasure.

Stands For Them clambered up, then awaited further encouragement by way of Cleve's nod to self-consciously sort through the junk in the wagon. He retrieved for himself a bag of rag-cloth, a lengthy strap of broken harness leather, and one woefully dented porcelain coffee pot. The old headman smiled up at Cleve in thanks, then climbed down clutching his finds.

Cleve shoveled the remaining trash into the draw, then together they sat on the cutbank to contemplate mankind's detritus. Sitting there near Cleve, the nut-brown eyes of Stands For Them showed a longing and regret born of inability to fully communicate.

Had they spoken each other's language, Stands For Them would have marveled at the perhaps unnecessary complexity of English; Cleve would have puzzled at a language with no swear words. Yet as sometimes happened Stands For Them found a way to convey, pointing to the glint of reflected sunlight of a distant and new brass survey stake signaling yet another invader of the reservation. The old man, turning palms upward in surrender, looked briefly at the cowboy. A wry smile played across Cleve's face, for was he not such an invader too?

Then as if with one mind, the pair slapped their knees and stood up. It was time to leave the dump to the buzzing flies.

While Cleve secured the wood-slat tailgate and made minor harness adjustments, Nawica Kicijin thought back to the middens attached to those campsites of the tipi days—his long memory easily recalling piles of bones, unusable hides, horse dung, canine and human feces, broken tools, dead birds, spoiled foodstuff. He recalled how a Lakota summer camp of 100-400 people became a rather foul place in as little as a week. Their semi-domestic dogs had helped scavenge anything remotely edible. But the full solution, conveniently synchronized with the need to follow buffalo, was to simply pack up and move to a greener, more pristine campsite. His band would return to the same series of campsites every summer, as by then vultures and beetles, rain, wind, and sun would have cleaned things up.

While clamoring back up into the wagon, but before sitting down, the pair cocked an ear towards a sound rarely heard near Cedar Butte— faint shriek of a far-off train whistle. Rare because the nearest railroad line, the Milwaukee Road connecting the Missouri River with the Black Hills, was some seventeen miles away.

But on this clear day on the rim above the cutbank, sound carried bell-like on a zephyr breeze. The train whistle brought a toothy smile to both creased faces, as always for opposite reasons:

"I never hear a train whistle but what I don't think of freedom," said Cleve to no one in particular. For a white man of his generation trains meant mobility, speed, adventure . . . and for him the whistle rekindled memories of that youthful summer spent riding the rails south to Texas. Cleve continued gazing to the north in hopes of hearing the whistle again.

Stands For Them had first heard the wail of a train whistle in 1869, the year America's transcontinental railroad was completed along the southern edge of the fall hunting grounds for his band.

Memories of that day flooded back. "I watched my father and his father, Santee Man, scramble up a high hill to better hear the first iron horse, or perhaps even catch a glimpse of the snake-like thing! When they returned it was to sit at a council fire of long-faced tribal leaders. Later when most had departed father called me to the fire. He said I was not to be excited or curious about this iron horse carrying the wasicu, warning that this fire-breathing thing will surely bring buffalo hunters. "These hairy men have already started killing our beloved buffalo, and for just the robes and tongues."

Riding back from the dump outing, both men heard again a faint echo of the train whistle. Cleve noticed the frown-lines and glistening eyes on his passenger's face. Then it dawned on him—to Stands For Them a train whistle did not mean freedom. It meant the beginning of the end of freedom, of the buffalo and the free-roaming life.

Back in the barnyard, Cleve's attention turned to Jessie's second request—refill the wooden water barrels. The only on-site water source was a windmill powered well, but it brought up only the bitterest of artesian water very nearly unfit for human consumption.

But what of pure spring water bubbling up from the very earth? Ah, for both men this was nothing short of a miracle. But only Stands For Them's allotment concealed just such a water source. This spring rose up from some unknown source, smelling of cracked-rock sweetness. Whether Celt, Christian, Cretan, Greek Delphi priestess, or elderly

Lakota, all believed there was something holy about a place where clean water bubbles up from the dusty earth. And this spring was less than a stone's throw from Stands For Them's house.

White and Indian alike came from great distance to fill wooden barrels at Stands-For-Them's spring—the sole sweetwater source between the Little White River and Black Pipe Creek. These waters gave Stands For Them, otherwise a "poor" man by wasicu standards, something to feel rich about. To trade with and to be generous with. Especially with neighbors such as Cleve.

There came a day when daughter Julia asked why their fine little house sat in such an exposed and dreary place:

"Here is why, my daughter. I, Stands For Them, was born Miniconjou, so water is in our band's very name. I am now Wazhazha by marriage and by my choice to restart life in this valley. In this same way you are considered Wazhazha. Wazhazha is an ancient word coming from the direction to the rising sun, a band name of our former allies the Ponca and Osage, a name connected to forces in the earth—of snakes and of invisible waters. For where the land meets the water is where the living meet the dead. When I heard of the spring on this allotment, how could I not ask that it be our home?"

By now Cleve had loaded up his four large wooden water barrels to start the three mile round trip to the Stands For Them place. The old man would be back there by now, and of course he'd be happy for Cleve to load 200 gallons of his spring water. The chore would take much of the afternoon.

On hearing the horses arrive, Stands For Them ambled out to welcome Cleve with his self-conscious smile. He'd changed clothes when the sun had disappeared behind clouds: Plain pants rough sewn from wool trade cloth, a shirt of burgundy topped by a knotted kerchief. His fur coat was of horsehide and tailored in wasicu style.

Together the men positioned the wagon and barrels below the spring. A homemade rough-lumber trough began slowly filling the first barrel.

Today while barrels filled the friends walked among grasses surrounding the ancient springs. It was a chance for Stands For Them to point things out, here and there. A grouping of old tipi ring stones. A patch of *timpsila*, the swelling tubers soon ready for digging. Traces of old buffalo trails showing that spring waters have always attracted the thirsty, whether two-leggeds or four-leggeds.

Circling back to start the next barrel filling, the men could smell moisture in the air. The northwest sky mixed shades of gray in anticipation of a spring snowstorm. Still the men walked, hungry for what they might find and share.

Stands For Them's practiced eye roamed left, then right. Then he froze. His chin tilted down, head slightly cocked, and mouth slightly open—striking an ancient, aboriginal pose. In it Cleve saw the scout that Stands For Them had been so many decades ago. But what was the *naca* seeing, hearing, perhaps tasting?

Another moment of suspension. Then Stands For Them took three steps and bent to extract an artifact that to Cleve's eyes was invisible in the mud-covered earth near the spring. Cleve thought it might be an arrowhead, but the old man rubbed the mud away from what was left of a stone ax. At this find Stands For Them visibly brightened, feeling again a connection to the ancients. He motioned Cleve to follow.

By holding his find just so, and walking with purpose towards the house, Stands For Them promised something still more impressive. On reaching the front door, Stands For Them looked back and then entered.

Cleve hesitated, despite Stands For Them's welcoming gesture. In these late frontier days one race generally did not enter the abode of the other. Even a tenderhearted homestead woman was sure an Indian in her home meant future bed bugs and lice. Cleve wavered, then gingerly stepped just over the threshold.

His first time in the dark interior of Stands For Them's house. His nose functioned before his eyes—jerked meat and eagle feathers and musty human odors from so many bodies living without benefit of tubs and running water. When his eyes adjusted, he saw no curtains, no floor coverings, few pieces of furniture. Army blankets substituted for interior doors. But here and there were colorful quilts and beadwork hanging from walls. A feather-festooned lance was propped in a corner. Now he saw a war bonnet, then an elaborately beaded backrest, a sacred shield, what might have been a young man's medicine bundle.

The items were beautifully bright, if slightly out of place in such a dark house. Cleve guessed these treasures were mostly the work of Cora, and would soon be moved to the nearby tipi recently erected to capture the cooling breezes of summer.

Soon Stands For Them emerged from a back room, holding up an object in both hands as a priest might present a communion chalice. It was a seven-inch-long stone spear point, expertly chiseled from obsidian, gleaming black with a faint green cast.

This lethal beauty seemed from the far past, meant for some prey bigger than either man could imagine. When Cleve made a gesture as to where it had been found, the old man pointed in the direction of the spring. *Of course,* thought Cleve, *the spring must have been a refuge for humanity thousands of years before the Sioux migrated here.*

Stands For Them rolled the stone from hand to hand, content to see it as "Big Mystery"—a courier from some forgotten time and race.

When offered, Cleve took the spear point in his hands, holding it to the light, turning it over admiringly. Seeing this, Stands For Them made it clear that Cleve was welcome to have the precious thing. Cleve was tempted to add the spearpoint to his box of collectables, but declined.

Stepping outside the house, Cleve noticed that certain bedding and clothing had been carefully placed over a grouping of nearby anthills. As a lad he'd learned this Lakota trick of using red ants to clean any garment contaminated by lice and fleas, for the ants love to feast in this way.

Water barrels full, farewell handshakes completed, Cleve turned Dick and Mollie towards home. He thought of the coming summer, and of October—by then the market cattle would have been trailed to the railhead.

When October arrived, the three Berry brothers, Cleve, Tom, and Claude, combined their market-bound cattle into one big herd as a thrifty way of driving the animals overland to the railhead at Belvidere. The animals could then be fairly easily separated by respective brands. The brothers' trained eyes could usually spot their respective critters. Tom bred Hereford calves sired by massive bulls. Cleve liked his calves a little smaller. Claude preferred southern steers.

A reporter caught wind of the big cattle drive and wrote a slightly exaggerated article claiming this Berry cattle shipment to be ". . . the largest live cattle railroad shipment in the history of the northern plains." That might have been so had the Berry cattle been from the same ranch instead of three separate shipments.

But things like cattle drives were fast changing here at the start of the Great Depression. On the very same day as the great stock market crash of 1929, Cleve leaned against the muscled flank of his new roping horse Babe, observing what with fleeting hope he thought might be a rain cloud. It was instead a dust cloud kicked up by a car approaching from the east. He put down the tool he was using to trim the hooves of Babe.

Straightening a sore back, he looked at hands as dry and cracked as the land—made worse by a morning spent gathering and curing prickly thistle. With no rains there would be no hay meadows. So in desperation he'd cut and stacked green thistle, knowing as a last resort that livestock might eat this weed as winter feed.

By now he could hear the rumble of the fast-approaching auto. It was a heavy four-door sedan, a DeSoto rumbling and billowing boat-like over the last cattle gate and up to the hitching rail. Cleve tipped his hat back, set his jaw and walked towards the car, knowing it held strangers which these days was rarely a good thing. The first head to pop out was mostly obscured by a white Panama-style fedora.

Just the week before there had come three long rings and a short, the party-line signal for Cleve to pick up the receiver. The baritone voice introduced itself as Miles Kennedy, Vice President of Loans, State Bank of Omaha. "Mr. Berry. This long-distance call concerns your mortgage as well as loans for the cattle feed, and the new breeding bull. I assume you are well aware that you're in default. If this situation is not resolved, State Bank has the legal right to recover sums owed by claiming either your house or your remaining cattle."

Cleve said little during that call. He had expected the bank to be a bit more lenient, as other financial institutions had been here in the Dust Bowl states. The conversation ended uncomfortably when Kennedy growled that he'd soon send representatives to the 33 Ranch to ". . . enforce a prompt payment."

That first fedora was followed by a second. Then a full view of the two bankers, wearing long-sleeved, sweat-soaked white shirts and holding wool suit coats. Each vainly dabbing at reappearing beads of sweat on forehead and temple with a handkerchief. Each glimpsed a land so dry as to have been stripped of all color.

The visitors had the trappings of power, but hardly the physical station to match. Neither slim nor heavy, the pair were to Cleve's eye a bit doughy in the few body parts visible—fleshy jowls, necks, hands.

Awkward acknowledgements followed. Cleve suggested they retreat to the relative comfort of the kitchen with its icebox-cooled lemonade. On entering, they passed a small table holding a half-filled basin of water and bar of lard soap meant for any dusty kitchen-bound cowboy. Even before seated, the bankers began lecturing Cleve on what he already knew—details of his outstanding loans.

With lemonade half-finished came the demand for payment. "Mr. Berry, we made this long drive so as to have a look at your operation, and to remind you time is up on the loans with State Bank. That means now."

Cleve got up and walked to the cupboard on the pretext of finding some napkins. He stood in his quirky way with more weight on one leg, the elbow akimbo on the hip. The bankers wouldn't notice what old-timers called Cleve's "double-sprung hips." They'd not know or care that such joints make a cowboy extra comfortable in the saddle.

He remained facing the cupboard for a moment, then turned around slowly. "These days I've got more dogs than bones. Same with every rancher in these parts. Cash is scarce. My Jessie is a very frail woman, and we're just getting by in raising our little girls, so I don't reckon you're about to take their home, are you?"

The bankers exchanged glances. Each held a pencil with which they circled unseen numbers on separate ledgers, and then the shorter one stood to speak, "Mr. Berry, we are not today going to take this house, even though it's your first listed collateral. However, we are going to insist you sell your remaining stock to satisfy the debts."

"That just don't wash. To sell my cattle at these low prices will not only put me out of business, it won't come close to the full amount of the loans."

Taut silence descended. No one budged. The bankers' doleful faces implied a willingness to take the partial loss. Cleve, accustomed neither to negotiating nor bootlicking, stared directly at one banker. Then the other.

At length Cleve went to the kitchen door, propped it open, and motioned with his arm towards the vastness of the ranch. So vast in fact that not a single cow was visible from ranch headquarters. He pulled out his tobacco pouch and papers, then said, "Hell fire, if you want those damn cows, then you go find 'em."

Cleve rolled his own as he walked back out to the gate to resume trimming Babe's hooves. The bankers left. In time Cleve was able to pay off the loans. Tenacity had won.

Babe whinnied, lifting his jughead south towards Cedar Butte. Cleve's gaze followed. He saw nothing, but dared not doubt Babe's sense—certain creatures were surely up there. Whether wild horses, predators, or rustlers, who could say?

Cedar Butte held a special spot in Cleve's heart, standing as the only height from which to survey all his many and growing acres. The easternmost point of the Pine Ridge escarpment, which arches westward through Nebraska to the Wyoming border, Cedar Butte is where prairie first meets badlands.

If Cedar Butte was heartfelt geography for Cleve it was perhaps even more so for the Lakotas. To them it was Hunte Paha, remote and lonely enough to serve as a perch for young males enduring their arduous vision quests.

Off the shoulder of Hunte Paha there rose up a minor mesa with further meaning to local natives. Stands For Them knew this flat-top as *Paha Wakan*, "high holy ground." The whites called it Coffin Butte. Treeless, nearly too steep to climb, it mounted to a perfectly level summit the size of a football field.

The Coffin Butte name came from early reservation days: for it was here that a locally curious custom played out—that of placing Lakota cadavers in steamer trunks, the lids weighed down with heavy stones. For traditionalists like Stands For Them, the practice accomplished three things— (1) it skirted the odd and frightening new law requiring burial deep in the earth, (2) the remains could rest on appropriately high hallowed ground and, (3) the butte's flat top made the rogue practice unobservable to white authorities.

Stands For Them's father had been of a generation fearing that a body buried six feet deep would mean a soul unable to escape. The scaffold of old was ideal, but steamer trunks were a reasonable compromise. Unknown to most settlers (including Cleve) but important to Stands For Them was this beautiful fact: Coffin Butte was his generation's high physical metaphor uniting the clash of cultures below. The thoroughly flat top of *Wakan Paha* as seen from the air but also as noted by observant persons afoot is the precise shape of a Christian cross, the top of the cross pointing towards the North Star. So, the holy butte of old native believers could double as the hill of Golgotha, a Calvary for native believers of the white man's religon. Such an intersection of faiths wasn't lost on the Lakota, nor on their light-skinned evangelists: The White Robes of the nearby St. Thomas Episcopal Church would each year lead native congregants on a short, steep pilgrimage to the top of the Butte. This happened just prior to sunrise each Good Friday, then again early on Easter.

Cross Butte was the new name, and it stuck. For forty years onlookers could see among the climbing congregants one a little taller than the others, eventually a little slower—the local *naca* Stands For Them, Cora beside him. Devoutly, humbly, Stands For Them would most often bring up the rear of the procession. In this way his incantations did not compete with those of the priests at the lead.

Every year when the Cross Butte service ended, Stands For Them could be seen stepping away from others—quietly greeting the rising sun in the old way. A moment to face the direction that is the source of all beginnings, all wisdom. At this hour an easterly breeze would often rise to brush his cheeks.

On one remembered morning as Stands For Them returned to the main group, he felt a tug on his sleeve. It was his nephew Good Voice, asking, "*Kakala*, in your prayers you mix the two faiths. Why?"

The old man thought for a long time before answering, "The spiritual truths of different peoples," he offered, "are as the many kinds of prairie flowers. Each dazzling and authentic in a way that neither duplicates nor competes."

As Cleve's gaze moved from the butte to the Red Road, he chanced to see Stands For Them rein in his wagon horses. Parties were too far away to shout or wave, but not too far to contemplate each other— Stands For Them holding the horses still, Cleve standing with a hoof trimming tool in each hand. Cleve wondered if the old man knew how sick Jessie was, perhaps explaining why he'd stayed away from the Berry house for nearly two weeks.

Jessie's health had never been good in this country. Rare was the winter day when she was free of a sore throat, a cough, or an earache. By November 1934 she had all three, and a swollen tongue too. Devoted mother of four girls, her youngest was barely out of diapers while the two oldest were away at Yankton College.

Cleve cranked the telephone handle, picked up the earpiece, dialed "zero." The operator sounded so very far away. "Hello, I need to reach my daughters. It's urgent. Please connect me with the house phone at the women's dormitory, Yankton College, Yankton, South Dakota."

Seven minutes later, "Daddy, is that you? Why are you calling?"

"Mother is not well. I think you need to take the morning train. I'll pick you up at the Murdo depot."

"How sick is she, Daddy?"

"Pretty bad." He choked on the words. Twenty-four hours later Marian and Phyllis stepped off the train at the one-room Murdo depot. On the drive home Cleve presented as a man worn out, worn down. "She has pneumonia. Can just barely breathe and talk, what with a very swollen tongue and throat."

"Oh Daddy, how much pain is she in?" Cleve hesitated, but then told them the doctor was administrating morphine. Would they understand what this meant? They were old enough to know the truth: "That's not something a doctor usually does for a patient that might recover."

When Marian and Phyllis entered Jessie's room, she brightened, and with effort whispered greetings, "Oh my, how healthy you two look. How wonderful to see you."

Years later Marian shared with her father, at his request, these five entries from her 1934 diary:

November 27: Horrible day and nights. Mother died at 1 a.m. She knew she was going to die. I could stand it if it wasn't for Daddy. I feel so sorry for him.

November 28: Don't see how Daddy will stand it, but he is so courageous.

November 29: Thanksgiving at Uncle Tom's. Everyone there so sorry for us.

November 30: Most beautiful funeral I ever saw. Mother looked so nice—white satin dress. Enormous crowd. Mountains of flowers.

December 4: Mrs. Chamberlain died and left seven little, little children. We are better off than they are. We sent many of Mother's flowers left here to this other funeral.

In the grey day after Jessie's death, people came from all points. Most stood outside the small house, made more so because Jessie's body was still in the bedroom.

Parked among the Model A's and Tin Lizzies was but one horse-drawn conveyance, that of the Stands For Them family come to pay their respects. James stood awkwardly at the fringes of the male mourners. Cora found a chair by the hitching post and by gesture made it clear that she wished to hold one of Jessie's quilts.

Had this been a Lakota wake, she surely would have joined the other females in loud keening—that death wail she knew would best release both mourners and the mourned. But not here, not among the wasicu. Instead she carefully folded the quilt from Jessie's own hands across her lap and stroked it for much of the morning. This she could do. When Cleve came near to offer a nod of welcome, Cora's return look of pained condolence was beyond anything language could convey.

Mostly Cora looked down at the quilt. But from time to time she looked up with sadness to see her husband standing there alone. Stands For Them did not however feel this sadness. He was accustomed to being invisible when in any group of wasicu men. For him, going unnoticed was simply a condition of being native.

By early afternoon most of the guests had departed. Still the Stands For Thems remained. Stands For Them and Cleve had retired to their little council tree, there to sip coffee and just sit. Cleve looked up often towards the long road to the mailbox. Stands For Them understood—His friend was watching nervously for the mortician's hearse.

Cleve took his eyes from the road, glanced at his coffee cup then up into Stands For Them's countenance looking oddly, fixedly at him. A way for Cleve to see something new in the wrinkled face: a man who'd many times stood where he was now—peering into the abyss. Cleve returned Stands For Them's gaze and whispered what did not need saying, "I see you see my pain. I see yours. Want this or not, we now share a thing deeper than friendship."

Two weeks later Stands For Them came calling. Not finding Cleve in the house he strode across the grounds to where barn doors were flung wide. What he saw caused him to retreat—for there sat Cleve bent to Jessie's mahogany-colored saddle on his knee. He'd taken down a cloth and saddle soap and was bringing a shine back to the fine-grained leather of the swell and cantle. Unseen, Cleve had first done this act of love shortly after the funeral. In coming years, he often shined the never-used saddle, seeking moments when he might yet feel her on his skin.

Chapter Eighteen

Flaming Arrows
1934, then 1864

Cleve and Stands For Them continued to meet regularly to conduct simple "business." There were also opportunities for congenial barter. Cleve loved these simple deals. Something about being in the presence of Stands For Them made him feel perhaps he would be able to hang on, to shake the blues.

On this blustery spring afternoon, there was a bit of business still pending. So they agreed to meet "tomorrow", both resorting to sign language to confirm it would be "before the sun is highest." Cleve knew that he dare not be more specific—for Stands For Them would not be ruled by the hands of a clock, this man who saw no sense in owning a watch even if he could have afforded one.

For Cleve, on the other hand, "time was money" . . . it was a linear commodity to be managed, guarded, saved like so many coins, exploited even. Stands For Them smiled at such a way of living, remembering maternal Grandfather Spotted Horse kneeling to place a hand on his always moving grandson Curved Horn to say, "Remember little one, he who hurries has one foot in the grave."

Cleve's youth had been spent watching his father, James Berry pull out that gold pocket watch multiple times a day, every day. It was an age when a fine pocket watch signaled to others ". . . there goes a man both punctual and reliable."

But there was more—James came to manhood during the Civil War, when almost all watches were still individually hand crafted, and beyond the reach of most. So for James, a pocket watch was a symbol of success.

This was Cleve's view too. Even so, he understood he was often a prisoner to time. He knew well the old Celtic saying: "When God made time, he made enough," while not himself fully believing it.

Next morning as Stands For Them harnessed his horses and set out for the Berry ranch, he too mulled the idea of time. His people had always felt the whites unwisely assigned a time and a date to every activity, big or small. *Was it not an obsession to measure everything in hours, minutes, even heartbeats? Then numbering all the days of the earth? How could this not pull humans away from the timeless center of all things?*

Stands For Them further puzzled over the confusing time zones of the land's white occupiers: How was it that one standing on Cedar Butte held a watch saying 12 noon. But in Kadoka, visible to the west, a similar watch would say 11 a.m.? Yet in his balanced way Stands For Them also thought, *Who can deny the wasicu live more comfortable lives? So perhaps this counting of heartbeats brings easier living.*

Just last month, Stands For Them shared the Indian concept of time with his youngest half-sister's first born, thirteen-year-old Good Voice. As maternal uncle he played a big role in raising this Lakota boy, equal to or even transcending a father's influence. In the custom of his people, he called Good Voice *Takoja*, "grandson." The boy was but one of many who called Stands For Them *Kakala*, "grandfather."

The discussion of time happened on one of Good Voice's regular visits—for he spent one sleep every other moon with his aged uncle and aunt. On this day as usual he waited with the long but patient face of a boy who'd rather be elsewhere.

They sat beside the ashes of a fire. "See these pebbles on the ground?" Good Voice nodded. "Today they will be symbols of the ticking pocket watch I know you've seen on a chain hanging from wasicu vests." At this Stands For Them picked up a dozen or so pebbles.

"You are clever in the new ways, Good Voice. You see that the tick-tocks of the watch are something a wasicu calls one 'minute.' Our ancestors might counsel that nothing in nature repeats in such a short, regular way."

A distant rumble of thunder summoned dual nickers from Stands For Them's nearby wagon horses. Good Voice frowned, afraid he'd not have time to hunt the nearby ravines for rabbits before it rained.

"Our people, your people, have always reckoned time in natural ways, bigger ways. The arc of the sun, the rising of the moon, the circling of stars. These were, and for old ones like me, still are our only clock."

Good Voice fidgeted, smiled, then did his best to listen, to comprehend.

"You will see, time has no beginning and no end, so it is best represented by the circle. Knowing time is a circle, you'll see it rolls fastest for those who do not recognize this cyclical order."

The old man again held his arm out, waiting, waiting, then dropping a handful of pebbles near Good Voice's feet. The boy looked up to see what lesson this might hold, as Stands For Them used a sharp stick to draw a circle around the heap of pebbles.

"Grandson, you will not be like me. You are compelled to live in the wasicu world. You must learn to keep a closer accounting of time. But remember, do not become a prisoner to the wasicu pocket watch."

"Look at nature, which does not hurry. Yet everything is fulfilled in each season. When I was your age, we moved as the sky and the land instructed. We often ignored time. Yet we had practices for dealing with important rendezvous."

"In what ways, *Kakala*?"

With his low gravelly voice and aided by images traced in the dust, Stands For Them told of a long-ago hunt with Good Thunder. They were young men chasing a herd of elk into Spearfish Canyon. Good Thunder had harvested a young bull elk, tying the best cuts to their only pack horse, then tying the horse beneath a pine.

The pair agreed more meat was required but that they would need to separate, for the hard-pressed elk had scattered. With sundown approaching, Stands For Them suggested meeting back at the pack horse in "the time it takes to erect a tipi." This span of time was known to both. The wasicu would call it forty minutes.

"One more thing Good Voice. Remember time cannot be lost, for it is nothing more than a tool to keep everything from happening at once. When nothing happens, as when we sleep, time stops. It cannot be gained or lost."

Finally, Stands For Them pointed with his stick to the circle, saying, "You have been to many a wacipi. I have seen you join others to dance around the circle. In the circle we are all equal, for there is no one in front of you or behind. No one above you or below. The circle is sacred because it gently brings unity. Our tipis were sacred circles. But when the wasicu put us in these square boxes," he said with a glance at his frame house, "much of our power was lost."

Stands For Them continued in this way to share Lakota essence with Good Voice, moon after moon for two years.

When Stands For Them was long dead and Good Voice very old, he counted himself among the handful who grasped the oral pillars of his people. And because Good Voice's eight years of schooling left him with one foot in each world, he later saw clearly why time is experienced so differently in the white and Indian worlds—He learned that wasicu saw time as history. For them and him there is a past, a present, a future and so time seems linear, like a stick. Yet he often smiled to think of the uncle who saw time as a hoop, with no beginning, no end. The uncle who said for Lakotas it only matters where an event happens, not when.

Who said time is an illusion, blinding two-leggeds to what we so rarely see—eternity.

He also smiled at uncle's last shared recollection: as a sixteen-year-old lad returning from a buffalo hunt, Stands For Them chanced to meet a young *Oglala* boy of ten: Black Elk by name. In 1906 Black Elk would marry Anna Brings Three White Horses, a relative of Stands For Them's patrol mate during the Wounded Knee days. (For among the Lakota it seems everyone is related or otherwise connected to everyone else.) Later, in the 1930s, Stands For Them learned Black Elk had been interviewed by the writer John Neihardt. Then came the slim book, *Black Elk Speaks*, eventually gaining worldwide fame. Why had no one sat down with Stands For Them to translate his wisdoms, Good Voice wondered. But Stands For Them knew. He knew the white man's printed stories were static, unmodifiable, in some ways dead. He would not have been interviewed if asked, for the puzzling printed words compared poorly to fluid oral Lakota stories, each able to be enhanced, expanded, having a certain life force when by tongue traveling down the generations.

At one memorable teaching session Good Voice seemed distracted, and Stands For Them wondered what to say. Then hitting upon it—*He is coming to the age where boys want to know about weapons.* He told Good Voice of admired Cleve's gun collection, mostly from afar. But there came a morning when he found his friend cleaning a carbine on his lap. Cleve happily handed the weapon to Stands For Them, his chance to balance a newer model Winchester in his big hands. To Good Voice he said, "Ah, such a fine weapon I had never touched." "What was your first gun, *Kakala*?" Good Voice said as he joined Stands For Them on a fallen cottonwood trunk serving as a rough bench on the shady side of the old man's house.

"In those years beyond the Medicine Line, I once traded for a Spencer carbine. This was the long-ago soldier fire stick. As a "single shot" it was nothing to be proud of. But that old gun made me a good shot— requiring sure aim if I was to kill a buffalo with but a single bullet. For if I missed with that one noisy bullet, the chance was gone. Lakota firesticks killed some buffalo, only what we needed. The wasicu money hunters wiped out our buffalo. We believe the beasts took many bullets meant for us. That is why the Lakota are still here."

"But tell me now of the time before the fire sticks," a smiling Good Voice said as he used this old term so new to him. "You have never boasted of your prowess with the bow and arrow. Yet I've heard other old ones, elders your age and older, making much of their aim with the bow."

The old man's eyes lost focus, and his voice grew distant. "I will tell you. When I first ventured from the mother lodge, like all boys I learned the bow and arrow skill. No exceptions. From our fifth winter on, we all played with the little bows and little arrows topped with bird points. Our great joy in those endless days was to shoot, to stun, or kill one of the many songbirds near camp. Not an easy target—for this was child's play with a purpose."

Good Voice nodded and tried without luck to imagine such a world. The plume of dust and distant rumble of an automobile bound for Belvidere caught their attention.

"In my youth, the steel trade arrowheads were nearly always used. In earliest memory I saw only a few arrows tipped with stone arrowheads."

"But I have seen among your possessions a few arrowheads, *Kakala*. Did you not make them?"

"Oh, no. Even in the last buffalo days, this skill was no longer being passed from generation to generation. But when I was first learning the art of bow and arrow, I can tell you of one ancient stone knapper who came to the great summer camps at *Mato Paha* (Bear Butte)." Good Voice slid inches closer along the log.

"Iron Mountain was his name. He was Hunkpapa Lakota, so we Miniconjou boys had to search him out among the campfires on the far side of the great summer circle. Iron Mountain welcomed guests only in the morning, and he was a man of deep ritual. When knapping he often touched his fingertips together over his head while murmuring a prayer, then using only fingertips he'd pick up the next charmed piece of stone. Somehow, he knew what was buried in this rough stone. Before the sun reached its high point, we watched him chip away useless parts to reveal the most artful arrowhead. A translucent living stone, shaped for flight. Magic."

"The greatest of the old knappers, men like Iron Mountain, took onto themselves a portion of the flint's character. Indeed, when finished the stone likewise took on a portion of the knapper's character."

Opening his eyes wider, Good Voice said, "I have found arrowheads. Maybe one was made by Iron Mountain. I have not found many."

"Do you know the old scout's secret for finding things difficult to find?" asked Stands For Them.

When the boy shook his head, Stands For Them said, "This is it. Scouts of old, the ones I learned from, taught the art of looking without looking. There are certain things in this world that are invisible to most eyes, like a partially buried arrowhead, a nest of fresh prairie chicken eggs, or a white buffalo. These holy things do not want to be found. So you cannot go looking for them. The best you may do is to be fully present when they choose to reveal themselves. Looking without looking."

Good Voice wanted more, "*Kakala*, what is your strongest remembrance of bow and arrow? I wish to close my eyes and make it my memory as well."

"There is a moment that still burns within. It was when I was a boy no longer at my mother's breast. The Long Knives of General Sully were pursuing our *Santee* brothers after the many bad killings in the forests where the sun is born among numberless lakes. But these soldiers had followed the sun's path so far that they were now in the middle of our nation . . . and the *Santee* fight became our fight.

"The bluecoats pushed us back, for they had guns so big they were pulled by mules. We made our last stand in the heart of Miniconjou hunting grounds at *Paha Tahkahokuty*. The wasicu renamed it Killdeer Mountain."

"In those days our war chiefs had learned that to win we must know when to kill, but also when to leave the killing fields. Knowing the land, it was for us to choose when and where to fight. I believe the horse gave us this wisdom. For from the back of a horse our ancestors could be the ones knowing when to attack, when to swiftly withdraw. Living to fight another day. They had all the watches, but we had all the time."

"There at *Paha Tahkahokuty* I'd never witnessed such excitement, and in this battle we young ones and women were sent back in the ravines. Our provisions were tied to pack horses, at the ready to retreat if need be. Word passed from band to band that the out-of-sight fighting was going poorly, and that a signal might come to melt into the badlands. If it should come at twilight or later, this signal would come by a great flaming arrow."

"Of course my little friends and I wanted badly to witness this sight. So when we saw the powerful archer Rattling Leaf move quickly out of camp and to the southwest, how could we not follow? Rattling Leaf did not go far, positioning himself atop one of the many rose-colored roundtops of the Little Missouri country. We quickly climbed a similar but smaller hill, careful to stay out of sight."

"Back in camp Rattling Leaf had used tongs to carry a hot coal from one of the small cooking fires. Now in gathering darkness, we would see this red-hot coal . . . but not much else. That's when he lit a fat-soaked linen wrapped 'round his arrowhead. In an instant he was half illuminated in the glowing light. Then we saw his shoulders roll back, sturdy arms pulling the taut bowstring to chin. He aimed high with the long bow, launching what others might have mistaken for a mighty shooting star."

"This flaming arrow made a beautiful arc, such as one sees in a rainbow, though there may be no words to describe it. At the arc's high point, the arrow slowed, hanging in the air before the flame finally went out. It left us boys wondering if the arrow, unseen, continued to float there." Stands For Them's eyes fairly blazed with this memory.

"At this sight there was a catching of breath across the land. Every manner of sound snapped into unnatural silence. But only for that moment. Then it was all craziness and commotion in camp below—dogs barking, horses braying, women calling out—the arrow signaling the break for the hinterland."

"With our mothers surely missing us now, we scrambled back to our proper places among families, presently fatherless as the men were still holding the battlefield. No scolding followed, for all energy was thrown into moving deeper among the badland peaks. We boys dared not talk about the sight of that arrow for many hours, as once in the vastness of badlands absolute silence was required."

"In this battle we lost 100 brave warriors, and the bluecoats only two. Yet on General Sully's orders, several Lakota's heads were cut off and mounted on pikes as a warning to all free-roaming Indians. We have never forgotten this barbarous act."

At this the pair sat for some time in silence. Stands For Them lifted his eyes to the western sky, spotted the evening star ablaze above a soft sunset, thinking of the one season when he carried both the old bow and arrow and the new fire stick. The gun had been a revelation, the emblem of full manhood, and an efficient killing tool. Yet it paled beside the experience of pulling back the bowstring—the archer feeling the energy of his right arm flow into the string, hence to the arrow, and hence to the quarry. It was as though his own life force traveled from heart to hand to arrow to buffalo.

At Good Voice's prodding, Stands For Them explained why he favored the older weaponry: "In the time I could load and fire a gun, and reload again, I could launch three, maybe four arrows. And from behind a bush, as an archer I could do this silently—no sound of thunder to reveal my position."

"Also," he said, "with the ancient weapon one could take a place of cover below a ridge and launch the arrow in a soft killing arch over the hilltop. The bullet travels only the straight noisy path. The arrow is the silent trickster."

"*Kakala*, tell me one final story of the days of the bow. For surely those days will not return." Stands For Them nodded yes before entering the house to bring his tin pot of coffee outside. He warmed up his cup while reaching back in time for a last story:

"Son, there was a curious custom of the bow among plains tribes that belonged to the age before my time. But it enjoyed a short revival in those years when I was called apprentice warrior." Good Voice brightened, encouraging Stands For Them to leave no detail untold.

"This ritual allowed boys of your age a chance to join in horse raids and even battle one year early. But only if this special ritual was successfully completed. It required the strength to pull the long bow, so not every boy tried. The elders called it Shooting the Sun."

"I was big for my age, so at the summer's first buffalo hunt, my father arranged with Chief White Swan for my attempt."

Good Voice had once heard of this obsolete ceremony, where a boy attempts to shoot an arrow directly at the sun. A ranking elder would serve as witness. If the trajectory was true, the arrow was lost in the sun's blinding fire, and in this way would appear to fly out of sight. To the sun.

Now self-consciously, Stands For Them continued, "White Swan took a position on my left shoulder. I pulled the bow string to my chin. To my ear. And let fly the arrow. I was lucky. Or White Swan was generous. For he proclaimed I had shot the arrow true and straight and to the sun. I heard a few shouts of joy from my tiyospaye. No one else much noticed. But it was enough, for on the strength of that moment I was allowed to join a horse raid against the Pawnee."

This ceremony had begun for Stands For Them a lifetime of watching the sky for wonders to come. The wish of a Lakota skywatcher like Stands For Them, as with aboriginals around the world, was to bring the obvious cosmic order down to earth. Stands For Them's mother's father once said it, her brother had often repeated it: "The sacredness of our high plains is in the sky. So look up Stands For Them, not down, when seeking nourishment for your soul."

For him one day there came a sky to exceed all sacred expectations. The back-to-back phenomena would have been unsettling had each not been so bewitching. The evening in question fell commonly enough, with Stands For Them riding as passenger on the way home after a day of visiting the sick with John Singing Goose. The team needed water as they rolled westward on a dusty Red Road. The solution was a short stop at the Berry ranch house. There Cleve could be seen rewrapping a coil of used barbwire that had too-long hung loosely from the gatepost.

"Yes, of course," Cleve nodded when he saw Stands For Them signal that his animals needed water while reining the team into the barnyard. Rather than requiring an unharnessing of the team to lead them to a nearly stock dam, Cleve instead grabbed two buckets of water intended for other horses.

He set the water down before each horse, and with skilled hands volunteered a slight adjustment to the harness where it rubbed the withers of one animal. He offered a few Lakota words of greeting to his visitors. Stands For Them left their English reply to bilingual Singing Goose. All caught the cordiality, if not the full meaning of every word. The horses drank every drop from the buckets. Together the trio turned to linger over the last sliver of what had been a crimson sunset.

Presently Singing Goose grabbed the headset of each horse and encouraged the team to pivot the wagon clockwise to complete the journey home. That's when something—a shimmer of pulsing light, swiveled heads to the north. What had caught their eye was a highly uncommon but not unknown spectacle this far south: the fluttering, wispy, unmistakable curtain of the Northern Lights.

Both Cleve and Stands For Them had spent time in Canada, a land where such light shows were not so rare. But here, in South Dakota, the sight lit astonished smiles on each weather-beaten face.

The younger men leaned on the wagon box, Stands For Them sat on the wagon seat, all sharing the wonder. But the red men and the white man read different stories into these lights. For Cleve, the story sprang from a modest knowledge of science . . . something about particles high above earth being bombarded by the sun.

Stands For Them understood the flickering lights as an unseen campfire beyond the northern horizon, in the spirit world, around which sat his grandparents, his father and mother, and Tall Woman holding little Nation. The longer he beheld the lights, the more comforting was this thought.

For a while longer the trio watched silver, blue, and green curtains shimmer then fade into a moonless sky. Then came an odd sense, almost a foreboding, as if this night might hold still more magic. But the feeling passed.

With a slap of both hands on his outsized arthritic knees, Stands For Them whispered a few words in Lakota that Cleve guessed to be a prayer of gratitude. Stands For Them beckoned Singing Goose to join him on the wagon seat. Offering no further comment or eye contact, he faced forward and handed Singing Goose the reins. Never mind the night's darkness, horses could use senses other than sight to safely navigate the Red Road's every twist and turn homeward.

Then it happened.

In a great flash, the black dome overhead turned startlingly white. Everything, down to blades of grass, was colorlessly visible as if at high noon.

Instantly, soundlessly, darkness snapped back in place.

Whether by unseen meteor or sheet lightning or some unknown incandescence, none would ever know. All three simply looked at the others. If silence is the best response to mystery, then their wide-eyed hush was as it should be.

Days later Cleve took his 16-gauge down off the rack above the fireplace, lightly oiled it inside and out, and found two boxes of lead shot shells. On this hunt he'd decided to leave the heftier 12-gauge at home, thus honing his marksmanship with the smaller gun. Perhaps this would impress his new hunting partner, for Bill was the type of person unexpected in rural South Dakota, circa 1934. A real live pilot . . . and better yet, a sportsman pilot!

On this late summer day Cleve hitched a ride with a friend eastward to Winner, South Dakota to stalk the recently introduced Chinese Ringneck pheasant. Bill had earlier determined where the birds were, so hunting was good and huntsman fellowship even better.

When time came to go home, Cleve's hitch ride had unexpectedly journeyed to Pierre. So Bill Hinselman made a stunning offer for that day and age—he would transport his friend the eighty miles back to the 33 Ranch—in an aeroplane!

Bill was in his fifties, noticeably well off, and 6'2" tall. His fluidity of movement suggested the middle-distance runner he'd been at State College. He dressed as hunters then dressed: all brown and rust colors, tweeds and double-stitched leathers, knee-high field boots. Bill's hands, seeming too small for his formidable body, were yet every bit as tanned and callused and capable as Cleve's. Thinning brown hair was hidden by a safari-style hat and framed by greying sideburns and an ample mustache.

Aviation in 1934 was barely out of its infancy, still a novelty in backwater South Dakota. Only recently Amelia Earhart had made the first female solo Atlantic crossing—and was plotting her ill-fated "round the world" attempt. Barnstorming pilots in biplanes were still celebrities when touching down at county fairs.

So when Cleve arrived back at his ranch home by dropping out of the sky, it was a big event. The aeroplane, Bill's slightly rickety little 1932 Waco, touched down with a bounce or two just north of the ranch house. Once on terra firma, Cleve turned to his aviation friend with a question, "Bill, do you suppose you could give a short ride to my little girl Jan? She'll never forget it."

Bill took a long draw off his Camel cigarette while smiling down at Cleve's impish, redheaded, and utterly astonished five-year-old daughter. She wore a green plaid smock dress with matching bloomers above black double strap leather shoes. Her appearance was such that despite misgivings about the makeshift landing strip, Bill could not bring himself to refuse.

Jan had no such misgivings and eagerly climbed into this flying machine, insisting on sitting up front beside pilot Bill. Her Aunt Dixie, at the ranch to serve as surrogate mother following her sister's death, settled somewhat skittishly into the jump seat in the back.

Contact. Ignition. Sputtering fire, then ever-faster spinning of the big wooden propeller. Bill maneuvered the plane so as to taxi into the wind. It figured to be a rocky takeoff. Bump, bump, bump over clumps of grass and prairie dog mounds. Then after one especially big bump, the rumbling plane was gliding smoothly on wrinkle-free air.

Little Jan was thunderstruck to see the badlands fall away in all directions. Sights included her now dollhouse-sized home. The family car similarly toy-like. Even mighty Cedar Butte looked pocket-sized. Pure magic as she imagined herself beholding nearly the entire world.

That big bump just before the plane became airborne? One of the wheels hit something. Likely a prairie dog hole. Unbeknownst to the now-airborne pilot and his passengers, the impact had severely bent the right wheel strut, and also knocked off the wheel casing and tire.

Little Jan never would forget this ride—but looking back at the ranch house she could not grasp why Daddy there on the ground was frantically waving his hat, pointing excitedly at the plane. But Bill knew something was wrong by Cleve's rapid arm movements and a part of the wheel he could see by leaning slightly out the window. With no radio to communicate, Bill yet construed Cleve's gesticulations correctly: "Do not land here. The plane is damaged."

Bill dipped a wing to circle the ranch three more times, gaining what knowledge he could from the fevered sign language below. He thought he understood Cleve's solution, for his cowboy friend pointed urgently southwest as if saying, "Follow me. I will lead you to a smoother landing place."

Cleve jumped into his aging pickup to attempt leading the plane across the badlands to the only level plot of land in this otherwise "broken" country: Stands For Them Flats. There he knew of a level field once plowed to corn, though it had lay fallow since the time of Wounded Knee.

Bill, in no rush to land, flew in slow circles to allow the pickup a head start. In this way, Cleve on the ground and Bill in the air, proceeded three miles to the west . . . the truck kicking up clouds of dust below the aeroplane's lazy slaloms. Lucky for all, both barbed wire gates on the Red Road were wide open. They could thank the Indians clip-clopping along the road, for natives had a habit of opening but not closing gates.

Waving his cowboy hat out the driver side window, Cleve squinted at the lumbering aeroplane, thought of wee Jan, and said a quick prayer. When Cleve reached the Flats he immediately jumped out, pointing repeatedly to the ground so as to make clear to Bill this was the chosen spot.

Knowing nothing about aviation but being a common sense sort of fella, Cleve figured Bill needed particulars on the wind direction and speed. So from his neck he undid a red bandana and held it aloft.

The fluttering bandana told Bill there was a southwesterly crosswind, making him consider either the "crab" or "sideslip" landing. *But no*, he thought, *the damaged wheel and struts require the lightest possible touch down.* So after circling twice Bill made his final approach, slowing to the point where he brought the Waco into a controlled stall just as the wheels met the old cornfield.

Light as a feather. But as the plane sputtered to a stop, its small tail wheel caught a series of timeworn plow furrows, making for a jarring end to the ride.

Cleve could breathe again. He ran to the plane and offered a hand down first to his sister-in-law Dixie, then Bill, and finally wee Jan, so eager to tell daddy all about the wonders of manned flight. Cleve was a patient listener, but in fact just wanted to hold his little girl. Over Jan's shoulder he could see Stands For Them and Cora some distance away.

A minute or so later, Cleve's hired hand, Emmett Wayne, rode up on his horse. The young man had been nearby mending fence. Cleve recruited Emmett to use the pickup to drive Jan and Dixie back home, but first retrieved the family Brownie camera from under the passenger seat. Then he tied Emmett's horse, his ride home, to the aeroplane's propeller.

Cleve quickly took this picture of damaged wheel and horse, and when developed scribbled on the back "Old Ride Meets New Ride." He rolled up his sleeves to be ready to help Bill on the needed repairs.

*****

Three hours later Bill wiped grease-covered hands on a rag and flashed a toothy smile. He'd completed a makeshift repair that would allow for a takeoff. Off he flew.

Cleve shortened the stirrups for the half hour ride home. He waved at James and Cora, frozen at their threshold as though dumbstruck by what had transpired.

Homeward, he encouraged the horse to a slight detour to the nearby tiny white Catholic chapel, there to bow his typically unreligious head in gratitude for Jan's safe return. The chapel had recently been constructed just twenty rods west of the Stands For Them house. Cleve found it a curious location, since all knew old Stands For Them had been baptized Episcopalian.

"So, what was it?" he mused. "Why a chapel in the middle of nowhere, close neither to Corn Creek Village or Running Bird Village." Cleve didn't know of the Catholic Church's long history of placing new houses of worship on sites already holding meaning for the indigenous peoples. In this case, the chapel was right beside the sacred Red Road. And so close to the powwow grounds, and the spring that served as a water oracle of the Stands For Them tiyospaye. Certainly the chapel location also honored wife Cora, a practicing Catholic since 1892. Soon would follow a burial ground, aptly named Stands For Them Cemetery.

Cora by this time had retreated inside, but Stands For Them could not take his eyes off the empty place where the plane had been. He had so far lived perhaps eighty years, though no one knew for sure. To the Lakota a toting up of years lived was trivial. Battered by a life of hardship, Stands For Them had come to accept that the marvels of earlier days would never return. But what of this flying miracle from the east? For him it was *Wakinyan*, the mythic thunderbird.

In summer especially the thunderbird was a favorite topic around pre-reservation campfires. Sitting at one of these campfires, Stands For

Them had first heard of the thunderbird. He had seen its image painted on many a tipi, on countless shields, and woven into his mother's beadwork. He knew one old seer claiming a visitation by a thunderbird during a vision quest.

In recent times, Stands For Them had seen aeroplanes. But only twice, from great distance, his eyes squinting at the noisy mechanical bird laboring high above the buttes. Today was different. Today's strange thunderbird floated just above the top of Hunte Paha, circled lower, lower, to all appearances looking for a place to "perch." Stands For Them and Cora were drawn by the droning sound into brilliant sunshine for a better view. Stands For Them's neolithic birth in a buffalo-skin tipi had not prepared him to witness an aeroplane landing in his front yard. He wondered, *Would any two-legged ever again see such change in one lifetime?*

Stands For Them put an arm around Cora as though to shield her. Lakota tradition said a woman having a vision or dream of the thunderbird was at risk of death by lightning strike. "For your sake Cora we must be cautious with this winged spectacle, and not move from this spot." Indeed, Cora had more than once told the story of her like-aged cousin, Morning Star. As a maiden Morning Star had a nightmare haunted by the thunderbird, obliging her to elect one of several sacrificial acts known to forestall the impending lightning strike. She chose to plunge her hand into a scalding kettle of stew to grab the severed head of a small dog. Her right forearm would ever after be discolored. Yet she was never hit by lightning.

For Cleve's part, he would not fly again for another twenty years. By autumn he was more worried than usual about his livestock and worsening condition of the range. His boots made a crunching sound on dried grass and dead pine needles. He walked under October skies hinting at overdue rain. Today he saddled Rex for the three-mile ride to his mailbox. There he chanced upon the mailman, who'd earlier spoken to the German emigrant neighbor who lived to the north: "Old Gunter says there's a stretch of fence down on your northeast pasture." Cleve had no choice but to trot Rex northward, hoping there'd be daylight enough to mend the fence. He found the broken wires, and the repair was blessedly routine and rapid. But it was clear from tracks that a few head of his livestock had gotten through the break.

Cleve headed westward along the fence line till he came to a "let down", where the wires were held only by hooks, not staples—the traditional way to get a horse across a fence when no gate is handy.

Letting the wires down one by one, then standing on them, Cleve coaxed his horse onto the vast Indian allotments to the north. In fading light, he followed tracks of his wayward cows where they'd meandered among ghostly badland spires. The further he rode, the fresher the tracks. A rising three-quarter moon gave Cleve hope that he could safely gather up the runaways and push them home. That was before a wind shift brought a wispy mist into the valley, followed by a thick fog and over-cast sky.

Cleve was disoriented. He'd come to know the dry creeks, canyons, and all forms of his land as well as his own hands but had rarely ridden here. He took a deep breath and dismounted so as to gain a closer view of the only thing visible—the immediate ground—in hopes of spotting anything familiar. Without the moon, North Star, or constellations to guide, he was simply lost. Remounting, he nudged dependable old Rex forward. Cleve gave up on retrieving the renegade cows. Instead, he sought a dirt trail, a fence line, or anything to orient.

That's when he stumbled onto a white-bluffed valley containing gar-gantuan skeletons. Sure that he had found a dinosaur graveyard, Cleve dismounted and walked among the elephantine bones, which he surmised had been exposed in the previous week's big downpour. It looked to him like at least five great beasts had died here.

How eerie yet lovely the bones lay, all scattered in the diffused light. Cleve picked up what looked like a femur, four feet long and thick as a yule log. He briefly considered tying the monster bone to the back of his saddle.

Cleve walked back and forth looking for a skull, hoping it might hint at the creatures he was dealing with. No luck. The fog showed scant signs of lifting. If anything, it was thicker.

Men of Cleve's ilk knew intuitively, or else were taught, that where human cleverness ends is precisely where animal senses shine. His father's words came back to him: "Only the hunting dog knows which bush holds dinner, only the woolly caterpillar knows the burden of a coming winter. And only the horse, come fog, blinding rain, or blizzard, has a sixth sense to carry its rider home."

So just before giving Rex his head, Cleve decided after all to tie the great bone just behind his saddlebags.

Rex led Cleve through the fog and back to the barn, but Cleve never could again find the "valley of bones." Wanting to tell someone but fearing they'd scoff at his "dinosaur" graveyard, Cleve could at least prop the femur bone against his water trough below the windmill.

It was some days later that Stands For Them and wife Cora came down the Red Road on their way to Rosebud Agency. Hot, heavy air meant his usual mid-trip watering hole on Cottonwood Creek would not do today. So they stopped where they'd be welcome, at the Berry homestead water trough.

Cleve was away. Stands For Them watered the team at the trough, and smiled to see the great bone, three times bigger than even the largest grizzly or buffalo bone. When Cora came up, he pointed and exclaimed, *"Wakinyan Wamakhaskan!"* The Lakota name for Thunderbeasts, for these bones were most often found after a heavy thunderstorm—and thus the ancients saw the bones as the remains of creatures among the storm clouds making the booming, crashing sounds.

There would be another interpretation for Cleve. It would come over thirty years later, when he unwrapped a Christmas gift copy of Cleophas O'Harra's *The White River Badlands*.

The book's many skeletal illustrations were a revelation to Cleve—his "dinosaur graveyard" was clearly the bones of Titanothere, beasts the size of Indian elephants from the Oligocene, the epoch of mega-mammals.

Chapter Nineteen

Beseeching His New Nation
1918

Cleve looked up from milking the cow to see yet another Indian wagon rolling down the Red Road with a hero of the Great War in the seat of honor. Even from such distance he knew it to be a returning veteran—for whipping in the wind off the back of the wagon was the Stars and Stripes.

He'd watched bemused as this stream of local young Lakota man returned from France. "Strange," he thought, "these lads volunteered but were not U.S. citizens." Abe Lincoln's Emancipation Proclamation had granted U.S. citizenship to most everyone born in America, slaves included, but pointedly excluding Native Americans. During the Great War, Indians volunteered to fight for America in high numbers. A few officials in Washington wondered if it was time to allow Indian veterans and a few other "good injuns" to become citizens, so there came citizenship ceremonies on a few reservations, all sponsored by the U.S. Department of the Interior. Finally, near the end of the Great War, a ceremony was announced for certain Rosebud Indians deemed worthy.

Stands For Them had been invited as one deemed worthy. He did attend, but stood with arms crossed near the back. By his presence, he brought a certain respect to the proceedings, though everyone knew he would decline the chance to become a citizen himself. Yet he watched the ceremony with keen interest, having heard rumors of a curious part requiring new citizens to shoot an arrow into the air.

Stands For Them smiled to see One Feather, his old army scout mate, standing as interpreter for the Interior Department Undersecretary sweating heavily in his dark wool suit. Stands For Them edged through the crowd to be just close enough to hear One Feather's translation:

"This is the Ritual On Admission of Indians to Full American Citizenship. The President of the United States has sent me to speak a solemn and serious word to you . . . He has provided papers naming some of you as worthy of American citizenship. I will read these names one by one, and you will come before me. Then I will say this:

What is your Indian name? You will answer.

I hand you a bow and arrow.

Take this bow and shoot the arrow.

You have shot your last arrow.

This means you are no longer to live as an Indian.

You are from this day forward to live the life of a white man."

Stands For Them turned his back to the next portion of the ceremony, choosing not to witness each candidate being asked to grip the handle of a plow, symbol of rural industry and work ethic. Others noticed his reaction.

Next, the Undersecretary instructed each candidate to renounce their tribal citizenship and consider themselves exclusively U.S. citizens. Finally, the compliant candidates were presented with a small American flag.

Six years later Stands For Them, nearly seventy years old, at last became a U.S. Citizen, not by choosing it but because Congress finally granted the same to all Indians.

Late in this summer of 1924, Stands For Them walked through the double doors at Norris Mercantile as he'd done a thousand times, today accompanied by lifelong friend Good Thunder. The pair came up short on seeing an unfamiliar and well-dressed woman at the counter. She spoke with an East Coast accent. It turned out she was a relic hunter—

one of a group of opportunists then scooping up artifacts, pottery, and regalia on the cheap, to be marked up and resold to museums, universities, and wealthy collectors. Stands For Them surmised that was her Studebaker parked outside, the finest motor car he had ever seen.

On hearing Stands For Them and Good Thunder enter, the woman turned from her discussion. She promptly judged these two Sioux elders as cash-strapped *and* likely in possession of desirable items. With a wink she enlisted the store owner as her translator: "Do either of you fine gentlemen have relics you would be willing to sell?"

Stands For Them pieced together the rough translation and firmly signaled his disinterest in such a transaction. But Good Thunder needed money for tobacco, so he stepped in front of his friend. "Yes. I have something I will fetch from my loggie. Home is not far from here." The woman signaled her interest with a nod. Stands For Them took a seat on the store's cracker barrel, content to wait for Good Thunder's return.

Good Thunder returned carrying a finely woven, golden-colored buffalo hair rope. Coiled now, but when uncoiled it was twelve feet long, trimmed in porcupine quills and wrapped in tooled leather at both ends. The woman seemed pleased.

Stands For Them watched with a sad face as yet another connection to nomadic days slipped away. Watched as Good Thunder's heirs lost a family heirloom that surely carried a significant story. The coins Good Thunder received were just enough for two small drawstring pouches of roll-your-own tobacco. Such was the depth of poverty on Rosebud Reservation in the twenties.

If cultural relics could not be preserved, perhaps some dignity could be. So Stands For Them paid attention three weeks later when word came that Congress had approved small pensions (as little as $20 monthly) for Indian irregulars employed decades earlier by the U.S. Military during the "Indian Wars." Recipients were to be men not formally enlisted but who had nonetheless served under the authority of military officers. Men like Army Indian Scouts. Men like Stands For Them.

Dotting an otherwise clear November sky were scuttled packs of puffy grey clouds that by late morning bunched above and around Cedar Butte. This made for a cool but not unpleasant day. When Stands For Them stopped at the 33 Ranch to ask for a dipper of water, Cleve could see his old friend had more than thirst in mind. So he led his friend to their usual seats under the little shade tree.

After draws of ice water, and shared nips from Cleve's flask, Stands For Them reached into his shirt pocket to self-consciously unfold and straighten a most unusual effect: A typed letter. Stands For Them handed the sheet to Cleve. As he did so, the old headman raised his eyebrows and smiled. Cleve took this to mean he was being asked to peruse the letter, and perhaps endorse what it contained. Cleve turned the letter right side up and read:

"Your Excellency,
Franklin D. Roosevelt, President of the United States
Washington, D.C.

Your Honor,
*   I have been trying to get a pension for my service as an ar-*
my scout during the Indian troubles in South Dakota in 1890.
My comrades, Brings Three White Horses and Bear Dog, are
getting pensions and I deserve the same . . .
*   . . . I have heard so much about your kindness that I want*
to write to you direct . . ."

The letter concluded with Stands For Them's thumbprint in lieu of a signature.

The upper righthand corner of the letter held the stamped proof of receipt and signature of Louis Howe, FDR's closest confidant and Chief of Staff. Cleve recognized the name, for it was just the month before that Howe's face adorned the cover of *TIME* magazine.

Cleve handed the letter back. Stands For Them refolded it with as much care as the unfolding. He then looked over at his friend.

Not yet knowing that the dispatch was but one of multiple letters across years of effort, Cleve extended a rather incredulous smile and a thumbs-up.

In coming months on street corners in Norris, Belvidere, and White River, Cleve heard more about Stands For Them's crusade. In total there were three letters to the White House, dictated by Stands For Them then translated, typed and mailed by others. One promising reply was from Chief of Contact Dr. G. M. Hyland, who wrote, "The President has requested that his interest in your case be expressed." On a later visit with Cleve, he brought forth from his shirt pocket a crumpled identification card confirming his service.

But for all the effort, Stands For Them was foiled repeatedly by the various and vague English translations of his unique name. Nawica Kicijin was, after all, a moniker in a society without a written language. This made for myriad ways to spell it using English letters. Some whites wrote it down as "protector," others "defender." Little wonder the War Department was unable to find Stands For Them's name in its' great vault of veteran records. Finally in the summer of 1935, as Stands For Them approached his eightieth birthday, came the emotionless letter that closed the matter—

Dear Mr. Stands-For-Them,
This is in reply to your letter of recent date, addressed to the President.

*It has not been possible to authorize any pension in connec-
tion with your alleged service as an Indian scout, inasmuch as
the War Department has been unable to locate a record of your
service.*

Respectfully,

George E. Brown

Director, Veteran's Claims Service

Bitter disappointment for Stands For Them, as over time the quest
had become less about the money—more about validation if not vindica-
tion from his adopted nation.

Oh, how sweet to be awarded his rightful pension from those unseen
rulers of the vast and muscular republic. But there would be no absolution. No squaring of accounts for a man who had first reluctantly then
graciously accepted the new sovereigns. This longing for justice was
captured at the end of a 1934 letter to John Collier, U.S. Commissioner
of Indian Affairs. The old scout's words hold echoes of the point in time
sixty-five years earlier when Stands For Them earned his name:

"I am seventy-six years old. As to this pension, I will stand up until I
do get it."

Chapter Twenty

Last Days of the Nomad
1937 - 1939

In the year after Stands For Them had given up ever receiving his Indian Scout pension, there came for the *wacanlica* a second friendship with a local wasicu. It grew to rival his formidable bond with Cleve.

This new friend was the young barber of Norris—an unlikely connection for Stands For Them, given his braided hair reaching nearly to his waist. Something to be cut only when in mourning.

Joe Desjarlais, like both Stands For Them and Cleve, resided beside the Red Road, his segment passing through tiny Norris before curving westward towards Wyoming. Dark-haired Joe was the kind of young man who other young men willingly follow. Born scant days before the turn of the century, this son of a son of a French-Canadian voyager was a drover on the last cattle drive to bring government-issue longhorns and shorthorns up from Oklahoma to the Rosebud Reservation during the Great War.

The trail drive ended at Wood, South Dakota. Joe plainly saw that cattle drives were fading into history. So in Wood he sold seven of his nine-horse string, giving up life on the trail for short-term stints as a ranch hand, then a handyman, a store clerk . . . anything for a grub stake. But it was hard to find steady work.

In fate's whimsical way, Joe drifted down to Mission, South Dakota. Prospects there were even bleaker than in Wood. He did manage to find a little work as a freighter, then briefly as an apprentice blacksmith.

Joe's lack of formal education was no disadvantage in this country. Nor did it dampen a naturally deep curiosity, and formidable intellect.

Like a jack-in-the-box, the twenty-year-old was spring-loaded for the right moment.

That moment came one chill morn when Joe and three other young men were warming their hands around the wood stove in Mission's roughshod barbershop. This day Klaus the barber seemed nervous, less talkative than normal. His ill ease finally spilled out in words: "Boys, tomorrow I'm packing everything up and leavin' this god-forsaken country for good."

"But Klaus," protested the shaggy lad to Joe's right, "How can you leave us? You're our only barber. Where would ya be headed?"

"Going back East a ways. Maybe Iowa. More krauts there. Around these parts the homesteaders, them that stuck, don't come down to Mission for haircuts much. And most Indians never ever cut their stinkin' damn hair." After a pause in which he stared at the ceiling, Klaus concluded, "I'm done here. But a guy ought'a get a buck or two for this shop. Any you boys know of anyone 'round who's tried a little barbering?"

Joe stood up to proclaim the falsehood that would change his life— "Oh sure, Klaus. I barbered some down on the Red River." His lie carried.

With that he walked across the street to the mercantile to purchase shears and a straight razor and was on his way to becoming the barber of Mission. His first twenty or so haircuts were ragged affairs sitting like roadkill porcupines atop razor-nicked faces. But then Joe was charging just ten cents instead of the going rate of ". . . shave and haircut—two bits."

By the time the Mission community was accepting Joe as the man to do haircuts, word came from further west that the village of Norris was advertising for a barber. The new town's offer was straightforward: a willing barber would get a shell of a storefront, and a used barber's pole—the red and white stripes once associated with blood-letting, for indeed barber and surgeon had once been allied trades. Even in the 1920s, in the absence of a doctor or dentist, a village barber might be called on to bind a wound or pull a bad tooth.

The modest offer was enough. In a fortnight Joe's Barbershop was doing a brisk trade, for Norris locals had no memory of his unsightly apprenticeship. Unsurprisingly his haircut and shave business also included the occasional tooth extraction, for which he had purchased medieval-looking tooth pliers. There came a day when one of the local Indians, Iron Bow, referred to Joe as *Pehzutah Tonkah*, "Big Medicine." Among the natives, this name stuck. Big Medicine had arrived.

Joe enjoyed meeting western Mellette County's immigrants from Bohemia, Austria, Holland, Slovakia. Heterogeneity suited him, for he possessed an uncanny ability to pick up foreign languages. It was said he could work beside a Swede or a German for as little as one day, and by sundown could carry on a simple conversation. By his second year in Norris Joe was nearly fluent in Lakota.

By 1927 a now well-established Joe, wife Angeliana, and six children had returned to the Roman Catholic faith. The local church made of him a deacon. There he met Father McCormick, priestly in long flowing robes and equine face. The Father was quick to note Joe's command of the Lakota language and appointed him local liaison between the church of the cross and the native church of the pipe.

Over the years, Joe overheard enough native conversations to have learned the old tribal mantra: "The oyate (nation) is only as strong as its women." This is not what Joe saw—to him Lakota women stood invisible behind the men, hesitant as rabbits to step into the headlights, dark eyes deeply suspect of a wasicu world. That perception died one heavily overcast February day in 1937.

Two winter-hairy horses harnessed to a worse-for-wear Indian wagon came to an uneven stop in front of the Norris barbershop. Hardly an uncommon sight to the few who noticed. Still, eyebrows raised upon seeing the lone driver of the team was diminutive Cora Stands For Them. Where was James? And had Cora caught the horses, harnessing them herself, and driven alone over the windy eleven miles to Norris?

Cora descended purposefully from the wagon seat and directly into the barbershop. There she saw Joe, his back to her, cleaning his various straight razors and scissors at the tiny porcelain sink.

"Hau, Pehzutah Tonkah," she greeted urgently.

On hearing her, Joe turned to face this normally retiring and now quite elderly Lakota woman. Her demeanor was all business. "You must help Nawica Kicijin," she said, "or he will rise no more."

"But what is wrong, Cora? Where is he?" Joe replied in his serviceable Lakota.

To which Cora headed out the door with a backward "follow me" glance. Joe followed. She scuttled to the back of the wagon to pull a rag quilt off of what seemed at first to be a pile of supplies. But it was the prone and shivering form of old Stands For Them, his hand to his face.

Beneath that hand on his right jaw was a red-streaked abscess the size of a grapefruit. The old man narrowly opened his eyes when Cora shook his leg as she then turned to the barber.

"*Pehzutah Tonkah*, you must save him by pulling the terrible tooth!" True, Joe had learned to pull an occasional bad tooth. But nothing like this.

"Oh no, Cora," protested Joe, "James needs a real doctor, probably a hospital. I cannot help him in his condition."

At this Cora rose up to her full height. Ignoring generations of female Lakota modesty, she squared up to Joe, nearly touching his hand

and leveling a gaze that flashed warrior eyes. *"Pehzutah Tonkah*, you *must* do something. You *must."*

Joe pondered if she might be right, for indeed Stands For Them was in no condition to travel any further on such a frigid day. By now a small crowd had gathered 'round the wagon. From this group Joe summoned two men to help him carry the old headman inside.

Not so gently they brought the semi-conscious Stands For Them to the chair, which was quickly tilted all the way back. Joe grabbed a bottle of Jägermeister which he asked Cora to administer to James as a substitute antiseptic mouthwash. And to take the edge off the pain to come.

Then Joe hurried to the back room to rummage for his tooth extracting pliers. By the time he returned with the gruesome tool, Stands For Them had taken a bit more than the suggested amount of liquor. Joe held the half empty bottle up to the light but smiled so as to tell his patient it was okay.

The 10x9 ft. barbershop room seemed too small for the moment— filled as it was with every manner of towel and box and bench, and smelling of hair tonic, old leather, and human sweat. And wedged in were a half dozen onlookers from the street.

Now began the challenge of simply finding the bad tooth buried in a mouthful of oozing and swollen gums. When Joe did find and clamp on the tooth, his typically muscular prying motion was not successful, nor was a repeat of the maneuver with still more robust pressure.

Backing off, Joe took a big breath and considered options . . . though it was clear there was nothing to do but extract tooth and root at all costs.

Seeking permission for stronger measures, Joe said, "Cora, as you see I try hard not to push against James. It is not the Lakota way to be pushed and touched by a person not of your family. But I fear I must take the difficult path to pry the tooth loose." When she glanced at James and he offered no protestation, she turned back to Joe with a look that said, "Go ahead."

So it was that Joe climbed up onto the barber chair to straddle old James. In this undignified way he applied all the strength and leverage of a man in his prime. When the bloody fang finally popped out, the collective sigh from the assembled was overtaken by subterranean groans from the old headman.

After half an hour's recovery and two more shots of liquor, Stands For Them was back in the wagon box, but this time he got there under his own power and assumed a position propped up on one elbow. Cora turned the team north and the wagon disappeared in the gloaming.

For the next fortnight Joe heard nothing from the Stands For Thems, nor did he make inquiry. It was high season for a barber—railroad crews were converging from the north and east, and the winter lull in farming and ranching activity meant men had time for that much-needed haircut. One memorable day Joe performed eleven shaves and nineteen haircuts.

It was on this very day that errand boy Billy came tugging on Joe's sleeve, then pointing out the window. Joe's throat tightened when he saw Cora's tiny form through the frosty window. But he relaxed when by lowering his head he could see her face wearing a tight little smile. Straight away Joe left the customer currently in the barber chair, and in five long strides was looking up inquiringly at Cora still holding the reins on the high wagon seat.

"For you," was all she said. Stands For Them was nowhere to be seen. Joe glanced into the wagon box where he saw two large elk skin bags bulging with the unknown.

"But Cora. You and James don't owe me a thing."

Then came her single Lakota word meaning "gift", sounding like a command brooking no allowable protestation: "*Waku.*"

Soon the bundles were safely on the rough wooden boardwalk in front of the barbershop. Joe could only shake his head as he undid a few of the leather parfleche straps to peek inside first one then the other leather bundle.

A stunned silence followed . . . for Joe had glimpsed the gifts a white man would least expect—the full regalia of Stands For Them neatly arranged in one bundle, and in the other the lovely ceremonial dress, leggings, and dance moccasins belonging to Cora. Upon further examination the headman's bundle included his ornate breechcloth and beaded moccasins, wrapped in a blindingly white ermine-pelt pouch.

As she drove away, Cora offered the only explanation Stands For Them would authorize and Joe would have to accept: "Because you saved his life."

Joe knew a headman such as Stands For Them did not simply decide to clothe himself in ceremonial garb. The PEOPLE clothed him, it being a labor of many hands . . . involving aunts, sisters, female cousins, and young men hiding long hours in eagle pits to acquire the needed feathers. None dared use the word "war bonnet" for the magnificent and spiritually-infused headdress—for to his people Stands For Them was a "peace chief." The shirt was no less magnificent—all trimmed in brilliant ermine tails and a mix of horse and human hair locks. The human locks were donated by a mourning person or someone wanting to honor the shirt wearer.

Days later, Cleve was paying for a roll of barbed wire at Cedar Butte Store when the clerk spoke of the strange episode in Norris—"Did ya hear? I got it from Etta Tinn. She said everyone down in Norris is talking about it."

Dropping the wire roll on the counter and taking a seat on a nearby keg of nails, Cleve listened with a smile and shook his head. Had Stands For Them really gifted away his magnificent regalia, seemingly the old man's very identity? Cleve knew well the Indian tradition of "give-aways." but this was generosity beyond the pale. What would the equivalent be for him? Giving the ranch away?

"Well, I guess this kinda turns the idea of an Indian Giver on its head," Cleve said to no one in particular as he headed outside to another day of hard labor on his ever-expanding spread.

For the aging Stands For Them it was not complicated—he knew eagle feathers must never be buried. And he felt power and freedom from this last big giveaway. Cora's sacrifice was no less, and he rested in the remembrance of her oft-repeated maxim: "One can be rich in three ways: by having much, giving away much, or needing little."

In this ample austerity they propped each other up through two more winters, rolling together towards March of 1939. The land was so brittle, so bleak.

Stands For Them fumbled with the stiff horse harnesses while looking over a homeland that felt empty compared to the same landscape of his youth. All the great beasts now gone. No wolf, nor grizzly bear, nor mountain lion. Saddest of all, no buffalo.

He pulled the Pendleton blanket more tightly around his shoulders and put the harness down when overtaken by yet another coughing fit, a rumbling, rasping hack from deep in the lungs that forced him back indoors and onto his bed.

In this his eighty-third winter Stands For Them had taken to thinking only of the solid past, never the ephemeral future. Memories of the buffalo seasons, mostly . . . those long sunny days of tipis with sides rolled up, horse adventures, big central fires, feasts.

He feigned sleep while listening to the little commotions of Cora as she adjusted his bedding and reordered the sick room. When sure she was out of the room, Stands For Them's hands felt for his body under the filthy blanket. His once mighty frame built on buffalo meat now so thin, so frail.

Touching first his ribs, then protruding hip bones, and withered thighs was his way of accessing health, weighing the chances that tomorrow he might rise from his bed of sadness. He concluded there could be no healthful tomorrows without a sacred intervention. Perhaps a small miracle would come if he found and consumed one of the rare and holy wild plants of old, as Red Badger had once done.

A distant rumble of midday thunder chased away the wisps of sleep he craved. Fat raindrops soon drummed the roof. Such a spring rain favored those searching for certain holy plants. So, Stands For Them propped himself on an elbow and called out for Cora. She appeared expectantly, hands clasped. He motioned for her ear. In a whisper he told of his wish to chew the pungent stem of the hallowed bear medicine plant. "Is springtime advanced enough that you might find a green sprig or two of the Bear With Horns plant?" Cora smiled. Perhaps, she thought, finding these uncommon plants would be possible in a sheltered south-facing canyon on Cedar Butte.

Even the youngest Lakota knew the story of Red Badger. Stands For Them had made his acquaintance in the buffalo days. It was at the Wagon Box Fight that Red Badger had dragged himself back to camp with deeply mortal wounds. But he was kept alive for four sleeps with four doses of 'bear medicine.' The bear is the healing animal for the Lakota, the animal that leads them to tribal medicines. When a bear was sick, it showed in the droppings, prompting the people to track the beast to see what roots *Mato* would dig up to cure himself. When they often saw the tracks leading to Bear With Horns plant, Lakotas used this same medicine on themselves. On the fourth day, Red Badger had emerged from his tipi to cheers, living nearly another year.

Stands For Them had asked. So she searched.

Cora was gone for two hours on that cold rainy day—she dared not stay away longer. Her hike was to the base of the butte, seeking the bear medicine plant despite the early season.

Walking through the door, Cora's long face told Stands For Them all he needed to know about his future. He would not receive the bear's healing plant. This did not surprise. What *did* surprise was the "peace of knowing" that now washed over him.

From youth he had been instructed that some things are unknowable. And he'd seen many sights beyond knowing—the thunderbeast, the magic arrows, many miraculous healings, the inscrutable wisdom of dreams. And so too would his death be beyond knowing—over the edge of the mountain to a place Lakota holy ones simply call the big mystery.

Word came one morning that there was to be a feast and young-man-honoring ceremony down at Corn Creek. These days the ceremony marked a young man's completion of school, or perhaps his enlistment in the army. The invitation had arrived by runner. Cora met the messenger at the door: "Would the wakanlica please come? If he is there it will bring good fortune to the youth named Bad Weasel."

She smiled to acknowledge the effort and sentiment, then she slowly shook her head side to side. "Tell everyone Stands For Them is now past the time for even short earthly travels. His next trip will be on the spirit road."

But the invitation made Stands For Them think of what could be done to influence this ceremony. Perhaps one or more of the old guard would take his place. So, he made a mental list of those older ones who might come to his house for one last council.

The list complete, he beckoned Cora come closer, "Long Soldier surely, and Holy Bear. They will come. Yes, and Brings Three White Horses, Sleeping Bear, Eagle Hawk, Singing Goose and perhaps even Thunder Hawk from over on the Little White River." Stands For Them's lifelong kola Good Thunder was unavailable, having traveled recently to distant Pine Ridge Village.

Cora pictured each elder as Stands For Them named them. Some had ridden with Stands For Them into the Grandmother Land. Some had ridden with him during the Ghost Dance troubles.

Cora hailed a youth from the Red Road to carry these words: "Come in two sleeps. We will feed you. Stands For Them is not well. He asks comrades to bring open hearts and open ears."

The appointed day's first light revealed four inches of fresh wet April snow. But the old wakanlica had asked, and so each man summoned would attempt the slippery horse-and-wagon trek to Stands For Them Flats. As usual, no meeting hour had been designated. Yet with the sun past its high point, wagons became visible rolling one after another across the flats—the last arriving just twenty minutes later than the first, a coordinated arrival divined rather than arranged.

Eyes downcast, Cora's whispered greeting was the same for each solemn arrival: "Hau, you are here!" Thunder Hawk was last to join the circle around their old tribesman. After murmured pleasantries and much silence broken only by Stands For Them's gurgled coughs, the old one opened his eyes wider than he had in weeks . . . looking 'round on the good faces.

He smiled, then with effort summoned words—"My old friends, we alone remember the days before the steamboat and railroad fire wagons, before barbed wire and plows, before the talking wires. We have for a few winters now been called 'citizens' of America. But we were born citizens of the Lakota nation. This is how we will die.

"Our nation is a shadow of what it was. America did not like a nation of a few thousand, owning a homeland vast beyond words. More than we needed, they said. So our homeland was made smaller and smaller.

Then men with tan faces but white foreheads took possession of the last of this land.

"Tomorrow I trust some here will attend the honoring ceremony in Corn Creek for young Bad Weasel. I cannot be there. Indeed, by then my spirit may have traveled to the far northern campfires."

No one moved. Every eye on the speaker.

"Some of you know that long ago I named my first son Nation. I held him up to the old high culture, that better version of ourselves, and this is what I ask you to carry to today's youth. My last wish."

With a start the assembled turned towards a low voice and fingernail scraping, as though the door were a tipi flap. It was Good Thunder. Entering, he nodded to Cora, uttered a word of greeting, grabbed a wooden chair, and slid it to the left-hand side of the death bed. On hearing that old familiar voice, Stands For Them smiled broadly but made no attempt to open his eyes.

Stands For Them spoke now as though there were no one else present save him and Good Thunder. Together they reflected on what was happening—Good Thunder listened as Stands For Them lamented his few options in the dying process. "In the old days we might be talking of the 'ancient one' death. Remember? When we were boys they told us to expect either the martyr's death, or else the old man's death." Back then many young or middle-aged deaths might qualify as a martyr's death—gored by a buffalo on the hunt, cut down while stealing horses, or best of all, dying in battle.

"But what of the very old, like me?" Good Thunder knew what his friend meant—In nomad days, when one reached a certain age, and usually prodded by the reality of not having enough sound teeth to chew meat, an elder might ride out on one last hunt, or even join the young warriors, with the purpose of not returning. Or, when camp moved and the moving was beyond painful, a wrinkled man or woman might honorably roll off the travois as it passed a gully or thicket. No one would question this, and there they would remain until wolves helped their bone and flesh blend perfectly with the swelling earth.

Presently Stands For Them opened his eyes with effort, vision blurry these days even on the face of his best friend. A face at once emotionless and faintly aglow with every emotion. "These honorable deaths are no longer available," said Stands For Them. "Now I have only a slow death no different from that of a coward."

Good Thunder nodded grimly, as did the others save Long Soldier, who was just then rising from his seat and stepping forward so as to be heard by his prostrate friend. "Wakanlica, I bear witness of what people are saying down at Corn Creek Village, also down at Bull Dog Village and even onto Red Leaf's camp."

"There the people have marveled at the strength of one such as you who can watch his wife die, then all his children, his brother in battle, all his grandchildren, and in the past year lose even his health. Yet still he rises, they say, to teach, to heal, to stand for the people. They say he has shown all how to suffer. And some say this suffering is as a prayer to the nation. An absolution for the people"

Stands For Them half opened his eyes as Long Soldier concluded, "I tell you this now as it may otherwise never reach your ears. Your life of suffering stands equal to the warrior's death."

Now from the cooking stove Cora brought in steaming bowls of a thin beef stew, one at a time. With help Stands For Them managed only a sip of his broth. The others emptied their bowls, one or two asking for refills.

Stands For Them stifled a cough, fearing it would bring blood to his lips, and thought of his still vibrant spirit body . . . how different from his earthly body, now frail and wrinkled and smelling of a putridness.

Ah, but it was not always so, he reflected. As boy of fifteen, sixteen, seventeen winters, he had finally grown into what others called a *washakah* youth—a "strong one" with proportionality for which his people were renowned—limbs lean yet clearly strong. Not so heavy that he would be burdensome to a horse in battle. Not so light that an enemy might easily bump him off his mount. It was this figure that friends spoke to that afternoon, not the skeleton in the bed.

Now one of those in the back—was it Thunder Hawk?—moved beside the bed and drew a sacred pipe from inside his long coat. He also fished out a pouch of tobacco, that most special of all gifts, which he parsed among those present as a priest might serve the eucharist. He twisted the redstone bowl onto the wooden stem—for one never kept the two together except for the holy smoking—and lit a small plug of tobacco within the bowl.

Careful not to contaminate the moment with words, each elder rose to join in a hoop 'round the bed . . . naturally, as a group forms around a campfire. Thunder Hawk presented the pipe to the four cardinal directions, then down to Mother Earth and up to Father Sky. Inhaling and then exhaling, he watched prayerfully as smoke circled upwards. Each in turn smoked the sacred pipe, until it arrived at the bedside in Good Thunder's hands.

The faithful kola knew Stands For Them's laboring lungs could not tolerate even a puff of smoke. This was reinforced by Cora's stern expression and folded arms as she leaned on the threshold to the kitchen. Thus, he took a puff on Stands For Them's behalf, exhaling a halo of smoke above the bed.

This benediction complete, Stands For Them gathered himself to speak of duties he wished others to assume—"Would you, Good Thunder, check in on Cora from time to time, and speak for me at the honoring of Bad Weasel? And you Singing Goose . . . would you continue the prayerful visits on both sides of Cedar Butte? Would you, Brings Three White Horses, now host the powwows, perhaps on the level ground south of your cabin?" Each in turn growled their ascent.

Good Thunder bent to say something, heard only by Stands For Them.

A fit of coughing interrupted the subsequent stillness, extinguishing the day's allotted energy for Stands For Them. Even so he could now see those assembled more clearly, circled so close.

That's when he noticed a stooped figure whom he did not recognize, unassuming and wearing a beaver cap pulled so low that others appeared not to recognize him as well. Then it struck Stands For Them—certainly here was the one come to help the soul escape his withering flesh. This was the headman called Death, welcome if unacknowledged among Stands For Them's other friends.

Hats in hand, the old friends knew it was time to move towards the door. Each offered a nominal farewell by way of a glance, a nod. With everyone gone but Cora, a hush descended. The minutes, hours, all such measures, had never meant much to these two, born as they were to a tribe which did not even have a word for "time." If illness was meant to prepare him for a state of complete timelessness, it was working.

Stands For Them had earlier given away the few personal possessions accumulated in a long life, including his fine roached dance headdress presented to Cleve. Being possession-free, the way Stands For Them came into the world, felt like a circle completed. It was the ancient way of making sure there is nothing to hold one back in the passing over.

Among all the gifting there was yet one exception, made clear to Cora when Stands For Them motioned her closer. Though he could scarce form words, his eyes traveled across the room to where from a nail hung a Presidential Peace Medal: one of hundreds given to ranking Plains Indians in 1850, originally a possession of his grandfather, then his father. Cora nodded her understanding. "Yes, my wakanlica. When you begin the spirit journey, I will place the medal around your neck before they close the coffin for the last time."

Now Cora began singing Stands For Them's death song for him, as he was beyond the ability to do so. His lyrics, his melody, composed years ago. She knew each word and note by heart.

Come early evening Cora spied a faint sparkle in Stands For Them's eye—his spirit force fighting to return to the body. She put aside her bead work and offered to recite a tribal tale for her husband's amusement. She knew hearing to be the last sense to flee:

"The craftwork I do today reminds me of that legend of the old ones, not of Lakota or even Nakota tellers, but from our distant Dakotah relatives. It speaks of man's coming and going on this earth. My father Eagle Wolf first told it to me. Perhaps you heard it in your boyhood." A flicker of eyelids encouraged Cora to continue:

"On a high mesa sits an old woman, alone except for the dog that never sleeps. She was doing what I often do—working the leather. Her wish was to decorate a buffalo robe. The designs she was adding, using porcupine quills and colored threads, would surely make it a buffalo robe too splendid for this world."

"Nearby was a boiling kettle of food above a fire. Now and then the old woman puts down the robe and gets up to stir the pot. At such times, and without fail, the dog that never sleeps gets up and pulls out the quills and threads, so that the old woman must start all over again. If ever the dog would fail to do this, the robe would in short order be finished, signaling the end of the world."

"So, I know you feel your work here is unfinished. It is not my place to say this to a headman such as you, but I repeat only what our parable tells us—we all must leave things to finish for those coming after us. This makes for a world without end."

Mulling this thought, both nodded off to sleep.

First Stands For Them then Cora awoke with a start deep in the night, though there had been no loud sound. As they looked at each other, Cora recognized in the dying one's face both the joy and sadness that always followed a dream featuring their deceased children and grandchildren. "They were all there, Cora. Baby Myra, strong little Nation, our dear Julia, poor baby Moccasin Face. By some mystery we were all together, happy, and tenting just east of *Mato Paha* on the very campground of my birth." At the shared memory, Cora's eyes welled with tears that dammed up before spilling down her cheek—one for each baby, each preteen, each young adult child and grandchild they had lost.

He raised his head from the pillow, "The angel of death seemed always to hover near my tipi, and later this wooden house. I do not know why that dark angel visited us so often. Or why presently he delays coming for me." By and by a rumble in Stands For Them's chest caused Cora to lean close to his face.— "Cora, I must know which of the Lakota women of Corn Creek are with child." Cora looked skyward, reciting names of local expectant women, names vaguely familiar to Stands For Them.

"These women are big with child—Medicine Blanket, Yellow Woman, Emma Eagle Horse." She paused, then said, "Wakanlica, these are women I know to be with a child not yet born. Those with baby at breast include White Rabbit, and also the younger of the two Leading Cloud sisters."

"And oh yes, little Herman Standing Bear is now walking and talking. I've seen it for myself, wakanlica." Stands For Them nodded smiling as Cora continued, "You remember. He is the baby brother of Richard Standing Bear, that fine boy of ten winters who has come to our house so often with big eyes for the dancing and drumming."

He seemed satisfied with this vision of new, fat, curious babies coming up from the earth. "I go to big mystery soon, and they have just come from big mystery. This is good."

Then his smile faded to a frown: "Still, I have this impossible wish, Cora. I wish for the funeral scaffold of old. When I was a boy, my *hunka* grandfather told me the meaning behind the scaffold, as told by one still more ancient than him . . . a *wicasa wakan* who remembered even the days before horses." Cora's eyes widened at this story, new to her.

"This *wicasa wakan* asked that future generations ponder the carcass of a bull elk or bighorn ram killed by wolves. Yes, much meat is eaten by the wolves . . . but look more closely—see how mouthfuls of the body are taken skyward by daring ravens, vultures, and magpies. Piece by piece, the body is carried on wings into the blue. This is the meaning of 'sky burial.' In this same manner, portions of our ancestors were also carried heavenward from the scaffold." So much talking now took its toll, the old eyes rolling back and closing as if for all time.

Cora could see death at the door. And yet he hung on. Something was oddly unfinished. Odd because Stands For Them's earthly affairs, simple though they be, were now complete. Still he lingered, dark eyes, when open, seeming to wait on something. Cora kneeled beside the bed, drawing close, seeking to know what kept him tethered.

In bits and pieces she gained this—Stands For Them yearned to say farewell to his ally and neighbor of a quarter century. To his silent-talking friend Cleve.

And so, the call went out from Cora to the community: "Bring us a strong runner. One to fly up the Red Road where it skirts the north slope of Hunte Paha to the home of the agreeable rancher. Time is short. See if young Dreaming Horse might come. He is a schoolboy who speaks enough of the white man's tongue." Stands For Them held young

Dreaming Horse in high esteem, having officiated at his honoring ceremony the summer before.

Soon the willowy teen was at the door, then shuffling nervously before his enfeebled headman but reluctant to draw near. Stands For Them's voice was now inaudible to anyone save Cora. She would relay her husband's wishes.

Dreaming Horse stared gravely at the dying old man as Cora spoke: "Do not linger, Dreaming Horse. Find the wasicu rancher wherever he might be. Tell Cleve that Stands For Them is very sick, and requests to see him one final time. Do not return 'til you have an answer."

"If the wasicu is not at his ranch, look for sign of fresh horse travel. Track him, as this one is often away with his animals in the badlands to the north."

Without taking his eyes off the dying one, Dreaming Horse reached behind to feel for the chair he knew was there. Seated, he changed from heavy hand-me-down cowhide boots to feather-light moccasins. In silence then he stood looking down at the frail wakanlica. When Stands For Them nodded, in a blink the boy was out the door and beyond shouting distance. He loped in that ground-consuming "wolf trot" of his people—the natural "barefoot" gait of old. Perfect for running uphill and down with brisk pace and minimal exertion. Feet barely touching the ground.

There was tradition in his strides—for had the Lakota not always used runners to spread the news? In rough terrain a good runner was almost as fast as a mounted messenger, yet moving with the stealth of the smaller animals. Unseen. Unheard. Moccasins so lightly brushing the earth that there was scant sign for enemy to see, to follow.

Breathing no harder than if he'd mounted a half flight of stairs, Dreaming Horse's strides in time brought him to the Berry ranch house, where he nearly ran into a startled young girl. But he could see no man.

Dreaming Horse was a stranger to the ginger-haired girl of ten, so she retreated to the house. Dreaming Horse paused briefly to consider options, then sprinted to the barn where he figured to pick up the spore of Cleve's horse. Cleve had departed earlier that morning to check fences across the windswept northern edge of his biggest pasture.

For Dreaming Horse, following fresh tracks of such a big creature and with the added weight of rider was a child's game. Urgency, but also pleasure in running through the "ocean" of bunch grasses rolling up to long, low brooding tabletops, interrupted here and there by badland canyons and alkali flats.

At the far end of this austerity Cleve was finishing his saddlebag lunch and gathering up fencing tools when a movement to the south caught his eye. Something running fast. Running towards him.

Within minutes, the sober-faced young runner was hesitantly approaching the rancher. "Stands For Them must be dying, he is coughing up blood. He has a last request—he said it was to see his old friend. That is you, Mister Cleve. Can you come?"

Cleve did not offer an answer there among the waving grasses, but instead invited the messenger to return to the house where they could both get a much-needed glass of water. This would buy Cleve time to consider his old friend's request.

Riding at a slow trot, he mulled his first instinct—to say "yes" and proceed to Stands For Them's bedside directly. "By car the long way around the Butte, or the short way on horseback over the old Red Road through those deep draws. With all roads dry, there is no time advantage one over the other," he thought out loud as if talking to his horse.

Then Cleve considered the harder realities. In those days the most feared and familiar death on reservations was tuberculosis. Stands For Them had lost two children and many other relatives to TB. It sounded like this must be the old man's fate as well. Cleve was torn . . . he'd lost a wife to an unidentified lung condition five years before. While tying the horse to the hitching post, he imagined entering Stands For Them's damp, dark bedroom to say goodbye. Would this risk bringing some scourge back to his young daughters? And what of those last three words dear Jessie uttered from *her* deathbed: "Protect our children."

Yet how could he say no to Stands For Them, the first native man to befriend him and Cleve's emissary to the Lakota nation all these years?

Having gained the kitchen door, he motioned Dreaming Horse to come inside to await a final decision. The young man shook his head and moved instead to wait on a tree stump near the hitching post. After fetching Dreaming Horse a glass of water Cleve wanted only to sit alone in his room. Yet he also felt a need to be with his girls.

Cleve now dropped to his knees in the kitchen to play marbles with Jan, ten, and Betty, thirteen. Then he retreated to his bedroom alone, knowing Dreaming Horse and ultimately Stands For Them awaited an answer. Closing his eyes for a moment, Cleve could "see" his old friend, and wondered if even in this moment Stands For Them already knew he would not be coming. After all, had not the old man proven in many seasons that he could "see" things across both time and space? Cleve thought of how each fall, on the very day when the winter steer was to be butchered, James and Cora inexplicably appeared with their team and wagon to claim those portions of the beast not appetizing to a white family.

Cleve's cowboy boots paced 'round and 'round the bedroom's hardwood floor as if movement might calm the dilemma: Betrayal to old Stands For Them, he of such a humble last request. Or similar betrayal of the girls, and a broken promise to a dying wife.

Then straightaway Cleve walked out to the tree stump, where Dreaming Horse waited. His eyes spoke of a deep resignation, while his lips said, "Young man, I cannot come. Please tell Stands For Them

362

why." Not fully confident that the reticent young courier would carry this message to Stands For Them, Cleve nonetheless shared his fear of the "White Death"—not for himself but on behalf of his young daughters. And of his wife's last wish.

Half an hour later Stands For Them received the news stoically. But glistening half-opened eyes confirmed to Cora her husband's deep sadness at forfeiting this leave-taking with a dear friend.

By next morning the eternal darkness could not be held back. It was filled with a thing neither dream nor waking thought—a sort of revelation about death: How could a crossing so natural, so universal, so necessary in making room for legions of new souls waiting their turn to be born, how could this passage be bad?

Cora started the last morning by making sure he was still breathing, then went outside to feed and water the horses. She returned to the deathbed to find pauses now appearing between what for eight decades had been dependably rhythmic breathing. Then a longer pause. She watched intently, not knowing if or when the once powerful chest would suddenly heave upwards again. Death and faint life in combat that could only end one way.

After one more long pause of breathlessness, a convulsive inward sucking of air was followed by a soundless exhalation—the silence of eternity. Thinking his eyelid fluttered, Cora leaned sharply forward. But he was not there. He was Heyúktan on the river bluff. Seeing the enemy, crouching. Then standing for the others. Becoming once again Stands For Them.

Cora sat beside the deathbed for a long time. Motionless, she felt the first of a long season of tears race down the deep furrows of her face.

But she'd not mourn alone. Mysteriously, without fanfare, a woman of Cora's age came to the door holding a red bundle carefully folded, the shroud for the end of days. Together and in silence the pair wrapped

Stands For Them's body in this red robe. Then this good friend, Black Winona, led Cora out to the fire pit and began keening and wailing—sisterhood sounds that at length would bring Cora small windows of comfort.

More women drifted up to the Stands For Them house as quietly as tumbleweeds. Maggie Wooden Knife, Betty Bull Dog, Iron Woman. As was custom the mourning women would be materially thanked for their keening and crying out—sometimes with food. Sometimes with money.

Time crowded in, for embalming was much too expensive—Stands For Them would need to be committed to the ground in two days, at most three if the weather stayed cool. Cora resolved to talk with the Black Robe who preached at the nearest Catholic chapel. Never mind that he lived twelve miles distance in Norris.

So under the setting full moon while others sat with the body, Cora and Black Winona walked overland to Corn Creek. When they entered among the log cabins clustered on the creek, there stood a sad-eyed young man beside a wagon. The horses were harnessed and her driver ready—as if by occult arrangement that did not visibly surprise Cora.

In respect for Cora's loss, no words were spoken. The women simply climbed in, both sitting cross-legged on the wagon box floor and facing north as the team trotted south towards Norris. The wagon rolled up Black Pipe Creek past log cabins half hidden among riparian cotton-woods. Cora knew her loss was already common knowledge, for here and there a red banner fluttered or a solemn face came to a window to witness the passing wagon. As the wagon continued southward, Cora looked wistfully up at Cross Butte. But no, Stands For Them had some-how made arrangements to be buried legally, in the ground. His eternal resting place the northeast corner of that cemetery so near his house and soon to bear his name.

In short order Cora completed necessary arrangements in Norris. Upon returning home she cut portions of her hair short, then turned the same blade on her upper arms and thighs, carefully keeping the bloody wounds in places that would not be visible—for the Catholic and Episcopal priests would disapprove of this "heathen" badge of grieving. At length Cora rose to feed a bundle of sweet grass into the stove. The resulting white smoke was sure to alert any who didn't yet know the sad news.

Late on the second day, male grievers began arriving by horse and wagon. First to arrive were men from the tiyospaye. They helped carry the body out under the sky, then into the tipi recently erected beside the house. A clean new buckskin shirt was brought forward. The men retired as the women washed the body with pungent sage and other holy plants in preparation for its long journey. So ended this day of the three-day wake.

As he began evening chores in his barnyard to the northeast, Cleve could faintly hear the mournful high-pitched keening of the women. *Not just another death,* he thought with regret. *Surely it is my old friend.*

Arrivals peered into the tipi to view the great brown lifeless face with those deep wrinkles. The observant noted two objects in his carefully folded hands, items to be buried with the wakanlica: His presidential peace medal, and a six-inch lock of Cora's own hair. Later Cora stooped unobserved beside the body to cut a similarly long lock of Stands For Them's still-black hair. In this way she'd retain his *nagila.*

In gathering darkness of this second day, unseen by human eyes, other beings approached the wake. Birds of prey circling, and four-leggeds coming in stealth. Chief among them were the little prairie wolves, in twos and threes, trickling silently down the canyons of Cedar Butte. In time there gathered nearly fifty coyotes, attracted perhaps by the commotion or drawn by some unknowable force. They came crouching low, even crawling on bellies, to lie hidden and motionless among the tall grasses of nearby ravines.

With buffalo, elk, grizzly, antelope, and true wolf all gone from the Rosebud, coyotes gathered as if on behalf of their larger and long-vanquished kin—gathered as if sensing the passing of one who had remembered when people and animals ruled the world side by side.

On one trip between the house and the death tipi, Cora hesitated mid-step at the sound of high-pitched yips. She alone raised her head and sensed instantly, though never seeing them, that coyotes had gathered in farewell.

Cora would not take the spirit tipi down any time soon. As was custom, she refrained from appearing at secular events in the coming four seasons. She held to the old belief that when a husband died, the wife must consider herself to have partially died too.

During this time, she resolved to move out of the valley of the Black Pipe, to be with her sister south of Horse Head Creek. But for the present his lingering spirit time kept Cora in the Stands For Them house, now drearier than ever on its windswept flats.

On the one-year anniversary of her husband's passing, Good Thunder would assume the role of local wakanlica. In that moon he traveled to the old Stands For Them house for a simple ceremony beside the spirit tipi. He brought offerings of the holiest of foods, *papa, wasna*, and *wojapi*, to feed the soul one last time. Together he and Cora performed the simple release-the-soul ceremony.

There followed a release-the-soul feast, with many of the prior year's mourners returning a final time to Stands For Them Flats. From inside the house Cora brought forth the household's few remaining items for the "giveaway," that ancient way of starting anew.

The next day, Cora began packing up what remained for the wagon trip to begin a new albeit short life with her sister beside the Catholic chapel south of Horse Head Creek. Cora died there the following year in the Moon of Seeding Plants.

Chapter Twenty-One

Fruit of the Tree
1940

In the busy but lonely years after Jessie's death, Cleve kept mind and body squarely focused on ranch work. For such daily brute force was needed to support four daughters.

He occasionally rode to a high point to survey the far horizons as a way of owning the old, immutable melancholy. On this limpid day, his still broken heart swelled, and distant coyotes sounded like bagpipes. Sadness doubled when he considered there were simply no single women near his age among the settlers. This meant for him a loneliness unlikely to ever end.

It was a late winter day, and as such the land lay barren. Not unlike his state of mind. But then, inexplicably, a sprout of hope poked through the landscape.

In coming months this hope took a form familiar to any healthy male, Cleve's unbidden mind occasionally manifesting the smoothness of skin, the scent and warmth, the very breath not of a particular woman but of universal woman.

Still, fleeting daydreams were no match for the thousand tomorrows holding no such promise. Five years since Jessie's passing was becoming six, her image enshrined in Cleve's heart—the slender one collecting wildflowers on the prairies of his memory.

Then, on a day seemingly no different from any other, it happened.

He heard her voice before ever he saw her, a lovely tongue that could only come from a lovely form . . . that form gliding along, speaking a lilting Lakota among a cluster of shawl-covered native women of similar age. After hearing the voice and stealing the barest glance, Cleve knew he'd encountered nature's most irresistible phenomenon—a beautiful stranger.

Cleve would glimpse the beautiful stranger only rarely. Once or twice in the general store at Norris, and then on a gusty fall day crossing the wide streets of White River. But had she caught his warm stare? Raven-haired, slender as a shadow, of pleasingly round face, Te'Mahpiya'Wiya was her name. For Cleve she was a nameless exotic. A Madonna of the Sioux.

It seems everyone but Cleve knew she'd recently arrived at Corn Creek community after many years up at Cheyenne River Reservation. Her husband, a troubled Miniconjou, had died in a drunken brawl at a relative's party. She had once come close to bearing twin girls, an event sure to dazzle the Cheyenne River folk. Tragically neither daughter survived a terror-filled midnight birthing.

Before and after that black night had come savage beatings. From a drunken husband, and twice from total strangers among the reservation's lawless. Beatings about the head and shoulders, legs, arms and stomach—sparing only her private place from the blows as this would be their site of ultimate contempt and pleasure.

In those days she found small comfort in the keeping of a length of stout rope coiled and hidden in her top drawer. Comfort in knowing there was at least this way out of the cage. A way taken by so many other girls and women of her generation, and less commonly of generations before. In an act both brave and humiliating the widow had returned, childless, husbandless, to the place where Corn Creek entered Black Pipe Creek. This was, after all, the valley of her birth tiyospaye.

During a long winter, Cleve's plausible interest in the woman was as fleeting as their encounters. For in those days, single white men simply did not talk with single Indian women of like age. Both communities held to this edict.

One morning as winter began relaxing its rimy blueness, Cleve drove to the ramshackle Cedar Butte Store in hopes of picking up a gate latch. It was a store like scores of others across this last western frontier, chaotically stocking all things a settler might need—roll upon roll of barbed wire with choices from Curtis Quarter-Twist to Shinn Locked Four Point, tar paper, stove pipes by the foot, great and small sheets of roofing tin, cowboy coffee pots, pitchforks in many styles.

And various gate latches. As Cleve set the brake on his '37 International pickup, he considered options if the store were sold out of the Wm. Rigby Co. gate latch he needed. With purposeful strides he advanced on the front door, hoping not to have to drive all the way to the White River or Norris Mercantile. The dusty parking lot held no other cars, just a half dozen horse-drawn Indian wagons.

Cleve walked through the door and into the dimly lit store, and there she was—in a shaft of filtered sunlight, bent in examination of a tray of seed potatoes. The grace-filled curve of her shoulders and back were outlined beneath an otherwise nondescript calico dress and brown crochet shawl.

Her personage, her manner of dress, bespoke a woman of small means but sizable pride and dignity. Tiny lines near her rather serious mouth hinted at a life where smiles were, if not more numerous than frowns, at least more prized.

But it was her neck that held Cleve's gaze. Exposed by the parting of long hair and kissed by a single sunbeam, the long neck was of natural bronze hue.

Did her limpid eye from beneath falling hair catch Cleve's . . . for but an instant? Was that the faintest smile on her lips? Perhaps not—after all, she was seemingly intent on selecting the proper seed potatoes. Walking past her as decorum and the day's tasks required, Cleve noted how the formerly dreary store goods, the wooden barrels, the kerosene wall lamps, had taken on a transcendent glow. *This woman walks in beauty*, he thought.

Pretending to sort through a collection of bolts until she left, Cleve stole the occasional glance. Later, he found and purchased the intended Wm. Rigby Co. gate latch and departed. An incandescence lit the remainder of his day.

In coming weeks Cleve made discrete inquiry on the streets of Norris and Belvidere regarding this newcomer. Finally, an old friend among the three-quarter breed Janis family confided, "Te'Mahpiya'Wiya is her name among the native people—She is a widow from up Cheyenne River way. Lived here years ago as a young girl."

"Blue Cloud Woman is how one might translate her name."

Cleve smiled and nodded in thanks.

In the coming busy weeks of calving season, Cleve ruefully slid the beautiful stranger out of mind. Most of the time. But another day would dawn for Cleve and Blue Cloud Woman.

It was a springtime day—though not typical of the damp, fickle springtime of the Northern High Plains. Rather, this was the one blessed day that comes each spring, the first short-sleeved day which foretells every other lovely warm-weather day to come. One knows this day by the first loud buzzing of insects.

On such zephyr breezes, a glance can became something else. It happened at the shallow wagon crossing on Black Pipe Creek below Sims Creek. He rode his fine buckskin saddle horse westward to the best creek crossing he knew of. She rode with head held high eastward, herding a neighbor's half dozen ponies to new pasture.

Fate ordained their simultaneous arrival at the crossing.

Maybe it was the unlikely meeting beside flowing waters, or the luck of no one else around to disapprove. Maybe it was the weather, spilling over the land with a warmth that made both overcoats and rules suddenly unnecessary. Whatever, on this halcyon day they could finally delight in seeing one another.

Perhaps Blue Cloud Woman was emboldened by the recent passing of her people's ranking wakanlica—for Stands For Them's moral leadership had surely included the taboo of any romance between a Lakota woman and a male wasicu. So when the soft-spoken, handsome rancher looked up to see her, Blue Cloud Woman returned Cleve's gaze, permitting him a few words of conversation.

Honey bees buzzed among plum blossoms on both sides of the creek. Cleve offered a warm "hello" from his side. Waiting a moment as she returned a faint smile and what might have been a small wave, he said, "I see one of your mares is lame."

"Akhe eya yo," she said, but then in English: "I fear I make it worse by herding her." With that modest invitation, Cleve spurred his mount across the narrow waterway and dismounted beside the lame horse, which stood slack-legged at the rear of her small herd.

Using a cowboy's measured motion so reassuring to equines, Cleve slipped his lariat over the lame horse's head. All the while the corner of his eye followed the equally graceful movements of Blue Cloud Woman. She encouraged all the sound horses through the knee-deep waters. On the far side they promptly dropped their heads to graze, allowing her to return on her mount to the painfully lame horse at Cleve's side.

Her boarding school English was better than Cleve had hoped. But it was not the pleasantries exchanged that so captivated Cleve. Rather, it was the utter grace of movement as she had encouraged the horses across the flowing water. Springtime seemed tangled in her long hair.

In short order he examined the lame leg, lifting the hoof and using his pocket knife to pop loose the offending sharp rock. This immediately relaxed the horse, which relaxed the man, which in turn relaxed the woman. The horse between them, Blue Cloud Woman now faced Cleve and leaned into the withers. Her shoulders then her head turned towards Cleve, penny-skinned, doe-eyed. Luminous. Smiles rendering words superfluous.

But before long, freed from pretense and sheltered from judgements by remoteness of place, they found their tongues. "I have seen you recently," said Cleve, "but I do not remember you from these parts."

"No," she said as another layer of shyness, like a sheer garment, dropped from her face and form. Her smile then retreated a little, and she continued, "I did grow up near Corn Creek, but you would not have noticed me. I have been up in Cheyenne River for many years, and now I return." Her expression begged Cleve to leave it at that, to find a new topic.

"Are these all your horses?"

"Oh no, only my paint and this lame one. The others belong to my neighbor, Mr. Thin Elk. Bringing them to water daily is easier than carrying the water so far."

Cleve nodded as he pondered the goodness of one who would help old Thin Elk, then appraised her two horses more carefully. Blue Cloud Woman jumped nimbly up onto the bare back of her paint, sat relaxed for a moment, then slid smiling back to the ground. Cleve saw by her movements that she'd been raised in a home where fine horsemanship, slowly vanishing from Lakota culture, was yet valued.

She considered the man before her. The engaging roughness of him—all calloused, raw-boned, tanned below. And above freshly shaved cheeks framing washed-out blue eyes from so much sun and wind.

They paused upon hearing the honking sound, then looked up together at the high "V" of snow geese winging upcountry.

"No more hard freezes," she offered. "My grandmother said the geese know such things." More companionable small talk followed.

Despite a modesty, her womanhood was now coming in harmonic waves that crashed over Cleve. Searching for a way to ensure they would meet again, Cleve feigned interest in a yearling dun pony by asking if it might be for sale. A slight grin, or was it a wink, suggested she'd seen his motive. But she did not embarrass Cleve. Even better, she played right along:

"The pony you speak of belongs to Mr. Thin Elk's daughter-in-law White Crane. She is also my neighbor. I will speak with her."

She then uttered a Lakota name-place Cleve recognized, thus half disclosing the location of her log cabin.

Further words weren't needed—they would surely meet again in this big country. With no telephone connection, Cleve would be obliged to come calling regarding the dun.

Both smiled and returned their attention to the horses. The sun had now thoroughly warmed the spring air. This encouraged lingering conversation, and what Cleve thought might be a knowing glance or two from his companion.

In a flash of black and white, a bird briefly alighted on the back of one of the horses. Blue Cloud Woman exclaimed with the Lakota name "*Halhata*' . . . Cleve concurred by saying "Magpie," thus chancing upon his future affectionate nickname for this woman.

Parting was without words in Lakota fashion. Instead, a last moment of contact by way of twinkling eyes. As the two rode now in opposite directions, a world of brighter, crisper colors rose up before each.

It was seemingly Blue Cloud Woman who carried Cleve home, not his horse. For he floated in a sort of rapture. The sun, warm on his forearms, might as well have been her touch. *Had it not already arrived,* thought Cleve, *this woman would surely turn winter into spring.*

Still, he could not help thinking any real bond was as unlikely as the sole tale of forbidden love he knew of—*Romeo and Juliet*. Yes, there was a sharp social taboo on even the most innocent friendship between a Lakota woman and a white man. How could his present joy end well?

It had not always been so. The sprinkling of French surnames like Bordeaux or Lamoureaux nested among Rosebud's Lakota testified to prior centuries, when a French-Canadian trapper/trader might openly take a Lakota maiden as wife.

Blue Cloud Woman was simultaneously suffering the same joy tainted with hard reality. But love, like youth, will be served. So four days later Cleve rode over to where he figured Blue Cloud Woman's cabin would be. Sure enough, there she was tending her small garden. He asked if the dun pony was for sale. She had spoken with the owner, and it was not. No matter.

The pair settled into comfortable conversation that stretched for an hour. "I've heard it said among my people that your sister married the grandson of Red Cormorant Woman. True?"

"Yes, you speak of sister Hattie and my bother-in-law George Lamoureaux." It was a connection of sort, as was their subsequent name-dropping of Lakota men who'd worked for Cleve over the years. Cleve saw in her wide eyes a wonder at how sister Hattie's marriage could be anything but a scandal. It had been.

Then Cleve proposed that they ride to a nearby ridge to take in what he knew was a lovely view of Cedar Butte, Pine Ridge, and the temporarily verdant Black Pipe Valley. By late afternoon Cleve had cradled Blue Cloud Woman's compact hand in both of his. So began their unlikely romance.

Even as they sat, shoulders lightly touching, Blue Cloud Woman thought of how often she'd been preached the merits of cultural and racial singularity. One of these times stood above the others—It was mere weeks after Blue Cloud Woman had relocated south to the Corn Creek community. She'd been invited into a lively circle of neighbor women who met weekly to pit chokecherries, to share gossipy laughter along with weightier topics. Here she could expect to hear the latest news, and perhaps a few old proverbs and admonitions. Often in attendance was a wry and energy-filled little woman, Cora of the Eagle Wolfs. She was a traditionalist. So when Cora walked through the door, all knew she'd bring needle and thread, beads, porcupine quills, quilting material, and squares of doeskin. Her brief but skilled instruction would set the circle of women to a cadence of cutting, stitching, stretching of leather and fiber. Activities that never interfered with conversation, but rather fueled it.

Cora was steadfast wife to James Stands For Them. They were a team . . . he passed on the best of Lakota healing ways, philosophies, folklore—and she matched him by passing along the most beautiful, most symbolic of Lakota handcrafting.

On this day, Cora abruptly dropped the beadwork to her lap while clearing her throat. It was her reply to tattling hearsay from Susie Lame Deer about a Lakota woman from Wanblee seen talking with a wasicu man on what passed for main street in Belvidere. When Cora spoke, everyone in the circle put their crafting down to look over at this woman of short stature but towering respect.

The subject of the valley's two cultures was a prickly one, but Cora took it head on: "Some things are not meant for casual chatter." Her gaze danced 'round the circle of women without quite making the reprimand of individual eye contact. "I thank *Tunkashila* for preserving some of our customs. I also thank our Christian Lord for the same reason. You see, Stands For Them and I believe these two are faces of the same sovereign, so we carry the cross *and* the pipe. And because we have not lost the Sun Dance, nor the *isnati awicalow*, our rite of purification that prepares us to become women and bear children, I believe the one Great Spirit made us all—he made my skin red and the wasicu skin white. He then placed us on this earth, and intended that we should live peaceably but differently."

"You see, my Nawica Kicijin and I believe that a baby from a wasicu father and Lakota mother is as much a miracle as any. But the only way for a culture such as ours to survive the centuries is to marry strictly within."

She then lifted her beadwork up as if making a point with it, and ended the discussion thusly, "Let us return to our handcraft and not talk of this Lakota woman seen with a wasicu man." After respectful silence, the lively conversation resumed. Many in the group were now pitting chokecherry and wild plum.

Later came a pause in the work so that the group's nursing mothers might suckle their babes. Then came murmurs of joy as juice-stained hands began passing the half dozen infants around the circle. Two of the little ones showed curly locks of hair, one in shades of red, the other auburn—the ringlets hinting at lusty tales of some French-Canadian or English trader from the not so distant past.

When the mixed-breed babes found warm cradle in Cora's arms, the old woman fussed over them for an extra-long time. Yet James and Cora's position was clear—beware the bed of the wasicu! And a deeper message was reaching some in the circle: The Stands For Thems sought not racial purity, but cultural purity.

Blue Cloud Woman did not take Cora's words lightly. Yet had she not once heard a story painting a quite different picture, told by Cora's own sister? A tale with some hope for a woman in her position . . . a tale she was eager to share with Cleve.

She waited, and waited. Then came a lovely evening outdoors where they sat together on a blanket, leaning against the fallen trunk of a great cottonwood and facing a hazy red sunset. Such a gloaming, Cleve commented, could only mean a great forest fire was raging upwind in Montana, or perhaps even Canada.

"Cleve," she said as her eyes flew up to his, "I wish to tell you of a pleasing story born in a long-ago winter count. You know of these painted skins that record our history, our Lakota way of remembering the years?"

"Yes, Magpie."

She continued, "This story was passed to me by Snow Bird, sister of the wife of Stands For Them. It is a story of one of our important holy women, Eagle Woman, from the winter count kept by Battiste Good. He is long dead but he was, I am told, a fine old man with the memory of a mountain."

Cleve smiled encouragement to Blue Cloud Woman, it being a treat to hear her speak at any length.

"In those days *Paha Sapa*, you call them the Black Hills, were the sacred center of everything that is. So when Eagle Woman had a vision on highest mountain *Hinhan Kaga*, the people listened. Her vision was as two stones. First, she said this voice came to her from the closest stone, " 'I am woman, and I decree that no blood shall flow in *Paha Sapa*.' "

"From that day forward our warring against both the whites and other tribes was never inside the Black Hills. Snow Bird then shared Eagle Woman's prophecy of the second stone: " 'Many, many years from now, the Lakota will move forward as one with the wasicu.' "

Here Blue Cloud Woman straightened her back as a way of insuring Cleve's full attention. Her eyes found his:

"And the year of her vision? 1856 as recorded on our winter counts. Snow Bird said further that this year, we call it The Year Good Bear Made War with the Crow, was the birth year of our departed *naca* Stands For Them."

Now Blue Cloud Woman stared at Cleve, a gaze inviting him to consider the hopefulness and gravity of the vision. Cleve knew this faint promise meant more to her than to him. But lacking words, he instead drew her into his arms and under his chin. Then cradling her face in both hands, as one might bear a lead crystal vase, her countenance ever more fragile and lovely.

As affections grew, there came a tumble of warm days and still warmer embraces. One humid day they rode bareback up to the line where scented cedars met the ever-singing pines atop Hunte Paha and together experienced an afternoon downpour. There followed the strange comfort of being rain-soaked, a feeling unique to new lovers. He never forgot the smell of that fresh rain on her skin.

A toasty sun soon reappeared, bringing a delightful tug of war between propriety and passion. Offering her shy smile and an attitude more playful than naughty, Blue Cloud Woman suggested they dry their clothes in the sunshine, using the long branch of a nearby dead pine tree. Cleve chuckled and then went first, quickly stripping off soaked clothes until left standing in underwear only. Blue Cloud Woman noted the ropey muscles of his arms and resolute shoulders—testament to long hours branding, sawing, fencing, and a thousand other cowboy chores.

Then it was Blue Cloud Woman's turn. She disrobed more slowly, artfully, half turning away from Cleve. As garments slipped from lean limbs, her crystalline eyes looked off at nothing in particular. At last she stood resplendent, trembling ever so slightly.

An emerald patch of clover would be their bed. It marked a first chance to know each other without limits, without hesitation.

Her winsome splendor made Cleve at first weaker, not stronger.

Honeybees buzzed over chokecherries partially hiding the lyre. He hesitated, then found the back of her neck with his mouth, her flowery scent with his nose. She did not move away, then found his arm to pull to her chest, his hand to her breast.

Breathing her in deeply, his eyes half closed as if once again inhaling the cedar-scented aroma of his rangeland. Magpie's amber hills and valleys, when touched or glimpsed, were for him an extension of fawn-colored badland curves and peaks. He fancied her more connected to the land than a white woman could hope to be.

Her eyelashes, Asian adornments borne genetically across the Bering Straits so long ago, brushed as butterflies on Cleve's cheek and chest.

His tongue, bee-like, tasted of her sweetness.

Nipples hard and hot as pebbles beneath a cooking fire.

He ran rough palms across the smoothness of tummy, of breasts, then with utter tenderness parted her thighs.

In coming weeks there would be nights of similar transcendence—the pair of hearts pressed ever so closely. Or afternoons stolen among midsummer's tall grasses, their hiding places damply verdant, vegetative, feminine.

Such liaisons always brought the same conundrum: When visiting her cabin, what to do with Cleve's saddle horse? Leaving Yellow Cat tied to his lover's hitching post would be as brazen as it was imprudent.

Then it struck him while out mending fence—on visits to Blue Cloud Woman he could mislead by tying a fence-stretcher tool and a loop of barb wire behind the saddle cantle, then tethering his horse to the west fence line of the Stands For Them allotment. Such a sight would not raise a single eyebrow—for Cleve was known to rent that pasture. It was then but a short walk to the Blue Cloud cabin, or some more hidden rendezvous. To add authenticity, he would when coming and going do a little fencing—the rancher's job that never ends. In this way they found the narrow path to a place of both discretion and romance.

He never forgot the first morn after the first night in her cabin. From deep sleep he awakened to the smell of fry bread, corn mash, and eggs. There she sat beside a tiny cook stove—needle and thread in hand repairing, unbidden, the small rip in his trousers while wearing only his unbuttoned work shirt. Through an open window floated the smell and sound of horses chomping.

Days rolled to weeks. Blue Cloud Woman and Cleve slowly, reluctantly, returned to the ground truth of 1940: their western South Dakota homeland was an impossible time and place for a mixed-race romance. Marriage was even more unthinkable.

But for the present, they continued to live and love as though the impossible were possible—the taboo subject of marriage dreamed of, but never mentioned.

Cleve's obligations at home were mounting. His daughters were, bar none, his first priority. He felt stretched, and the childless Blue Cloud Woman knew this. Higher cattle prices of the looming world war hadn't yet materialized, so making the ranch mortgage was a nip-and-tuck affair each month. Still, Cleve's work-a-day life was as it had ever been— mostly alone on or near a horse, sunup to sundown, six days a week. One such day as he cut, trimmed, and stacked cedar fenceposts on a ridge, the crystal view north and west beckoned. Even unto Horseshoe Butte. And even unto Blue Cloud Woman's barely visible cabin. Pausing to sharpen his axe with a whetstone, Cleve straightened and rubbed a sore back, then calculated the hours of sunlight remaining by stretching forth his fist, each fist above the horizon equaling an hour of sunlight. And he thought of Sunday morning.

Lovely were Sunday mornings when Blue Cloud Woman awoke to snorting and shuffling of hooves, cracking the door just wide enough to see a smiling Cleve astride the buckskin Yellow Cat, and holding the reins of a blood bay he called Topper—saddled and ready for her.

If he arrived without the second horse, well, then his intentions were pleasantly clear to Blue Cloud Woman, and she would beckon him into her warm featherbed.

But time was not with them. Theirs was becoming that bittersweet love with no place to go. The gray portend of some final goodbye was as a serpent slithering between, then coiling up.

Sooner than later there came a mellow, hazy morn when Cleve rode up to the cabin without the second horse. But there would be no ardor on this particular day. Blue Cloud Woman swung open the door and met her cowboy sober-faced, balancing a package wrapped in yellowing newspaper, tied with baling twine. She held it out to him.

"Please do not open this now, Cleve. Put it in your saddle bag," was all she said.

"But why, Magpie?" his eyes pleading but voice steady. She ducked just inside the rough-hewn log cabin door as he followed. Turning now, the pair stood facing each other though not touching. He placed the package on the bed.

"I cannot presently tell you. One day you will know."

"But what is in this package, with your face so serious? I am not ready for sad things today or talk of the future."

She allowed him to envelop her in his arms, before saying, "It is not a goodbye, Cleve," her gaze was squarely on his boots. "It is what is in the package. I have no words to add."

Then, as calloused, barbed wire-nicked hands both gently and firmly held the slim Lakota waist, these words tumbled from her trembling mouth:

"In the moon of ripe chokecherries," she said, "I was so honored when you rode up to my small house with your oldest daughter. On horseback, in that warm sunlight, you both looked so wonderful. That visit, the chance to meet your Wynona, your first born—For me it was a moment filled with brightness and honor."

"For me as well," said Cleve. "For me as well."

She hesitated, smiled, looked Cleve full in the face. Choosing words carefully, haltingly, she went on, "My people are kinsmen of social connection, but not of social ceremony. Not for husband and wife rites anyway. I believe you know this. You may *not* know what your introduction of an eldest child meant to me."

Then blushingly, "It confirmed our connection."

Despite her insistence, these words in past tense fell on Cleve's ears like the beginning of a long, slow goodbye. By the cabin's low light he could see her bright eyes were now tear-filled. His kindly but unsmiling eyes mined her every expression.

She continued. "As you know, I have no close family here anymore. So I have no such introductions to offer you. And of course no hope of wearing the white lace of your people."

"For many weeks I have thought of what you gifted me that day. And of what I might now gift you. Today's package is my response."

"We must open it now . . . and together," Cleve replied as he lifted the package.

"No. Please, later," she blushed. "One day you will understand. It is not so very important now."

Except that Cleve could see it *was* important. He put his arm lightly on her hip and guided her to a seat on the edge of the bed. There he slowly opened the package to reveal a new pair of men's moccasins, ornately beaded in blues, whites, greens, and reds.

"You made these?" he asked, effectively hiding a wasicu *'s* bemusement at such an unlikely gift.

Her face perked up a bit. "Yes. They are a simple gift. Of course moccasins are not meant for a cowboy to wear. They are ceremonial."

As together their glances tracked from his big black riding boots to moccasins and back, the absurdity of it all brought mutual grins.

"They are wonderful," he beamed, "But help me understand this gift."

She answered in Lakota, as she occasionally did when wishing to be inscrutable. But Cleve thought he heard the word "*Tawechoo*", which he knew meant wife.

She returned to English: "Today they mean only what you see before you—a humble gift from my hands for the man who walks beside me. In future memories, they might come to mean what they did in the old days."

Without fully understanding, by degrees it dawned on Cleve that before him was the feminine acceptance of a proposal.

A toss of her head cued a lighter, less pensive mood. "Let us walk together down to the crossing at the creek, the crossing where we first met."

As the sun rode its arch from warm-golden to hot-white, the lovers strolled to the creek crossing—that place of first shared smiles, first conversation. Separated yet united then by the big bodies of their horses. Separated now by a darkness neither would speak of.

Shortly after the first hard freeze, the lovers began experiencing, here and there, disapproving glances from their respective races. Discretion had ensured that none could know anything for sure. But neither could they now ignore that neighbors of both communities were forming suspicions.

The loving rendezvous, fewer and fewer, still held fathomless joy. But a day came when Cleve knew that for her sake he would need to act. Thus, he resolved to reach Blue Cloud Woman's cabin at an hour when she would surely not be home.

Cleve's young daughters were finally in bed. He fired up the humming generator to light the three incandescent bulbs in his house, took his stubby pencil from the breast pocket, and rummaged for suitably elegant stationary among Jessie's old things. As he began writing, Cleve struggled to find fitting words: The writer with the eighth-grade education, the reader for whom English was a second language.

When words came, they belonged less to him and more to this strange cross-cultural love. Satisfied and a little surprised, he folded the stationary, and placed it in an over-sized envelope, the only one he could find. Hesitating before sealing the envelope, he proceeded instead to the upper drawer of his dresser where he found the only handy photo of himself. From the Black Hills Roundup—the faded and crumpled Brownie snapshot also showing Stands For Them with a pure white horse between them. *She will appreciate seeing me with such an important man of her people.* Photo and letter in the envelope, he secured it in the saddlebag hanging from a peg on the aromatic cedarwood back porch.

Late on the following day, Blue Cloud Woman returned home to see the corner of a manila envelope just peeking from the bottom of her door. A letter received—most unusual for a Lakota person. In fact, the first and last letter of her life. And though her brimming eyes deciphered only every fourth word, a sad meaning to letter and snapshot, both clutched to her breast, seemed likely.

Four miles to the east Cleve was musing over whether she had the letter in her hands, wondering what parts her reading skills would recognize. Worse, he belatedly considered who could read it to her? Not the priest, surely. Not the adolescent Lakota students of Corn Creek. And certainly no wasicu of any station should read this most personal of letters.

But Blue Cloud Woman was not without resources, so after carefully placing the photo with keepsakes, she rode off to find Ruth Earth Maiden, her better-schooled friend and confidant who'd surely understand every word of the letter. Ruth lit a candle, and with trembling voice read:

"My dearest Magpie,

I write this to protect you. I will miss you always in this world.

Do not wait for me, but know that in another world I will come for you on horseback so we may ride away together.

Until then, my fondest farewell.

Love, Cleve"

Blue Cloud Woman recognized this "riding away" from a beautiful dream she had shared where dappled horses with churning hooves carried the pair up past the impossibilities of 1940 and into a far-off country at the dawn of a gentler age.

And now through a veil of hot tears Blue Cloud Woman looked back, back to her one special evening with the hallowed Stands For Them. There among a dozen others at the rare ceremony known as *Hocoka Ohomni Wacinyekiyapi* (Gathering in a Circle, With Hope).

Had not Stands For Them, in the chill air, addressed her present heartache? His words had closed the ceremony, floating like sparks over the campfire's last flicker—"What we do in this world influences the next world. Whether we fall in love or drop an enemy in battle, we establish a relationship with that person that lingers in this lifetime and surely crosses over to a place of meeting beside the Holy Road."

In coming weeks, separately Blue Cloud Woman and Cleve shared that ache in the breast known only to the star-crossed who lose love even before the "falling in love" is fully finished.

Then came a chill morning in the Moon of Popping Trees when up through layers of heartbreak Blue Cloud Woman felt a more physical discomfort. Her vague suspicions were soon confirmed—new life stirred within. A rare smile lit the fine face, for now she carried a piece of the lost love, a piece of Cleve.

She discretely moved an hour's ride south to Red Leaf Village, there to live a quiet life ensuring that Cleve need never fret over this feisty little child of copper skin and wavy nut-brown hair. Indeed the lovers would never see each other again, excepting in night reveries.

Chapter Twenty-Two

Riding the Rustler's Moon
1941

Cleve had often wondered over Stands For Thems warrior past, but lacked both the spare time and the handy interpreter to ever learn much. Still, he did know the old man's approximate age, the years of the great Sioux battles, and the finery of his regalia. With these, he could make calculated assumptions of a warrior's past. He did not consider himself a warrior. Those lucky lads born in 1886 were spared: conveniently too young for the Spanish-American War, and just a bit too old for the First World War.

But he'd known two or three "warlike" periods as a young man. That winter in a tent on the Niobrara. The treacherous year in the Canadian Rockies. Yet his longest battle was in simply trying to wrestle a living from a badlands ranch. For in this time and place a man might claim he owned the land, but always the land owned him.

It had all started with the wolves. Back then "keeping the wolf from the door" was not just a turn of phrase. But there were other sinister forces—cattle rustlers and horse thieves.

"The fences were so far-flung, those dirt roads running alongside the biggest pastures too lonely. This was the challenge for those of us on the bigger spreads," recollected Cleve years later, "We had no solid way to keep track of our cows. And they were our only living."

"But it was exciting." He was talking to daughter Jan, who since girlhood had been a collector of homestead stories. Leaning back in the chair, Cleve appraised the evergreen-stubbled badlands as only a person can whose dream landscape precisely watches the view from the picture window. In his mind's eye and to his audience of one, he was riding beside Tom in the twilight of a March day. Tom was astride a gaited horse, as was his recent preference. They rode downhill into a sparsely wooded coulee, dodging dirty little snowbanks, seeking a missing Shorthorn cow and its weanling calf.

This was one cow-calf unit best kept closer to the house. The calf was not yet branded, but old enough to survive without its mother. A tempting target for rustlers.

The horses picked their way over rough ground as the brothers deftly rolled and lit cigarettes *and* had a conversation—all at a trot! They spoke of the business at hand, of cattle prices, of troubling finances. Then a mutual nod to a Rustler's Moon rising to their right as twilight beckoned. The Rustler's Moon. That waxing orb rising just as most ranchers were sitting down to supper—prime time for stock robbers.

The brothers sat their horses and discussed the rumors then circulating of rustler activity in the area. That's when they saw their intended cow, '33' brand and flopping udder, bellowing and running just ahead of a snarling yellow dog.

Cleve did not hesitate to enforce a "Law of the West" that endures still—a strange dog chasing livestock is a dead dog. From the saddle, in what seemed like a single motion, Cleve pulled rifle from scabbard, shouldered it, and squeezed off a single shot. A shrill whine. And then silence.

The brothers traded looks that confirmed a shared belief that a dog meant some human nearby. The commotion spooking a coyote out of the brush, lean as a fox and rolling uphill at a flat-out sprint. It was increasingly clear something was amiss. Cleve and Tom saw no calf. And the cow was bawling and facing the east fence-line of the ranch. Unsure, Cleve scratched his head.

The men spurred their mounts not towards the cow, but on a line past the dead dog. If their hunch was right, it belonged to cattle rustlers, perhaps just out of sight.

Cleve knew rustlers were often unemployed cowboys or failed homesteaders. Their method was to target the bigger, less defensible spreads.

The brothers were not surprised to top the rise and see two men astride hard-ridden horses, one with a rifle at his shoulder firing wildly at the spooked coyote still loping eastward. They were in the middle of a dirt road paralleling Cleve's barbed wire property line. A seldom-used wire gate just to the south lay oddly open.

Who the hell were these men? Something in their overdone nonchalance brought that old "Irish" throb to Cleve's neck and jaw muscles.

"Rein up here until the big one holsters that gun," cautioned Tom. "Do you recognize either?"

"Yup," said Cleve, "saw 'em walk into Norris Merchantile when I was buyin' fencing staples last month. It's those Ritz brothers."

Common knowledge across the Horseshoe Butte/Cedar Butte communities held that the luckless Ritz boys had resorted to occasional cattle rustling and even horse thievery to make ends meet. Problem was, nobody could catch 'em redhanded. Not to mention the conundrum of what came next if a farmer or rancher did attempt a citizen's arrest.

This time was different. Cleve had backup.

The bigger of the two riders slipped his gun into the scabbard as he and his sidekick unhurriedly turned their attention, and physically turned their horses, towards the rancher brothers.

Equally unruffled, Cleve and Tom continued riding to within fifteen yards of the strangers. "What in hell you two doing here?"

"Shooting that gray wolf," came the response, possibly to elicit small sympathies from any rancher . . . if only it had been true.

"Hell, you surely know that's just a coyote, boys." At this wry correction, Cleve urged his horse closer til only the barbed wire separated him from the big intruder. Cleve felt without needing to look that Tom had likewise ridden up on his right side.

Cleve was sure there was a stolen calf nearby. The open gate his confirmation. So he leveled an icy glare at the pair demanding, "Where's my damn calf?"

Sides were now close enough to see the flash of opposing eyes, all the more menacing in the failing light.

The only sound the snorty nickers of horses unfamiliar with each other. No one blinked. No one spoke.

The taut silence, however, carried nuanced male signals back and forth across the fence: starting with the Ritz brothers' response to Cleve's question by uncoiling legs so as to take a deeper saddle seat, by way of saying, "We call your bluff."

Unhurried, Cleve now considered the situation.

The strangers' horses where unremarkable. This only raised Cleve's suspicion, as outlaws were known to avoid easily identifiable mounts such as pintos, appaloosas, or dappled greys.

As seconds passed, a palpable fearlessness bristled on both sides. For Cleve, this was his hard-fought livelihood, his cattle. He could brook no larceny, as this surely was. He also had the law on his side, albeit small comfort in a rangeland without telephones—and the sheriff a full day away by horseback.

Tension rose from simmer to boil, as with a nod Cleve drew Tom's attention to the tall rider's long unkempt hair, falling over his cheek and nearly to his shoulders.

True, frontiersmen had chosen long hair for decades. Wild Bill Hickock, George Custer, and Buffalo Bill Cody for sure. But also your average cowboy, who often worked and lived nowhere near a barber.

But starting around 1890, when horse thieves and rustlers risked losing the upper part of their ear if caught, long hair among cowboys was viewed suspiciously. *Is he covering up a cropped ear?* wondered Cleve.

Both Berrys scanned the intruders for other weapons, when Cleve's eye lit on something telling. Peeking out from behind the scabbard of the second rider was the curved end of a running iron. Heated red hot, this was a rustler's tool of choice when altering a brand. With a running iron one could change "O" to "P", "J" to "O." In this pasture, perhaps they were ready to change "33" to "88" or "66."

Cleve stood in his stirrups, pointed, and said "We see your damn running iron."

Further accusation was unnecessary. That "33" mother cow bellowing back in the draw was calling out for her calf, likely hog-tied with mouth taped shut. Probably somewhere in the tall roadside grasses. The open gate, the running iron, and the sullen attitudes completed the picture.

Light was fading. A grass-waving breeze heaved 'round from south to northeast even as a calm descended on both Berry men. Tilting his hat brim back, Cleve spoke as though he were vigilante law . . . which under present circumstances he was. "I just shot some rustler's cur dog. Yours, I reckon. Pick up the flea bag if you'd like. And how 'bout saving us time by pointing out where you hid my damn calf."

Cleve figured a full citizen's arrest was out of the question, but he had to defend his ranch. Then it struck him—demand the Ritz brothers turn over the stolen calf, and then confiscate their horses. Make 'em walk home.

"This is your one chance. Talkin' is now over. Where's the calf?"

In unruffled fashion Cleve leaned forward to pull the Winchester out, balancing it crossways on the saddle's high pommel. Tom simply reached a hand under his long duster, to grip what might or might not be a hidden sidearm.

The following silence contained that vibration of air when equally armed and mounted men face off across a fence line. A shootout seemed probable.

Men of the frontier understand—at such moments the first to speak, or move, is almost always the beaten one.

The big fella pursed his lips in what was not quite a smile and pointed to a tall stand of Big Bluestem on the fence line, where with effort one could see the white ears of a hog-tied calf.

At this, Cleve and Tom rode through the open gate and right up to the now seemingly beaten strangers. But when Cleve reached down to grab the reins of one of the rustler horses, the bandit deftly flipped his bridle over the horse's head, spurred his mount, and Cleve was left holding the empty headstall. The other Ritz brother followed at a flatout gallop.

Cleve sawed his horse around as if to give chase. But the moment had passed. Unwilling to leave a young calf and distressed mother cow in twilight, the Berry men simply sat and watched as the would-be rustlers loped southward over a low hill.

Minutes later Tom had retrieved and untied the calf. He carried it to his brother, boosting the young thing up in front of Cleve's saddle for the short ride back to a visibly relieved mother cow.

Hats pulled down and collars turned up, they leaned into a blue wind while herding the cow and calf back to Cleve's home place. Each retreated into Scots-Irish taciturnity. The tension of the day rode with them, especially with Cleve.

With house and barn in sight, Tom broke the silence. As they slowed their mounts to a walk, Tom asked his brother if he'd like to hear a relevant family story. The one where as small boys Tom and an older brother hid under a bridge as the notorious Kid Wade horse thief gang galloped overhead, followed minutes later by a like number of vigilantes, their faces covered by red bandanas. It had been an occasional topic of family discussion—had their father ridden with his vigilante neighbors that day? A white-haired Papa never did deny, or confirm.

But now Tom offered parts of the story that Cleve had never heard: "I know this for sure cuz I saw it—Papa sent a message every day to Kid Wade by taking his big .44 revolver out the backdoor for target practice on that junked cast-iron stove halfway up the hill. You were too young to remember. People took note."

"Here's the best part. One night in the early '90s Papa was pretty sure Kid Wade was hid out in our barn. The next day some of our horses went missing. That's when Papa and Uncle Bill gave chase, only to realize they were themselves being chased!"

This was news to Cleve. He flicked away his cigarette.

"They could see the pursuers were Sioux warriors. By looking down at the many hoof prints on the trail, Papa said he figured Kid Wade's men had also stolen cayuse ponies belonging to the Sioux. That's when the Berry men pulled over to let the speedier Indian ponies lead the chase."

"Again, you were too little to know this. But imagine how happy we were to learn the horse thieves were caught that day. Not sure what happened to the thieves but the Sioux got their ponies back, and returned all our horses! That's what Papa called frontier justice."

As the pair arrived now at the barn, Cleve wondered to himself if Stands For Them had known this Niobrara Valley story—or had even been one of the Sioux riders.

On entering the warm barn, familiar smells of sawdust, leather, and straw dissolved lingering tension for the brothers.

Dismounting his muscular but compact Shocky, Cleve recalled that frontiersman adage: "Admire a big horse, but saddle a small one." By thin yellow lamplight in the stalls, Cleve stowed his tack while Tom dispensed a snack of oats to his mount for the night ride home.

"Do you think I handled this right then? Are those two just free to try again?"

"Well, I figure you made your point. They rode off with their tails 'tween their legs, you shot their damn dog, *and* got your calf back. And hell, you even got a new bridle!"

"S'ppose you're right—I'm not sure what we would'a done if we'd held 'em."

Cleve finished wiping down his horse with a curry comb and brush, content to have another cowboy's validation.

With a tug of his hat Tom closed the matter, led his horse to the barn door, mounted, and swung his horse's head towards the last narrow trace of sunset for his ride home.

Like Indians, the brothers never ever said "goodbye."

Cleve walked quickly towards the house, intent on telling the girls a safer-sounding version of the standoff. But he also knew that tomorrow he could tell someone the full story, for after the achingly long sadness of losing his "Magpie" there had arrived a possible companion.

Rose was a comely, unassuming woman of a certain age who'd come from Bohemia as a child. She was a widow and had recently hired on as assistant postmistress of the little White River Post Office. He'd taken a shine to her, and the job made it easy to see her often—maybe buy a few more postage stamps than he really needed. Never failing to touch the brim of his hat: "Any packages for me today, Miss Rose?"

"No, Mr. Berry. Just this Sears Roebuck catalogue."

"I'll take ten of your postcard stamps, too. I sure wish you'd call me Cleve. Say, do you know what today's special is down at the café?" She looked up sharply from the cash register, wondering if this might be the start of an invitation to lunch. It was not. But in the coming weeks the bashful cowboy did find the words that began their High Plains court-ship. A courtship hidden from public view almost as well as Blue Cloud Woman's had been.

Theirs was an age of courting when a woman could tell a suitor that making love was impossible outside of marriage—an arrangement serving mostly to advance the date of said ceremony. Yet this too was but fodder for a relationship peppered by as much humor as passion: "Now Cleveland, you watch where you put your hands." Then with a self-conscious smile she shined up at him, "Why would a man buy the cow if he gets the milk for free?!" The look they then exchanged was better than a promise.

When she fully committed to the handsome, quite well-established rancher from near Cedar Butte, others whispered that as an Eastern European she was "marrying up." But hers was not a devotion born of desperation or subservience. She didn't marry just the man, but the ranch and family too. Cleve's love for her, though perhaps not the springtime love of one holding her face in both hands, was to the bone.

Chapter Twenty-Three

The Phantom Rider
1952-1956

In his later years, Cleve wistfully followed the passing seasons. For they no longer felt endless.

Autumn, 1952, was such a bittersweet season. Glorious for Cleve the hunter, but for Cleve the rancher oscillating weather and low cattle prices put new creases in his forehead. The last few days had been suffocatingly hot and humid.

That pesky cough would not go away. Sometimes during a smoke, it became a coughing fit. But on this day he smoked without coughing while taking a seat close to the radio. He could no longer lean into the speaker, on account of a paunch that had grown steadily in the years since marrying Rose. He liked to level a mock glare at her and say, "I guess you're just too damn good a cook."

Static filled the air. But with fine tuning Cleve coaxed a human voice out of the wood paneled Philco radio. A familiar gravel voiced announcer on the cattle markets show was barking out big news.

To keep up with cattle markets meant being home for lunch, where sandwich in hand he would spin the dial to 570 WNAX. On this day, Cleve pulled the radio closer as the announcer revealed new higher prices for good growthy yearling Herefords at the Miller, South Dakota sale barn . . . likely to be the month's best prices in the Northern Plains. Instantly Cleve knew he could make a tidy profit by borrowing his neighbor's big truck, loading up thirty head of cattle, and driving 200 zigzaggy miles to Miller.

The prospect was exhausting, coming as it did on top of an already tough week. But he said to Rose, "I need to do this. Thirty fewer head will help our grasses bounce back if we ever get rain. I'll round up the critters this afternoon, get 'em in the loading corral by dark, load 'em at first light. Then leave right after breakfast." She frowned.

He glanced again at the Philco, then back at her as she wiped her hands twice on the red-checked apron and cleared her throat.

"Cleveland, remember I'm heading the spring cleanup at church, so I can't come. Promise you'll call when you get there."

Next morning while drying her hands on that same apron, over and over, Rose watched the receding cloud of dust that was Cleve full throttling the big truck towards Miller. On the road he smoked one Pall Mall after another. Hadn't rolled his own in years.

Maybe it was the sweltering eight-hour drive, there being no truck air-conditioning in those days. Maybe it was the stress of hauling thirty bawling heifers on short notice. Whatever it was, as Cleve used a pole to prod the beeves down the ramp to the yards at Miller he felt a lightheadedness, then a throbbing in his throat followed by crushing pain in his chest. It brought him to his knees.

A yard hand offered to drive the old cowboy to Miller's small medical clinic. Cleve could not speak, and at first shook his head "no", but then nodded "yes." An hour later the town's only doctor entered the room with clipboard and furrowed brow. "Mr. Berry, you just survived a moderate heart attack. You'll need to make some changes."

This news required a rare long-distance call to Rose. "Can you drive out here and get me. I'm not feeling so great. Bring along Marvin Starkjohn. He'll have'ta drive the empty truck back."

It was a day where there rose up in Cleve the first undeniable recognition of his mortality. But it also signaled the beginning of maybe the best years of his life. For having glimpsed the end of time he could for once "hear the train whistle" and surrender to that travel yearning.

But first there was cowboy work to do, once Cleve felt sufficiently healed. On his second day back in the saddle, he rode to fix a bad spot in the fence on the east boundary of his empire of grass.

Riding through a dawn ground fog, his horse nearly trotted into a three-strand barbed wire fence—distracted as they were by a surprise appearance of an out-of-place critter. It was ol' #22, a bull who'd serviced the herd for nearly seven years. Lame in the right rear hock, and unable or unwilling to keep up with the heifers, the beast was in a bad way.

Cleve could see without dismounting that the bull had gotten tangled in the barbed wire fence, then pulled free. Fortuitously #22 was not far from the ranch's Cottonwood Creek corrals. So by alternately driving the bull ahead and pulling him by lasso, Cleve, horse, and bull arrived at the corrals by late morning.

Cleve closed the corral gate from horseback in that ballet-like maneuver of top man-horse partnerships. Dismounting, he moved cautiously for a closer look at the exhausted bull, its head lulling close to the ground. By sight and touch, Cleve determined the gangrened wound was beyond any economical healing. Looking skyward at high cirrus clouds promising more hot weather, Cleve considered slim options for disposing of this animal. Balmy conditions and the lack of a freezer nixed the home butchering option. Plus, it was late on a Saturday.

He tossed a pitchfork of hay to the bull, remounted and rode past the ranch house and up the path to the mailbox on the Belvidere road. Hoping the mailbox might hold the latest issue of his beloved *Field & Stream* magazine. The mailbox was empty. But the forking road to Running Bird village was not. Old Andrew Long Soldier was just then walking past. Cleve invited Long Soldier to share scant shade under a nearby boxelder and a swig from his canteen.

Long Soldier spoke a bit of English learned from his grandchildren, so the two shared simple conversation as a breeze rippled the rye grass at their feet. Long Soldier proudly recalled long-ago summers when Cleve hired him as one of the Indian teamsters driving ten-horse hay mowers through meadows on the 33 Ranch.

Then it hit Cleve—"If I simply tell Long Soldier that I have a bull to donate to the tribe, nothing will go to waste. I've done it before, but it's been awhile. Tell just one Indian, and you tell every Indian." This he did, setting in motion what locals called the "moccasin telegraph."

Cleve could predict that within hours, and no later than a fast-approaching Sunday morning, he'd see scores of Lakotas arriving from all points. This phenomenon was somewhat mysterious, for the Lakotas had no telephones, few cars, their tiny hamlets widely scattered over the land.

Before going to bed, Cleve short-tied the bull to a gatepost just south of his barnyard to await butcher by the sure-to-arrive native visitors.

Sunday was the one day a rancher might ignore the urge to be up an hour before dawn. So 7 a.m. did not seem early when without leaving bed Cleve lifted the curtain to spy Andrew Long Soldier conferring with a trio of Lakota women near the freshly killed bull. Having snubbed the creature even closer to the gatepost, Andrew had neatly sliced the beast's throat, its single bellow having awakened Cleve. Two large cooking fires were being stoked to red hot.

Cleve rubbed his eyes and looked again. Down the road came the first of a steady stream of tribal people arriving by all manner of conveyance. Some on foot. A few on bony cayuse ponies. Now and then a carload in pre-WWII jalopies. Many commenced at once to erect old army wall tents for what promised to be a two-day feast. Only one couple arrived in a horse-drawn wagon. Tied close behind their wagon was Stands For Them's doddering old white horse. Cleve puzzled at the sight, but as day lengthened he observed many Indians approach this horse to pet it and offer handfuls of green grass. Perhaps they were still honoring the old headman fifteen years after his death.

The recent Korean War was the beginning of the end of the wagon days, for the Sioux had volunteered in record numbers—and when discharged, many had just enough cash to buy an older used car. For themselves. For their parents.

Once dressed, Cleve looked out from the front door. He noticed the gathered, nearly 100 now, had split into four or five distinct groups. What he could not know is how this reflected the sub-tribes of yester-year—Sicangu doing most of the butchering, Oglala sharing news under the elm tree, Wazhazha in storytelling cells nearer the gate, and a small grouping of Miniconjou gathering timpsila by the creek.

Never in prior beef donations had Cleve enjoyed such a front-row seat. He noticed the oldest visitors were most organized, most assured of how to proceed—they moved as if reenacting the buffalo butchering of old. Indeed, a few had participated in the last big hunts in Canada.

Cleve beckoned Rose to the window. Together they watched as the elder women skinned the bull with four legs pointed skyward while the hide was stretched out to form a protective "tablecloth" for the rendering. Three and sometimes four women worked cooperatively over the carcass. Arms bloody to the elbow, they nimbly harvested even those body parts that would not have struck a non-native as edible.

Meanwhile, several younger women took stomach and intestines down to the small creek running behind the Berry ranch house. Taking turns, they thoroughly rinsed clean each piece of what would become offal.

After a light breakfast Cleve and Rose, coffee cups in hand, took up seats on their front porch. Patrons of the feast, they accepted many nods and smiles.

The frenzy of the day's feasting became apparent to a rather astonished Rose. Less so for Cleve. The stomach was eaten both raw and cooked, the cooking done by simply flinging pieces onto the coals at the fire's edge. The tongue was roasted and devoured by the older men at the gathering. Followed by the heart. Not a drop of fat wasted. Tripe was likewise consumed to the last, both raw and cooked. Choice cuts were sizzling on what amounted to great shish kabobs. And certain of the women had begun jerking and drying the lesser cuts for next month's meals. Prime cuts were saved for the evening fires.

The feasting now commenced earnestly and would not abate soon. Through evening and into a black night. For this was no powwow, no storytelling or drinking party. This was a feast for a hungry nation. Eat. Eat more. Rest. Eat again. For a recently nomadic people, the question was always the same: Who can say when such bounty will come again? Best of all, the feasting was on foods similar to olden times—the "guts and grease" diet of tipi days.

By morning all were gone save old Long Soldier, looking among the trampled grasses for a misplaced knife.

When this feast was a months-old memory, there came a series of glory trips inspired by Cleve's semi-retirement: A successful Canadian moose hunt north of Lake of the Woods. The memorable Old Mexico trip with Rose. There to glimpse the ranchos of the world's original cowboys, the vaqueros. Best of all, an excursion to Alberta to share with Rose those grand views of a half century ago—the Canadian Rockies cradling great hanging glaciers.

On the long car drive home from Alberta, Cleve had an especially bad coughing spell. Try as he might to hide it from Rose, she spied one of his blood-stained handkerchiefs. She insisted they stop at the big hospital in Rapid City before heading home.

Tests. Waiting. More tests.

A doctor they'd never met entered the room wearing his emblems of authority—a long white lab coat, a stethoscope, a clipboard. And a face either very tired or simply emotionless.

From that face came what many would call the darkest word of the 20th Century.

"Mr. Berry, I'm very sorry to tell you that you have cancer of the lungs. It is rather advanced."

With these words a slate grey curtain dropped around the couple. It would never fully lift. For the old cowboy it was as if every knot he'd ever tied was in that hour untied.

In coming days, a bit of relief came from the sheer volume of things to do. A whirlwind of medical and legal undertakings. Some vaguely hopeful. Most meant only to insure ". . . all affairs are in order." And of course, the great ranch still to be managed. Though blessedly a competent son-in-law and a burly hired hand were by this time doing most of the physical work.

Flying and driving to a Minneapolis hospital, back to the Rapid City doctor, a visit to the local doc, back to Minneapolis . . . then down to Mayo Clinic. Somewhere in this haze of painful travel and jumbled words came the only sentence that mattered. The unsurprising second opinion: "Mr. Berry, your cancer is inoperable. Modern medicine has no ability to prolong your life."

Cleve set his jaw to this news, to a painful grinding down, for his generation lacked the gentle passage of hospice.

He understood after a lifetime of living with cattle, horses, and dogs that for him, for his species alone, no mercy killing was possible. No gentle bullet behind the ear—the coup de grâce he had so often granted his very old or very injured animal companions. His would be the slow-motion train wreck, the obscene death.

By the conduct of our life, he'd heard it said, we "earn" our death. Cleve may have earned the good and bad details of his passing. He was, after all, a lifetime no-filter, roll-your-own Bull Durham tobacco smoker. Like all good cowboys, he could roll and light one from the back of a moving horse, mostly one-handed. Into a stiff breeze. Nicknamed "The Old Reliable," Bull Durham tobacco came in a soft white muslin sack with drawstrings, fitting neatly into a stockman's vest pocket. Since 1902 Cleve had found a good smoke, like a tin cup of hot coffee, a pleasure making all the sweat and saddle time manageable.

He could squeeze thirty-one cigarettes out of a ten-cent sack of Bull Durham, quite the bargain considering each sack included a small book of cigarette papers. But on this day in 1956 it didn't feel like much of a bargain.

Cleve thought of all the death he'd seen on this earth. Death of livestock, family members, friends. He regretted not so much that it was his turn . . . but rather that he'd not have a fitting cowboy death. Quick. Clean. Fierce. Somewhere out on the range. He'd always lived with the sense that he'd someday die. But damn it he didn't like knowing when.

And when he considered dying, he thought of old Stands For Them. For only now could Cleve fully appreciate Stands For Them's urgent deathbed request to see him. And his own inadequate response. He reminded himself that the decision was in the best interests of little Jan and Betty. Still, that refusal of a dying friend's request bubbled up now in Cleve's mind as betrayal.

As the heaviness of his sentence spread like a fog over Cleve's world, he yet found islands of solace—in loving talks with Rose, in baiting a fishhook, in a hundred tasks needed to leave the ranch in good shape for wife, children, grandchildren.

And if Rose could not find Cleve late in the day, he'd likely be sitting in the barn on a bale of hay—close enough to smell, and hear, and feel his beloved horses. Here he found a comfort and timelessness unavailable among his own species. An equine lack of pity so right, so steadying.

Here among the herd he was not a dying man, simply a man. The horses told him so.

When not with horses there came dreams of horses. Recent horse dreams were on Cleve's pillow for that last trip to Minnesota. A sad trip, but it did provide a chance to breathe easier for three days under an oxygen tent.

Lying there in his white hospital bed, in the white room behind a white door leading to a dismally white hallway—was there some way, even at this late date, to die in his world of western colors, to die with his boots on?

As a young man, boots on and fourteen hours in the saddle, there'd been time to formulate his loose yet lifelong philosophy of spiritual matters: religion was for times when a man needed help. Some needed this help all the time. Those at the other extreme, the men he modeled himself after, professed to need it only rarely.

Cleve had not pondered such things enough to even have spiritual questions. But now spirituality seemed like the only question. So when a cherub-like face above a clerical collar peaked through the hospital door, Cleve hesitated, then beckoned him enter. It was the second and as it turned out last conversation with hospital chaplain Blaine Smith.

Blaine had first invited himself to sit with Cleve one afternoon when Rose was running errands. Barely thirty, pleasantly meaty, his alabaster skin told Cleve that this visitor was no outdoorsman. Still, Blaine was surprisingly informed on topics dear to Cleve's heart: ranching, hunting, the Black Hills, the Badlands.

Today the chaplain would not stay long, seeing the thinness of the old cowboy's energy. Cleve was pleased by the frankness of Blaine's one question, "Mr. Berry, what do you wish for in these remaining days?"

"I wish to return to my ranch. To die there."

That night, Rose slept in a nearby chair as the great hospital building retreated to hushed stillness. Through an open window Cleve heard the hoots of barn owls. An incongruous smile lit his fine face, for he knew the Lakota legend: that these dwellers of the dark are hooting to call home the dying of all creation.

The owls, he knew, were calling his name.

By morning Rose no longer saw a trace of fear in her husband's eyes, eyes which often and gently now closed for blessed interludes of sleep. During one lovely dream Cleve, half awake, thought he heard a distant train whistle, on tracks hugging the river separating life and death, then curving magically through his beloved ranchland and disappearing up Black Pipe Valley.

The bliss of the dream caused him to twitch as though in a nightmare. Which it was not. But Rose did not know this—so she interrupted the reverie by wiping his forehead with a cool washcloth.

The end was now near. Ever devoted, teary Rose kept rearranging the pillows so Cleve's hideously ravaged lungs could steal just enough oxygen to maintain consciousness and perhaps a bit of comfort.

Now as the eastern horizon proclaimed predawn of December 10th, there came the death rattle, a series of shuttering half breaths marking the end. Individuality melted away, and with it the pain of self. His last flicker of life had a twin: a first flicker of timelessness. The tiresome chain of thoughts and breaths ended.

Cleve Berry's body died in what cowboys might call the bleakness of the big city. His soul, though, floated to the cedared badlands and from there melted to some secret place known only to newborns and the dead.

Word of the plainsman's silent heart drifted in unhurried fashion westward across the prairie. By telephone, by postcard, in barbershops, sale barns, and saloons. Gray-headed cowboys smiled to recall a man who sat the saddle deep and solid. Finally, even the Lakotas knew.

One week later there came a morning when not a person stirred among the Wazhazha cabins. For overnight the tide of winter had rolled in like ten thousand pale tumbleweeds. Utter whiteness, utter stillness cloaked Black Pipe Creek. Eleven inches of snow filled the bowl between a waxing half-moon setting, and a watery sun rising.

There was but one witness to the scene—the recently appointed itinerant Episcopal preacher just starting his rounds on horseback. His mount advanced slowly, as though recovering from mild lameness.

Jim was his name. He was in his late twenties, of average height, on the gaunt side. His scholarly forehead topped an otherwise accessible and earnestly freckled face framed by curly red hair.

The morning had been cold enough to foil his car battery, so he'd resorted to borrowing his wife's saddle horse.

As the roan gelding snorted and shuffled along the wagon road beside Black Pipe Creek, Preacher Jim noted how being atop a horse lent itself to a more careful observation of one's surroundings.

He saw unlikely bursts of color among the normally grey Indian loggies—here a red blanket tacked to a door or peeking from a window. There a red kerchief fluttering from a hitching post.

Preacher Jim believed he was witnessing a tribute to a recently deceased tribal member. He could not know the Black Pipe band was bestowing the honoring "red robe" of death to the *waste* wasicu—the good white man.

Here and there the flag was a Hudson's Bay blanket showing plenty of the sacred red, marking the family as descendants of those Canadian exiles who escaped north after the Little Big Horn. As the mounted preacher advanced, he witnessed one or two cabin owners smearing the door frame with a plant-based crimson medicine paint.

Some miles south of the village, he saw from the corner of his eye a shrouded female figure leaving her abode by wagon team. No color adorned her tiny cabin. She dared not fuel the rumors that still occasionally floated up and down the valley. She dared not arouse her tiyospaye, some of whom had surely heard the gossip of seventeen years past. She traveled today because she would not feel invited to the white man's church for the funeral, which anyway was a long wagon ride to the town of White River. Instead, she journeyed through the snow to what would be her private memorial prayers at the little brick Catholic Church in Norris.

The woman paid scant attention to the rider behind her as both plodded southward. Preacher Jim could not recognize her, bundled as she was against the cold. By the time she was half a mile down the trail, Blue Cloud Woman smiled the "beautiful sadness" smile. How could she not, with red tribute banners flying from so many snow-topped cabins.

Her smile was also for headman Stands For Them. His living influence had made intimacy between the races taboo, in a kindly yet undeniable way. Then his death had made her impossible wasicu love seem possible, if only for one shining summer.

Blue Cloud Woman's horse team, normally stubborn as mules, were today willing to trot up the trail leading to Norris. She still called it the Red Road, not the Norris Road.

Preacher Jim followed some fifty paces behind. That's when he saw a lone rider approaching from the south. A male in his late teens. The boy and horse moved as one.

Meeting Blue Cloud Woman's wagon, the young rider reined up and the pair engaged in conversation. The preacher overtook them, tipped his hat in greeting, and noted they conversed as a native mother and son might: Without making improper eye contact. In hushed tones of the Lakota tongue. The youngster briefly turned his face to the preacher, nodding.

The preacher looked back one more time to see the young man step down from the stirrups to stand in relaxed conversation—weight on one leg, the elbow akimbo on a flexed hip. Behind him the sun reflected flashes of silver to his saddle.

As the preacher rode on towards Norris, he wondered how such a young native came to own a silver-trimmed saddle. Then he remembered the name, Grover, and that they'd briefly crossed paths at Frontier Days just that summer.

It was common knowledge that Grover had been presented with the silver saddle at his honoring ceremony in May, that "coming of age" ritual for worthy Lakota youth. The ceremony had been conducted down by the Little White River, officiated by Samuel Ghost Head with Richard Standing Bear assisting.

Grover had used this fine saddle in a Wild Horse Race at Frontier Days, a fierce contest requiring teams to subdue and saddle a wild bronc before riding it to the end of the arena and back. His all-Indian team finished first, but nearly every team member suffered significant injury—Grover had broken his ankle. With the ankle now healed, he'd reclaimed his bunk at the XX Ranch, earning a modest living as a hired hand.

Most everyone knew of Grover's natural ways on horseback. Even the new preacher. By age fourteen Grover was a consummate roper, with a wrist that could catch a calf on the first loop. It made him the up and coming roper at many roundups and brandings.

Before riding north towards the XX, Grover asked, "Mother, what gets you out in such weather?" She tried to conceal her trip as one to buy items at Norris Mercantile—a little white lie, for now was not the day to speak of Cleve's death, nor of the big secret. When this felt inadequate, she fought to hold back tears, then found a distraction by pulling from her shawl the faded Brownie snapshot Cleve had slipped in the envelope to her years ago and handing it up to her now mounted son. "Please take this old photograph of our departed headman, a face to go with his wisdoms that I shared with you in your childhood."

He brightened at the visage of a headman in full regalia. "Ah, it can only be him! Thank you, mother. In this valley he is so often recalled and described." She only nodded, so that together they might keep an uncommon man's name from becoming common.

Grover did not inquire of the horse or the other man in the photo as he secured it in his saddlebag. Departing then, and soon entering the village, he looked curiously left and right at the red banners festooning so many log homes. Wondering who of his tribe had died, who warranted such a display of the honoring color?

Only upon reaching full manhood, standing beside his mother's hospital bed, would Grover at last learn the source of his nut-brown hair, and of those red banners. For only then, in halting voice, would "Magpie" share her great secret: "Your father's name was Grover Cleveland Berry, but everyone just called him Cleve. His good people still ranch on the Red Road below Cedar Butte. They are your people too."

He smiled in hopes this would make his glistening eyes less noticeable, and bent still closer to the bed. He took her hand, for she was beyond the ability to extend it.

"Son, I am sorry for not telling you earlier. In this community it might have been a burden. I was never ashamed of your story. And you should not be. I am so proud of you."

Then as though jolted he leaned back: "The snapshot you gave me beside the Red Road of Stands For Them and the white horse? The other man must be my father." She squeezed his hand.

Lakota Cowboy

In that hour of partings and anointings Grover Cleveland Blue Cloud was become, in every sense, the Lakota Cowboy.

At present the winding Red Road has mostly returned to grass, more cattle trail than road. The primeval natural way through the badlands is as inviting as ever, but nearby modern highways speed people and goods much more efficiently. And jet planes simply vault over this seemingly empty country—a million eyeballs fixed on screens and pages, none peeking down at the once storied Red Road below.

*****

Today the graves of Cleve Berry and James Stands For Them are as different as casual observers assumed the men were. Cleve's resting place is in a groomed cemetery with a view down towards the Little White River, and on clearest days even onto Cedar Butte. Cleve's bones lay beneath twin cedar trees once too small to notice, but which today seem robust enough to live the species' allotted 700 years. Below Cleve's name the granite gravestone perhaps should have read simply "Cowboy." Instead, it says "1886 – 1956."

Stands For Them's grave is presently unmarked, and thought to be in the northeast corner of Stands For Them Cemetery—a burial ground still intermittently used and maintained by local Lakotas. If in 1939 his resting place was marked by a wooden marker and cross, these have long since weathered away. Instead, only native prairie grasses and summer wildflowers rise above root-tangled sod on the windswept flats.

The researching and writing of Lakota Cowboy

For nearly a dozen years this book has been an active part of my life. So much so that I have at times dreaded its publication, for as a writer I will now be closing the book, saying goodbye to Stands For Them and Cleve.

In the early years I very much enjoyed the research involved. This was much easier for Cleve Berry. He was, after all, my grandfather. He was a faint, big-booted memory in my early boyhood, but when I started the research Cleve had many living persons who had known him as adults.

Stands For Them was another matter entirely. To put more flesh on his character, I would need to turn to diverse sources, and began using the Freedom of Information Act, Mellette County will and probate records, and outside experts such as Kingsley Bray of Manchester, England. He is one of the world's leading experts on Lakota clan history and genealogy and was very generous with his time.

Two moments of the research stand out, and both were when I was deep within the online collections of the Library of Congress and later the National Archives. Moments such as these brought a joy bordering on ecstasy in the researching, the hunt: The first was an obscure Indian census, hand-written, that listed Stands For Them's father Elk Robe as "head of household", and detailed his wives and also his children. One name jumped out at me: "Julia, born 1879 in Canada." This would have been a half-sister of Stands For Them. Because I knew on this date that Stands For Them was not yet living on his own, this meant that Stands For Them had been among the many Lakotas who followed Sitting Bull into Canadian exile after the Little Big Horn and other battles of 1876-1877. I was dumbstruck, for it was the link connecting his nomadic life with his reservation life.

Another pivotal moment was when I gained access to the vast Native American records of the Church of Jesus Christ of Latter Day Saints (Mormons). There I came upon a photocopy of an ID card listing Stands For Them as an irregular in the Army Indian Scouts, 1890. This firmly established Stands For Them's role in the tumultuous events of the Ghost Dance troubles and Wounded Knee. Again, I was dumbstruck.

The crux of *Lakota Cowboy*, the paradox, remains unresolved. It outlived both Cleve and Stands For Them. As it will surely outlive us all, clinging as we do to a melting pot globe that spins, homogenizes, becomes ever smaller, ever less unique—Not a single village worldwide without Nike t-shirts and Apple smartphones. The kernel is this: who can argue the love Cleve felt for Blue Cloud Woman, and the glory of their son straddling two worlds? And yet, who can argue Stands For Them's dream that a people and a culture deserve to remain intact? In the end how can diversity and homogenization both win? I believe that in time Stands For Them came to see assimilation as looking more like erasure.

Acknowledgements

Of the two main characters in the book, understanding and then sharing the main events for my grandfather's life was not difficult. The Lakota headman was another matter entirely—necessitating a hunt through museums, into Congressional records, tribal records, probate and other court proceedings. Slowly a picture of James Stands For Them came into focus. But in the end, it was not records but people who helped me pull something of James and Cleve back from their graves. Those people are acknowledged below:

My cultural editor of the project was Jhon (not John) Goes In Center. Examples of his lifetime of achievement are many, but Goes In Center is proudest of his elder status and citizenship in the Oglala Lakota nation. Honors for Goes In Center, a museum curator by training, include Research Fellow with the Smithsonian National History Museum, stints on various boards of directors such as the Denver Art Museum and more recently as cultural advisor to the Indian Museum of North America located on the grounds of the Crazy Horse Memorial in the Black Hills.

Mr. Goes In Center provided advice and editorial direction on the most culturally sensitive portions of *Lakota Cowboy*, but his deep knowledge was not required for every chapter. For certain passages I relied on my several conversations with the Standing Bear brothers, Charles "Jumbo" Standing Bear (1927-2018) and Herman Standing Bear (1936- 2020). They spent most of their lives in the valley of Black Pipe Creek, and at various times worked for one of the Berry ranches. Charles shared vivid and reverent memories of both James and Cora Stands For Them.

It is important to state that any cultural errors, omissions, or inadvertent misuses of the beautiful Lakota language in *Lakota Cowboy* are mine alone.

I owe so much to book editor Anita Mumm, as her rural West Kansas upbringing and avid interest in Lakota culture provided both "cowboy" and "Indian" perspectives. My cousin Dan Rasmussen, 64, a cattleman and grandson of Cleve Berry, was a further highly valuable resource on cowboy culture. Plus, Dan's lifelong relationship with the native Corn Creek community meant that his introductions to various Lakota elders provided interviews that I otherwise could not have arranged. Many were the days Dan left ranch duties undone to drive me here and there among the Lakotas. His sister Amy Lehman was equally helpful, her forte being the tracking down of old photos and documents.

My Aunt Jan Rasmussen is the youngest daughter of Cleve and Jessie and was a friend of Stands For Them. She not only provided several of the tales woven into this novel, she lived some of them.

My three adult sons, Adam, Joel and Andrew, at various times and in various ways provided concrete improvements to this work.

Also, I sought and welcomed input from Cal Thunder Hawk, enrolled member of the Rosebud Lakota Nation, and a descendant of the 19th century Thunder Hawk appearing in Chapter 13 of this historical novel.

I owe a special thanks to friend Renae Bottom, whose love of good writing guided me through many of the final edits. With so much of action in *Lakota Cowboy* taking place in Nebraska, it seemed only right to have a native Nebraskan like Renae contributing. Special thanks to my wife and my daughter-in-law. Wife Lori Hafnor was both supportive and very patient through the many years of my obsession with this book. Trish Becker Hafnor was there when I needed cover ideas and other support.

Finally, I've been honored these years to have as a friend and confidant a man who was born in the fading frontier of Montana in 1917. His 104-year-old memory and voice are still clear and strong. Clair Michels is his name, and his first job as a teen was to ride herd on cattle on the open range between his family ranch and the vast Indian reservation hugging the Canadian border. When not on horseback or behind a plow, he and brothers would collect buffalo skulls and bones then littering the prairies. Delivered to the railhead, the bones might mean one dollar in Clair's pocket for a day's labor.

Clair's wisdoms influenced many a page of *Lakota Cowboy*. Here in his words is one example: "Well, when I was a boy most farm and ranch work was done by horses, but it was a time of transition to steam powered and gasoline powered machines. I kinda preferred working with the horses. Being creatures, they needed a little rest now and then, which meant I could rest in the shade they provided. But those newfangled machines never needed a rest, so for me it was go, go, go all day long."

Lakota was originally not a written language, and even today there are unique letters in written Lakota that do not correspond to the English alphabet. There are also alternate spellings to certain words and phrases, including in this brief glossary.

Akhe eya yo - Please say that again.

Akicita - a band's appointed enforcers or policemen.

Arikaree - a tribe living along the Missouri River. Traditional enemies of the Lakota.

Blotahunka - War party leader.

Canku Wahatuya - meaning High Backbone, this was a formidable leader of the Eat No Dogs band.

Cansasa - a special tobacco made from the inner bark of red willow.

Chanku Luta - The Red Road.

Chagusica - "the cough that kills." The Lakota word for tuberculosis.

Chanupa - the sacred pipe.

Chonsusbecha Wahzeyahtah - A Lakota constellation named for the salamander.

Heyokha - a thunder dreamer, the humorous or contrarian "clown" of the people. A bringer of strange wisdoms.

Heyokha Kaga - a traditional healer.

Hoka Hey - similar to the American expressions "Let's do it!" or "Let's roll!" Often incorrectly translated as *"it's a good day to die"* because Lakota leader Crazy Horse famously exhorted his troops *"Hoka hey, today is a good day to die!"* which meant something like *"Let's go men, today is a good day to die!"*

Hunka - a "relative" by adoption or mutual consent. This willingness to adopt was common practice among the Lakotas.

Hunte Paha - Cedar Butte, a notable escarpment rising at the eastern terminus of the South Dakota badlands, just east of the Corn Creek settlement. As the easternmost manifestation of the White River Badlands, the butte was a site of vision quests and other Lakota ceremonies.

Intancan - The leader or "chief" of a band or larger unit of Lakotas.

Istawicayazan Wi - the Moon of Sore Eyes (snow blindness), aligned with either February or March moon, not necessarily a calendar month.

Kangi - Lakota for Crow or Absa Indians.

Kakala - term of endearment meaning "grandfather," though not necessarily a biological grandfather.

Kazuta Sapa - literally translated as "medicine that is black," this is the Lakota phrase for coffee.

Key kta yo - Means "wake up"

Kola - A dear friend for whom one would die, as close or closer than siblings. There are two levels of friendship depending on the pronunciation.

Mako Sica - Badlands. More specifically "land bad or eroded."

Mato - A bear.

Mato Paha - Bear Butte.

Mila Hanska - the "long knives," a reference to U.S. Cavalry's use of long sabers.

Miniconjou - One of the seven council fire bands of the greater Lakota tribe.

Mita' kuyepi – The meaning is "Attention, my relatives." Relatives is used broadly here.

Naca - Refers to a headman, or alternately an assembly of leaders.

Nagila - ones soul, spirit or essence.

Nawica Kicijin - The one who stands up for others. Stands For Them.

Nunge Yuza - The meaning is "Listen up," from the phrase wash or clear (yuza) your ear (nunge).

Oceti Sakowin - The Seven Council Fires of the greater Lakota, Dakota and Nakota nation.

Paha Sapa - the Black Hills. Also "He Sapa" in Lakota.

Pte - Bison or buffalo.

Pte Oyate - Buffalo Nation.

Santee - The eastern Sioux people, mostly from the woodlands of Minnesota. Otherwise called the Dakota, they were considered "cousins" of the Lakota.

Sicangu - One of the seven council fire bands of the greater Lakota tribe.

Sunka - the dog.

Sunkamanitu Thanka - the wolf, or literally "true dog."

Shunka Yute Shni - the Eat No Dogs, an esteemed band of the larger Miniconjou division of the Lakota nation.

Ska' Yuhas - a distinguished Lakota hunter society.

Takoja - grandson.

Tasunka Witco - Crazy Horse.

Tatanka - alternative word for pte or buffalo. Often specifically denoting a bull buffalo.

Tawechoo – Wife.

Tiyospaye - An extended family unit composed of several families related by blood, marriage, or adoption. Sometimes called "Big Family."

Timpsila - the wild turnip of the northern Great Plains.

Tos - an emphatic yes, certainly, of course.

Tunkasila - the "grandfather" Creator.

Unci Maka - grandmother earth.

Unci Maskoce - Grandmother's Land, and in the years following the flight north after the Little Big Horn was used to refer to the land of Queen Victoria or Canada.

Wacipi - Powwow or ceremonial dance.

Wagmu l'eju ta - the holy wild gourd.

Wah Yahwah - To read, or one who reads.

Wakanlica - philosopher, or "one who commands stones."

Wakan Tanka - universal spiritual power, sometimes translated as God.

Wakanyeja - the Lakota word for a youngster but which translates literally as "the child is also holy."

Waku - A shortened expression for "to give" or denoting a gift.

Washakah -Various meanings, including a strong-bodied youth.

Wasicu or wasichu - White person, but originally and more literally "takes the fat," or by implication "greedy person."

Washasha - the sacred hue of the color red, often associated with an honored death.

Waste – Good.

Wasigla - One who mourns a close family member's death.

Wazhazha - A traditional and once powerful band of the Lakota nation who in early reservation years lived between the Oglala and Sicangu peoples.

Wicasa wakan - a Lakota priest of the old religion. Alternately Pejuta wacasa - a Lakota healer, somewhat erroneously described as a "medicine man."

Wi-wanyang-wa-c'i-pi - The Sun Dance ceremony.

Left photo: Nawica Kicijin and unidentified woman. 1923

Right photo: Cleve and Jessie Berry, wedding day. 1914

Nawica Kicijin 1899

Cleve Berry at his sod bunkhouse with coyote pelts. 1916

Nawica Kicijin with Cleve and Jessie's daughters,
Phyllis and Marion Wynona. 1921

Nawica Kicijin with wife Cora Eagle Wolf. 1923

On Sale Now!

2019 ELMER KELTON AWARD WINNER
APACHE LAMENT

SPUR AWARD-WINNING AUTHOR
PATRICK DEAREN

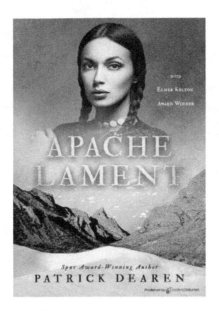

For more information
visit: www.SpeakingVolumes.us

Sign up for free and bargain books

Join the Speaking Volumes mailing list

Text

ILOVEBOOKS

to 22828 to get started.

Message and data rates may apply.